# Early Praise for
## *Secrets of Nanreath Hall*

"Alix Rickloff's debut is a delight—beautifully written with fascinating characters, rich historical detail, and an intriguing family mystery that keeps the pages turning."

—Hazel Gaynor, *New York Times* bestselling author

"In this compelling and heartwarming novel, Alix Rickloff shares with us two women, mother and daughter, whose tragic and triumphant lives intertwine through two world wars. The story pulls us into the universal struggle of all women to find their places in their worlds. I was deeply moved by *Secrets of Nanreath Hall*."

—Karen Harper, *New York Times* bestselling author

"Two women and two wars separated by a generation filled with secrets that kept me turning pages to get to the mysterious truth. At the heart, this is a novel about searching for one's identity. The vivid writing combined with such an intriguing story make Alix Rickloff an exciting voice in historical fiction."

—Renée Rosen, bestselling author of *White Collar Girl*

"Telling an elegant tale about a mother and daughter trying to find themselves in the midst of two very different world wars, Alix Rickloff establishes herself as an up-and-coming talent in the historical fiction genre."

—Stephanie Dray, author of *America's First Daughter*

# Secrets of Nanreath Hall

# Secrets of Nanreath Hall

## ALIX RICKLOFF

WILLIAM MORROW
*An Imprint of* HarperCollins*Publishers*

SECRETS OF NANREATH HALL. Copyright © 2016 by Alix Rickloff. All rights reserved. Printed in the United States of America. No part of this book may be used or reproduced in any manner whatsoever without written permission except in the case of brief quotations embodied in critical articles and reviews. For information address HarperCollins Publishers, 195 Broadway, New York, NY 10007

HarperCollins books may be purchased for educational, business, or sales promotional use. For information, please e-mail the Special Markets Department at SPsales@harpercollins.com.

FIRST EDITION

Designed by Diahann Sturge

Library of Congress Cataloging-in-Publication Data has been applied for.

ISBN 978-0-06-243318-3

16 17 18 19 20    OV/RRD    10 9 8 7 6 5 4 3 2 1

*For Mom and Dad, who have waited for this one*

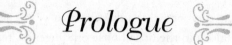

# Prologue

London, England
February 1923

"I am dying."

Prue puts down her sewing and eyes me through her cheaters, but in no other way does she reveal the shock she must be feeling at my news.

"Cancer, so Mr. Porter tells me." I blunder on before she can gather herself to speak. "He suggests I put my affairs in order while my strength remains, but what's there to organize? The last payment I received for modeling was just enough to pay the doctor's consultation fee. By the time Andre returns from Biarritz or San Remo or wherever he's gone in search of lucrative commissions, I won't be in any position to pose for him or anyone else."

We are taking advantage of a mild winter's afternoon to take the air in Prue's small back garden. Laundry flaps on the line, and in the corner by Graham's potting shed, the earth has been turned in preparation for planting cabbages and cauliflower. My journal lies open in my lap where I have tried to capture the poignant intimacy of the scene, but my mind won't focus. Memories laced with regret and grief simmer too close to the surface for me to concentrate on my work.

I chose my moment carefully. Graham is at the pub, leaving Prue and me alone in the little house on Queen's Crescent. I know I can no longer hide my illness from her. She is far too observant and has already noticed my lack of appetite and how quickly I grow tired from the least strenuous of activities. It's just as well. I need her counsel and her quiet common sense. She'll not burden me with useless sympathy. That isn't her way. For good or ill, life must be faced head-on. She has taught me that if nothing else.

"There's Anna," she says simply, as if reading my thoughts. "You must make arrangements for her."

Anna. My daughter. My dearest treasure.

I sent her to school this morning in a crisply starched pinafore, her wild red hair tamed into two slick braids. She made me leave her at the corner, too old at six to be seen holding hands with her mother. But at the last moment, she threw her chubby arms around my neck and kissed me on my nose. I wanted to crush her close and never let her go. It took every ounce of strength I possessed to release her. Too many times have I watched silently as those I loved walked away. As she marched proudly, back straight and head high, down the sidewalk, I clamped my jaw shut to keep myself from calling her back.

"Of course, but I don't want her to know, Prue. Not about the cancer. Promise you won't say anything." My throat aches, and I shiver with unexpected cold. My fingers knot, and I'm surprised to see how knobby my knuckles have become, the veins running blue under the translucent skin of my wrists.

"Are you certain that's wise?"

I force myself to relax my hands so they lie flat on the pages of the journal, but I can't make myself leaf back through the pages. Not yet. "I've weighted her with enough burdens, don't you think? I won't add to her load."

Prue pours out two cups of tea, adding four heaping spoonfuls of sugar to mine, just the way I like it. The sweet, syrupy heat coats my throat and warms my stomach. I take a deep breath and the ghosts of the past recede, though they never completely leave me. Now I am glad of their company.

"You should write to your family," Prue urges, her own tea prepared with only a thin slice of lemon. Her expression is grave, though I can see she is already looking ahead to what must be done, checklists mentally ticked off in her head. "Tell them what you've told me. Ask them for help. If not for your sake, for Anna's. She's a Trenowyth, no matter what side of the blanket she was born on."

Next door, crazy old Mrs. Vaisvilaf begins playing the piano. Some of the neighbors dislike the noise, but I enjoy her concert-worthy performances of Haydn and Mozart as she relives her youth on a St. Petersburg stage. Perhaps because I know how she feels when the past becomes more real than the present. "You make it sound so simple. You forget that in their eyes Lady Katherine is already dead and has been for years."

Despite my protest, Prue's suggestion makes perfect sense. Anna *is* a Trenowyth. I've made her one through my own arrogance. And I wish I had the courage or, perhaps, the shamelessness, to write and beg my family's aid.

I imagine Anna moving from room to room at Nanreath Hall, her shoes scuffing the same crooked floors, her fingers trailing along the carved oaken banister as she is led downstairs for her daily obligatory visit with the grown-ups, staring out the same nursery window toward the glittering gray-green sea and listening to its purr as she lies in the narrow iron bedstead with Nanny snoring a comforting room away.

But I know even as I imagine it, that it is a dream with no hope of coming true. Nanreath is lost to me. There is no going back.

I close my journal and run my hand over the tooled calfskin cover, worn smooth over years of use. It is warm to the touch, as if the souls of the people and places within might be conjured with a word and a breath. "It's funny, but I'm not frightened of dying. I'm more terrified that when Anna understands who and what she is, I won't be here to explain. That she'll despise me."

"And why would she do that?"

"Bastards are rarely treated gently." I hate the taste of the word. Prue winces, too, and she catches back a little breath. "Sometimes I regret not feigning a marriage," I continue. "It would have been easy enough after the war. There were so many widows, who would question one more? I know you thought I was mad not to."

"I didn't want you hurt any more than you already were. You were so fragile, so lost. I didn't see the honor in wearing your shame like a badge."

"Perhaps not." I give a little shrug. Now that the confession has been made, I find I am weary, my strength deserting me. "But I'd lied to myself for so long that when I finally realized the truth, I couldn't lie anymore. Not even for Anna's sake."

"She won't despise you." Prue reaches across to take my hand, squeezing it gently in a wordless note of comfort. "Graham and I will make sure of that."

Her motherly gaze behind her glasses holds the reassurance I seek even if I don't ask outright. I could not have wished for a better friend or a better guardian for Anna when the time comes. But not even Prue knows the whole story.

There is no one left alive who does.

The sun chooses that moment to break free of the clouds and spear the sea of belching chimney pots, falling warm and golden upon my face. Spent, I close my eyes, and though I am in London where my life is ending, I see the glittering expanse of ocean stretching on forever and feel the June sun burn my cheeks as a briny wind tosses my hair into my face. Mrs. Vinter's house sits at the bottom of the lane where riotous beds of camellias and jasmine and verbena frame a pink front door, and Nellie Melba on the gramophone floats through an open window to war with the cry of gulls.

It is Cornwall the summer before the Great War, and though I am already twenty and, to my mind, quite grown up, my life is just about to begin.

# Chapter 1

*September 1940*

"T his is London." American newscaster Edward R. Murrow's nightly send-off repeated itself in Anna Trenowyth's head as she emerged from the Aldersgate Tube station into the dusty yellow glare of a late summer afternoon.

This certainly was not the London she knew. In the weeks since German bombers had begun concentrating their nightly raids on the capital, the city had taken on a surreal feeling, as if the entire population clenched its fists and held its breath. Even the air seemed charged and heavy, coating the back of her throat with a taste of grit and cinders.

Damaged roads had been roped off, so that just navigating the short distance between the station and Graham and Prue's house became a game of snakes and ladders, with every move forward requiring three moves back. Homeless queued in front of a burned-out department store where volunteers handed out blankets and coffee. A group of boys rooted near a rubble-filled crater, hooting and whistling over bits of shrapnel and twisted metal. A family hustled, heads down, toward a bus, carrying a few bits of scarred luggage.

She'd been warned what to expect. She'd listened to the news reports from her hospital bed in Surrey, fingers clenched white in her lap, stomach tight and tense. Whitechapel, Clerkenwell, Holborn, the names familiar and dear. Places she could picture when she closed her eyes. Her city. Her home. But not even Mr. Murrow's impressions of devastation had been enough to prepare her for the harsh reality.

"Pardon, miss. Street's closed off. Unexploded bomb." A policeman barred her way, twirling his whistle round his finger, rolling back and forth on the balls of his feet. "Bomb disposal's on its way, but you'll have to go round." He eyed her dark blue gabardine Red Cross VAD uniform and the valise she carried, the weight of it dragging against her bad shoulder. "Home for a bit?"

"A week's leave. My family lives just north of here. I thought I'd surprise them."

His frown deepened. He caught his whistle in a closed hand. "A good daughter, you are, miss. I hope you find them well."

Anna nodded her thanks and began the roundabout track that would take her east then back north. At this rate, it would be dinnertime before she dragged herself into the small front parlor in Queen's Crescent. It was Friday, so Graham would be at the pub for his weekly pint of bitter and a jaw with the lads. Prue would be in her chair by the radio, listening to Vera Lynn or the comedy of *Band Waggon*, chewing nervously at the end of her spectacles.

Anna hadn't seen either of them since July, when they'd visited her in hospital. She'd tried talking them out of the difficult trip from London to Surrey, but Prue had insisted, and Anna hadn't the stamina to argue. It took all her energy just to scribble a few hackneyed lines on a postcard each week. There was no way she could make them understand her desire to be left alone without sounding cold and unfeeling. And she'd not hurt Graham or Prue even if it meant gritting her teeth through their hovering attentiveness.

Just as she'd expected, it had been an awkward reunion. They'd not known what to say as she lay plastered like a mummy, her face gaunt and marked by the constant nightmares that left her sick. She'd had too much to say and no words to speak of the horrible images seared upon her heart. By the time they left, she'd felt nothing but guilty relief and an overwhelming urge to be sick.

Then she'd received her new orders, and she'd had to speak to them. They were the only ones who might understand her emotional tug-of-war. She'd foregone a letter, choosing instead to ring them up with the news, spilling her confusion and doubts over the wires. Graham had listened to her calmly before handing the phone to Prue, who urged her to come home for a long-delayed visit. They needed to talk with her—about her mother.

Anna had hung up the receiver with shaking hands and arranged for leave to travel up to London. Now, a week later, she was finally home, though home seemed sadly changed.

She shifted the heavy weight of her valise off her shoulder to relieve the growing ache of stiff muscles as a trickle of sweat ran down her spine. The day was warm, and it had been months since she'd walked so far. But she'd not the fare for a cab even if one could be found. Besides, she couldn't very well complain at being passed over for a posting due to her injuries and then wilt at a bit of effort. There would be effort and more if she returned to the front.

No, not if . . . when. When she returned to the front. There was no *if* about it. She had not become a VAD to sit safely in Blighty making tea and playing cards while others risked their lives.

She passed the church and the greengrocer's, rounded the

corner, her steps hastening as shattered glass crunched under her boots. Her hands slid clammy on the leather strap of her bag, and her damp skin itched beneath the heavy wool of her uniform.

Buildings leaned drunkenly on their foundations, their windows blown out, doors knocked from hinges. A jagged gap like a missing tooth was all that was left of the butcher's shop. The pub looked comfortingly unscathed until she approached, then she noticed a tumbled slide of bricks and shingles where the roof had collapsed. A gleam of brass railing poked up through fallen plaster and splintered beams. A pint glass stood half-filled on a table in a corner. A dart stuck dead center in the dartboard still hanging on the back wall.

Ten paces. Twenty. The damage greater, the houses tumbled and spilled like a child's toppled building blocks. Smoke hung low like a morning fog across the Thames. A few firemen replaced their hoses upon a truck. A policeman unrolled a coil of rope across the pavement where a set of marble steps led to . . . nothing.

No.

Anna's chest tightened. Her throat closed around a hard painful knot. Pain lanced down her leg, buckling her ankle. The awkward weight of the valise knocked her to her knees. Dirt bit into her skin, scraped her hands raw. She retched, but there was nothing in her stomach except the weak tea she'd drunk this morning on the train. Still, she felt her insides shriveling, darkness crowding the edges of her vision.

It couldn't be. There was some mistake. She was having another nightmare. She would open her eyes to see curtains at the windows and geraniums on the stoop. Graham and Prue standing on the steps to meet her.

"Here now, miss. Are you all right? You took a nasty spill on these cobbles."

One of the firemen.

Anna opened her eyes, her memories as ephemeral as the smoke blowing east toward Shoreditch. She swallowed down her horror, clamped her mouth over the sobs threatening to overwhelm her. "The people who lived here . . . do you know what shelter they might have been taken to?"

The firemen exchanged awkward glances before one shouldered the burden for all and faced her, shaking his head. "I'm sorry, miss. Ten died in this block alone. Seven more around the corner."

He need say no more. There would be no welcoming embrace. No comforting advice. And no revelations about her mother. She stared disbelieving at the wreckage.

"Have you a place to go?" the fireman asked in a deep, smoke-harshened voice. "Someone you can stay with?"

"No," Anna said, finally looking away. "No one at all."

The grammar school served as a temporary shelter for those who'd lost their homes in the air raids. With nowhere else to go, Anna climbed its steps as the sky purpled to twilight, the streets emptying of crowds, the growing dark slashed only by the sweep of arcing spotlights from antiaircraft batteries.

The building was packed, a lucky few finding seats on the narrow benches, the rest making do with the cement floor. Sleep was impossible, though a few managed catnaps curled on blankets, some wrapped in their coats, heads on their arms. Every now and then, the heavy krump of Bofors guns could be heard, followed by distant dull explosions and the constant moan of sirens.

Anna was handed a cup of coffee and a sandwich upon her arrival, but she'd no stomach for food and the coffee cooled untouched to a black tarry goop. With fumbling fingers, she pulled her locket from its place at her throat. What began as a childish charm against the bogeyman when she was six had become a talisman during her long, painful months recovering in hospital. A link to the familiar when the rest of the world seemed bent on chaos.

She ran her thumb over the enigmatic inscription engraved upon the back—*Forgive my love*—before flipping the locket open to stare at the grainy photographs nestled within: the woman's delicate features at odds with her mulish chin and defiant posture; the soldier's lean good looks still obvious beneath his battle-weary scruffiness.

As always, she sought shades of herself in these two ghostly figures, the curve of an eyebrow, the slope of a nose, the firmness of a chin. Did she have her mother's laugh? Her father's smile?

She snapped the locket shut with a disgusted snort.

Mother? Father?

Those terms should signify more than egg and sperm and a name on a birth certificate. The faces immortalized in her locket might be better termed sire and dam; clinical names that didn't confuse conception with parenthood.

In every way that mattered, Graham and Prue Handley had been her mother and father. They gave her a home when it would have been all too easy to send her to an orphanage or workhouse. They had comforted her when she broke her arm falling out of a tree at seven years old and when she had her appendix removed at twelve. They had tolerated her teen complaints at being forced to practice the piano while other girls her age were going to the cinema with boys. And when they introduced her to strangers it had been as their daughter, a statement of love and belonging she'd always taken for granted.

Where did she belong now?

"Anna? Anna Trenowyth? Is that you?"

She looked up to see her old next-door neighbor Mrs. Willits pushing through the crowds toward her. She wore a flower-printed nightgown under a man's mackintosh and gum boots on her feet. Her hair was wrapped in a red chiffon scarf, and a string bag dangled on her wrist. She barreled her way through a group of chattering housewives and stepped over an old man curled on his coat, who grumbled and turned his back.

"It *is* you," Mrs. Willits announced, as if she were broadcasting for the BBC. "I thought I recognized that ginger hair of yours."

Anna smoothed a curl back from her forehead, suddenly self-conscious of the wild tangle of red-gold curls barely contained beneath her storm cap.

"What on earth are you doing here, my dear?" Mrs. Willits shoved herself onto the bench beside Anna with a huff of breath. "We'd all heard you were still recuperating in Surrey."

"I came up on the train this morning. I . . ." Anna disguised her emotion with a sip of her cold coffee.

"Oh dear, yes, I see." Mrs. Willits patted Anna's knee. "Not the homecoming you were expecting, I daresay."

Rage and grief sat like a sour weight in the pit of Anna's stomach, but it was regret that gnawed at her nerves until she shook as if she were fevered. She had taken them for granted, imagining they would always be there as they had always been. As unchanging and familiar as the cluttered little terrace house that forever smelled of Graham's Grousemoor tobacco and Prue's rosewater perfume. Anna stared hard into her cup, vision blurring, but now was not the time to fall apart. She blinked back her tears and forced herself to straighten her shoulders, though she felt as if her spine might snap with the effort. "Forgive me, Mrs. Willits. I'm all at sea."

"Of course you are, and there's nothing to forgive, child. I know it's hard, but we mustn't lose heart. We must carry on and keep faith in our soldier boys and Mr. Churchill." She pulled a perfumed handkerchief from her cleavage and handed it to Anna. "The Handleys wouldn't want to see you all red-nosed and blotchy. Not when you've only just got yourself healthy again after that horrid mess in France."

Anna dabbed at her eyes with a weary smile. "It doesn't seem real yet. I mean, I know they're gone, but I can't feel . . . I don't want to feel. If I do, then I'll have to face the truth that they're really gone, and I can't do that. Not yet. Is that wrong? Is it disloyal?"

"Of course not. When you're ready, you'll mourn them properly, and until then, you can take solace knowing they were happy in each other to the end, and few can make that claim, can they? They were proud as peacocks of you and your war work. Always bragging to the neighbors, reading us your letters from France to let us know how their girl was getting on over there."

She crushed the handkerchief in a trembling fist. "But I wasn't their girl, was I? Not really."

"Pish tush! Of course you were. Has someone been needling you?" Mrs. Willits eyed the sea of weary faces, as if seeking out a perpetrator to confront. "Has someone been talking out of turn?"

"No, nothing like that." Anna paused to gather her breath and her scattered thoughts. Spoke before she could think twice. "Do you recall my mother? My real mother?"

Mrs. Willits leaned back with a lift of her brows. "Of course I do. She was a dear sweet thing. Not at all what you'd expect from a . . ." She pressed her lips together, as if threading through a difficult problem.

"Earl's daughter?" Anna offered. "Or fallen woman?"

Mrs. Willits's shoulders gave a quick, agitated jump before she recovered with a shrug and a wave of her hand. "Take your pick. She was quiet but always polite and never standoffish. You'd never have known the one by her demeanor nor expected the other if you weren't toddling about the back garden."

"What about my father?"

Mrs. Willits's open gaze grew shuttered. "Your mother never spoke of him and it wasn't my place to pry. I don't think even the Handleys knew who he was, only that he'd perished in the Great War and left your mother with a child but no wedding ring." She paused. "What do you remember, Anna?"

She gave a sad shake of her head. "Not much. I was only six when she died. She's more like a dream than a real person."

Not that Graham and Prue hadn't tried to keep the memory of her mother alive. They had told Anna stories until in her eyes, Lady Katherine Trenowyth became imbued with the same glamour and mystery as the most fantastical characters in her Grimms' fairy-tale book. A tragic princess driven from her beautiful home by evil forces. But where did the fairy tale end and the truth begin? Who was the real Lady Katherine? And did Anna really want to find out?

She'd hoped her parents might be able to help her make that decision. Now they were gone. Who would help her now?

Her gaze fell on Mrs. Willits, who watched her, eyes pinched with sorrow and her own losses.

Reaching into her pocket, Anna pulled out the crumpled letter, the letterhead stark and businesslike. "May I ask you a favor?"

"Of course, my dear, anything."

"I received this last week." Anna passed her the letter. "I'd wanted an overseas posting—Egypt or the Far East. Somewhere I could be of use. Instead, I was assigned to . . . well, you can see for yourself."

Mrs. Willits scanned the letter with a pursing of her lips. "Yes, I can understand your dilemma."

"I know I've been refused because of my health. Still, of all the convalescent homes in England, did it have to be Nanreath Hall?"

"It does seem a cruel twist of fate to be sent to your mother's old home."

"I came to ask Graham and Prue what I should do. Now I'm asking you."

Mrs. Willits folded the letter carefully, tracing a line across each pressed seam, her penciled brows drawn low in thought. "Perhaps you should look at this chance as a gift rather than a curse. You've been given the opportunity to step into your mother's world, to meet the family you never knew. Who's to say what doors might open?"

Anna snatched the letter back and stuffed it in her pocket. "Or what doors might be slammed in my face. Why should I want to meet them? They certainly never cared a tuppence for me."

Mrs. Willits tapped the locket with her finger, a knowing smile curving her lips. "Perhaps you have questions only they can answer."

The sky was a perfect blue with high, thin clouds stretched like fingers toward the Continent. Birds called in the yew hedges and far off could be heard the hum of morning traffic. A postman cycled by with a ring of his bell. A woman walked her dog. A normal day but for the red, raw cemetery earth and the mourners clinging round the new graves, taking comfort from one another.

Anna stood beside Mrs. Willits, who had shed her mackintosh and gum boots for a donated skirt and blouse, serviceable but sadly out-of-date. Her gas mask hung in its cardboard box from her shoulder. "Is there anyone you can call on now that Graham and Prue are gone?"

"No, but I'll be all right." Anna offered a game smile. "I'm used to being on my own. What about you?"

"I've had word from my daughter in Cardiff. She's asked me to come stay with her."

"Ginny's in Wales?"

A clever, popular girl, Ginny Willits had been in Anna's class at school, and the two had been close friends until Anna's enlistment with the VAD took her from home. Even then, they'd kept in touch until the evacuation from France left no time for letters. And afterward . . . well, silence had been easier.

"Nah, my Ginny's a WAAF, working here in London for the War Office. You should see her. Looks spanking in her uniform. This is my eldest girl by my first marriage, I'm talking of. Her husband's been called up and she could use the company."

Anna laid a bouquet of autumn flowers on each grave, her hands steady, her eyes dry, only a painful tightness in her chest and a lump that made eating impossible. "I'm glad you'll be safe out of London. I'm sure Ginny feels better knowing you're safe, as well."

Mrs. Willits sniffed her disdain. "It's too much like running away for my tastes, but there's no help for it, I suppose. And to look on the bright side, I'll have a chance to spend time with my grandchildren. George is seven and little Kate almost three."

"It sounds lovely."

"It does, doesn't it? Perhaps if I concentrate on that bit of it, I won't fret over the rest." She slid her gaze toward Anna. "Family can be a boon in hard times. Nothing better than kin when you've your back to the wall."

Anna ignored her clumsy salvo as she sent a final prayer heavenward. Graham and Prue were gone. That stark fact hammered against her mind until her head ached. She would not wake from the dark tunnel of this nightmare to the soothing murmur of a nurse and the quiet calm of the hospital ward.

"Have you decided what you're going to do yet? Whether you'll take the posting?"

The mourners began to filter away. Anna turned to follow the rutted gravel path toward the lych-gate. Or rather, where the gate once stood. It, along with the rest of the iron fencing surrounding the cemetery, had been pulled up and taken away for war scrap.

"I know it's not my place, Anna, but I feel responsible for you. I don't like the thought of leaving and not knowing what's to become of you."

"You think I should go."

"I do. The Trenowyths are your blood, and in times like these, blood is important. Knowing who you are and where you come from is important."

"And if they toss me out on my ear?"

"Then you'll know that, too, won't you? You won't spend your life wondering what might be. You'll know what is, and that's good, steady ground to start on."

"Mrs. Willits, you knew Graham and Prue better than anyone. When I told them about my posting, they asked me to come home. They said they wanted to discuss my mother. That it was very important and they were afraid they might have left it too long." She kicked a chunk of concrete from her path, eyes cast on the pavement ahead of her. "Do you know what they might have wanted to tell me?"

"I'm afraid not, dear."

Anna tried to hide her disappointment. "Oh well. I just thought . . ."

Mrs. Willits patted her hand, sympathy shadowing her motherly gaze. "I'm glad you asked, dear, and if I think of anything, I shall write and let you know immediately. You have my word. And write to Ginny if you can. She'd be happy to know you're better and doing well."

"I will. I promise." Ignoring the hustling passersby, Anna stopped in the middle of the pavement and hugged the older woman. "Thank you for everything. I don't know what I would have done without you."

"Pish tush, dear. I've done nothing but pry my nose into your business and offer you a lot of unwanted advice, as if you were one of my own girls."

"No, you've made me see clearly, just as Graham and Prue would have done had they been here." Anna jerked her chin sharply in decision. "I'll report to Nanreath Hall as ordered. Even if the high-and-mighty Trenowyths brush me off, I'll still be able to work hard and help as I can. Perhaps if I do a very fine job, I'll get the posting abroad that I want."

"That's the fighting spirit, my girl. And who knows, Anna—the high-and-mighty Trenowyths may surprise you."

Her smile felt awkward and uncertain, but Anna's heart lifted and the lump in her stomach unknotted. She threaded an arm through Mrs. Willits's, and together they walked briskly down the street away from the church. "They may, but one thing is for certain—I will definitely surprise them."

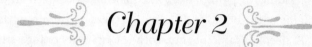

# Chapter 2

*Nanreath Hall, Cornwall*
*August 1913*

L ady Katherine, I would say this is a surprise, but I woke this
morning with the most delicious premonition that you were
coming to see me today."

Mrs. Vinter welcomed me with her usual exuberant, patchouli-
scented embrace, so different from my parents' parsimonious affection.

A somewhat mysterious and glamorous figure, she had retired
to the village of Melcombe after an exhilarating, globe-trotting, cos-
mopolitan life I could only imagine and envy. And while most of her
neighbors considered her nothing more than a harmless eccentric,
I alone knew her true worth. She was a stiff wind of freedom and
unwavering approval where everything about my life was planned
and every shortcoming noted with weary resignation.

"You see? I had Minnie lay the best china and bake those jammy
cakes you enjoy so much."

I followed her billowing, parrot-colored figure into the tiny breakfast room where sunlight streamed in through windows thrown open to the sea air and an extra plate had been laid for tea. Puccini's "Addio di Mimi" from *La Bohème* wove itself into the softer strains of the ocean and the maid's pleasant humming as she worked. A sleeping cat kept time with the tip of its orange-striped tail.

I shed my hat and gloves, feeling a release from familial expectations with each article removed. "I'm sorry it's been so long. Lady Boxley's been ill and Mama needed me at home."

Mrs. Vinter merely nodded sagely, and I had the feeling she knew all too well what truly ailed my new sister-in-law. Since William, my elder brother and heir to the earldom, had left for London, Cynthia dragged about the house like a martyr, her growing stomach and shrinking temper setting everyone's teeth on edge.

"You're a good girl, Lady Katherine."

"I don't know about that."

"Take it from a very bad girl, I know your kind well. You make the rest of us appear positively beastly." She winked, her fingers clacking the long strands of beads she wore in excited agitation. "Now, let me look, let me look."

She clapped her ringed hands until I handed her my portfolio of sketches. Then as I poured the tea and sliced the cake, she intently studied each work, her brows furrowed, her gaze solemn and assessing. I never spoke during these critiques but sat silently on pins and needles awaiting her judgment.

She reached the final drawing, sat back in her chair, a smile creasing her lined parchment face. A small sigh of pleasure escaped her lips. "This one, Lady Katherine. This one is your best yet." She laid a picture of William on the table beside her cup of Lapsang souchong.

I sat up in my chair. "Really? But it's just a quick pen and ink. Barely more than a doodle."

"And yet you can feel his patient frustration, the unhappiness he seeks to hide behind the quiet solemnity of his features, and then there is perhaps a touch of the hangover behind the eyes . . . just there."

"You can see all that?"

"I see it because you put it there. You are a talented artist. You have a gift."

I looked upon my sketch with new eyes, trying to see what Mrs. Vinter did in the hasty dash of my pen over the page. I had done it in the final moments before William's train had come. We sat on the station platform, just he and I, with nothing to say that wouldn't embarrass us both. I had understood his desire to leave. I had longed to go with him.

That was a month ago.

My desire had only increased over the ensuing weeks.

"Have you given any more thought to my suggestion about sending your work to my friend Mr. Thorne at the Slade?" Mrs. Vinter asked. "The school would welcome a talent such as yours. You could study under some of the best artists of the day."

I choked down my last bite of cake. "I have. And I want to. But Mama would never allow it. She would say it's not what a proper lady should do with her life."

Mrs. Vinter leaned forward, her face alive and intent. "Then the question you must ask yourself is this—are you a proper lady?"

I folded and refolded my napkin. "I am. At least I want to be. It's complicated."

"I know well this tangle of loyalties, so will say no more about it—for now." Her eyes twinkled, and I knew she would bring it up again and again until I surrendered. Her vision for my future might be different from my mother's, but her persistence was very similar.

"You chafe at your fetters like a wild thing, Lady Katherine. One day, you will fight your way free. I only hope I'm alive to watch you soar." She spread her arms wide, the scarlet and yellow drape of her scarves wafting in the sea breeze as she laughed with joy.

We finished our tea in pleasant accord, chatting about the latest London exhibitions, the newest novels, and the most provocative plays. It was an exhilarating afternoon, all too soon over. The brass ship's clock she kept on her mantel chimed four, sending me into a mad panic. I threw myself from my seat, shouting for Minnie to bring me my hat and gloves.

"We're expecting guests this afternoon, and Mama wanted me home in time to bathe and change. She's going to kill me . . . worse, she'll offer me one of her freezing stares that makes me feel the size of a worm."

"I know well that maternal stare, my dear. Think no more about it. But come again when you can. Minnie and I shall be here with tea, cakes, and conversation."

I gave her one last wave as I hurried across the meadow toward the stile separating her property from the edge of our park. Cutting across the fields would take a mile from my walk back to the house. I might even be able to slip inside and to my rooms unnoticed.

"Katherine Trenowyth, why can you not remember simple instructions for more than two minutes together? Your father's guests will be here any moment and here you are, looking like a gypsy hoyden."

So much for my grand plan. Mother waited for me on the terrace, a hand shading her eyes against the afternoon sun, her tone expressing her all-too-familiar disappointment. "Amelia's already dressed and waiting."

"I'm sure she is," I muttered under my breath.

"Why can't you be more like your sister?"

"And spend all my hours planning out my wedding? No, thank you."

"Green has already drawn your bath. If you hurry, you can be dressed and in the drawing room before your father realizes you're late."

"An awful lot of bother for one of Father's tedious friends, if you ask me," I continued to grumble. "All they do is complain about Lord Asquith's government and smell up the house with their cigars."

"If you must know, it's not one of your father's political allies this time. He has commissioned portraits of the family, and the artist is arriving today, Mr. Balder or Balzac. Something like that. It's quite a coup. He painted Ena, the late queen's granddaughter, you know."

"Arthur Balázs?" My disgruntlement faded.

I'd read about Balázs in *Country Life*. The great families of England were lining up to have their likenesses painted by the talented Hungarian-born artist. Every noble heiress and prominent peer in the country passed through his studio in London. How on earth had Papa convinced the sought-after painter to leave the center of the social universe to travel all the way to Cornwall?

I couldn't help but catch some of Mama's excitement as she ushered me into the house. Not even Cynthia's moods could sour this unexpected treat. Perhaps that was why I lost myself for a moment and let my normally wary tongue run away with me. "Mrs. Vinter says I have real talent, Mama. Good enough to attend art school in London if I chose to. She has a friend there who—"

Mama swung round, a cloud heavy upon her brow, lips pursed. "Don't say any more. You know full well there is no question of art school, and any talent you have would be better spent assisting me."

"But Mr. Thorne is a famous professor there. He's exhibited his works at the Grafton and the New English Art Club."

"Enough. You're too old for these childish flights of fancy. It won't be long before you're married with your own household. It would serve you well to know how to run it."

"But what if I don't want to marry or . . . or . . . settle down with a family? I want to be an artist. I want to travel and experience the world. I want to do something important with my life."

"And raising children, making a good and happy home, isn't enough?"

"No . . . at least not yet."

"Green is waiting for you. We'll discuss this later."

But we wouldn't. I knew that for certain.

She drifted up the staircase on a cloud of lilac perfume and gray silver-shot chiffon.

I dropped my gaze to the floor to follow meekly in her wake. I never even noticed the young man until he spoke, his voice hitting me like a hammer blow between the eyes. "Have you ever seen such an architectural monstrosity? It must be like living inside a wedding cake."

He was loose limbed and confident, dark hair brushed back off a broad forehead, a mocking twinkle in his deep-set eyes as he set down the luggage he carried and wiped his brow.

"It is a bit, but one gets used to it," I replied boldly.

The man's startled gaze met mine, and a cold shiver splashed across my shoulders as if I'd been dunked in the ocean. A humiliating heat crept into my cheeks.

He offered a sheepish smile and held out a hand. "The name's Simon Halliday. I've come to assist Mr. Balázs. And you are—"

Mother's rules of proper etiquette had been drilled into me from birth—servants were to be treated kindly, but never encouraged into familiarity—yet something about this brash, handsome young man with his expressive eyes and paint beneath his fingernails caused me to blurt, "How do you do? I'm Kitty. Kitty Trenowyth."

If someone were to ask me my favorite place in all of Nanreath's acres, it would have to be the ancient cliff ruins. Perched at the mouth of a deep, tree-lined creek, the moss-covered remains of an ancient fortress guarded the coast between Hendrum Point to the north and Dizzard's Pool to the south. In days long past, Bronze Age soldiers manned the ramparts, scanning the sea for potential invaders. Today there was little left but a tumble of crudely carved stones outlining the old perimeter, like an architect's floor plan, and a gaping archway leading to a set of worn stone steps that climbed to a crumbling watchtower.

Simon and I walked there after a morning spent working; or rather I sat unmoving in a girlish confection of lace and ruffles that made me look twelve while Simon ran about fetching and carrying for Mr. Balázs. The painter had turned out to be a lively man with bushy side whiskers and a jovial laugh, who immediately put me at ease. He treated Simon more like a prized pupil than an assistant, and I envied him such support for his artistic ambitions.

"We used to clamber all around this place when we were children," I explained as I reached the small, sheltered platform of rocks and old lumber built years ago with childish ingenuity and enthusiasm. I had spent many an hour battling dragons with William or braiding daisies into my younger sister Amelia's hair. Now William was gone and Amelia had no interest in such grubby pastimes. These days I came alone with my journal to watch the scuttle of clouds overhead and plan out my life as if I actually controlled my fortunes.

I would be a great painter and travel the world—Spain, France, the Orient, perhaps even Africa—and when I was old and gray, I'd come to live in a cottage by the sea, keep cats, and dine when I wished and wear what I wanted.

Those dreams seemed as high and thin as the haze above me this afternoon, and I scolded myself as sternly as Mama ever could for being a ridiculous little girl.

"Then William had a bad fall and broke his ankle. My father forbade us from coming here after that. He said it was too dangerous."

"Why do I have the feeling you don't follow Papa's orders?" Simon high-wired his way along the parapet to stand at the very edge where cliff met sky. His face had a distant eager quality as it scanned the ocean, his eyes bright and fixed upon the horizon, as if he might step out into the very air and take flight.

"It's a good place for thinking . . . and dreaming."

He shot me a smirky glance over his shoulder. "And what does a top-drawer earl's daughter dream about? Parties and fancy dresses and a handsome young man to sweep her off in his expensive motorcar?"

If he'd been talking to my sister, Amelia, he'd be right, but I felt his joke like a punch to the stomach. "Is that all you think I'm good for? Parties and shopping and chasing men?" I swallowed my disappointment. Why did I care what he thought of me? I stared out at the sea, thunderclouds gathering like mountains along the horizon.

"I'm sorry, Kitty." Simon joined me on the platform, a boyish flop of hair curving over his brow, an apologetic bent to his features. "Can we start fresh? Pretend the bit where I made an ass of myself never happened?" His eyes twinkled as he spoke, fluttering my heart.

"I don't know. Can we?"

His shoulder felt nice where it touched mine, and his cologne smelled woodsy and masculine. He lit a cigarette, offering me a drag, which I tried, coughing madly as my eyes watered like faucets.

"I see what you mean about thinking and dreaming." The tip of his cigarette turned to ash. He fumbled in his leather bag, retrieving a pad and a sharpened pencil. With deft, precise movements, his hand moved over the paper; a line here, a curve there. A bit of shadowing with the side of his finger.

I watched mesmerized, my body crackling as if an electric current passed through it. Even my scalp tingled.

"What do you think?" he asked.

I paused for only a moment before taking the pencil and pad from him, adding a stroke here, a shadow there. Working quickly and with purpose, lost completely in my desire to capture the truth with a bit of lead and my imagination.

I handed the pad back, my stomach tight, my fingers trembling.

There was no way to discern his thoughts from the strong line of his jaw or the flecked green gleam of his eyes. I could only grip the rough plank of my seat and wait.

"I stand corrected, Kitty Trenowyth," he said quietly.

A slippery excitement curled up my spine, and I shivered.

"So if you aren't dreaming of jewels and a closet full of ball gowns, what *do* you want?" he asked.

Dare I speak? I felt his eyes on me, a little curious, a little admiring, and courage spread warm like honey along my stiff limbs. "I want to attend art school in London."

I waited for his laughter. Instead, he nodded thoughtfully. "So why don't you?"

"You've met my parents. I'm destined for an advantageous marriage with a young man of good family and the proper political aspirations."

"They can't force you to marry some dull clod with an upper-class lisp and the right school tie."

I hugged myself against the chill as the day's heat was replaced by a cool storm breeze and stared out at the ocean, now sullen and white-capped. The air smelled of rain.

"Are you happy, Kitty?"

His question hung suspended in my mind. Three little words that I could not adequately answer. Was I happy? I had everything a girl could want: a family that loved me even if they didn't understand me; a beautiful home, fine clothes, freedoms other young ladies my age would kill for. So why was I so discontented? Why did I feel the need to escape at every opportunity? Why did the security of family and rank and wealth feel less like a net and more like a noose?

He leaned close, and before I understood what was happening, his lips touched mine. A soft brushing that sent my senses tumbling. I knew I should recoil with a slap to his cheek to put him firmly in his place, but I couldn't breathe for the glorious expectation of something . . . though I knew not what at the time, only that I ached for it with every cell in my body. His body was hard and muscular. I could feel his strength as he held me and smell his aftershave and hear his breath.

When it was over he smiled, not the impish grin or the cynical smirk but a smile of genuine warmth and respect. "Papa would definitely not approve."

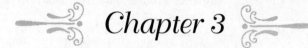

# Chapter 3

*Cornwall*
*October 1940*

Anna stood on the station platform, bags at her feet, heavy
coat slung over her trunk. By the light of a crescent moon,
she strained to check her watch against the station's ancient clock.
Eleven on the button. Six hours later than she'd been expected, but
there had been no help for it. Her train had been sent to a siding
twice to sit idle as endless cars of freight rolled by toward the coastal
ports at Southampton and Portsmouth.

She wandered the platform, hoping to locate a telephone or a
porter, but neither seemed available, and the doors were locked
tight. A village lay in a shallow valley below. No welcoming lights,
but the gray and silver outlines of rooftops and chimneys gleamed
in the frosty moonlight, and Glenn Miller floated on the cool breeze
ruffling her collar. Perhaps someone there could drive her to Nanreath Hall.

Leaving her trunk for collection in the morning, she hoisted her duffel on her shoulder and set off down the road, praying some nutter with dimmed head lamps didn't come whizzing round a curve in the dark and smash her flat. As she clung to the verge, she listened for the telltale growl of a motor, but aside from the strains of distant music and the creak of tree branches, all was quiet.

At the crest of an old stone bridge, she paused to rest and catch her breath. What seemed a short walk from the top of the hill had become a long, tiring slog on narrow, winding lanes lined by high hedges and thick copses of trees. Wiping a sleeve across her forehead, she stretched and windmilled her bad shoulder before leaning against the baluster, watching the sliver moon shimmer and ripple among the mossy rocks below. The wind smelled sweet and loamy, but she tasted the brine of salt at the back of her throat along with the tartness of sea air.

Leaving her bag, she clambered down to the shore where she scooped up a handful of water and splashed it against her face and ran a damp hand over the back of her neck. She dipped her hand in again and impulsively put it to her lips. Icy, the water bit against her tongue and cramped her empty stomach.

The low drone of planes drowned out the faint notes of "Begin the Beguine." Anna stiffened. Her hands trembled, and her throat closed around a sob. The muscles in her calves tightened as she crouched like a rabbit caught by the poacher's lamp, and she squeezed her eyes shut, whispering under her breath.

This was not France. The road was not clogged with panicked refugees, their hands outstretched and eyes pleading for help as the ambulances crawled ever west and north toward the beaches. These were slow, ponderous Junkers, not the deadly German Stukas. Her hands were not covered in Harriet's blood; her shoulder was not shattered and useless as she struggled to escape the sinking cruiser.

This was England . . . this was England . . . this was . . .

She took a deep breath, letting the past wash through her. She refused to fall to pieces, yet still she reached to massage her opposite shoulder as a ghost pain seared her right side.

The bombers continued eastward, the terrible drone of their engines fading beneath the normal country night sounds of creaking branches and nesting birds. She struggled to her feet. "You'll never get posted to a forward hospital that way, Anna old girl," she chided herself.

Beyond the eastern horizon, flashes of light burst across the sky accompanied by a string of earth-shaking thumps. She jumped, shoulders twitching toward her ears, heart leaping in her chest. So focused on the *whump-whump-whump* echo of falling bombs, she never heard the bang and rattle of a horse-drawn wagon heading toward the bridge until it was skittering on the road above her.

"What the devil?" Gravel spat as the wagon racketed to a halt. "Ho, boy. Easy now. Easy."

Anna scrambled up the bank to the bridge to find a broad-backed gray horse stomping and tossing its head and mouthing at the bit.

"You there," a man shouted from the wagon's bench seat. "Are you trying to cause an accident?"

"I'm sorry," Anna began politely. "I only meant to—"

"Who leaves their bloody luggage in the middle of the road at night where anyone could blunder into it?" He set the brake and tied off the reins before clumsily lowering himself to the ground. "I nearly ran into the creek avoiding a collision with your unmentionables. Bloody fool woman."

She hoisted her duffel to her shoulder. "You needn't be insulting. How was I to know you'd come charging down the road as if the hounds of hell were after you? This isn't Oxford Circus, after all."

He soothed the horse with a murmur and a pat on its flank,

rubbed its nose until it butted at him, whuffling its contentment. "A good thing. God knows what sort of mayhem you and your luggage would create there." As he approached, the moonlight shone on a thin, pale face, long, narrow cheekbones, and eyes of a luminous gray that narrowed as he studied her. "What are you doing wandering around out here in the middle of the night anyway?"

Anna adjusted her cap. Straightened her cuffs. Set her coat round her shoulders. "My train was delayed and I've missed my ride. I'm due at the convalescent hospital at Nanreath Hall."

His gaze traveled from the top of her horrible navy-blue "egg cup" hat to the RAF gold eagles on her collar down to her sensible shoes. "You're a nurse?"

"Red Cross Voluntary Aid Detachment."

"So you're here to do the muck work the proper sisters don't have time for."

"I'll do whatever is needed for those who need it most." She took in his disheveled state of dress, wrinkling her nose at the powerful scent of alcohol, cigarettes, and stale perfume, adding, "I'm very good at dispensing aspirin and making strong coffee."

"I'll wager you are." He snorted his disdain. "Come along. I'll take you. If I leave you to walk to Nanreath alone, you're liable to be shot as a spy by some overzealous farmer or wander onto the moors and be trampled by a sheep."

"I wouldn't want to put you to any *more* trouble."

He took her duffel and tossed it into the back of the wagon. "No trouble. I'm headed there anyway."

"You work at the hospital?"

"That's one way of putting it. The name's Hugh, by the way."

He didn't sound like a local farmer, but then what did she know of the inner workings of grand estates? Perhaps he was part of the medical staff or a governmental functionary.

"How do you do? I'm Miss—" She hesitated. If he'd been working at Nanreath Hall for any length of time perhaps he was acquainted with the Trenowyth family. Even if he was part of the temporary staff, he might have gossip about them to pass along, a hint of what she might be getting herself into with this ridiculous posting. "I'm Miss Handley." She swallowed the lump in her throat along with the white lie. "Miss Anna Handley."

"It's nice to meet you, Miss Anna Handley. Now that the social niceties have been dispensed with, can we be on our way? It's been a long night and my bed awaits. I might even manage a few hours' sleep before I'm routed out at dawn."

He helped her onto the bench, where she smoothed her skirt over her knees and folded her hands in her lap. With another awkward clamber, he was beside her, taking up the reins.

"Is it far?" Anna asked.

"A few miles south of here. It won't take long unless we come across more of your lot tramping the Cornish hills." He slanted her a skeptical glance. "An army of misplaced VADs wandering in circles?"

"Just me."

"Not sure whether to be relieved or disappointed. Well then, let's be off."

A slap of the reins and the wagon jerked forward, nearly tossing her into his lap. Hugh steadied her with an arm around her shoulders. Anna moved away with a cool stare down her nose until he slid to the far side of the bench with a chuckle.

"You can't fault a lad for trying. It's a pretty night, you're a pretty girl, and I'm properly soused. But I'll not push where I'm not wanted. Don't worry."

She couldn't help the smile twitching her lips. "Oh, I'm not worried. I grew up in the city. I know how to deal with rats."

He laughed, his surliness easing into friendly sociability. "I like you, Miss Handley. You can leave your luggage scattered about in the road anytime."

They set off, the village falling behind them until it was finally lost from sight behind a wrinkle of hills as the ground rose toward the western cliffs.

"It was very patriotic of Lord Melcombe to donate his house to the war effort, don't you think?" she ventured.

He gave a twitch of his shoulders, his gaze fixed on the road. "It was donate or have the government conscript it. Besides, the drafty old pile might as well be used for a worthwhile cause. The family only occupies a few rooms anymore."

Anna ran a finger along her locket's chain. "Are they nice?"

He shot her a sidelong look, his mouth a thin, stern line. "About what you'd expect from an old aristocratic family clinging to its privileges with every ounce of influence it still possesses."

"You don't sound as if you like them very much."

He shrugged again, his face turned away from her and lost in darkness. "I don't."

Anna subsided into silence, letting the rocking wagon ease her into a half doze, letting the pain in her heart bloom and spread. Her face hurt, and her throat closed around a lump the size of a football, but she couldn't cry. Not even for Graham and Prue. She'd tried in the weeks since she'd departed London, but her tears had dried up. She had none left to shed. Only a dull ache that pressed against what was left of her heart.

The wagon turned onto a narrow avenue overhung by sheltering lime trees. The growl of the ocean was louder now and the wind snapped at her curls and stung her cheeks. Across a wide meadow, chimney pots and a slice of crenellated roof appeared and disappeared between the curtain of trees.

"Is that the house?" She turned to see Hugh slumped at the reins, his cap pulled low over his face, as he snored lightly. "Here now, are you mad?" She shook his shoulder. "Wake up!"

He thrashed, eyes wide and staring, body vibrating with rage and fear. "Shit all! Scotty, look to your tail! Jerries at—" Slowly his unfocused gaze settled on her face with visible relief. "You," he said gruffly. "You're determined to stop my heart one way or another, aren't you?"

"You could have put us in a ditch—or worse."

Hugh wiped a sleeve across his forehead. "Napoleon knows the way home better than I do. Why do you think I take him when I want to go into the village? He's far less bother than a driver, and he never breathes a word of what I've been up to, no matter how Mother might snoop."

Anna's stomach began a slow sink into her shoes. "Mother?"

"The chatelaine of the lordly manor, Lady Boxley."

"Oh dear. So you're . . ."

"Host and chauffeur, the Earl of Melcombe." He tipped his hat. "At your service."

Here now, shut that door. You'll have the ward sister on us for violating blackout rules." The young woman hurrying down the stairs toward Anna was dressed in the familiar VAD ward uniform of blue dress, white apron, and veil.

"It's my fault, Tilly." Hugh—her very own cousin Hugh—slid in behind Anna. "I thought I'd bring her in the back way so she might snatch a bite to eat and maybe a doze before she faced the onslaught."

The change in the woman's demeanor was immediate. She put a hand to her veil with a coquettish smile, her brisk scurry slowing to a hip-swaying saunter. "Lord Melcombe, I should have known you were up to your tricks again." She wrinkled her pert little nose as she came closer. "Phew! You smell like a distillery. Your mother will be fit to be tied if she catches you in such a state."

"The second reason we came in through the sculleries, my dear. I can slip up to my rooms and none will know the extent of my inebriation."

Hugh—should Anna call him Lord Melcombe? No, he had introduced himself as Hugh. He was smelly, drunk, and dissolute, a far cry from what she had imagined a peer of the realm should look like. But he was her cousin. And he had a mother, presumably making her Anna's aunt. She'd gained two relatives in the space of thirty seconds.

Tilly gave Hugh a kittenish pout. "You just leave everything to me, my lord."

"I always do." He gave her a quick buss on the cheek before swinging his attention to Anna. "This is where I take my leave of you, Miss Handley."

Heat crept into Anna's cheeks at the reminder of her lie. She thought about confessing, noted his bloodshot eyes and drunken posture and chose to keep silent. He'd probably not even remember her in the morning, much less her last name.

"Nurse Jones will see you settled and pointed in the right direction. She's a whiz at avoiding Matron when she needs to." He winked.

"But I don't want to avoid her," Anna replied, feeling slightly besieged.

"It's nearly one in the morning, you're a wrinkled mess from a long day on the train, and you're swaying on your feet. None will expect you to report until morning. In the meantime, Tilly can find you a billet, and when you present yourself tomorrow you'll be spruced up and in fine fettle for the old dragon."

"I shouldn't . . ."

But Tilly had already grabbed the duffel from Anna's hands and was making for the stairs. "His lordship's right. Matron's gone to bed and the sisters on duty are busy on the ward. Best to come along with me, but be quick. If Sister Murphy catches us, we'll be scrubbing until our hands fall off."

Anna followed as they climbed the narrow stairwell up to the slope-roofed attics.

"Keep your voice down and step lightly. The floors creak something terrible."

An uncarpeted corridor stretched for about fifty feet before branching, a lamp set on a table giving off a stark, ugly light. Tilly hurried Anna down and around the corner, finally stopping in front of the last door before another broader stairwell. "Home sweet home." She dragged Anna into the small room and flipped on the light.

Three narrow iron bedsteads took up most of the space, two in various stages of tidiness and one stripped bare to the ticking. A locker and ladder-back chair stood sentinel beside each bed. Someone had managed a dressing table out of four fruit crates and a plank, prettying it up with a piece of frilly fabric in a sickly shade of mauve. A silver framed photo of a young man sat atop it beside a cut-glass bottle of expensive Après L'Ondée perfume and a jewelry case with a gold key in the lock. Thick flannel blackout curtains stretched across a single window. A mirror hung on the back of the door, photographs and magazine clippings haphazardly shoved into the frame.

"We'll get your kit sorted tomorrow. In the meantime, that one's mine." Tilly pointed to the messier of the two made beds. "Get some sleep. I'll wake you when I come off duty."

"Thank you," Anna said, eyeing the thin mattress, army-issue sheets, and lumpy pillow with lust in her heart.

"My pleasure." With a last friendly smile, Tilly dropped the bag, snapped off the light, and vanished back the way she'd come.

Anna sat on the bed with a tired stretch. Flopped backward onto the pillow with a whush of spent breath to stare up at the ceiling. She closed her eyes as every muscle slowly unkinked, but her thoughts ran in ever-tightening circles. She pulled the locket free of her blouse and snapped it open. As always she was met by Lady Katherine Trenowyth's serene and unchanging expression. "I've done it. I'm at Nanreath Hall, Mama. Now what?"

L ight roused Anna from her nightmares. Not the soft, seeping light of a new dawn, but the glare of a handheld torch. A hand shook her by the shoulder. "It's all right. It's just a bad dream. You're safe now."

Heart racing, Anna struggled up through a soupy fog to find a pert, oval face framed in dark chocolate curls hovering inches from her own.

"Better now?"

She sat up, running a hand over her face. "Yes, much. Thank you."

The face and the torch withdrew. "You had me worried. I thought you might knock my teeth in the way you were thrashing about in the bed."

Anna squinted to see the clock. Three A.M. She'd slept an hour at the most, and that had been a fitful, anxious rest leaving her drenched in a cold sweat, temples throbbing. "Sorry to be a bother. Miss Jones let me stay here. I'm to report to Matron in the morning. I'm Anna, the new VAD."

"I'm Sophie Kinsale. How do you do? Always nice to meet a fellow worker bee." She spoke in plummy Mayfair tones as she snapped on the overhead. "Are you quite certain you're feeling well? I've seen cadavers with more color."

"Much better, thank you. Suppose I'm a little skittish about starting in a new place."

"Seemed more than skittish nerves to me."

Anna offered her best reassuring smile, an expression she'd perfected after weeks in hospital. "That's a . . . uh . . . lovely overcoat."

Sophie wrinkled her nose. "It's a flea-bitten mess, but it belonged to my father and reminds me of home. Charles says it's like hugging a mammoth."

She shrugged out of the ankle-length raccoon-skin coat. Skimming off her tunic and loosening the top button on her blouse, she stood in front of the mirror, lip chewed between her teeth as she tilted her head side to side in close examination.

"I think you're safe," Anna offered finally.

Sophie stiffened, meeting her gaze in the mirror. "I beg your pardon?"

"Your neck. It's fine."

Sophie spun round, cheeks flaming red. "Please don't say anything. Matron would have my head."

Anna leaned back on her pillows, her nightmares naught more than a vague unease now, though she knew if she closed her eyes they would return. They came every night without fail. Dark and insidious, dragging her back to the chaos of France when the world seemed on fire. "Your secrets are safe with me."

Sophie's shoulders slumped in relief. "You must think me a horrid flirt or worse, but I'm really not a Sodom and Gomorrah type, I swear. Charles . . . that is . . . Lieutenant Douglas is shipping out. Tonight was our last night together. I suppose we got a bit carried away." She undressed, neatly tidying away each article of clothing before donning a pair of silky pajamas straight out of a Hollywood picture.

"It's hard saying good-bye."

Sophie dabbed at her eyes with the edge of her washrag. "I didn't realize how hard until I left him standing alone at the railway station. In that moment I would have happily thrown my reputation away for five more minutes."

Anna felt a leaden weight choking off her breath. If only she'd opened up to Graham and Prue during that last visit. If only she'd shared her heartbreak and her fear. If only she'd told them she loved them one last time.

With quick, deft strokes, Sophie removed her makeup and began the arduous process of brushing out her hair then putting it up in curlers. "You're a real sport. Matron would rake me over the coals for breaking the rules."

"What would she do to you?"

"I don't know, but she once caught a nurse and a young man in a broom cupboard. Sent the young woman packing."

"What did she do to the young man?"

Giving her scarf-covered curlers a final pat, Sophie snapped off the overhead and slid into bed. "Oh, he returned to his outfit and was shot down during the Norway campaign. Lost his leg." She paused and drew a soft, sad sigh. "Now he drinks too much, smokes too much, and when he's not behaving outrageously, he putters about this rackety old place like a lost soul."

Anna's hands curled around the edge of her blanket. "Are you talking about Lord Melcombe?" That explained his awkwardness around the wagon tonight, and why he wasn't in uniform now.

"So you've met him, then." She gave a helpless sigh. "Hugh's always been a bit wild—he was a positive fiend in London before the war—but it's grown worse since he lost his leg. Charles says he needs to get away from Nanreath before his mother swallows him up. That this place will pull him apart bit by bit if he lets it."

"He knows Lord Melcombe?"

"The two of them were at Eton and then Cambridge together."

Of course they were. Sophie oozed wealth and breeding. She probably took tea at the Savoy, wintered in Biarritz, and played badminton with princesses, too. And now she served meals, scrubbed floors, and gave sponge baths. Just like Anna. War united them in common purpose. Bombs and bullets didn't discriminate. Rich and poor bled equally.

"Luckily, Charles is a third son so he doesn't have the weight of an earldom hanging round him like an anchor," Sophie said, her voice already heavy with sleep. "Hugh has been carrying Nanreath Hall like a burden since he was four."

"What happened to his father?"

"He was wounded and gassed in the last war. Never regained his health and died shortly after. The family never recovered. Scandal, debt, and now poor Hugh. It's enough to make you wonder if the Trenowyths are cursed or something." Sophie's eyes closed, her breathing slowed. "Wake me at six, would you . . . uh . . . what did you say your name was again?"

Even as Sophie relaxed into slumber, Anna rolled over, her face to the wall. "It's Trenowyth."

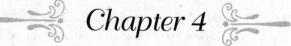

# Chapter 4

*London*
*October 1913*

Mr. Balázs's London art studio inhabited a narrow, redbrick creeper-covered building in the Grosvenor Road. The ground floor was taken up with sculleries, offices, and storage, from which seeped the acrid aromas of glazes and varnishes, paint, linseed oil, and turpentine. On my way up the stairs to the first floor where he lived and worked, I caught teasing glimpses of canvases stacked three deep, easels, and long sink counters cluttered with bottles and jars, brushes and old rags—an Aladdin's cave of artistic riches.

"Welcome to my abode, Lady Melcombe," he said with a continental bow and a kiss for my mother's hand. "Please, make yourself comfortable. I've sent for some refreshments."

My mother nodded graciously as she took a seat on a velvet-covered sofa, arranging her skirts in a pose of patient serenity. One I could never duplicate in a thousand years.

"And Lady Boxley? She is well?" he inquired politely.

"Much improved, now that we are assured of the child's survival."

Perhaps if one's definition of *improved* included wild swings between sullen indifference and smothering attentiveness. I smothered my cynical snort in a bout of coughing until Mama shot me a stern look.

Hugh Xavier James Roland Mannering Trenowyth had been born far earlier than suggested by the specialist Papa had hired as an accoucheur. Barely bigger than a kitten, he hardly stirred in his cot or made a sound, and for some weeks, we hovered in a painful state of expectation and dread.

"Lord Boxley must be so proud," Mr. Balász proclaimed. "A man's son is his guarantee of eternity."

Besides a flicker behind her eyes, Mama's mask never wavered. "He is the most satisfied of fathers."

More coughing. Mama handed me a peppermint and then studiously ignored me.

In fact, William had returned to Nanreath Hall only briefly after Hugh's birth. A whirlwind visit that left no one satisfied. He spoke little and nothing of consequence, though I pressed him more than once. He would laugh and turn aside all seriousness, as if he'd not a care in the world, though there were moments I caught him staring at the baby with a look of confused sorrow, as if facing a calamity that left him without hope.

"I expect Lady Katherine's final sittings won't take too long." Mama's imperial command was couched as a polite request.

"No time at all, my lady." Mama started to rise, but Mr. Balázs motioned for her to relax. "I do not like distractions as I work, you see. We will leave the door open, and she will be well looked after, I assure you."

Mama subsided, and I followed him into a bright, airy room

lined with north-facing windows. A large easel took up one corner, the canvas hidden from my view. In the middle of the room, a simple straight-backed chair had been placed.

"I wore the same gown as you instructed," I said as I removed my wrap and draped it over a convenient column to reveal the gaudy confection of sea-green silk. In the autumn chill of his airy studio, I felt goose bumps rise along my bare arms and up the back of my neck.

He moved quickly and efficiently, arranging palettes and brushes and small jars on his worktable. "Would you like to see what I have accomplished so far, Lady Katherine?"

"Oh yes, please," I said, my discomfort forgotten.

The portrait set me in Nanreath's rose garden on a white metal bench. Even unfinished, one could sense the drowsy peace and muted late-summer colors in the meticulous strokes of his brush. But I saw nothing of myself in the roughed-in charcoal sketch of the girl almost glaring out at the artist, her hands twisted in her lap as her hair lay twisted against her head, chin hard, lips thin. Did I really look like this? So . . . unhappy?

"You don't like it?" he asked mildly.

"I suppose it's always a little surprising to discover how the world views us, isn't it?"

"And it is perception as much as observation. So much of what we believe is hidden is actually visible if one has the eyes to see."

I thought of Mrs. Vinter's comment on my picture of William; she had spoken of my ability to capture emotion with my pencil, the spirit rather than the facade.

"If I'm not mistaken, you understand when I speak of these connections between the soul and the mask," Balázs said quietly.

"I understand. I only hope my father does, as well, or you'll be minus your commission. No offense intended, but he's not likely to hang me among the family's elite looking as if I've been sucking lemons all day."

Balázs continued watching me for another long, penetrating moment then laughed, his mustache wobbling in amusement. "Perhaps you're right. And I certainly wouldn't want to deny you your place among Melcombe's generations. We shall bend honesty a bit and in the doing make Lord Melcombe pleased as a pig in mud."

A clatter from the outer sitting room followed by the murmur of conversation caught my attention.

"I'm just back, sir." Simon Halliday, windblown, paint spattered, and incredibly handsome, poked his head round the door, carrying a paper parcel. His face stiffened when he saw me. "Good afternoon, Lady Katherine."

I remembered those lips touching mine, the cautious exploration that left me breathless and yearning before sense reasserted itself. The way his heart beat under my hand, the pulse in his throat and my own swaying of limbs.

"Mr. Halliday, how nice to see you again."

"You're late," Mr. Balázs snapped. "I sent you over an hour ago. See to Lady Melcombe and then get about your business. The day is half over and you've barely begun."

"Of course, sir." With a quick smile and a roll of his eyes, he was gone, but that heady, bubbly feeling I'd once felt in his presence returned, and I shivered.

"Please, my lady. Be very still!"

I subsided, and for the next hour and a half I sat unmoving, until just when I thought I must scratch my nose or die, he laid down his brush and wiped his forehead with a large spotted handkerchief. "We are finished for today."

As if on cue, Simon reappeared with a restorative cup of tea. "Helps get the blood flowing after sitting still for so long."

I rose stiffly, my foot asleep, a crick in my neck. The tea was hot and thick with milk and sugar, just as I liked it. "Thank you."

I barely noticed when Mr. Balázs departed to speak to my mother. Instead, I sipped at my tea, nibbled on a biscuit, and tried desperately to think of something—anything—to break the stilted silence between us. What was it about this man that emptied my brain and tied my tongue like no other person I had ever met? "I hope you've been well."

Simon handed me my wrap. "Very well, thank you."

"Mr. Balázs sounds like he's keeping you very busy."

"I don't mind. Hard work helps me forget for a little while."

I started to question him about what he wanted to forget when he suddenly moved away and to the painting. "I sometimes think I've mastered my craft and then I see a portrait he's done and I'm struck all over again by how much I have yet to learn."

I joined him, stomach tight, hands clenched. Reluctant to be faced once more with Balázs's unflattering version of my discontent.

Instead, the braced shoulders had been softened so that I looked at ease as I bent toward the sun that filtered green and gold through the leaves to gild the bench and the pearled comb in my hair. Subtle shading and layering of color had transformed the pinched, sour expression into one alive with an almost iridescent radiance. A smile barely touched my lips but shone clearly through my wide, clear eyes.

"He's captured you perfectly," Simon said quietly.

We stood shoulder to shoulder, and though the room remained chilly and clouds cast a gray, cheerless pall over the room, warmth dampened my skin and heat burned in my cheeks, for I recognized immediately what Balázs had perceived in those minutes while I sat, body immobilized, mind flying free.

My journal became my confessional as I spent the following days recounting every look that passed between us and each word we'd exchanged, plumbing them for hidden meaning and import. When facts failed me, I daydreamed our next meeting, our next conversation . . . our next kiss. Daydreams seemed all I was liable to have. I'd no idea how we might ever meet again. Papa had visited Mr. Balázs and deemed the portrait a success. It had been wrapped, crated, and sent on to Nanreath Hall. My time with Simon had run out before it even began.

Or so I thought.

"Good afternoon, Lady Katherine. Are you enjoying the exhibition?" he asked, appearing as if by magic as I wandered the National Gallery, catalog in hand. Soon we were discussing the merits of Maris and Pissaro, the hours passing in a blur of heated conversation and congenial argument.

"How wonderful to see you tonight, my lady. Looking forward to the performance?" This time we met by the stairs to Covent Garden's upper balcony during the interlude. He bought me an ice and we laughed over the horrid dialogue and the plodding plot until the bell sounded us back to our seats.

"Let me take those packages before you topple," he offered, accepting my latest Selfridges purchases as I tried to summon a cab. In company, we meandered down Bond Street, stopped at a tearoom for late-afternoon sustenance, and ended in Hyde Park feeding the ducks from the crumbs.

Each arranged accident was more exhilarating than the last. Each hour spent in each other's company cemented the notion more firmly in my mind that Simon Halliday was a man who would be very easy to love.

Taken up with their own comings and goings, neither Mama nor Papa paid close enough attention to note the increasing number of wild coincidences, and my maid, whose job it was to act as duenna, was easily persuaded by Simon's charming, careless manner to allow us more than the usual privacy as we visited galleries and exhibits, attended concerts and musical revues at Bechstein Hall and the Palladium, and window-shopped along Bond Street.

October slid into November. Days stretched golden and warm beneath blue, cloudless skies, the entertainments were endless, and when women cast sidelong glances at Simon, as they always did, I would smile in secret delight that someone so polished and handsome cared for me.

I should have known it wouldn't last and that when the storm broke, it would break in spectacular fashion.

The day didn't start out dark and brooding. Rather, the afternoon clouds bunched like cotton across a deep blue November sky, and the temperature had warmed enough to make me perspire beneath the jaunty poplin jacket I sported as Mama and I made the short walk from Reville's in Hanover Square to the family town house in South Audley Street after a long session of dress shopping.

"Kitty, slow down. We're not running a foot race." Mama paused to dab at her brow. "And I'm not as spry as I once was."

"Sorry, Mama. I can't help it. Everywhere I turn, there's always so much going on. I suppose I feel that if I dawdle, I might miss something."

"That's no excuse for scurrying as if you were eluding a constable."

"No, Mama." I slowed to her pace as we continued onto Bond Street.

"I want to find something nice for Cynthia. It's been a difficult time for her these last few months. Pearls, I think. Or perhaps sapphires. They would look perfect with her golden hair."

"Isn't this something William should be doing? I mean it's *his* wife and *his* son."

"What goes on between your brother and his wife is none of your concern."

"But doesn't it seem odd to you that he's only been to Nanreath once since Hugh was born? I would think he'd be over the moon, or at the least mildly excited," I pressed.

The corners of Mama's mouth turned down, her hand upon her bag tightening. "Marriage is a complicated matter, Katherine."

"What's complicated about love?"

It was my turn to hurry after Mama, who plowed ahead, leaving my questions behind.

We turned off the busy thoroughfare and into a side street, letting the current rush past us. Here the way was narrower, the buildings and shops closer together. Held to Mama's pace, I had the time to study the passersby—two nursemaids pushing prams, a maid flirting with a footman in a doorway, a workman with a barrow of building supplies.

"Dearest heavens! What on earth?" Mama's voice faltered as did her stride. "Katherine Trenowyth, what have you done?"

I joined her before a cluttered bow window displaying a series of framed paintings on easels; a few pastoral landscapes or dour still-life interiors, but high in a corner framed in a light golden wood was a small portrait of a young woman.

I couldn't breathe, and I glanced around in helpless desperation, as if I might wake to find this moment a horrible nightmare. "It can't be."

But it was.

The artist had caught me as if I'd just turned, a smile of joy upon my sun-browned, freckled cheeks and dancing in my blue eyes. My tangled red hair spilled free of its pins to curl around my ears and over my bare shoulders. I reposed upon a couch, sheets tangled over my hips and artistically draped to insinuate without completely revealing.

"Shameful." Mama's voice had gone icy and remote, her eyes hard as agates. "You look as if you just rose from . . . well . . . I shall say no more."

She was right. This was the pose of a woman in love; a woman made for love, body ripe, lips kiss swollen, a gaze both knowing and coy. Shocked, I couldn't turn away. Is this what I looked like? Surely not. This woman possessed a dashing confidence I would never have in a million years. She exuded lust and satisfaction and wisdom born from experience.

"It's not me." Shame washed over my back in a cold sweat, leaving my knees trembling. "It can't be."

"Who could possibly have created such an abomination?" Mama asked, the merest thread of panic entering her voice.

I looked at the gold lettering above the door—WEISS AND MESSER.

"Whoever it is, I shall put a stop to this immediately." She pushed past me and into the gallery as I followed, not knowing whether to be appalled or flattered.

A beetle-browed shopkeeper met her before she'd gone ten steps inside. "Good afternoon, madam. How can I help you?"

Mama drew herself up, as if preparing for battle. "The portrait of the girl that you have in your window. Take it down this instant."

He rubbed his hands in anticipation of a sale. "Ah, *The Red-Haired Wanton*. A fine choice, madam. We've had quite a lot of interest in that one."

"I am not interested in purchasing it. I am interested in burning it."

His smile faded to a confused frown as he looked from Mama

to me, as if for reassurance he wasn't dealing with a raving lunatic. Then his face cleared with instant comprehension and admiration. "You. You're the wan—"

"Don't say that word if you value your life." Mama clutched her handbag, as if preparing to beat him with it while all I wanted was to sink into the floor. "Her name is Lady Katherine Trenowyth. You will remember to address her as such."

"Mama, please," I pleaded, heat scorching my face. "Let's just leave. I'm sure there's been a mistake."

"That is no mistake, Katherine. That is libel." She stared me down until my stomach shriveled. "Or worse." She spun round to spear the poor man with a cold look down her long, perfect nose. "I want that scandalous indecency you have displayed in your window for the world to gawk at removed immediately or my solicitors will descend to drive you back under the rock from whence you came." She fairly radiated righteous vengeance from the tip of her wobbling peacock feather to the toes of her black button-strapped shoes.

"I'm sorry, madam, but that's not up to me. I just attend to the accounts. Mr. Weiss is the owner of the gallery. He's busy with a client at present, but I can let him know of your concerns."

"If you won't remove it, I will." She shoved past him, all grace and elegance gone in her wild agitation.

"Madam, please. If you'd only wait a moment." He grabbed her arm. She yanked herself free.

By now the tumult had drawn attention. An older gentleman with a long, sallow face and a pear-shaped body entered from the back. But it was his companion that froze then heated my blood and made me tremble.

"Lady Melcombe. Lady Katherine." Simon Halliday acknowledged each of us with a gentlemanly nod. "What a delightful surprise."

I was thinking more along the lines of unmitigated disaster myself.

"You!" Mama jabbed Simon in the chest, nearly knocking him off his feet. "You are a serpent." Another hard poke right in his sternum. "A defiler. A base creature slinking into the bosom of our family to wreak havoc and destruction."

Before she could strike a third time, Simon caught her wrist, his own ire increasing. "Lady Melcombe, I assure you I haven't defiled anyone. If the Red-Haired Wanton resembles Lady Katherine, it was mere chance. My painting is solely a creation wrought from my imagination." His diamond-sharp gaze found mine, and a tremor began in my legs before spreading upward to infect my heart until it raced and jumped. In that moment I hated Simon for bringing down this catastrophe on my head, and yet I found myself reveling in his obvious desire.

Perhaps Mrs. Vinter was wrong. Perhaps I was a bad girl, after all.

Mama huffed, her lips pressed tight. "It's more than obvious what you were imagining."

He paled but remained firm.

"Fine." Mama crossed her arms, her voice icy and regal. "Then I will purchase it from you. How much?"

"It's not for sale."

"Fiddlesticks. This is an art gallery. The intent is to sell the paintings. I wish to purchase that one."

Mr. Weiss stepped into the fray, a brave man seeing his profit about to slip from his hands. "Let's not be hasty, Mr. Halliday. Of course, Lady Melcombe, if you're interested in the painting." He paused as if calculating in his head. "It's marketed at one thousand pounds."

Mama blanched. I gasped. And Simon went a few shades of pink then gray.

"You must know I haven't that sort of money on me," Mama seethed.

Mr. Weiss spread his hands in a gesture of helplessness. "Then I'm afraid, there is nothing I can do for you, my lady."

Mama continued to bluster and threaten, all but dragging Mr. Weiss into his office.

Simon used the distraction to sidle his way close to me. His words were a low purr that shivered along my skin. "Mr. Balázs's sister is hostessing a party tonight. Come with me."

"You're mad," I spat under my breath. "I'll be lucky if I'm not packed off to a convent posthaste."

"I'm sorry, truly. I had no idea anyone who knew you personally would ever see it, but I can't stop thinking about you."

"So it would seem," I huffed, straining to remain resolute despite the mounting heat dewing my skin as his hot gaze burned through me.

"Please, Kitty. I want you to meet my friends, and they want to see who's finally managed to knock me head over heels."

Would it be wrong to say I was flattered? My resolve weakened along with my outrage.

"You're a grown woman, and Sophia Comersby is a perfectly respectable matron of impeccable reputation with a house in Bloomsbury," he cajoled. "What's stopping you?"

I couldn't help the flick of my eyes toward my mother, still arguing with the gallery owner, though it was obvious by Mr. Weiss's firm chin and gleaming eye that he'd already won this round.

"What happened to the girl who doesn't like to follow orders?" Simon dared me.

"Come along, Katherine." Mama's reappearance drew me back from a heady brink. "Your father will know how to deal with this effrontery."

"I'll wait for you at the corner of Curzon and Piccadilly," Simon whispered. "Meet me at ten."

I shot him a cornered are-you-trying-to-get-me-killed look.

He just smiled. He knew I would come.

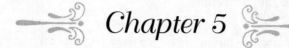

# Chapter 5

October 1940

A s an auxiliary to the military hospital in Southampton, we're used mainly for soldiers recovering from disease rather than injury, and those cases which would most benefit from the quiet of the country. We're a small staff, but I assure you, no less dedicated to our mission."

Sister Millbank, the hospital's matron, had the commanding bulk of a battleship and a voice that could cut glass. She sat behind an enormous desk littered with ledgers, forms, and a steaming cup of Bovril. Sun streamed through the window behind to halo her like an avenging angel, wimple wobbling in stern agitation. "I'm pairing you with Kinsale. She can teach you the day's routine, which is strictly enforced, and introduce you to the orderlies on your ward. Do not bother our MO, Captain Matthews, unless absolutely necessary. He has enough to do." She puffed up like a baker's loaf, chest and chin jutting equally. "I run a taut ship, Trenowyth. You're here to do a job, and I won't offer you any favors despite your connection to the family so don't expect them. Ask Kinsale if you don't believe me. She's been given the same stern warning."

"No, ma'am," Anna replied. "I mean . . . yes, ma'am. That is . . . it's a very distant connection."

"Well, all to the better. They're not happy to have us here, and I'd rather not have to put up with even more nonsensical complaints about the way in which the military's ruining the family mausoleum than I already do. Now, I've work to complete. I leave you in very capable hands, don't I, Kinsale?"

Sophie looked as if she were tempted to drop into a curtsy, but gave a submissive nod, instead.

The two of them had risen promptly at six, though Anna had already been awake, lying in her borrowed bed as she turned over Sophie's words, sifting them like sand for the answers she sought. The Trenowyth family never recovered. Scandal, debt, injuries, death. None of these things had been mentioned in the *Debrett's* she'd scanned among the stacks at the lending library, curled in a chair and hidden away from prying eyes, as if she were ashamed. Dry facts were all she'd had to go on: names, marriages, dates, coats of arms, honors, and benefits bestowed by various kings and queens over the centuries.

There had been nothing about a runaway daughter and a bastard child in the formal paragraph. No hint of the tumult such an occurrence must have caused. No clue to the identity of the man who had led a petted daughter of the house astray and then died forgotten in the mud of a French battlefield.

Would she learn anything more here, or would Nanreath Hall keep tight to its secrets?

With Matron already turning back to her desk and her Bovril, Sophie motioned Anna to follow as she led her down a second-floor corridor to a set of curving stairs and thus into a warren of storage rooms.

"Most of the house has been turned over to the war effort," Sophie explained, her tone clipped, her movements as crisp as her apron and veil. "Lady Boxley wasn't happy about it, but in the end, there was nothing she could do. She and her son keep a few rooms in the west wing. We don't see them unless they want to be seen."

"Hugh seems to move back and forth between realms at his leisure."

Sophie paused at a door, sliding a key from her ring into its lock. "Hugh does what he likes, as you must already know, Miss *Trenowyth*."

"Let me explain—"

The room they entered held shelves upon shelves of bedding. Racks contained mounds of freshly cleaned laundry, while in another corner piles of dirty stood waiting to be washed. "Sheets and blankets need sorting then we've got equipment to clean and sterilize," Sophie continued, her manner briskly business. "I'll show you around the wards this afternoon when we're expected to help the sisters with daily rounds. Tea is promptly at four. Matron doesn't like us to be late. It upsets the men's schedule."

Anna grabbed her arm, dragging her around to face her. "Sophie, listen to me. Please."

Sophie glared. "You let me prattle on last night when all the time you were laughing at me. Why didn't you say who you were then?"

"Because I was curious. You *know* them. I only know what I've read in books."

Sophie folded her arms over her chest, but her icy expression held the first signs of thawing. Perhaps Anna hadn't destroyed this hint of a friendship.

"My last name might be Trenowyth, but I'm not part of this family. I'm not part of any family. Not anymore."

"I don't understand. You told Matron you were related."

"My mother came from here, but I never knew her—or them. She left Nanreath Hall before I was born and died when I was six. I never knew my father, and the people who raised me died in an air raid last month in London."

Sophie's brows crumpled in sympathy. "Oh no, Anna. I'm sorry. I didn't know."

"Why should you? It's not usually how I begin most conversations." Anna pushed her sorrow away before it consumed her. If she didn't think about it, it couldn't hurt her.

Seemingly mollified by Anna's apology, the two of them worked through the morning's list of tasks laid out in Matron's neat handwriting.

In the corridors outside, orderlies moved with quick efficiency, conversations came and went, doors banged, shoes scuffed past, and wheels squeaked as trollies were rolled back and forth between the basement storage rooms and the medical wards, which had taken over the drawing rooms upstairs. It might be late October, but down here, the steam and heat from the nearby laundry saturated the air with damp humidity. Sweat trickled down Anna's spine and turned her well-tamed hair to a frizz of red beneath her veil, now sadly wilted from the heat.

Each time she thought they were coming to the end, another orderly would arrive with a fresh batch of linens to be folded and stored for use. Anna's arms ached, her stomach growled, but the repetitive monotony of the job and the industry beyond the door soothed her into a state of unthinking numbness.

Sophie worked beside her, the silence congenial now rather than cool until, "Does Hugh know who you are?" she asked.

Anna looked up from the form she'd been filling out, confused until she realized that while she had laid the conversation aside, Sophie had continued dwelling on it. "I don't know. It happened a long time ago."

"That won't matter. Families like ours have long memories." Sophie turned back to a cart filled with enough pajamas and robes to clothe a battalion. "Is that why you came to Nanreath? To find out about your family?"

"I came to Nanreath because I was assigned here. I don't expect a warm welcome. I don't expect any welcome." She felt foolish proclaiming her intent among heaps of pillowcases and stacks of sheets. "I'm here to do a job. That's all. And at the first opportunity, I plan on transferring to a real hospital with patients that need me."

Rather than being dismayed by Anna's outburst, Sophie smiled, her eyes alive with a curious excitement. "Meet me outside the library after visiting hours. I have something to show you."

"What is it?" Anna asked.

Sophie continued to look like the cat with the canary. "Let's call it 'a long memory.'"

Despite the linoleum on the floors and the ugly hardboard paneling nailed up to protect the walls in all the downstairs rooms, Nanreath Hall maintained an air of country house serenity. Patients relaxed in the salon, browsing newspapers or listening to the wireless. Knots of men congregated in the armory, where tall windows looked out on a sloping expanse of lawn toward the sea. Down the passage, a threesome belted out the latest hits on an antique spinet.

Anna loitered at the base of the grand staircase, hoping Matron didn't pass by and question her momentary inactivity. Technically, she was still on duty, but the hospital's medical officer, Captain

Matthews, was making evening rounds, and she'd been sent to grab a quick cup of tea and a sandwich by one of the sisters who'd grown tired of hearing Anna's stomach growling while they worked checking in an ambulance of new arrivals. "Be back here in an hour," Sister ordered. "We've got to see these men settled before the night nurse comes on duty."

The sandwich had taken the edge off Anna's hunger, but she could gladly have devoured three more and still not been satisfied. She'd had no desire to eat since leaving London, but long hours of hard physical work had broken the numbed loss of appetite. If only it helped her to sleep soundly, she'd be satisfied.

She checked the watch pinned to her bodice. Half past. Sophie was late.

"Trenowyth, so glad you're able to enjoy a lounge while the rest of us are run off our feet."

Anna spun round to find Sister Murphy glaring at her with beady-eyed indignation. A veteran of more battle campaigns than most generals, the QA military nurse had a long, disapproving face, a knifelike sarcasm, and the stealth of a jungle cat. No wonder Tilly was terrified of her. Even Captain Matthews seemed a bit in awe of the woman.

"Should I bring you a cup of tea and a cushion perhaps?" she sneered. "A nice bit of cake?"

"I've had dinner, thank you, Sister."

She shoved a pile of folders into Anna's arms. "Take these to the MO's office. He'll need them before tonight's appointments."

"I don't know where the medical officer's—"

"Upstairs, girl," she said with a jerk of her head toward the staircase. "And get a move on. He can't wait on Your Highness's laziness all day, can he?"

Word of Anna's connection to the family must have leaked out.

Now she'd have to put up with the staff's unwanted curiosity and, apparently in some quarters, outright hostility.

She'd hold off on unpacking. She might be back on a train by tonight.

Perhaps she'd get that overseas posting, after all.

"Yes, Sister. Right away," she answered, clasping the folders to her chest as she hurried up the steps, her mood brighter than it had been all day.

"And wipe that ridiculous smile off your face," Sister Murphy shouted after her.

The upper floors had been given over to the medical staff. Bed-chambers that once slept dukes and duchesses now housed Captain Matthews, Matron, and the QA sisters of Queen Alexandra's Imperial Military Nursing Service. Rooms had been set aside to be used as a private mess and an officers' parlor. Filing cabinets, type-writers, and telephones replaced what must have once been graceful tester beds, draperied dressing tables, and polished cheval mirrors. Yet the air possessed a hint of perfumed graciousness beneath the layer of ammonia-laced disinfectant, and light shone golden and watery through tall lattice-paned windows.

Poking her head in and out of doorways in hopes of discovering the MO's office, Anna rounded a corner to come upon an enormous room ornately paneled in oak. Groupings of comfortable chairs and couches centered on thick, richly patterned carpets. But it was the paintings that drew Anna's startled gaze. Women in ruffs and col-lars, men in wide-brimmed feathered hats and scarlet sashes. Fami-lies perched upon benches with Nanreath's facade as backdrop. A woman seated with a spaniel, her great Georgian silk skirts floating around her ankles, her hair piled high and powdered on her head. A young man leaned against a tree, a brace of pheasants laid at his feet, a musket in his loose-limbed slender arms.

"You heard about Villiers and Crangle, I suppose."

Anna stopped dead, a foot paused above the floorboard, breath clogging her throat.

"I did. What the hell happened, Tony? We've lost close to half the lads with us at St. Barnack's. Cambridge's hallowed colleges must echo like tombs these days."

Hugh was in conversation on the far side of the room where a pair of armchairs had been pulled to a window. She must have stumbled into the family's apartments. Should she retreat as silently as she entered? Announce her presence with a cough or a clearing of her throat?

"Villiers was on the *Triad* that sank off the Italian coast." A deep voice with the trace of a brogue about it. "Crangle plowed his Spitfire into a field in Sussex."

"And here I sit playing the doddering fool for a bunch of blasted nurses."

"Do you know how many men would kill for your blasted nurses, Melcombe?"

"They can damn well have the lot."

Every moment Anna delayed only worsened her position, yet she couldn't quite bring herself to back away.

"I expect your mother is glad to have you safe at home."

Hugh stretched as he relaxed, his trouser leg riding up to reveal the unnatural shade of a wooden prosthesis. "Of course she is. She can wrap me back up in packing wool to be trotted out at dinner parties and village fetes for the neighbors to hail as the conquering war hero."

"Rumor has it you're doing your best to dispel them of that notion."

The laugh that followed was harsh and bitter, full of regret.

Nothing like last night's boyish amusement. "First you ask about my mother. Now you're starting to sound like her."

Anna decided retreat was her best option. One step. Two steps. Slowly. Carefully. Gauging each footfall to avoid the squeaky spots.

"Don't let her hear you say that. She'd never stand to be compared to a miner's grandson from Glasgow."

Anna never noticed the table until she banged into it, setting a lamp wobbling.

Hugh sat up, his leg disappearing from view. "I hope whoever you are, you're enjoying the conversation," he called out.

Conscious of the heat flooding her cheeks and the tremble in her fingers gripping the folders, Anna swallowed her panic and stepped forward boldly. "I'm sorry. I didn't mean to eavesdrop. I was looking for Captain Matthews's office."

Hugh levered himself awkwardly to his feet, a hand resting lightly upon the chair back. "Tony, this is one of those nurses you were envying me."

His companion turned out to be an RAF flight lieutenant whose square-jawed, broad-shouldered vitality only accentuated Hugh's pallid lanky air of dissipation. He smiled, his dark eyes sparkling with laughter as he shook her hand. "Hello there. Tony Lambert. I'm a neighbor of yours over at St. Eval airfield. It's very nice to meet you, Miss—"

"Trenowyth," she answered, her chin lifting in unconscious defiance. "Anna Trenowyth." She couldn't help the quick slide of her eyes toward Hugh, who stiffened, his face wiped clean of every emotion but astonishment. So much for lying low and easing her way through without a ruckus.

"Is this a joke?" Hugh demanded.

Lambert's surprise had been fleeting. Now he eyed the situation with smug amusement. A reaction that was oddly reassuring. "I didn't know you had any family living, Melcombe . . . well, except that crazy aunt of yours and her Yank daughter."

"This is *not* Lucy," Hugh argued, adding under his breath, "thank God for small favors. Who are you really, Miss whoever you are?"

"I can show you my identity papers if you'd like."

"You told me your name was Handley. I don't remember much from last night, but I do remember that."

"Not to take sides, but I think she might be telling the truth," Lambert interrupted. "There's definitely something similar about the eyes and perhaps a bit round the mouth. A little rouge and lipstick, Hugh, and you'd be her spitting image."

"Ha bloody ha. You're not helping."

"Maybe I should leave you two to sort the mystery out without my interference." Lambert rose, taking up his cap. "It was very nice meeting you, Miss Trenowyth. Good luck with this clod. He's not a bad sort despite his snarling."

Hugh continued to glare, his hands twitching at his sides, as if he wished to punch something. "Look, Miss Handley or Trenowyth or whatever name you're using today. I'm not sure what you hope to gain, but—"

"Anna! Golly, I wondered where you'd gotten to." Sophie came careening into the gallery, pulling up out of breath. "Oh dear." She sighed. "I'd no idea you'd have companions."

"Don't mind me," Hugh complained. "I'm just trying to relax in my own home. A pointless endeavor as it turns out."

"Don't be dramatic, Hugh. It doesn't suit." Sophie waved his sarcasm off, as if whisking away a tiresome child—or an irritating servant.

"Miss Trenowyth?" Flight Lieutenant Lambert stood just to

the left of the chimneypiece, an odd expression darkening his easy, pleasant features. "You might want to see this."

Anna followed his gaze. A young woman in a sea-green gown stood with one hand resting upon a metal garden bench. Her head was slightly tilted, as if she stared at something or someone just beyond the edge of the canvas. A smile hovered over her lips, her gold-flecked blue eyes dancing with pleasure.

"It's an incredible likeness," he said, looking from the painting to Anna and back again.

She swallowed, unable to pull her gaze from the riveting intimacy caught by the artist. So different from the solemn reserve of the locket's photograph. This woman glowed from within.

"You found it." Sophie's voice broke the spell. "As soon as you told me your name, I immediately remembered this painting and put the two together. It must have been done shortly before the last war."

"Who is she?" Lambert asked.

Anna sensed Hugh's presence at her shoulder. She felt the tension in his frame like a vibration through the dusty air. "My father's younger sister," he answered. "Lady Katherine Trenowyth."

Anna moistened her lips as a strange, quivering excitement centered in her chest. She lifted a hand, as if to touch the swell of alabaster cheek. "My mother."

Night hovered just beyond the dim glow of the green-shaded table lamp, peopled with silent generations of Trenowyths all watching Anna with unblinking eyes and fixed smiles. Did they welcome her as one of the family? Or did they stiffen with indignation, as Hugh had done just before he'd offered her his hand with all the cool politeness of the very angry?

She knew the gallery was off-limits to staff and if she were caught, there would be hell to pay, but she'd returned at the end of her shift to sit among these men and women in silent introduction.

Her eyes burned with lack of sleep, while her shoulder throbbed, the ache moving down her arm into her fingers. She had fixed herself a cup of tea, but what she really wanted was a whiskey. Something to ease the pain in both her shoulder and her heart.

She turned her chair so that her mother's portrait was just off to her right. She had merely to cock her head to see the lively smile and clever gleam in Lady Katherine Trenowyth's blue eyes. Anna pulled her locket from her blouse, snapped it open. There was no comparison between the laughing, vibrant woman in the painting and the solemn, rigid features caught by the photographer's camera.

What events lay between these two disparate portrayals?

Would she ever know, or had those answers been lost with Graham and Prue?

A stir of the dusty air and the creak of a floorboard signaled someone's approach. Tilly was right. Sneaking was impossible in this place. She braced herself for the inevitable reprimand.

"Miss Trenowyth? Is that you?"

"Good evening, Mr. Lambert." She straightened, stuffing her bare feet back into her shoes. Combing her fingers through her thick hair. "I know I shouldn't be here and I'm sorry to intrude, but . . ."

He offered her a weary smile. "Say no more. I'm relieved it's you sitting there. For an instant, I thought I'd been snabbled by Her Ladyship and all my sneaking about was for naught."

"Why are you sneaking?"

"I was depositing a parcel."

"At midnight? A bit late for the post, isn't it?"

"Actually, this parcel was rather the worse for drink."

"Hugh?"

"Afraid so. He should be fine by morning. I think he left most of it along the side of the road between the village and the house. Not all, more's the pity for my poor borrowed motorcar."

"It's my fault. I shouldn't have spoken. I suppose my turning up like a bad penny came as an awful shock."

"Losing his leg came as an awful shock. You are a welcome surprise." His eyes had a nice way of crinkling at the corners when he smiled. "Besides, Hugh's love affair with the gin bottle began long before your arrival."

He gestured for her to reseat herself while he perched against a table. Pulled a silver cigarette case from his tunic pocket, flipped it open, and held it out toward her.

"No, thank you."

He took one for himself and lit it, settling himself more comfortably. He had a nice face, all sharp angles and straight lines, large brown eyes and a mouth that seemed always on the poise of laughter. That, and she'd always been a sucker for a whisper hint of an accent.

"Is Lady Boxley that bad?" she asked. "The staff makes her sound like a cross between Attila the Hun and Bloody Mary."

Tony chuckled. "An apt comparison on both counts. She can be difficult, but Hugh's been all she's had for so long, she's a bit proprietary. Still treats him as if he were in nappies. His injuries in Norway only made it worse."

"She doesn't sound like someone who would welcome a stranger into the fold."

"I expect His Majesty King George would find it hard to completely meet with her approval, but don't let her scare you off. She might be able to tell you more about your mother." He paused. "If that's what you want."

Maybe it was the compassion in his eyes or the humor in his

voice. Or maybe it was simply the late hour and her own exhaustion, but she found herself confiding in him. Quiet words that fell in the solemn dark of the gallery like a sinner's confession.

"I'm not sure. I had the chance to ask. The Handleys—the couple who took me in after she died—never hid the facts from me. But when they offered to tell me more, I refused. I did everything but hold my hands over my ears and whistle."

"Why?"

Anna shrugged in helpless incomprehension. "Guilt. Duty. Denial. A desire to be like every other child on my street with normal parents and a normal family. I didn't want to be different."

"What child does?"

Talking ripped open a wound barely healed over. Grief pressed against her chest like a weight, and it was as if she were back standing on the sidewalk, staring at the ruins of her world. "I suppose I always thought there would be time."

He stubbed out the cigarette butt in an ashtray. "A lot of us thought that, didn't we?"

# Chapter 6

*November 1913*

M r. Weiss has managed to sell four of my paintings. I've begun
to think about leaving Balázs and setting up my own studio.
There's a building in Ralston Street. It has space below for display
and a flat above. Not much more than a few rooms and a bath, but
more than I need."

"That's wonderful, Simon. It's exactly what you wanted."

The two of us had found an out-of-the-way corner in Mrs. Comersby's busy front parlor. Mr. Balász's sister was just as I'd imagined
she would be; a wide-hipped, apple-cheeked hausfrau wreathed
in welcoming smiles who plied us with food and drinks until my
initial uneasiness was overcome, and I felt myself melting into the
loud, uninhibited chaos of her bohemian salon.

A shout went up as the door opened to admit new guests. I
could just make out the drape of a fur coat and a sleek bob of dark
hair from my corner.

"It is what I want, but not at the expense of seeing you hurt. I'm very sorry about the painting." Simon sipped at his cloudy glass of absinthe. I had left mine untouched, the strong aromas of anise and fennel not to my taste. But wine I'd imbibed in plenty until I was quite relaxed and a bit buzzy-headed.

"I admit it was rather a shock to see myself in such a . . . manner, but I've decided I quite like it." The guests moved into the front parlor, two gentlemen in evening dress, and the woman who had removed her fur to reveal a daring Worth gown in sky-blue silk and Brussels lace. "Mr. Balázs once said what we believe is hidden is actually visible if one has the eyes to see. Perhaps the Red-Haired Wanton exists locked somewhere deep inside me and all I need to do is"—the woman turned her head and my mouth dropped open like a codfish's—"hide!"

I leaped from my seat as if I'd been scalded, ducking into the relative safety of the kitchen, which was thankfully empty.

"Kitty, are you all right?" Simon had followed and now eyed me as if I'd run mad. "You look as if you've seen a ghost."

"Worse. It's Lady Ashdown. She's one of the biggest gossips in London. If she sees me and gabs it to my mother . . ." I furtively peeked round the swinging door to see if I'd been spotted.

"I see." Simon's clipped and icy voice drew me back into the kitchen long enough to observe that his expression bore all the marks of one having trouble chaining his temper. "I'm good enough for you, but not for your family." I sensed deep hurt beneath his anger.

"Don't be absurd. Of course you're good enough, but you don't understand my family. They need time to accustom themselves to the idea. I need to ease into it slowly."

"Like you eased into telling them about art school?"

The accusation struck me like the tip of a lash, and I gasped.

"A cage is still a cage, Kitty, no matter how gilded the bars.

When are you going to finally stand up for what you want? When are you going to let them see what I see? That you're a strong, smart, beautiful young woman who doesn't need Mama and Daddy telling her how to live her life?"

I had no answer to that. I was still trying to adjust to being called strong, smart, and beautiful. It dawned on me that the only time I felt that way was in Simon's company. He gave me confidence because in his eyes I was confident. "You really think I'm all those things?"

His voice softened. "Of course, you darling idiot. Why do you think I've skulked about like a criminal to be with you?"

His kiss took me by surprise, but I didn't shrink from it as I had his first attempt so many months ago. This time I savored the slow exploration of his lips and the wickedly daring dip of his tongue. My bones turned to jelly as the knots in my stomach tightened, and excitement flushed my skin so that when the swinging door into the entry hall opened, the blast of cooler air was like an arctic shock.

"Hi-ho, good people!" A gentleman giddily waved a bottle of whiskey in one hand while his other arm was thrown about the waist of a blowsy woman dressed in yellow silk. "What have we here? An interrupted tryst?"

Terror splashed cold across my shoulders as I drew in a ragged breath. "Good evening, William. Funny meeting you here."

If being found out by Lady Ashdown would have been a disaster, to be tumbled by my own brother was a hundred times worse. To say I was surprised to see him here was a mild understatement. It would be more accurate to say I was at once astonished, appalled, and sick with nerve-tightening fear. If William's initial reaction was any indication, he suffered from the same powerful mix of emotions. I clung to that with every ounce of quickly disappearing hope as his initial euphoria sank to a brooding silence, helped along by a few strong cups of Mrs. Comersby's potent Turkish coffee. He sat at her kitchen table, staring into his cup, his face gray-green and jumping with mental agitation.

Of his companion, I had seen nothing since Simon stepped into the brittle, ugly shock of our first meeting and whisked her away. His eyes met mine, and I saw in that moment both sympathy for my potential disaster and a reassuring strength I could lean upon no matter what befell me. It made me brave despite my quaking knees and jittery stomach.

"I met Letitia at the Alhambra," William mumbled into his coffee. "Charles Blakeney introduced us. She's a friend of a lady he . . ." His words trailed into a quiet mumble.

Not that I needed him to finish his sentence. I could well imagine what sort of lady both Letitia and her friend were, though I didn't express this aloud. To cast stones seemed not the wisest course at present. And there was a part of me that thought if I remained quiet, perhaps William would finally reveal what kept him from Nanreath, his new baby, and bad as it was to say—me.

I was not used to secrets between us. William might have been five years my senior, but we connected in a way I'd never been able to duplicate with Amelia, for all we were sisters. William and I shared a similar nature, though behavior deemed acceptable and even encouraged in the son and heir had always been seen in a daughter of the house as less than ideal. Still, when no one else seemed to understand me, it had been William who championed me time and again. I wondered what he would think of my dubious celebrity as the Red-Haired Wanton. Would he laugh it off as a grand joke or would he play the stern, protective older brother?

Until now, I could have answered with certainty. Now I was not so sure—about that and about a lot of things I had always taken for granted about my brother.

"I'm surprised we haven't seen you more in South Audley Street since our arrival. But I suppose your friendship with Letitia occupies all your time," I said, hoping to sound mature when in fact I felt completely out of my depth.

He looked up from his coffee, his eyes starting to focus in the same direction, his long face seeming longer in its inebriation. He rose, grabbing his jacket from the chair and swinging it across his shoulders. "Come along, Kitty."

I had no choice but to follow, leaving Simon and my increasingly horrid evening behind.

We walked the empty dark streets, slick with rain from a passing shower. The gas lamps flickered their greasy circles of light along the pavement, and in the distance someone sang a plaintive love song from an open window. It made me unaccountably sad and very lonely, despite having William by my side.

He broke the silence first. "She doesn't mean anything to me. She seemed a good sport and up for a lark. That's all."

"Her kind usually are," I grumbled.

"Kitty!"

So much for remaining nonjudgmental. "I'm not a child, William, despite what everyone in this family thinks."

"But you *are* a well-bred young lady . . . out alone in company with a gentleman." My head snapped round. "Or did you think I wouldn't notice that part of your adventure?" he added with an air of wilted triumph.

I jerked my chin upward, as if preparing for a fight. "Don't turn this into an indictment of my behavior. I don't have a wife and child waiting for me at home."

He had the grace to look away, his shoulders stiff, hands shoved in his pockets.

"William, what is going on? I know Cynthia isn't the easiest person to get along with, but she's your wife. You love her."

His laughter was cold and ugly. "Kitty, you tell me you're not a child, but then you say such beautifully ridiculous things. Do you really think love had anything to do with our marriage? It was her money for our connections. Simple as that."

"You didn't have to agree to the marriage."

He responded with a snort that told me I was being a sentimental female. "You know the impossibility of defying Father once he's made his mind up. One would have greater luck holding back the tide. And since my duty was to marry, it may as well have been Cynthia as anyone."

It wasn't that I didn't understand the pressures and expectations, but that didn't make me any less nauseated by William's plainspokenness. "You've only been married a few years. Perhaps given time, things will change between you, especially now that you have Hugh."

"Yes, Hugh. He does change things, doesn't he?" William said with a puzzling ambiguity. He took my hand in his own. "Come on, Kitty. Let's get you home before Mother realizes you're gone."

"You won't tell?"

His eyes met mine, deep hollows shadowing the pinprick gleam of his irises. "Not if you won't."

"Never."

He chucked my chin. "That's my girl."

And just like that, we were pals and comrades once again.

Simon's painting eventually turned up at an exhibition at the Freeman Gallery in New Bond Street, and within days *The*

*Red-Haired Wanton*—and the model who'd inspired her—became the talk of society.

I knew I should have been upset or embarrassed, but there was only a feeling of inevitability, as if my life were unrolling toward some unknown end beyond my control. Unfortunately, my parents felt none of my serenity in the face of such public scorn. Raised voices behind closed doors and the arrival of Mama's personal physician had the household walking on eggshells. Even the servants cast me furtive glances, their manner cheekier, as if I'd already lost my respected position within the family.

I ignored them all as best I could, though each passing day grew harder to endure. The morning after a particularly galling evening, I rose as dawn crept steely gray over my windowsill. Taking up my journal, I tried writing out my wild swing of emotions, hoping the soothing act of putting pen to paper would untangle my tumultuous thoughts, but there was no peace to be found even in that familiar refuge.

Looking round my room with its girlish frills and naive innocence, seeing my flushed and agitated reflection in the mirror, the desire to step into the unknown nearly overwhelmed me. In that moment I would have traded every elegant trapping of my privileged upbringing for the confidence and poise Simon had rendered with a few dabs of oil paints and canvas. I didn't want to be Lady Katherine, whose fear held her captive. I wanted to be plain Kitty Trenowyth with the courage to fly.

Dressing quickly, I took up my journal and workbox and left the house. As Burton opened the door for me, I let him know, should my parents inquire, which was doubtful since neither would rise before ten, that I had walked to Green Park and would be back in time for breakfast.

A skittish wind had picked up overnight and the clouds sat

thick and damp in an unsettled sky, causing the normal city sounds to seem muffled and forlorn. I headed south past the dawn inhabitants of South Audley and onto the busier thoroughfare of Curzon Street, and from there to the early-morning bustle of Piccadilly, ignoring the admiring looks and occasional greetings shouted from passing omnibuses or mumbled shyly with a tip of the cap and a nod. I entered the gates at Green Park where the fog hung in tattered veils along the ground and the grass dragged against the hem of my skirts as my heels sank into the earth. I chose a likely spot looking west toward Buckingham Palace and spread a blanket upon the ground, settling in to work. Soon enough the whirl of my thoughts focused down to the movement of my hand over the page.

"You'll catch your death on that damp ground."

Immersed in my own imagination, the shock of his voice sent a startled shiver up my spine, and I dragged my pencil like a pale gray thread across the page. "Bother! Now look what you've made me do."

Simon knelt beside me, laughing. "I thought for sure you'd seen me clomping up the hill toward you."

My hat shielded my face from close scrutiny, but I was sure my answering smile was obvious. I'd not seen him since our illicit rendezvous, but the brief pleasure of that one evening returned tenfold. "I was consumed with trying to manage that shadow along the path, but my pencil's gone dull and I've forgotten a knife for sharpening."

"Allow me." He joined me on the blanket, pulling a pocketknife from his jacket and whittling away at the little nub. "It's awfully early to be out, isn't it?"

"I couldn't sleep."

"Neither could I." His eyes cut sidelong toward me, and his

hand upon his knife tightened. "I haven't been able to do much of anything since I saw you last. Even Mr. Balázs has started to notice I'm off my feed."

"So you decided to stalk me?" I said it with a small laugh, but his eyes remained on his work and my joke fell flat.

"I don't know what I meant to do. I suppose stare at your bedroom window like some lovesick Shakespearean swain. When I saw you coming along Piccadilly, I couldn't believe my good luck."

"How could you tell it was me?"

He frowned, and there was a solemnity to his features that seemed at odds with his usual breezy wit. "I could pick you out in a crowd of a thousand."

I felt the heat rise into my cheeks as I fought the battering of stomach butterflies.

He reached for the journal. "May I?"

I closed it and put my hand on the cover. "It's private." To soften my refusal, I added, "You wouldn't be interested in any of my silly scribblings anyway."

"Don't let your family's opinions define you, Kitty." His gaze met mine in a look of near challenge.

Reluctantly, I opened the journal, flipping closer to the front, where he'd not accidentally come across anything I might have written about him. He was bold enough without knowing how much I began to care.

"You're a dream at landscapes, but it's the faces where you truly shine." He paused. "This one of the boy with his dog. Such pride in both their eyes." Another page. "And the fishmonger there. Look at the way he holds his load. He's tired, but he daren't put it down lest he not be able to pick it up again." He skipped to a third page. "And this one of your mother is dead-on. Look at her, so prim and proper. So smug with herself and her Victorian attitudes." He sobered, his eyes seeming to spear me to the ground. I felt myself waiting with held breath. "Are you in much trouble?"

"They never knew I was missing." I took back the journal and flipped to my half-finished sketch as a way to avoid meeting his shrewd gaze.

"That's not what I meant. The painting . . . my painting . . . are you in much trouble over it?"

"I'm to be shipped to Great-aunt Adelaide's in Glasgow until the furor dies down. I don't want to go, but . . ." I shrugged at the inescapability of fate.

"So refuse. Tell them about your plans for art school. Make them listen."

I couldn't help the tears that pricked my eyes and made my throat burn. I snatched the book from him. "What's the point? They'd never allow it."

But Simon was no longer paying me any attention. He scrambled to his feet, alarm quickly replaced by his usual easy self-assurance. "Good morning, Lady Melcombe."

I turned in time to see my mother storming toward us like an avenging angel, her lady's maid, Green, following in her wake, smug in her moral superiority. "Burton informed us you had sneaked out. I should have known."

"Had I been sneaking, I'd not have told Burton where I was going." I shoved my journal back in my bag and rose to meet her, trying hard to keep my knees from knocking and my voice steady. "Mr. Halliday happened upon me while I was sketching."

"It's nothing untoward, my lady. Your daughter was merely showing me her work. You have my word."

"I wouldn't give a ha'penny for your word, Mr. Halliday." She dismissed him with a final icy glare before turning her wrath on me. "I've been tolerant of your whims, Katherine, but I have reached the end of my patience. I'll have you packed and on the next train north. Aunt Adelaide will know how to deal with your waywardness."

I recalled Simon's words. "No, Mama. I won't go."

By now the frustration and swallowing of emotion over the last few months came to a boil. My vision narrowed. My throat burned. And there was a welling of every swallowed complaint and irritation I had ever felt. It could not be contained. Nor did I want it to be.

"I'm not a parcel to be passed among the relations nor must my life be arranged as if I haven't the sense I was born with. If Aunt Adelaide wants a companion let her find some poor appreciative Glaswegian relation."

"You're overwrought, and this is neither the time nor the place. We'll return home where we can discuss this in private. I'll not be made a public show for the titillation of every passing stranger."

Here was my chance to be the confident woman of my imagination. "No, you'll listen to me now. My whole life, you've shut your eyes and ears to everything I try to tell you of how I'm feeling or how I want to proceed with my life. You want me to be good and be quiet, but I can't. Not anymore."

Mother stared in the same way she might have stared if the sofa had started complaining about being sat upon. "We've offered you everything a daughter could want. Is this how you repay us? With insolence and cheek?"

"You've offered me the world, but then you snatch it away and tell me I'm not allowed to step foot into it. I can't accept that."

Mother's face clouded over, her features alive with barely tamped fury. "You're naught but a spoiled child and not too old to be switched and put to bed without supper."

My heart threatened to pound from my chest, and my throat closed around the words so that I struggled to say them, but say them I did. "I won't be returning home. Not now. Not ever. I'm leaving."

"You haven't the courage," Mother dared me.

That was the final straw. I turned on my heel, still high on the drama of the moment, and set off down the gravel path.

"You want to be independent?" Mother called after me. "To step foot into the world? We'll see how long you last. I'll wager you're back by the time dinner is served."

Her words fell like a gauntlet at my feet. I lifted my chin, squared my shoulders, and continued walking.

Too bad I had no idea where I was going to go.

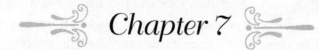

# Chapter 7

December 1940

November rains were gentle, a drizzle that silvered the air and greened the park until it glowed like an emerald carpet. December rains turned the park into a sodden mess of drowned shrubbery and hip-deep mud. After a day, the tennis court flooded. After three days, part of the nurses' showers collapsed. After an entire week, a tree fell across the main drive, causing no end of headaches for vehicles. From her window at the top of the house, Anna looked out on the white-capped froth of ocean beyond the rows of razor wire and the ominous ugly hump of pillboxes. The surf's dull roar echoed like constant radio static. The damp seeped cold and clammy against her skin.

Despite the best attempts at insulation, drafts infiltrated every crack and wind whistled down every chimney. The patient wards were kept warm, but the staff was left to shift for themselves as best they could on the upper floors. Anna's attic billet had a wheezing, clanking radiator that either gave off sauna heat or none at all. She never knew whether she would be pulling on the extra layers or shedding garments like a soldier's pinup.

In the months she'd been at Nanreath Hall, she'd seen little of Hugh beyond a nod when they met in a corridor or a few moments of small talk when to ignore him would be outright rude. Hugh's mother, Lady Boxley, made only one appearance to the hospital while Anna was on duty. As if on regal procession, she swanned through the wards accompanied by Captain Matthews and Matron, dispensing pained smiles and stilted conversation, though her permanent expression of displeasure contradicted her otherwise encouraging words.

Anna could have sworn Her Ladyship's hard gaze sought her out where she stood half-hidden behind a trolley of magazines and newspapers. But when Matron brought her forward to be introduced as their newest VAD, there was not even a flicker of recognition nor the barest twitch of an eyebrow.

So much for the idea of approaching Lady Boxley for information about her mother. It was clear she wanted nothing to do with the consequences of the family's scandal.

Downstairs, Anna's life had fallen into a routine that allowed the sharp edges of her grief to smooth until she could remember Graham and Prue without feeling as if she'd taken a bullet to the chest. Up at six to wash and dress and eat in a hasty clatter before reporting to the wards by seven. Once on duty, there were endless rooms to scrub, equipment and instruments to sterilize, bandages to cut and prepare, laundry to wash, fold, and put away, and meals to arrange and serve. But it was the time she spent attending to the patients that filled the empty places inside her.

Anna listened to their jokes as she handed out squill oxymel or the ubiquitous M. & B. 693 tablets, learned of sweethearts and family back home as she took daily temperatures, removed stitches, or checked bedpans, and heard more than one heart-thumping tale of life at the front during afternoon tea or one of the countless cut-throat games of cricket the men engaged in on the small patch of lawn cut and rolled smooth for the purpose.

"Nurse Trenowyth's got pluck. She served in France before it fell," one of the orderlies volunteered with pride as a lanky sergeant with a wrenched ankle recounted a dogfight over the Kentish countryside. She'd been handing round cups from a loaded trolley, the setting winter sun casting a stark light over the room. But as all eyes swiveled in her direction, she felt her breath catch in a throat clogged with unexpected fear.

The men noticed none of this. They peppered her with questions, showing their new respectful interest.

"Were you at Le Havre?"

"My brother made it out on a minesweeper the last day."

"What were the beaches like?"

"Were you afraid?"

Caught off guard, she could think of nothing to say as her heart raced, and sweat washed cold over her back despite the warmth in the room. She stumbled, the cups and saucers on the trolley rattling dangerously. A glass wobbled and fell.

A hand caught it before it hit the ground. "Easy or young Newsome will be wearing his tea."

She looked up to find Flight Lieutenant Lambert, concern etched upon his strong, handsome face.

"What are you doing here?"

"One of my fliers is recovering from rheumatic fever." He continued to regard her with unspoken curiosity as he placed the glass back upon her tray. "Glad I was nearby to avert a disaster."

"It was an empty glass, not a hand grenade."

"You wouldn't know it by the way you looked as it fell."

She shook off her memories and turned to the young soldier with a forced smile. "Did you ask me if I was afraid? My greatest fear was fending off a shipload of homesick soldiers with only a tongue depressor."

The young man laughed, and the moment passed on smoothly. She completed her round of the salon with no further trouble. Only in the corridor, away from the eyes of the men, did she slump against the wall, hands fast under her ribs to slow her frantic heartbeat.

"Miss Trenowyth? Are you all right?"

Tony Lambert again. Couldn't he see she wanted to be left alone?

"I'm fine. Why do you ask?" She straightened, adjusting her apron, touching her veil as if assuring its crispness.

"Because you're pale as chalk and look as if you've seen a ghost. Did the men upset you with all that war talk?"

"Do you really think I can't take hearing about the war without falling to pieces? I wouldn't be much of a nurse if that were the case."

"But sometimes the talk stirs memories we'd rather keep buried."

"I have nothing to bury."

"No? I served at an airfield in Poix. The stories I could tell about the evacuations would turn your hair white."

"I don't need to hear your stories. I have my own." She cleared her throat. "If you'll excuse me, I have patients to see to."

As she crossed the hall to return to the main ward, she felt his gaze tickling her spine like a blade. "Remember what we talked about? Don't let another chance pass you by, Anna Trenowyth," he called after her. "In these times, there's no guarantee it will come your way again."

"You're awfully brash."

"No, just very mortal."

It took a closed door and a gruff order from Sister Murphy before she let out the breath she'd been holding.

But it took until the very end of her shift before she stopped hearing his words over and over in her head.

Saturday night. A rare evening off. Anna sat cross-legged on her bunk with emery board and polish at the ready. Not all the hand cream in the world could put right the damage done by constant scrubbing in hot water, but at least her nails would be tidy.

She'd just finished writing to Mrs. Willits, who'd been true to her word and kept in touch. Anna welcomed the weekly letters from Cardiff, filled with the trials and tribulations of ration coupons and overzealous AR wardens. She usually answered with colorful tales of hospital life and her fruitless attempts at befriending her aunt and cousin, though Tony Lambert's name seemed to crop up in this latest letter more than she'd intended.

Anna chose to ignore what that might mean. She wasn't cut out for a reckless fling, and anything more serious was unthinkable while the war news continued to be so bad.

"There you are, Anna. I've been looking everywhere for you." Tilly burst into their room, bringing with her a frigid blast of air from the corridor.

"What do you want to borrow tonight?" Anna asked, unable to hide her smile.

"I resent that." Tilly jammed her hands on her hips and puffed out her bottom lip. "How do you know I'm here to borrow something?"

Anna cast her a long, skeptical look.

"Oh, very well," Tilly answered hastily. "It's that dreamy blue jumper, the one with the pearl buttons. You don't suppose . . . I mean, you're not going out tonight, are you?"

"A date with a bottle of Young Red or At Ease pink?" Anna said, waving two bottles of nail polish for Tilly's opinion.

"The red definitely. I hear it's Captain Matthews's favorite color."

"And why would I care what the MO's favorite color is?"

"Only because he's completely smitten with you."

Captain Matthews was the comfortably middle-aged medical officer in residence at the hospital. At least two of the nurses and three VADs were madly in love with him, despite regulations putting him firmly out of bounds.

Anna was not one of them.

"Don't be ridiculous," she said firmly. "He's merely being polite."

"He's polite to the rest of us. He gushes over you. If I have to hear one more time how Trenowyth knows just the right way to give an enema, I shall scream." Tilly changed out of her ward dress and into a pretty floral skirt and white blouse.

"He doesn't do that."

"He does. That's the act of a smitten man, and I should know."

"Who's so smitten with you that you need to borrow my new jumper?" Anna asked, in a desperate attempt at changing the subject.

Tilly swung round from her mad primping, wearing a cat-with-the-canary expression, her blue eyes dancing with excitement. "Lord Melcombe asked if I'd go into Newquay with him for a pint and maybe some dancing."

"Are you certain that's a good idea?"

"And why wouldn't it be?"

"Only that it would be awkward if things didn't work out. You could hardly avoid him, could you?"

"Is that why you haven't accepted Captain Matthews?" Tilly smirked as she brushed her golden hair until it crackled.

Anna rolled her eyes. Tilly really *was* incorrigible. "You have to see that Hugh's different from Captain Matthews. I mean, he owns the hospital . . . this house. He's not like us."

"He's exactly like *you*. You're cousins, aren't you?"

"You make it sound more than it is."

"Last time I checked, he pulls his trousers on like every other man, one leg at a time. That's good enough for me."

"It's how he takes his trousers off that worries me."

Tilly turned back to the mirror, reapplying her lipstick, tucking an errant curl in place. "You leave his trousers to me."

"That's a picture I didn't need to conjure."

"Really, Anna. It's one evening out. It's not as if I'm planning a walk up the aisle at Westminster Abbey or anything."

"The jumper's in my locker."

"You're the absolute, Anna love," Tilly said, rummaging through until she found it. "Thanks heaps."

She departed with an airy wave of her handbag and a waggle in her hips, leaving Anna alone . . . for almost a complete five silent minutes before Sophie wandered in to collapse in a chair with an exhausted sigh. "Every muscle in my body aches. I've just finished cleaning, organizing, and double-checking labels in the drug dispensary. Even the thought of primping for a gin and a jitterbug is enough to send me into a swoon. I think I'll take a shower and then curl up in bed to write Charles a lovely long letter full of hearts and flowers." She heaved herself out of her chair long enough to pour two tiny glasses of hoarded sherry, handing Anna one of them. "I had a letter from him yesterday. He says it's spiffing Hugh has a cousin. Apparently, his only other family is an aunt living in Singapore with rich husband number three and her wild daughter. Compared to them, you're practically a nun."

"Thanks . . . I think."

"Oh, you know what I mean. You're sensible, clever, kind, frugal . . ."

"In other words, dull."

"I was going to say perfect."

Anna studied the sherry shimmering in the glass. Downed it in one gulp. "Right. Perfect."

Christmas threatened to be a sorry affair. Between fear over the new offensive in North Africa and the heart-wrenching reports of the terrible bombing raids on Manchester and Liverpool, there seemed little to be festive about. In a valiant attempt at merrymaking, the nurses strung tinsel and colored paper streamers throughout the wards. One of the orderlies came up with the brilliant idea to tack army-issued socks up on one of the carved mantels in hopes of a visit from Father Christmas. And hymns and carols replaced the wild strains of Glenn Miller and Count Basie on the music room's piano. Even Sister Murphy was caught humming a few bars of "Good King Wenceslas" under her breath.

Anna spent the afternoon of Christmas Eve walking into the village. She quickly found a box of pretty stationery for Sophie while a lovely green scarf caught her eye that would be perfect for Tilly. Both were wrapped and hidden at the bottom of her locker until the morning. She pondered the idea of purchasing Hugh a gift, even going so far as to stroll the tobacconist's for a box of cigars or a new cigarette lighter, but turned coward at the last, and departed empty-handed. She would not push where she so obviously was not wanted, but it was hard not to look back to past Christmases in the little house on Queen's Crescent; the small spruce in the front room heavy with paper snowflakes, pinecones, and pretty dried leaves gathered on walks, and Graham, Prue, and Anna sitting round the table in their paper crowns while Lessons and Carols played on the radio, and not wish with a heavy heart for a return of those carefree days.

"'Libby has knitted you this scarf,'" she read aloud to a young man seated in a wheelchair beside her. "'Your sister spent all the fall working on it so you are to be sure and tell her how much you like it the next time you see her . . .'"

"As if that will happen anytime soon." He stared blankly into the distance, a lumpy blue and brown scarf wrapped round his neck over his pajamas and robe. His hands clutched at the arms of his chair, his hair brushed low across his brow to hide the scars upon his forehead from an accidental paraffin explosion.

"I'm sorry. That was an ill use of words, but you may yet regain your sight. The MO was quite optimistic."

"And if I don't?" he asked, his mouth twisted into a bitter, ugly sneer. "What do I tell my sister then? Do I lie and tell her it's beautiful even though I can't see it?"

"You thank her for the kind gift and tell her you hope to be home with her soon."

"Easy for you to say."

"No, but I wish it were, Lieutenant. I wish I had someone who cared for me so much that they spent hours knitting me a scarf. You're far luckier than you can possibly imagine."

"Nurse Trenowyth?" An orderly stood at her shoulder. "A letter's come for you."

For a moment hope leaped in Anna's chest. There had been a horrible mistake. Graham and Prue had been in hospital this whole time, unconscious and unable to write. Or better, they'd been away on a trip to come home and find the house wiped out and no word of her. It had taken them this long to locate her through the proper channels. A fool's hope destroyed as soon as she took the envelope.

She recognized the handwriting as her own. A great red stamp across the face of it read RETURN TO SENDER. UNDELIVERABLE ADDRESS.

Cardiff had been one of the cities heavily hit by German bombing. Mrs. Willits had been concerned that by leaving London she was running away from the war. In the end, there had been no safe place to run. The war had found her anyway.

A weight seemed to anchor Anna to her chair, a pain like an old wound reopening with the agony of a scalpel blade. "Thank you, Price. I . . . uh . . . I appreciate you bringing it to me."

"Nurse?" the young soldier asked gently. "Are you all right?"

"Of course, Lieutenant. Why do you ask?"

"My sight's gone, miss. My hearing's sharp as ever."

Her chest and stomach ached, but she dragged in a shaky breath. She mustn't lose heart. She must stay brave for the men who needed her to be their strength and their hope when theirs was gone.

"Ho! Ho! Ho!" Hugh bellowed as he and one of the hospital fire crew hefted the top of an enormous Scotch pine through the doorway. His cheeks were pink with cold, and he wore a set of old jingling sleigh bells round his shoulders. "What's Christmas without a tree?"

Immediately, the room came alive with laughter and conversation. Someone struck up a chorus of "O Christmas Tree." Tilly appeared draped in long red and green paper chains. "They're not pearls but I think they suit me better, don't you?"

Stuffing the letter into her apron, Anna rose to take the top box from an overloaded orderly. "The boys worked wonders. They'll look lovely."

"I hope so. We've run out of real paste, and the flour and water glop Sister Louise concocted in the kitchens to use in its stead nearly had me retching my breakfast."

Space in a corner of the room was cleared and Hugh, with much shouting of instructions, hoisted and secured the tree in its stand, the top nearly scraping the ceiling. The crisp smell of pine replaced

the mingled scents of antiseptic and sweat. Melting snow dripped
from its broad green branches.

"Perfect!" Hugh stepped back out of the way, hands on his hips
in admiration, though Anna noticed the way he held himself uncomfortably, as if his leg pained him, and his face bore a grayish
cast. "Go to it, men."

Like children let free on Christmas morning, the men rummaged through the boxes, pulling out elaborate ornaments in glass,
tin, lace, and wood. Laughing and chattering, they jostled for space
around the tree as they worked. Trays of cider and biscuits appeared. A gramophone belted out carols. Tilly flirted and teased as
she helped drape the paper chains, her easy charm pulling even the
grumpiest soldier into the festivities.

Anna placed a tin soldier in scarlet coat and busby. A delicate
robin's egg–blue glass ball. A set of crystal icicles in various colors.
With each ornament, she couldn't help but compare what must
have been her mother's sumptuous childhood holidays with her
own joyful, if frugal, Christmases. Had Katherine, like Anna, only
realized the preciousness of those childhood memories once they
were all she had left?

Kneeling beside a crate, Anna pulled aside crumpled newspaper
to find a beautifully rendered miniature of a young man framed in
delicate woodwork. His solemn gaze seemed at odds with the smile
tugging at one corner of his mouth.

"I haven't seen that in ages. I almost forgot it existed."

Anna looked up to see Hugh standing over her. His hands were
stuffed into his pockets, and without the animation of the tree raising, she could discern the tight lines at his mouth, the shadows
haunting his pale gray eyes.

"Your father?" she asked.

"Yes." He bent and took it, running his thumb over the glass. "I was four when he died. According to Mother, he was a paragon of every male virtue, cut off in the prime of life, leaving her helpless and alone amid a family of wolves. At least that's how she portrays her life after his death."

"You don't believe her?"

"My mother has never been helpless in her life." His lips curled in a cynical smile. "Grandfather used to hang this ornament himself every year. Wouldn't let anyone else touch it. Not even Mother. It must have been packed away when he died."

"You're fortunate to have grown up surrounded by people who knew and loved your father. I have so many questions about my mother and no one to ask."

Hugh continued rummaging through the boxes. Anna had almost decided their one and only conversation was at an end when he straightened with a glass star in his hand and an odd almost expectant expression on his face. "Is that why you came to Nanreath Hall?"

"I came because the powers that be have a twisted sense of humor, but if I keep a stiff upper lip and do a good job, they might just send me to the front, where I could be of some real use."

"I would think discovering where you came from would have been too good a chance to miss."

"Yes, well, I didn't come from here, did I? I was born and raised in London. And you can see how well the touching family reunion has turned out. You've barely spoken to me."

"I'm a bloody bastard. Ask anyone who knows me. But it's not every day one has a brand-new relation spring like magic from the ether." Together, they began to unpack the box and hang the ornaments.

"No, I suppose not."

"God knows I've enough horrid relations as it is without adding to the bunch. Luckily, they all live on the other side of the world."

"I don't want anything from you if that's what you're worried about."

"You'd be disappointed if you did. The earldom of Melcombe is tottering on a precipice built of death taxes and devalued land. A push in the right direction and down we come like so many others of our kind before us. It's the rising families like Lambert's with the cash and clout these days."

"Tony Lambert?" She paused, the crystal icicle still in her hand.

"His grandfather shoveled the coal. His father bought the coal mine. If Tony inherited even a tenth of the family's ambitions, he'll have the blunt to buy us all by the end."

"He seems so . . . so normal."

"As opposed to me, the mincing, lisping fop?"

"That's not what I meant." She laughed and continued her work.

"Lambert's a good chap. He's the one who told me what a horse's ass I was being. Gave me a verbal thrashing until I promised I'd apologize to you, and here I am." He made a stage bow from the waist complete with a wrist-twisting flourish.

"Lord Melcombe? Would you like to do the honors?" Tilly held the angel for the top of the tree. "After all, this was your idea."

Was it Anna's imagination or did Hugh tense? Did his expression harden with wild panic before settling into its usual loose smile? "Let Corporal Keller have it. No lords a-leaping for me. I'm not too good with heights these days."

Tilly blushed as she handed off the angel to a balding, cherub-faced orderly who scampered up the ladder, wobbling as he leaned over the tree, settling the angel upon her perch to the accompaniment of much cheering and applause.

"Can you forgive me, Hugh?" she asked with a pitiful begging scrunch of her face that only seemed to enhance her vivacious attractiveness. "It never even occurred to me you'd have trouble with the ladder."

He looped his arm with hers. "Which is exactly why I adore you, Tilly, my sweet." He glanced upward. "Now, if I'm not mistaken, that's mistletoe."

Anna turned her gaze upward. "Actually, I believe that's a sprig of—"

Hugh shot her a look as Tilly moved in for a kiss.

"Never mind," Anna mumbled. "Must be mistaken."

Tilly broke away with flushed cheeks and a twinkle in her eye. "Crikey, my lord. I think I need a drink after that." She looped her arm in his. "Care for a cider?"

"Sounds ghastly, but lead on." Just as Tilly began to steer him toward the tables, he leaned toward Anna. "Mother's roped me into attending a local fund drive for wounded soldiers on New Year's Eve. I thought you might go with me. Another Trenowyth to impress the local bigwigs."

"They'll be so busy ogling me, they won't have time to pester you. Is that it?"

"Am I that obvious?"

"Yes."

"Well? What do you say . . . cousin?"

Was this her chance to step into her mother's world and find out if there might be a place for her? "Are you sure? Won't it be awkward?"

But Hugh had already accepted her long pause as a yes and wandered off, leaving Anna queasy with anticipation. She picked up the ornament, staring once more into the handsome frozen expression of the young man lost so many years ago.

"New Year's it is," she whispered.

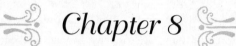

# Chapter 8

*February 1914*

"Come on, Kitty. Get a move on or we'll be late."

The entire basement bedsit in Islington I shared with Doris Price, a young woman working as a typist in the City, was smaller than my sitting room at Nanreath Hall. The only natural light to be had leached in through two grimy narrow windows set nearly flush with the ceiling; the privy was at the end of the back garden, and we had no means of cooking other than a spirit stove that served for tea or a pan of beans, which we ate on toast. Thankfully for our meager coal supply, the winter had been mild. But tonight a thick green fog seeped through every crack and crevice, clinging to the skin and making breathing difficult. Coughing left my stomach achy and my throat sore.

"If we pool our week's wages, we have the threepence each for entry and enough left over to get coffee afterward," I said as I counted out the precious coins from my change purse with chapped and trembling fingers.

"Are you all right?" Doris asked as she fastened a small gold cross around her neck. "You look a bit flushed."

"Brilliant." I offered her a game smile. "Now, let's go. Agnes and Jane will be wondering what's happened to us." As a last thought, I grabbed a scarf to wrap around my neck against the night's damp.

Doris eyed the square of expensive Liberty's silk for a moment. "That pretty scrap must have cost a bob or two." Her derisive tone didn't completely conceal her envy.

"A birthday gift," I replied, not quite meeting her gaze as I felt a stab of dread to add to my already churning stomach.

Did Doris hold my gaze a moment too long? It was hard to tell. Perhaps I was just being paranoid, knowing her rabid socialist tendencies.

Simon had introduced me to Doris over cups of thick sweet tea at a Lyons just off Islington Green. He had offered her a story of solidly middle-class parents in Cornwall displeased at their daughter's decision to leave home for work in London. Being the first in her family to leave service on a northern estate, Doris had understood familial expectations and immediately sympathized with me. But in the two months we'd lived together, she'd made very plain her resentment of the upper classes and their life of parasitic privilege. I was certain that if she ever realized the truth about me, I'd lose her friendship and my accommodations in one cruel blow.

Just as I thought she must have unraveled my secret, she smiled as she checked her reflection in the mirror, pinching color into her cheeks. "Any word from Simon?" She shot me a teasing look over her shoulder.

Heat flooded my face though I continued to shiver with cold. "Not since yesterday."

Simon had departed for Italy with Mr. Balázs, who had commissions that would keep the pair away from England until spring at the earliest. It had been difficult waving him off at Southampton docks after an idyllic few months spent almost continuously in each other's company. His letters had become a rare bright spot amid an otherwise dismal winter of chilblains, aching muscles, and the degrading realization that all I had learned to this point in my life was of absolutely no use to me. A child of five knew more about how to get on than I did; a fact reiterated at least ten times a day by my employer.

"Be careful, Kitty. You know what they say about those artist types." Doris fanned herself as she batted her lashes.

"You're mad." I clutched my handbag and tried to sound natural and easy. "Quick! There's the bus!"

The conversation was dropped in our race to catch the bus that would take us to Upper Street and the new cinema that had just opened. By the time we joined Jane and Agnes outside the movie house, I was laughing and chatting as we made our way through the evening crowds to our seats.

I had yet to grow used to being unremarkable among a population who cared nothing for my imperfections of carriage or conversation, didn't gossip over my matrimonial prospects or leap on the smallest social gaffe with malicious glee. The independence was exhilarating and unnerving at the same time. As far a cry from the quiet streets and velvet-draped drawing rooms of Mayfair as my new friends were from the simpering, sulking debutantes I'd associated with up to now.

Jane and Agnes both worked as mannequins at Madame Duchamp's, showcasing the fashionable Soho couturier's designs to her wealthy, influential customers. They were worldly-wise in a way I could never hope to be, and their racy stories always left me blushing, even as I pretended to laugh along with them.

"You should have seen the young gentleman who came in yesterday with his sister. The son of a duke." Jane giggled.

Agnes shook her head. "You're such an innocent, Jane. That woman was no more his sister than I am. His fancy piece, more like."

Jane gave a dreamy smile. "I don't think I'd mind being a kept woman. Not if it were by the son of a duke. All those lovely clothes and jewelry and a motorcar and a sweet little flat in Kensington with a maid and a cook all for a bit of how's your father now and again."

"Well, if you find a duke's son ask him if he has three well-to-do friends then, will you?" Agnes advised. "Though I *might* settle for an earl if you come across a handsome one."

We all laughed, though mine came out a little shaky as I imagined Agnes and William together. She might not know the proper use of a fish knife or who took precedence going in to dinner, but she was kind and amusing and down-to-earth—all things Cynthia was not. She'd have made William a good wife; or at the least a loving one, and surely, love must rate higher in selecting a mate than wealth and position.

I sank onto the theater's wooden chair with the same relief I might once have reclined on a plush chaise longue. Even among the crush of the audience, I clutched my coat tighter around my shoulders against the pervasive chill that seemed to settle in my very bones. The others didn't seem to notice. Perhaps they were more used to drafty auditoriums and thin cotton coats, but I sighed with relief when the lights dimmed and the flickering glow of the cinema drew everyone's attention. If Doris suspected I was under the weather, she'd insist we return home, and our rare evening out would be ruined.

Doris rose before dawn each morning so she could commute by

Tube and bus to her office in the City and sometimes didn't return home until eight or nine at night. My job as a kitchen girl in a café was only two streets away, but sometimes the effort to rise, dress, and make it to work before the breakfast rush was almost too much to bear. Having no marketable skills whatsoever, it had taken me longer than expected to find work. I had only gained this position through sheer luck—the previous girl had taken ill. The days were interminable; hours spent on my feet as I scrubbed the endless stream of dishes and glassware from the dining room along with the mountains of dirty pots and pans that seemed to always fill my enormous stone sink. My hands grew red and chapped, blistered, broke, and callused over. My knees and feet ached, and my shoulders seemed locked in a perpetual hunch. Had William come upon me now, he'd have passed me by without a second glance. My silk scarf was all I had left of home.

Doris leaned over and offered me some peanuts from her bag. Agnes and Jane giggled over the handsome young man seated three rows in front of us. I sat quietly and tried focusing on the screen. My head hurt, and the piano music vibrated around my skull like an entire pit orchestra.

"You really don't look well, Kitty." She put a hand to my forehead. "And you're burning up. I knew you were ill."

By now all I wanted was my bed. I nodded dumbly.

"Come on. Let's get you home." Doris rose from her seat and took me by the arm while Agnes and Jane hailed a cab.

"It's too expensive," I argued.

"Well, I can't shovel you onto the bus the way you are now so there's no help for it."

"I have to be at work tomorrow by six," I moaned through chattering teeth. "What on earth will I do?"

"You'll rest in your bed until you're well. That's what."

"They'll sack me."

"So you'll get another job. You won't be a lick of good to them as you are now, will you?"

I wanted to argue, but that would take energy I didn't have so instead I let Doris lead me to the waiting cab. The lights and excitement of the cinema were left behind as I leaned against Doris and closed my eyes.

An arm wrapped around my trembling shoulders. I snuggled closer to try and warm myself. "Are you here to take me to Nanreath, William? Did Mama and Papa send you?"

"Aye, Kitty," a voice whispered back. "I'll see you get home safe."

I wanted to believe, but I knew I'd never see home again.

It turned out that what I thought was merely a bad cold turned out to be scarlet fever. I lay in my bed, too tired to do more than sip at the hot sweet cups of tea Doris fed me, my hands too shaky to even hold the mug. By the time I began to feel as if death might have passed me by, the position at the café had been filled by a young, able-bodied girl just off the train from Lyme, and I was out of a job. I sold my scarf and paid Doris as much of the rent as I could, but I had nothing of value left.

A girl in the upstairs flat suggested a suitable occupation for someone with naught but the clothes she stood up in. When I began to seriously contemplate her suggestion, I surrendered to the inevitable, tucked my tail between my legs, and returned home to South Audley Street.

Mother and Father welcomed me back into the fold, though they made very sure I understood the depth of their compassion at forgiving such a wicked and ungrateful daughter. Within a week, I was whisked north to Glasgow to be sequestered away from the public's eye while I repented of my appalling behavior and regained my strength.

And if I happened to meet someone of the right sort—meaning wealthy, of good family, and willing to overlook my shameful reputation—all to the better.

That potential future husband's name turned out to be Sir Lachlan McKinley, who was tall, broad, and weathered as the mountains ringing Aunt Adelaide's house in Strathblane. He'd been to dinner almost every evening in the three weeks since my arrival, recounting tales of his years as a minor military attaché in India's Punjab province. He was home, now that his prospects had unexpectedly improved upon the death of his cousin and his sudden elevation to a baronetcy.

I wasn't stupid. I knew exactly what was in the works, especially after he cornered me in Aunt Adelaide's conservatory, pressed his sweaty pink hand against my waist in a vain attempt to steal a kiss, and murmured his happiness at our "understanding."

I taxed Aunt Adelaide with his actions after the guests had left—Lachlan and his sister, as mountainous as her brother; the local doctor and his wife; and the vicar—because apparently it's obligatory to have at least one vicar at every dinner party.

"Did my parents arrange this with you?" I asked.

She looked up from her book, her spectacles sliding to the end of her nose, her snowy white hair pinned beneath a lace cap like some matron from the last century. Anyone who met Aunt Adelaide for the first time assumed her a fragile wisp of a woman with the heart of a saint and the manners of a duchess. I knew her better. She ruled her household and tenants with an iron fist, and if it was sheathed in a velvet glove, no one was in any doubt she'd crush you if she found it necessary.

"I don't know what you're talking about, my dear. Arrange what?"

"This very crude attempt at matchmaking."

"If you are referring to Sir Lachlan, I should think you'd be flattered that a gentleman so obviously eligible would wish to attach himself to you after that horrid kerfuffle. There aren't many men who would overlook your unsavory fame."

"He isn't interested in me. He's interested in bagging an earl's daughter to secure his place in society. I'm the means to an end."

"Be happy you are still a marketable commodity" was Aunt Adelaide's tart response, and that was that.

From then on, I avoided being caught alone with Sir Lachlan, spoke only in pleasant generalities so as not to encourage his attentions, and ignored the increasingly blunt attempts by my aunt to force the issue.

Winter in Strathblane was a dreary affair of heavy snows punctuated by gale winds, driving rain, or, on the rare nice days, a rolling fog that smothered the hills and curled musty, damp fingers into every crevice of the old house until I spent most every waking hour wrapped in layers of itchy wool topped with rugs, shawls, and anything else that might keep the piercing cold out. For amusement, I had Aunt Adelaide's ancient spinet, a library full of agricultural tracts and Methodist sermons, and my journal, which I read again and again, as if it were the latest D. H. Lawrence novel and nothing to do with my life at all.

Letters arrived regularly to let me know what was going on outside my wintry cocoon. Mama and Papa wrote frequently, though these tended to be missives directed toward my proper behavior, my family duty, and their anguish at my ongoing racy reputation. Amelia's reports were taken up with dress fittings and morning calls as she prepared for her first London Season. Even Cynthia sent me the occasional newsy letter from Nanreath Hall, where she remained with Hugh and a seemingly unending string of houseguests.

I tried not to notice William's continued avoidance of the family, but it was hard to ignore, especially when his pages would arrive, recounting dinners and parties in London with old school chums, shoots he'd attended, and possible plans to travel abroad, but no hint about the reason for his continued absence from Cornwall and no date for his return.

There had to be more at work than the ambivalence of an unhappy marriage, but the heavy fog out of doors matched the thick, cobwebby funk within my own head and I could make neither heads nor tails of it. Besides, I had my own unhappy marriage to prevent.

As spring made a tentative appearance in the hedges and meadows, my strength returned and with it, my desire to stretch my legs and wander, pad and paint box to hand.

On a particular nice day in the earliest weeks of May, I bid Aunt Adelaide farewell as I snatched a piece of toast and two or three pieces of bacon from the sideboard. "I'm thinking of walking toward the summit of Dumgoyne today. Cook's prepared a basket, so I won't be home for luncheon."

She laid down her paper and reaffixed her spectacles with a troubled expression. "Ring round the moon means rain coming soon. You'll catch cold, and a red sniffly nose is never appealing in a young woman, Kitty. Besides, Sir Lachlan is due for dinner."

"Then I shall see you by six and be sure to powder liberally and carry a handkerchief." I gave her no chance to respond before I snatched one last sip of my tea and dashed from the room.

A groom waited with the dog cart and Cook's largesse, and soon I was bowling along the lane taking me into the rocky hills and wild meadows overlooking the estate. From my bedchamber, I had often watched the clouds riding heavy along the ridges to the north, and this was my destination. The landscape's stark beauty and the odd combination of light and air that gave the whole area an ethereal quality would test my rusty skills and hopefully give me the space and quiet I needed to ponder my uncertain future.

Dumgoyne was farther away and the roads less direct than I had thought. It was early afternoon before I ascended the summit and was able to spread a blanket on the ground and set up my portable easel in preparation for work.

Despite a freshening breeze, the sun was warm on my back, and I soon shed my coat and rolled up my sleeves as I sought to paint the scene before me. My hat cast a shadow on the page, and I removed the pins securing it and laid it aside. Aunt Adelaide would be scandalized, but she was far below in the valley's bowl. What she didn't know wouldn't hurt her. I nibbled on a chicken wing, sipped at the flask of tea, and enjoyed the quiet away from my aunt's ringing bell and her overly officious household. I had yet to decide how best to deal with Sir Lachlan, but here I could concentrate on the wash of color across the paper and leave the rest to worry over later.

So caught in my own head, I never heard the spill of stones or the crunch of boots on the track until the back of my neck prickled and the acrid whiff of cigarette smoke itched my nose. I had no idea how he'd found me. Perhaps a talkative groom had a few extra pennies in his pocket this afternoon.

He hiked the final incline to where I sat, his figure dark against the pale green and silver of the hills. He used a stick for the last few hundred feet, and his curses rang out as the scree tumbled and slid beneath his feet.

"Damn, that was a brand-new pair of trousers. I remember now why I left for milder and less steep environs. Too bloody . . . rustic."

I smothered a laugh as I turned to meet him, my insides jittery as I wiped my suddenly damp hands over my skirts.

He paused with a heaved breath, running an arm across his forehead to wipe the sweat from his brow. His dark hair clung to his scalp, and there was the shadow of a beard on his square jaw. "I hope you've gin in that flask. I'm parched."

"Tea." I handed it over.

Instead of the flask, he grabbed my wrist, dragging me to my feet. He was harder than I remembered, his body all muscle and sinew. Taller, too, I had to look up to meet his eyes, splinters of gold gleaming within the emerald green depths. "Welcome back, Mr. Halliday. How was Italy?" I said, dropping my eyes, suddenly shy.

He tipped my chin so I must look up into his face. "Lovely, and yet all I could think of was getting back to dreary old England as fast as I could." He wrapped his arms around my waist, pulling me close. I loved the way I fit against him, the smell of his skin, his sharp, angled brows drawn close as he studied me. "You're naught but bones." He fingered a curl by my ear. "And so pale the light shines right through you. What the hell happened while I was away?"

If only Sir Lachlan's bearlike embrace affected me this way, how easy my life would be. I stood on tiptoe and kissed him. "Nothing at all. I was merely waiting for you."

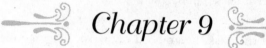

# Chapter 9

*December 1940*

"Charles says they live on bully beef and biscuits and he's already had to shake three scorpions out of his boots."

"Ugh." Tilly shuddered with disgust. "Sounds horrid."

It was New Year's Eve, and Sophie and Tilly were helping Anna prepare for the night's village social with Hugh. Well, perhaps "helping" might be a stretch. Tilly sprawled on her stomach across her bed, a cigarette in one hand, a glass of sherry in the other, and a copy of *Tatler* open between her elbows. Sophie lounged in a chair, her hair in curlers, reading a letter from her fiancé. Anna rummaged madly through her wardrobe, looking for something even halfway acceptable for an evening out.

"He makes it sound like a grand adventure, but I know he's only doing it so I won't worry," Sophie said. "Sometimes I wish I were there. Not to be with him, of course, but maybe Cairo or Alexandria, somewhere close. That way if the worst happened and he was wounded . . ."

"Try not to even think like that," Tilly cautioned. "He'll be fine. You'll see."

Sophie drew in a cleansing breath and gave a shaky smile. No one would admit it out loud, but all three knew the dangers he faced. One tried to lock the fear away and live as normally as one could, but grief hovered close and devastation was never far away. A sister on C ward received a telegram about her husband just last week, and there were two Home VADs who'd lost brothers. Anna grieved for Graham and Prue, but that pain, while still tender, was behind her. She didn't think she could live through that stomach punch of raw anguish ever again. She didn't want to.

"How's your yummy RAF flight officer?" Tilly asked, blowing out a thin stream of blue smoke.

And yet . . .

"He's not my officer," Anna said a bit more sharply than she'd intended. She'd not seen Tony Lambert in months and spent most of that time regretting her unnecessary harshness. How could he have known she equated speaking of France with having her appendix removed with a dull fork? Smarter men than he had tried to get her to open up. Catharsis, they called it. She called it prying and buried her feelings deeper. Armored over them more thoroughly so no cracks showed.

"You're cruel, Anna," Sophie said. "He's nice and he obviously likes you. He asks after you whenever I see him down at the pub."

"He's just being polite," Anna argued. "Why are you two so determined to pair me off anyway? Why don't you focus your energies on someone who actually needs a man—like Sister Murphy?"

"I think Hitler's already taken." Tilly laughed as Sophie heaved a pillow at her.

"Really, Anna," Tilly badgered. "Tony Lambert's lovely. You should give him a chance. What have you got to lose?"

*Everything*, Anna wanted to say.

"Leave her be, Tilly." Sophie folded Charles's letter and tucked it inside her blouse against her heart. "Not everyone is out to snabble a husband."

"Good. Leaves more of them for me." Tilly stuck her tongue out at Anna and rolled up to refill her sherry glass from the bottle on the nightstand.

Anna pulled out her red and white cotton—too frumpy.

The black linen with the yellow piping around the neck—too tight around the middle.

A gray tweed skirt and white blouse—too boring.

"Ugh! I give up. I have absolutely nothing that hasn't been let out, taken in, or isn't hopelessly out-of-date."

"What about your jumper with the pearl buttons?" Sophie suggested.

"I'd love to wear it, but Tilly"—she shot her a long-suffering glare—"mislaid it somewhere in Newquay last week."

Tilly blushed and eyed the pile of castoff clothes with renewed vigor. "What about that one?"

"A stain on the sleeve."

"And that one?" Sophie asked.

"It smells like camphor."

Sophie and Tilly exchanged smothered smiles that made Anna want to throw something at them.

"So you're asking for our help? Is that it?" Tilly asked sweetly.

"I thought that was what you were supposed to be doing from the start."

Sophie began looking through the dresses, as if she might stumble on a Chanel that Anna had overlooked.

"Here's what you need." Tilly pointed to a picture in her magazine of actress Vivien Leigh staring up into the eyes of Olivier.

She wore a gorgeous patterned silk gown that would probably have taken Anna's entire yearly salary to purchase.

"Right," Anna answered tartly. "Add my family diamonds and a tiara and I'm ready for Cinderella's ball."

"That's it. Of course." Sophie moved aside the sherry bottle and opened a steamer trunk serving double duty as a nightstand, emerging with a tissue-wrapped package that she laid on the bed. "Mother made me bring it with me—just in case." She unwrapped the tissue to reveal a deep red velvet gown trimmed across the collar in gorgeous hand-tatted lace. "I can't exactly wear it while emptying bedpans or folding sheets, can I?"

"Crikey! Is that a Madeleine Vionnet?" Tilly breathed, stroking the velvet's soft nap.

"Mother and I bought it in Paris the summer before the war."

"You're mad. I can't possibly borrow that."

Sophie shook it out, the fabric spilling down to the floor in a soft sweep of vibrant color. "Don't be silly. Of course you can. I'm hardly going to be drinking champagne and dancing while Charles is sweating in the desert with scorpions and snakes."

"And Jerries," Tilly added.

"Exactly. So wear it, Anna. Then I can at least tell my mother it was worn. She doesn't have to know it wasn't me wearing it."

Anna slipped out of her skirt and blouse and slid into the gown. Sophie zipped her up the back, fluffing the skirt around her ankles as Anna admired herself in the mirror.

She should say no. She really should. If anything happened to this gown, she'd owe Sophie Kinsale her firstborn. But after a year of making do, wearing this exquisite dress was a dream come true. The color was a deep rich crimson. The lace looked as if it had been spun by a battalion of spiders, and the fit accentuated her less than ample bosom while making her waist look positively tiny.

"Just so you know, I was joking about the Cinderella bit," she said, unable to keep the smile from her face.

"Shut up, Anna. You look lovely," Sophie said.

"If Sophie's your fairy godmother, what does that make me?" Tilly asked. "An ugly stepsister?"

"Um . . . about that. Are you certain you don't mind my attending this dance tonight with Hugh? I mean, he didn't really ask, it was more like a direct order."

Tilly leaned back against her pillow. "Of course I don't mind, dearie. You're part of his family, not some siren on the make. Besides, Hugh's jolly good fun and I like him a lot, but he's not exactly the type to bring home to my mum and da, is he? What would they talk about? Da's job at the shipyard? Ma's victory garden? I know my place, and lady of the manor isn't it."

"Don't sell yourself short, Tilly Jones. You'd be the best thing that ever happened to him," Sophie scolded. By now, she'd guided Anna into a chair and was brushing out her hair before pinning it up. The movement of her hands as she worked hypnotized Anna. She felt her eyes close, her shoulders relax, and her roommates' voices seemed to float to her through a haze.

"Ha! We'd kill each other within a month. It's different with you and that lieutenant. The two of you have things in common, lives that make sense together. When Charles comes home, you'll marry in some big wedding with a train of twenty bridesmaids and a reception at the Ritz and have beautiful babies and live a perfect life."

Sophie paused. Her hand trembled upon the brush. A bunch of pins clattered onto the floor at Anna's feet.

"Sophie?" she asked, attempting to glance through the hair hanging in her face. "Are you all right?"

Sophie sank into a chair, tears leaking down her cheeks. "I'm so scared. I try not to be. I try to be strong and carry on like they say we should, but I can't help it. I hate not knowing what's happening to him or where he is or whether he's alive or dead."

Tilly threw Anna a look of helplessness. "Maybe you *should* ask for that transfer to a forward hospital, Sophie. If nothing else, it would keep you too busy to fret."

"My parents would never allow it," she answered through her sniffles. "It was bad enough when I joined the VAD in the first place. Father wanted to arrange for me to get a comfortable clerical job with one of his cronies at the Ministry of Food so I could live at home. If I told them I was going overseas and into harm's way, they'd probably lock me in a room for the duration."

"That's right. We're so bloody safe here with the Germans knocking at our door," Tilly snorted.

"You know what I mean." Sophie's breath came in quick spasms as she fought to calm herself. "You served in a battalion hospital in France, Anna. What was it like?"

Anna's muscles tightened with an all-too-familiar sense of dread. She stared down at the red of the gown's skirt as it draped across her lap. How had she not noticed it was the exact color of fresh blood? She swallowed down the bile rising in her throat. "It's a different world. The men come in caked head to foot in filth. Some are terrified or weeping for the mothers. Others are deathly quiet. It's chaotic and heartrending and terrifying and you've never worked so hard in your life or been so tired, but at the end of the day, you feel as if you've done something important, as if you really mattered."

"Who was Harriet?" Sophie asked, her voice barely more than a whisper.

Anna's nerves skittered, the hair along her arms rising as she stiffened.

"You call her name sometimes in your sleep."

Tilly nodded in agreement.

Anna didn't want to talk about Harriet. "No one." She rose from her chair, grabbing up her handbag, a false smile pasted on her lips. "So, where's my pumpkin?"

Despite wartime restrictions and a somber restraint on the part of the organizers, the church hall was beautiful. Electric lights had been replaced by candles, which flickered amid centerpieces of fragrant holly and pine on every table. A small stage had been set up at the far end of the room where a rather haphazard band played carols and the occasional dance tune while guests mingled.

"It's lovely, Hugh." She took his arm as they entered, admiring the way he looked in his RAF uniform, his blond hair slicked back, cap under his arm. This was what he must have looked like before injury and then bitterness had dulled the golden glow. "As are you. I'd no idea you'd scrub up so well. You're positively dashing."

He grimaced. "Not sure how I feel about being called lovely, but thank you all the same. It's part of the job. I'm here playing double duty as lord of the manor and local wounded soldier. Might I return the compliment? You're looking jolly good yourself." He leaned close. "You smell nice, too."

"Down boy."

His laugh ended on a strangled bark and he stiffened, the muscles of his arm hardening under her fingers. Anna followed his gaze, her own tension curling cold up her spine. Lady Boxley approached them through the crowd, the vicar and a few local dignitaries following in her wake like ducklings. Despite the make-do outfits of most of the partygoers, Lady Boxley stood out in a sequined crepe de chine midnight-blue gown gathered just under the bust, her face and hair arranged to perfection. All she needed was a scepter and a ruff and she'd be the spitting image of Good Queen Bess just before she sent Raleigh to the gallows.

"So good of you to make an appearance, Hugh," she snipped. "We've been waiting over an hour. Mr. Lester was hoping you'd make a speech, rallying the troops for the cause." She nodded toward the gray-haired vicar hovering at her shoulder.

"It's my fault, Lady Boxley," Anna interceded. "Hugh waited for me to go off duty, and I was delayed due to some patients arriving unexpectedly."

Lady Boxley acknowledged Anna with a sharp, raking glance and a smile that never reached her eyes. "It's Miss Trenowyth, isn't it?"

"Oh for God's sake, Mother. You know bloody well who she is."

She put out a limp-wristed hand for Anna to shake—or perhaps kiss. "Yes. Of course. Hugh, may I see you a moment—privately?"

He shot Anna a long-suffering look but followed his mother, leaving Anna alone to face the crowd. Head up, she made her way to a table heaped with food. It was obvious more than one household's weekly butter and sugar ration had gone into the spread before her. Anna hadn't seen such delights for ages. She politely chose a slice of pound cake from a tray and forced herself not to fill her pockets.

"You're one of those girls from the big house, aren't you?" A tall, thin woman with a helmet of steel-gray hair eyed her curiously as she ladled out a glass of pink fizzy punch.

Anna had the uncomfortable sense she'd been caught at something. "I'm a nurse there."

It might have been her imagination, but she would swear the woman looked at her with narrowed speculation. She whispered to a woman beside her, " . . . daughter . . . back to Nanreath Hall . . . from London . . ."

Obviously, news of her arrival had reached the locals. By now the pair had been joined by two more. All of them regarded her with expressions ranging from mild interest to outright curiosity.

One of them juggled punch and a plate and stuck out a hand. "I'm Mrs. Crewe." She nodded toward the other women at the table. "This is Mrs. Polley"—a fussy middle-aged woman in a gray dress prettied up with a chunky red beaded necklace—"Mrs. Thompkins"—round and buxom and pink-cheeked in a loud floral print with a gold brooch—"and the old sourpuss ladling punch is Miss Dawlish." She continued to regard Anna with a disapproving eye.

"How do you do? I'm Anna Trenowyth."

"Funny you coming back after all these years," Miss Dawlish commented in a voice that held no hint of laughter. This pronouncement seemed to break the dam of conversation.

"She can't be *coming* back. She's never been here before."

"That doesn't matter. She's Lady Katherine's daughter. Nanreath Hall is her home."

"Natural daughter, and I'd imagine Lady Boxley might have a say in that."

"It's Lord Melcombe's say, though, ain't it? He's the one in charge."

"You believe that, Emmaline Crewe, you're dafter than a turkey chick. It's his mother what calls the shots."

"I don't know about that. He's such a good boy."

"Good? He took out a whole stretch of my laurels with that motorcar of his and nearly ran down Tom's old dog."

"He's grieving."

"He's drinking."

"It's a mean, smelly old dog anyway."

"That's not the point. It could as easily have been a child."

"Not lying in the middle of the road at midnight."

"You don't make sense, Emmaline."

As their voices rose in war with each other, Anna flushed with embarrassment. She shot a pained look toward Hugh, but he remained in unhappy conversation with his mother. "It's been lovely to meet you all. I never thought I'd get the chance to see where my mother spent so much of her childhood."

"Wouldn't have got the chance if the old earl were alive," Miss Dawlish grumbled. "He was a stickler, that one. Not an ounce of bend in him. He'd have sent you packing like he sent her when she run off with that man and got herself in the family way."

"Hush, Louise. Don't be such a prude. Lady Katherine wasn't the only girl that made a mistake. It was the time, wasn't it? Things were topsy-turvy."

"Topsy-turvy doesn't make it right."

"Maybe not, but it's over and done a long time ago and no sense behaving like you're shocked."

"Heard he died at the Somme."

"No, it was Passchendaele."

"No, he ran off with a French dancer and lives in Venice."

"They said you looked like her, but I didn't believe it." This new voice cut through the women's babbling like an ax. All turned to a faded woman wearing a faded dress. Her face bore the creases and complexion of one who's worked hard with little thanks, her knuckles knobby and bent, her back slightly bowed. Only her eyes stood out, bright as two turquoise beads.

"Wanted to see for myself if it were true. Imagine, Minnie, I said to myself. Imagine Lady Katherine's little daughter is come back at last." She smiled. "Could tell you were hers the instant I clapped eyes on you. That hair couldn't belong to no one else, now could it? Red as a sunset."

"You mustn't mind Miss Smith," Mrs. Crewe cautioned. "A bit vague these days."

The woman bristled. "I never am. My mind's clear as crystal. Can see them days like it was last week."

"You knew my mother, Miss Smith?" Anna asked. Out of the corner of her eye, she saw Hugh and Lady Boxley's conversation had grown heated. Hugh wore a hard-jawed petulance while his mother's countenance reddened by the moment. Finally, Hugh walked away, leaving his mother to glare after him. Anna turned her attention back to Miss Smith but not before catching the angry gaze Lady Boxley leveled in her direction.

"Call me Minnie. All my friends do. Of course I knew your mother. What they call a real English rose. Sweet and pretty but with plenty of thorns to keep you guessing." She chuckled at her own joke. "Lady Katherine spent more time at my mistress's house than she did her own. Always a smile for me or a how-do-you-do. Not like some of them others at the big house. Never flaunting herself as if she was better." Minnie's accusatory gaze swung over the room, lips pursed thin with resentment. "When she came back here round as a pumpkin, I told her I was sorry it didn't work out with that boy of hers. She smiled at me and gave me a hug just as if we were friends and not lady and maidservant. Like I said, a real English rose."

Hugh returned to Anna's side, strain tightening his lazy smile. Amid flustered greetings from the bevy of church ladies, he handed her a glass that upon closer inspection turned out to be whiskey rather than the punch everyone else seemed to be drinking. "Some grease to ease your way through this ordeal."

She accepted it gratefully. "Hugh, this is Miss Smith. She knew Lady Katherine when she lived at Nanreath Hall." She took a swallow of the whiskey. "Did you know my mother had come back here when she was pregnant?"

"It makes sense. Unmarried with a child. Where else would you turn but to the people who profess to love you?"

"Yes, too bad they didn't see it that way," Anna replied tightly.

Hugh's gaze sharpened, but Minnie merely smiled. "You come see me, miss. I'll fix us a pot of tea and we'll have a nice comfy coze. Anyone can point you to my house. Just tell 'em you're looking for the Smith place." She cocked a glance across the room to where Lady Boxley stood surrounded by a coterie of hangers-on. "Bet the fox is in with the pigeons now with you coming back, isn't it, miss? She must be jumpy as a cat in a thunderstorm and no mistaking."

"Why would that be?" Anna asked.

She gave a little shiver and smiled. "I'll just be getting along. They're saving a bit of pudding for me to take to Dad. Feeling poorly, he is. I've to get home to him before too late." She patted Anna's cheek. "Take care, my girl. And remember. Come for tea when you can."

The evening rolled on with dancing followed by a buffet supper laid out on long tables and a whist drive in which fifteen pounds was raised for the local wounded soldiers fund. Lady Boxley moved easily among the guests, a born hostess, gracious, witty, and charming, but occasionally Anna felt a prickle shiver along her spine. She would look up to catch Hugh's mother watching her, lips pursed, eyes inscrutable and dark.

Hugh, on the other hand, seemed gauche and ill at ease. He stood morose and silent, a drink never far from his hand, as older women asked after his health and sighed over his injuries or younger ones giggled and cast sidelong glances at him from across the room. Occasionally, he would grow animated, though even his laughter possessed a wild edge as he drank with the older men who swapped stories of the last war and toasted his heroism with blustery guffaws and tasteless jokes. There were few younger men besides Hugh.

By the time he rose to make his speech to herald the New Year, he needed to steady himself against a table, and bright spots of red burned high on each sharp cheekbone. As the crowd quieted, he lifted his glass. "I want to thank you all for coming tonight and for making this event such a success." He paused, his glassy eyes raking the crowd. "What would us wounded soldiers do if it weren't for the pity of a nation?"

A ripple spread through the crowd. Anna tensed.

"In Wellington's day, old soldiers who'd outlasted their usefulness ended on street corners begging for pennies. Now we end in church halls begging for shillings and half crowns. Not much has changed, has it?"

Lady Boxley looked as if she wanted to do murder, her face stone-white and frozen. The rest of the room moved and shifted uncomfortably. Some laughed nervously. Hugh wobbled, dropping a hand to Anna's shoulder. He glanced down at her, and Anna swallowed hard. This was not going well and was bound to become very much worse.

"Maybe you don't all know it yet, but we have a new addition to the family. Oh, don't look so excited," he said as a murmur rose from the audience. "I'm not shackling myself to any dewy young thing, as if any would have me with this metal leg of mine. But we have here the prodigal sheep come home to us. Stand up, Anna. Let the people ogle you."

Now she was the one who wanted to do murder. Her jaw clenched as she shot him a dagger look.

He lifted a brow in inebriated nonchalance. "No? Suit yourself.

Anna here is a Trenowyth. Those of you old enough, and by the gray hairs I see, most of you are plenty old, will remember Lady Katherine Trenowyth, the aunt I'm not supposed to speak of except in a shameful whisper."

Oh God, was he really doing this? Was she really going to sit here and let him? But how on earth could she stop him without causing more of a scene? She looked to Lady Boxley, hoping his mother might charge in and stop the onrushing disaster, but she remained poker-straight in her chair, her face completely wiped clean of any expression. Only her eyes spoke her fury.

"Smart woman, my aunt," Hugh maundered on, oblivious to the growing unease . . . or rather reveling in it. His mouth curved into a hard, brittle smile. "She had the good sense to run as far and as fast as she could from this godforsaken little back corner of the world. But now her daughter has returned. Why, I have no bloody idea. Why *did* you come back, Anna?"

She felt the blood rush to her face before dropping like a stone into her shoes, leaving her breathless and a bit sick.

Hugh waved an unsteady hand toward Lady Boxley. "My mother finds it terribly embarrassing. I can't see why. It's not like it's her illegitimate child, now, is it?"

Someone laughed. Anna thought it might have been Minnie Smith.

The clock struck midnight. The crowd shifted again. Some raised glasses. Others gave a halfhearted cheer. Anything to drown out Hugh's performance.

Lady Boxley stood, shoving roughly back from the table. "Sit down, Hugh."

"I've not finished with my toast, Mother."

"I believe you've given us adequate words to chew on at present."

Hugh glanced at Anna, who silently pleaded with him to agree.

He raised his glass. "Here's to Lady Katherine and her daughter, Anna. Welcome home, cousin."

Uncertain, the captive and captivated audience followed suit. Anna wanted to sink into the floor or just die on the spot.

The vicar, finally breaking free of the train wreck unfolding before him, stood and took over seamlessly with words about the ongoing struggles ahead and our determination to continue the fight no matter what. Anna barely registered the toasting of 1941. She pushed her way through the crowds toward the door. Anywhere she could get away from the curious stares and murmured whispers.

"Anna!" Hugh shouted after her, but she didn't stop. He tried following, but stumbled, his bad leg catching hard against a table, sending plates smashing to the floor, a candle falling to smoke and spit in the evergreens. People flocked to put out the smoldering fire. Women clucked like chickens while the men laughed and cheered him on.

Outside, the cold soothed her burning cheeks. She stared up at the distant stars. She couldn't breathe except in quick, snatching gasps that froze her lungs and cramped her stomach.

The door opened and closed behind her. She braced herself for Hugh's babbling drunken apologies but it was Lady Boxley whose words cut the brittle, icy silence. "My son won't remember any of this in the morning—but I will, Miss Trenowyth. I can assure you of that."

Anna never took her eyes from the faraway pinpricks of ancient light until the door opened and closed once more.

Nanreath's gallery was dark but for a lamp by the door. Heavy blackout curtains drawn across the west-facing windows cut off even the tiniest sliver of winter moonlight but couldn't completely muffle the distant roar of the surf.

Anna had come here as soon as she'd returned to the house. The walk back from the village had been cold—her feet still hadn't thawed out—but it had given her time to calm down. By the time she'd skirted the main gates to avoid nosy sentries, followed the same grassy track Hugh had used to bring her to Nanreath that first night, and climbed the stairs to the deserted gallery, her kicked-in-the-gut feeling of nausea had subsided. Now she just had a horrid headache, eyes that burned from cigarette smoke and lack of sleep, and the realization that no matter how much she wanted to belong, this wasn't her house and these people weren't her family. But damn it, that was her mother up on the wall, no matter how they tried to erase her embarrassing existence.

She shifted uncomfortably in her chair, unused to the heavy weight of her borrowed gown. A gown fit for an earl's daughter with its lace and its velvet. No wonder they laughed at her tonight. She was no more meant to wear a gown like this than take tea with the queen. She was not one of them. She never would be.

"Coming here was a mistake. I should have known they'd want nothing to do with me. I let myself believe and then hope and then . . . who was I fooling? You're still the trollop who stained the family honor and I'm still the embarrassing reminder. Nothing will change that. And I'm a fool to ever believe it could be any other way." She tilted her head back to stare into the dark. "God, I'm cracking up. Now I'm spilling my guts to a painting."

Her mother smiled down from her place on the wall, but not at Anna. No, she seemed to stare at some hidden delight just beyond the portrait's edge, her body poised, as if waiting for the artist to put down his brush so she might flee the stiff formality of her pose, a radiance about her and yet a shyness in her expression, a pensive sweetness, as if she were in love.

As if she were in love . . .

Anna fingered the inscription and snapped open her locket to study the picture of her father, as if she didn't have every line and shadow memorized from his soldier's cap and corporal's stripes to his sleek dark hair and thick-lashed gypsy eyes. Was this who she swayed toward as a flower turns to the light? This stranger whose blood Anna carried in her veins, a man who had cared so little he left her mother with neither ring nor name? There was a scholar's ascetic about him and yet he bore the broad shoulders of an athlete, the lean, chiseled features of an aristocrat. Had he known of her birth? Or had he been long gone by that time? Had her mother wept over him? Or had she been relieved at his abandonment?

*Forgive my love.*

What did the mysterious inscription mean? What had Graham and Prue wanted to tell Anna that was so important they'd called her home to London?

A door slammed. A draft whistled cold around her ankles. She fisted her hands around the locket. Damn. She'd thought she didn't care if they discovered her trespassing, but faced with being caught red-handed, the idea of being dragged in front of Matron for a harsh reprimand sent nervous butterflies through her stomach.

She'd only time to draw deeper into her chair when Hugh staggered into the room from the far doorway, his steps unsteady. Gone was the polished RAF officer. His cap was gone, his hair mussed, a lipstick stain smeared his collar, and his left eye bore the marks of someone's fist. He stiffened when he saw her, his every movement possessing a drunkard's precision. "Happy New Year, cousin Anna."

He lifted a hand as if raising a glass, swayed for a drawn-out moment then buckled to his knees, as if taking a slug to the jaw to go with his black eye. Without thinking, Anna leaped to catch him before he landed on the floor in a heap. Instead, they both ended in a tangle, his artificial leg twisted awkwardly underneath him, his trousers yanked high to reveal the ugly prosthetic, the hinge of his false knee. She brushed the steel clamps attaching what was left of his thigh to the leg. He winced. Her fingertips came away stained faintly red. "You're bleeding."

"It's nothing."

"It's not nothing." She gripped the cuff of his trousers and tore with a nurse's strength. The fabric ripped along one seam, revealing the raw, ugly flesh of his upper leg where the straps bit into it with every step. "You never say anything."

"Would it do any good?" She saw the tight-lipped, hard-jawed strain for what it was, constant pain held at bay with drink and determination.

"Oh, Hugh," she sighed.

"To hell with your pity, cousin," he snarled. "To hell with all of them and their damned smothering compassion. I should have gone down with the plane. Better to die a hero than live on as a pathetic cripple tied to his mother's apron strings."

"Don't say that. Don't ever wish for death."

He lay back on the floor, staring up into the dark reaches of the ceiling. "I never meant to hurt you, Anna. I'm such a bloody awful bastard."

"You'll get no argument from me."

He closed his eyes, his breathing ragged but steady.

"Let's get you to bed. A good sleep and you'll feel a hundred times better."

"Doubtful."

She wrapped an arm around his shoulder and together, they

managed to maneuver him back onto his feet. By then his face was white, his hands shaking. "I can make it the rest of the way on my own."

"I'm sure you can," she said as she continued to assist him. They hobbled from the gallery, slow, unsteady steps taking them down a long hall and up a flight of stairs. He stepped on and ripped the hem of her gown. "Blast. Sorry about that."

"Tell Sophie when you see her next."

"I'd buy her a new one, but I have a feeling I couldn't afford it."

At the door to his bedchamber, she leaned against the wall as she scooted close enough to turn the handle and get him inside. By now his green face had grown gray, white ringing his clamped lips, a rapid pulse beating under his jaw.

"I can't go any farther or I'll toss dinner all over your shoes," he said through clenched teeth.

"I'm a VAD. Remember? I do all the muck work the proper sisters don't have time for."

"Ouch. Hoist with my own sword." He gave a rough bark of laughter. "Careful. There's a step down . . . oof."

Her foot missed the drop into the room, and she came down hard, his awkward weight dragging her almost to her knees. He pinned her against the doorjamb. His bloodshot eyes seemed to drink her in, as if seeing her for the first time. He pushed a strand of hair behind her ear.

"No one could ever dispute the relationship. Your resemblance to Lady Katherine is uncanny," he said. "I've never seen such a shade of red before."

She swallowed around the lump in her throat, tried to keep her voice cool and no-nonsense. Hugh was drunk and remorseful—a bad combination. "Lady Katherine was much prettier. My mouth is too wide and I have big ears."

He traced the edge of one lobe. "Did he have big ears?"

"Extremely. Like father, like daughter," she said in the same chirpy tone she used with her sickest patients, hoping it would break Hugh's whiskey spell.

"Who was he?"

"I have no earthly idea. Now, are you going to let me go, or do you plan on chatting all night? Because I just want to go to bed and put this disaster of an evening behind me."

Neither one of them noticed the shadow slicing the floor between them like a cleaver until a voice thundered from above like a crack of doom. "I believe leaving is for the best, Miss Trenowyth. You needn't worry about Hugh. I can take care of whatever he needs."

Anna snatched her hand from Hugh's waist as if it had caught fire. So much for a battalion hospital in North Africa or the Far East. She'd be lucky if she weren't scrubbing lavatories in Greenland for the duration of the war.

"Good evening, Mother . . . or should I say good morning?" Hugh smiled at Lady Boxley, who hovered like an angel of doom. "Anna here was helping me to bed."

Anna shot Hugh a venomous look. As if Lady Boxley didn't already resent and despise her, Hugh had to throw fuel on the fire out of some perverse need to shock his mother. She found herself remembering Sophie's tale about the last nurse caught in a compromising situation with the master of the house, and sympathized with the poor girl.

"Miss Trenowyth is a credit to the Red Cross, I'm sure. Her talents are wasted on such a small hospital as Nanreath." Her attention flicked to Anna. "If you'd like, I know more than a few people associated with the Joint War Organization who could assist you if you wished to transfer."

Lady Boxley's expression was unreadable, but her meaning more than clear: leave or be sent away.

Anna wanted to laugh. Here was her chance to be sent to a battalion hospital close to the front. They'd turned her application down, but they wouldn't refuse Lady Boxley.

"I don't want her to go," Hugh groused, his voice petulant as a small boy's.

"It's for the best, Hugh dear. For everyone," Lady Boxley replied.

He looked from his mother to Anna and back. Then threw up.

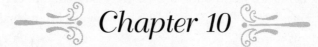

# Chapter 10

*May 1914*

Simon and I arrived at London's Euston Station close to midnight. A cold spring rain drenched the streets, quickly overcoming our shared umbrella, and by the time we were settled in a cab, I was soaked to the bone and trying not to regret my wretched impulsiveness. If I'd chosen differently, I could have been tucked up in a warm bed with a crackling fire and a glass of milk with naught to worry over but how best to please my new fiancé. Instead, I had defied Aunt Adelaide and fled Strathblane with her dire predictions blistering my ears.

*Wretched, ungrateful girl.*

*You'll come to a bad end. Calf love has ruined cleverer girls than you, Katherine Trenowyth.*

And with the finality of a funeral, her last words before slamming the house's great double doors. *Good riddance to bad rubbish.*

For better or worse, I had tied my fate to Simon.

As if sensing my thoughts, he smiled reassuringly as he directed the driver to Digswell Street. We had decided as the train clacked its way southward from Scotland that the best course of action was to seek out Doris's assistance. If I was fortunate, she'd offer me my old lodgings back. If less so, she might know where I could find suitable rooms to rent.

"Tell me again about this job you've found for me?"

"The woman's name is Evelyn Ferndale-Branch. She's a respected member of the new art school started by the artists Byam Shaw and Vicat Cole in Kensington. She's willing to take you on as her assistant. The pay won't be much, but you'll be able to take classes at the school in your free time."

"I can't believe it. It's a dream come true."

"You say that now, but what about your parents? I doubt they're going to be happy."

By now my parents would have been informed of my precipitate departure. I could well imagine their reaction. If I returned home this time, I'd be handed a one-way ticket to Australia or some other equally distant destination where my troublesome existence might be swiped under the rug. "I don't care. Or rather I don't care enough to do as I'm told. After all, they say in life you only regret those things you didn't do." I tried to sound brave and indifferent. Inside, I was terrified.

"It will come out all right, Kitty. I promise." He touched my chin, my cheek. Locked eyes with me until I nodded dumbly in agreement.

He pulled me close, his hand curving around my waist as he nibbled wine-scented kisses up my throat to my ear. My skin grew hot and tight as my hand flattened against his chest, the beat of his heart like a drum beneath my palm.

Before we got too carried away, the cab pulled up in front of the narrow terraced house. A light shone through the basement window. Someone was home—and awake.

"You've a nerve coming back here after all these months, Lady High-and-Mighty." Doris answered my tap on the door in a belted dressing gown, her hair in a braid down her back, her expression nearly matching Aunt Adelaide's for outraged displeasure.

"Let me explain."

"You don't need to," she cut me off. "You're like all the rest of the bleeding toffs, lying to get what you want with no care about who you hurt in the process."

"It wasn't like that at all."

"No?"

Was this the same girl I'd laughed with over dinners of bread and butter when we'd not two pennies to put together? The same girl with whom I'd commiserated over long days, small pay packets, and men who thought every unattended female was deserving of their unctuous attentions? The same girl who'd nursed me through the worst of my fever even when it meant missing a day of work?

"Please, Doris. Let us in. It's raining, and we've had an awfully long journey."

She cocked a narrowed glance at Simon behind me.

"He's found me a job. I'm to work for an artist at the Byam. I'll finally be able to do what I've always wanted."

"Good for you. It still doesn't explain why you lied—or what you're both doing here begging in the middle of the night."

I tried to collect myself, but my heart jumped in my chest and the breath I drew into my lungs reeked of fish, cooking oil, and latrines. "Please, Doris. I never meant to deceive you. At first, I was afraid no one would hire me if they knew who I really was. Then you had such strong views on the greedy aristocracy that I was afraid to tell you the truth. I couldn't lose you."

"Me or my flat?"

I drew back. "That's unfair."

She dropped her eyes to the frayed cuff of her dressing gown, face splotchy and mulish. When she met my eyes once more, there was doubt, but I knew I'd not convinced her. "Yes, well . . . that's all fine and good, but you can't stay. It's late and Sally's sleeping."

"Who's Sally?"

"My new roommate. I'll wager she won't disappear and take her share of the rent with her," she spat with renewed venom. "I had to pawn my gold cross in order to keep a roof over my head, and that was a present from my mum."

"I didn't know. I'm sorry, Doris."

"'Course you didn't. You were off hobnobbing with dukes and duchesses and never a thought to those you left high and dry. I can't help, Kitty. If you're smart you'll go home and stop pretending to be something you're not." She closed the door in my face, the thrown latch a hollow, painful sound.

"Damn," Simon muttered. "That's done it, then."

The loss of Doris's friendship hurt like a slap to the face, and my breath came in small, stuttering gasps, but I tried not to panic. "Is she right?"

"About what?"

"That I need to stop pretending to be something I'm not. Simon, I think I've made a terrible mistake."

"What happened to all that about regretting the things you don't do, not the things you've done?"

"When I said that, I wasn't drenched to the skin in the middle of the night wondering what was to become of me."

He ushered me back to the waiting cab. "Ralston Street."

His expression was hidden, but for the flickering reflection of passing streetlights in his eyes. A strange, quivering anticipation settled in the pit of my stomach.

This time the cab ride seemed to last forever. The rain intensified until water streamed down the windows. I knew we headed south past Ludgate Hill and the Houses of Parliament and along the Embankment but I could see nothing beyond the bleary rain-smeared glass. Simon lit a cigarette. Neither of us spoke.

At Ralston Street, Simon held his umbrella for me and we dashed for the door. He fumbled with his key. Drops slid cold beneath my collar and down my neck. I tried to convince myself this was the cause of the shivers running up and down my spine.

Inside, we ignored the door opening off the narrow foyer and instead climbed the staircase, which ran up to a landing and bent before rising to the first floor and another two doors. Simon opened the left and entered a cluttered set of obviously bachelor rooms. They smelled of unwashed dishes and unwashed socks. A few pieces of furniture in the front room, a tiny kitchen at the rear, and behind a set of heavy, dusty velvet curtains could be seen the corner of a bed and a dressing table.

He set down my case, took my coat and removed his own. "I'll put on a pot of tea. That should warm you up."

I removed my hat and tried to look as if I belonged.

A few minutes later he handed me a steaming cup and sat beside me on the couch. "You'll stay here. It's for the best anyway. Much more convenient than a bedsit all the way in Islington."

"Simon, I . . ."

"I know what you're going to say."

"I don't think you do. I may have left my great-aunt Adelaide's house for the promise of a job and a place at the Byam, but I came to London for you."

He did not smile as he took the cup from my hands and set it down. His expression bore a dark, questioning intensity as he leaned forward and kissed me. The sweet, smoky taste of him was dizzying, like drinking too much champagne. He drew a pin from my hair, then another. Slowly. Patiently. As if he had all the time in the world. As if each tress that fell about my shoulders was another promise between us. "The first time I laid eyes on you I thought you were a meek little mouse like all the rest," he said quietly. My hair hung loose, curling to my waist in a fiery tangle. This time we had no stern cabbie to hold us in restraint. He kissed me again, deeper, longer. I felt a greedy heat pooling low in my belly, my blood rushing hot through my veins. "I was wrong, Kitty. You're not like anyone I've ever met."

His hand moved to the buttons on my frock, his breath shivering my bare skin. I should have been frightened or nervous. I should have had Mama's imprecations on suitable female behavior ringing in my virgin ears, seen the error of my wicked ways, and run from this place and this man, but I did not. "Not a mouse." My answer came breathless but firm. "A wanton."

He smiled and drew me up from the sofa, leading me back to the velvet curtain and that glimpse of bed beyond. "My wanton."

I woke suddenly, completely disoriented. For a heart-stopping moment, I imagined myself in my bedchamber at Great-aunt Adelaide's house, the last days naught but a hallucination brought on by a return of my fever. Then a body rolled over to spoon warm against my back, an arm snaked over my side to pull me close. He breathed evenly in sleep, though parts of him seemed very much awake and more than alert. I held very still. Not out of fear, but because I wanted to savor this brief exhilarating moment as long as I could before the reality of my situation intruded.

When the sun rose above the rooftops, I would be no more than a cautionary tale to be whispered about in horrified yet eager undertones. But in these small rainy hours as the breeze curled chilly through a crack in the window, and the faucet in the kitchen dripped a steady tempo to match my heartbeat, the man I loved held me in his arms and I was perfectly and utterly at peace with what I had done.

When I woke next, I was alone in bed. Rain streamed down the window and the smell of toast and bacon filled the tiny flat. Simon whistled as he cooked.

I had an irresistible urge to pull the covers over my head, but Simon poked his head round the door before I could feign unconsciousness. "Good, you're awake. Come eat something and then I'll take you over to meet Miss Ferndale-Branch. She's usually at the Byam, but she owns a small studio south of the river."

I washed and dressed quickly, tidying my hair as best I could, ignoring the wreckage of my damp, wrinkled clothes. I ached in unusual places, there was a mark on my neck that no amount of powder erased completely, and my body felt strange and heavy, limbs stiff, breasts tender, and my freckles seemed to congeal across my face into one huge scarlet letter. I half expected a lightning bolt to strike me down where I stood.

"We're going to be late if you don't hurry," Simon called.

I pulled myself together with a deep breath and gave my reflection in the speckled mirror a stern talking-to. I had wanted a life of my own with the man I loved. I'd not go pudding-hearted now.

I strode into the kitchen as if laying claim to it. Simon sat at a rickety table, a dressing gown over his shirt and trousers. His feet were bare, which I found indescribably sweet. "There you are. Waiting for the maid to help you dress? Afraid it's her day off."

My confidence faltered, then I realized he was teasing and returned his smile. "By the looks of things, I'd say she's been absent for a while."

He grimaced. "It is a bit of a muck, but it won't take long to put to rights."

True. It was only three small rooms and a loo on the upper landing. And I'd had a few months' practice at scrubbing. I'd soon have the place sparkling. I snatched a piece of toast and suddenly felt much better. "What's Miss Ferndale-Branch like?"

"If you want the truth, she can be damned disconcerting," Simon replied. "Very straightforward and brutally honest. She smokes like a chimney, drinks like a sailor, and has the vocabulary of a dockworker, but she knows her craft. You couldn't be in better hands."

"Oh." I chewed slowly and tried to look nonchalant.

He smiled as he ate. "You and she will get along fine. She knows your history and can't wait to meet the infamous daughter of Lord Melcombe. She thinks it's all a great laugh."

My toast seemed to stick halfway down my throat, my newfound poise shriveling along with my stomach. "Does she?"

A great laugh? Is that what I was? Is that what Simon thought, too? He'd not mentioned last night, instead behaving as if waking with a woman in his flat was nothing out of the ordinary. My already deflated stomach turned over, and I had to lock an ankle round the table leg to prevent myself from fleeing like a wronged maiden.

Simon paused, his cup of tea halfway to his mouth. His brows wrinkled, his expression endearingly puzzled and worried. "Kitty? Are you feeling well?"

My face grew warm, my hand fluttering to the powdered spot on my throat. "Simon, last night . . . I mean we . . . that is . . . you and I . . ."

He nearly knocked the plate of bacon on the floor as he came round the table and scooped me from my seat. "You delectable, ridiculous, stammering creature, don't tell me you've grown cold feet."

"You might have done this before. It's all new to me."

"Do you truly think I go about seducing young ladies like some modern Casanova?" He pulled me close, tucking my head under his chin. I liked feeling small and protected in the cocoon of his arms. "If you must know, my dear, you are the first . . . and the last . . . young lady I have ever worked my sexual wiles on. Too many places to see and things to do to settle down."

I tipped my neck back and my head up so I could look into his eyes, clear gold and green like the creek water running below Nanreath Hall. No clouds gathered there. No deceit. I smiled and kissed his neck. "And now?"

"I've found someone worth settling down for, I suppose. Simple as that."

It wasn't simple at all, but my bubble of panic subsided, and I was calm enough to finish my breakfast and accompany Simon to the narrow town house in Southwark where Miss Ferndale-Branch occupied the two topmost floors.

The rooms were big and airy and painted white with two tall curtainless dormer windows overlooking the noisy street. A platter of half-eaten cheese and bread sat on a table beside a bottle of Veuve Cliquot and an ashtray littered with butts.

Miss F-B (as she implored me to call her) wore baggy trousers that accentuated her leggy height and a blouse that clung to every voluptuous curve. Her hair had been cropped short and tied back in a beautiful silk scarf, and when she smiled her rather severe face melted into a cherubic pout that made you want to immediately smile back. "So you're the innocent Simon has gone over the moon about. I hope you've skills beyond the bedroom. I need someone who knows what to do and how to do it as well as the diplomatic temperament I lack. I teach. I don't coddle. And I don't mince words. I'll tell you what I think, good or bad. If you're good, you'll do fine and be paid accordingly. If you're a fraud and a failure, I'll tell you so and you can go groveling back to Mummy and Daddy in Cornwall. Fair?"

She frightened me to death, but I liked her bracing acerbic tongue. So different from the veiled cushiony aggression I was accustomed to. "Fair."

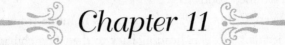

# Chapter 11

*January 1941*

A delay on the line stalled all underground traffic indefinitely, leaving Anna stranded at Blackfriars Tube Station with a long walk ahead. As she stepped out onto the pavement, she drew her coat closer around her. Winter clouds threw London's already dingy gray streets into shadow, and a knifing January wind burned her cheeks and made her nose run. Tomorrow she had a meeting scheduled at the Joint War Organization about an overseas posting. She hoped for Africa or Palestine; a place of activity and purpose, a place where she could begin anew.

A spiteful part of her toyed with the idea of sending Lady Boxley a note of thanks for her assistance. Nanreath didn't want her? The feeling was definitely mutual, thank you very much.

Her months tucked away in the Cornish countryside had dulled her to the harsh reality of London's distress. As she drew closer to the West End, the crowds thickened to a sea of khaki. Enormous barrage balloons floated low over the city, and wherever she walked were signs of the months of nearly nonstop bombing. Boarded windows and smashed glass, rubble piles and war-hardened citizens ignoring the destruction as they went about their day with stoicism and a determined goodwill.

The West Country was by no means immune from the war's effects. German bombers heading back to their French bases had a dangerous tendency to drop their surplus bombs on any convenient target, while Plymouth was increasingly being battered by intense nightly attacks. But among the rocky cliffs and deep coombes it was easier to pretend life went on unchanged and uninterrupted.

It was easier to forget.

She had managed to avoid any glimpses of Aldersgate and the ruins of Queen's Crescent. Twice she'd traveled from her small hotel to the stop where she'd so often disembarked to walk the few streets home. Twice she'd let the doors of the train close again and carry her away from the truth she would be forced to face.

Still, the shades of Graham and Prue hovered close. Anna glimpsed them in every crowd of afternoon commuters and every clutch of haggling housewives. She even thought she'd spotted Mrs. Willits in mackintosh and gum boots standing outside a restaurant until the woman turned to reveal a rough bun of grimy yellow hair and vacant eyes. Anna countered these moments with a true soldier's will, walling her memories away where they couldn't touch her, couldn't hurt her. Avoidance, the doctors in hospital had claimed when she'd lain there for weeks refusing to speak. A way to shelter the mind from a pain too great to bear. Anna merely knew it as survival.

She rounded the corner onto St. Martin's Place, feeling in her pocket for the scrap of paper she carried. One word penned quickly as she'd hurried to catch the lorry that would take her to the station—Balázs. Three pictures in Nanreath's gallery bore his name; an enormous canvas depicting a young and glamorous Lady Boxley, a watercolor of a teenage girl, purse-lipped and sulky as she held a small dog in her lap that Hugh had told her was his aunt Lady Amelia, and the richly detailed oil of Lady Katherine smiling at someone standing just beyond the artist's frame. Someone who would have been present at her sitting. Someone Lady Katherine might just have loved enough to risk all she had ever known . . .

Anna tugged on the gallery's doors.

"Closed, dearie," said a gray-haired man seated on the pavement alongside the portico. He clutched a beat-up leather satchel and an umbrella, his wiry hair standing like a halo around his narrow seamed face. "They even moved the pictures out to keep them safe. Just a few staff left behind to keep a watch. That's all."

Anna pulled uselessly once more on the door handles, as if willing the man to be wrong. The door remained firmly shut; the National Portrait Gallery was closed for the duration.

"Have to wait for the end of the war, I guess, dearie. Same as the rest of us what got let go."

"You worked here?"

"Aye. Twenty years. Never missed a day. Not many can say that, eh?"

Just then, a gentleman approached. He carried a briefcase, a newspaper beneath his arm, a ring of keys in his hand. "Hello, Mort. Good to see you today."

"G'day, Mr. Jamison," the man answered with a tip of his weatherworn hat. "Spent another night in the Tube. Hell on my back. Bloody Jerries."

"Well, come in and get warm. There's a lecture at eleven and a concert at four. Then out you go for the night."

"Excuse me, sir. Do you work here?" Anna asked the gentleman.

"Yes, I do. Is there something you need? The place is empty, but a botany lecture's been planned. You're welcome to come in and wait. Nasty weather out."

"Actually, I'm looking for information on a certain artist. Balázs was his name. Have you ever heard of him? It's awfully important."

"Is it?" He eyed her for a moment as if considering then nodded. "Come with me to my office. I'll fix us a pot of tea and we can talk."

Emptied of its contents, the building echoed as they crossed the central hall beneath the blank walls and took the lift downstairs. Mr. Jamison's office turned out to be barely bigger than a broom cupboard and cluttered with books, papers, and heaping folders. He removed a pile from a rickety chair and offered her a seat. "Sorry for the mess. You'd think there would be less to do with everything stored off-site. Instead, I feel as if I'm working double time to keep up." He put a kettle on a small electric burner and dusted off two mugs. "Now, what can I help you with, Miss—?"

"Trenowyth. I'm interested in finding out anything you can tell me about a portrait artist by the name of Balázs. I believe he painted in the years before the last war."

"You must mean Arthur Balázs. He was a sort of artist to the stars—society portraits, figures high in the government and the military, even a few members of the royal family. Quite popular. For a short time, everyone who was anyone wanted their likeness done by him. What did you want to know exactly?" He handed her a cup of strong, unsweetened tea.

"Would you know where I might find him? Or have his telephone number or an address? I need to speak with him."

"I'm very sorry, Miss Trenowyth, but he's dead. As a Hungarian national, he was interned as a foreign alien toward the end of the last war. Don't think he ever quite recovered. His heart carried him off in the late twenties."

She put her tea down with a disappointed rattle. "Oh dear. Was there anyone . . . anyone at all who might have known him that I could speak with? Family? People he worked with?"

"I really can't say. It was before my time, I'm afraid. You seem very keen. What did you want Mr. Balázs for if you don't mind my asking? Perhaps I can help."

"I'm interested in a painting he did just before the Great War. It was of a young woman by the name of Lady Katherine Trenowyth, a daughter of the Earl of Melcombe. I know it sounds mad to think he'd remember one painting among so many after all these years, but you see—"

"Trenowyth . . . Trenowyth . . ." Mr. Jamison tapped a finger to his lips. "Of course. I thought the name sounded familiar." He began frantically rummaging among the books and folders. "Astounding coincidence, you coming here and me just happening on it so recently. I suppose it's one of those odd moments when you spot something and then it turns up everywhere."

Anna nodded as she watched him search the office.

"Here. I knew I'd had it last week." He pulled an oversize art catalog from underneath a stack of such. Flipped through it until he found what he was looking for then handed it over. The left page bore text only, but an enormous photograph on the right page showed a painting of a young woman rising from a tousled bed. Waves of curling hair tumbled over her alabaster shoulders, her full-lipped, half-lidded expression hinted at her earthy sexuality and the knowledge of her own power to attract. The same face as the painting in the Nanreath gallery, but this woman . . . this woman bore a siren's curves and a courtesan's talents.

"It's called *The Red-Haired Wanton*," Mr. Jamison explained. "Lady Katherine Trenowyth served as the model. See here?" He pointed to a paragraph outlining a short history of the work.

"Balázs did this?" Anna asked.

"No, an artist by the name of Simon Halliday. Unfortunately, he's dead, too. Killed during the Battle of the Somme in 1916. The painting is coming up for auction."

She set down the book and rose from her chair. "Thank you for showing me this. I'm quite grateful."

"You can have the catalog if you wish. I've too many to keep up with as it is. I wish I could have given you more to go on about the Balázs painting."

"No, you've done splendidly."

He escorted her back to the front doors. "You bear a striking resemblance to the wanton." He flushed. "An odd thing to say, I know, but there you are. You did say your name was Trenowyth?"

"I did. Another one of those odd coincidences, I suppose."

"Yes, of course." He bid her good day and disappeared back into the gallery.

"Find what you were looking for, dearie?" The old man from earlier remained at his post beside the portico.

"Not really, but I may have found something even better. Cheers." She dropped a shilling into his open briefcase.

Walking briskly, she headed past Trafalgar Square and the Admiralty, Horse Guards Parade and across into St. James's Park, finally pausing to rest on a bench across from the lake. She pulled the catalog from her bag and flipped once more to the page of *The Red-Haired Wanton.*

Even pictured in black-and-white, the portrait bore a striking luminescence, the woman's body rising from her bed, seeming to almost glow as she reached for her lover with one outstretched arm. Intent radiated from her eyes, a look of blatant invitation and the promise of paradise. Anna felt her cheeks warm, as if she intruded upon the most private of moments.

"Anna Trenowyth? Is that really you?"

She jerked her head up as she closed the catalog. Tony Lambert stood over her, a corner of his mouth turned up in a hesitant smile as if unsure of his welcome.

Her heart fluttered uncomfortably. "What on earth are you doing here?"

"Here in London or here with you?" he asked.

Shoving the catalog back in her bag, she scooted over, giving him room to sit beside her. "To start, you can tell me what you're doing in London."

"I wrangled a few days' leave and decided to come up to meet a friend from home. What are the odds I'd bump into you in this muddle, eh?"

"Barely measurable." By now an uneasy suspicion tickled the base of her brain.

"Exactly, but here you are . . . and here I am."

Was it her imagination or did his enthusiasm carry shades of a guilty conscience? "You have yet to tell me how on earth you managed to *bump* into me among millions of people."

Yes, now he definitely had a sheepish look to him. He didn't quite meet her gaze and his jaw worked as if he were mulling his options. "If I pleaded an amazing coincidence, would you believe me?"

"No."

Tony inhaled a deep breath and shifted on the bench, his eyes meeting hers. Funny but she'd never noticed how dark they were, nearly black in the dim winter afternoon light. Or the small silver scar high at his hairline that slashed downward into his right brow. For some reason, this awareness frightened her, and she dropped her gaze to the ground, at the pebbles mixed with the sand of the park path, at a puddle by her foot, black and slick with ice.

"Sophie Kinsale told me what happened," he began.

She gave a strangled laugh. "I should have known."

"Hear me out, Anna. Sophie told me because she's a good friend and she was worried about you."

"So why are *you* here and not her?"

"Because I was worried, too. And I'd like to be a friend if you'd let me past all those prickles."

She finally found the courage to face him and was relieved that whatever insanity had possessed her, it had passed, along with the clammy twisting of her stomach and the odd lightness in her head.

"If it's any consolation, Hugh's sporting a wicked shiner," he said.

"You *didn't*."

"Not me. It was Tilly's doing, but mum's the word. She's sure Lady Boxley would have her transferred to a British outpost in Bora Bora if she knew a lowly VAD planted her precious boy a facer."

Anna let out a sigh. "It wasn't Hugh's fault. Not completely. I knew why he'd brought me to the party. I just didn't know the lengths he'd go to in order to throw the pack off his scent."

She shoved her hands under her arms. Hunkered into her collar. It really was bloody cold out here. Tony must have noticed. He removed his scarf, tucking it around her neck against the damp, clinging chill. The wool smelled musty and acrid, not unpleasant— she'd smelled much worse—more like what she imagined a boy's dormitory smelled like or perhaps the bottom of his kit bag, an indefinable masculine smell. She burrowed deeper into the soft thick folds and smiled her thanks. "It was awful, Tony. Absolutely horrid. I had every woman in the village offering me their blunt opinions on my mother's lack of morals and my own ulterior motives for turning up out of the blue. Hugh just happened to be the icing on the cake. It was as if he despised them."

"He doesn't despise them. He despises himself."

She must have shown her confusion.

"You really don't understand, do you? Hugh was the petted

heir then the dashing flyboy. That crash took more than his leg. It stripped him of everything that made him special."

"That's rubbish."

"Nevertheless, it's true. What has he got now? His mother manages the earldom, such as it is, and shows no signs of handing over management to her ne'er-do-well son. If she didn't already wrap him in swaddling, his behavior these days certainly wouldn't convince her to trust him with more than a few meaningless responsibilities."

"What he needs is a swift kick in the pants. There's no use feeling sorry for oneself. Not in times like these because for certain the chap next to you probably has it worse."

"Someone should tell him that." He slid her an encouraging glance.

She dug at the path with her boot; the ice cracked under her heel, fracturing outward in a million tiny slivers of white. "I see what you're trying to do."

"Am I that transparent?"

"Says the man who accidentally *bumped* into me in the middle of London."

"I won't say another word. But you came to Nanreath Hall to learn about your mother. You can't let Lady Boxley scare you away from your best chance at getting to the truth." Anna opened her mouth, but he stopped her. "Now enough about Hugh and his woes. Let's you and I celebrate. Come out with me tonight."

"What's the occasion?"

"Friendship." He rose from the bench and held a gloved hand out to her. "And second chances."

The dance floor of the Café de Paris shook under the weight of dozens of madly jitterbugging couples hoofing it to Glenn Miller's "In the Mood." It hadn't taken Anna but a few hesitant steps to be drawn into the music, her feet following the familiar rhythms, her heart leaping at every spin and shimmy. By the time the bandleader slowed the tempo and a singer in a slinky black dress stepped to the microphone to begin a heart-wrenching rendition of "I'll Be Seeing You," Anna's blouse clung to her skin and she had to pant to catch her breath, but her mind seemed sharper, and her body seemed lighter, as if she'd laid down the burdens she carried for the space of a song.

Tony pulled her close. Shadows lay in flickering bars across his face, the light from the chandeliers caught and refracted in his dark eyes. He smelled good—soap with a hint of cigarette and whiskey. His hand in hers was roughened by work, the palm calloused. But as he swung her around the floor, there was surprising catlike grace in his movements.

"Enjoying yourself?" he asked.

She laughed, suddenly awkward in his presence. "What a ridiculous question. All my life I've heard of this place. I think I saw Cole Porter when we came in, and I'm certain it was Margaret Rutherford taking a powder in the loo when I went to fix my lipstick earlier."

"So are Cole Porter and Margaret Rutherford the only reasons you're enjoying yourself?" His breath tickled her ear.

"Another ridiculous question," she replied quietly.

His arm tightened around her waist, and she felt rather than heard his deep rumble of laughter. A bubble of happiness grew in her chest.

The bandstand, the winding, elegant stair up to the balconies, the crowded tables, the other dancers—they blurred and spun in a feverish whirl with her and Tony at the center. Anna grew dizzy, her head swimming, her body alive with a crackling heat as if she were feverish. The singer's smoky alto spoke of loneliness and longing, emotions Anna understood too well. She laid her head on Tony's shoulder and closed her eyes, letting him guide her, giving herself up to the music and the moment, the glittering excitement around her and the steady man holding her safe.

In that instant of surrender, her guard faltered, and all the memories she'd so firmly locked away spilled free. Cold sweat doused her feverish skin. Her heart raced until it felt as if it would propel itself right out of her chest. No! Her eyes snapped open, focusing on the bandleader, a thin Negro man elegantly dressed in a dinner jacket, hips swaying as he led the orchestra in the final refrain.

Tony cast her a glance, but in the dim light of the club, it was impossible to interpret the odd quirk of his mouth and contraction of his brows. He continued to carry her through until she regained her composure, his arm always there, his steps unerring until the last note fell into an uneasy silence, as if she were not the only one affected by grim thoughts.

A few in the audience clapped, sporadic at first then growing until the place roared, as the singer bowed and moved offstage. The bandleader moved into another tune, and Tony led her from the floor to their table.

"Phew! I haven't danced in ages," Anna said, working to calm herself with the deep breathing exercises she'd been taught in hospital. "I'm positively dizzy."

"Ginger Rogers couldn't have cut a more elegant rug."

She slid into the seat across from him, her smile a shade too bright, her manner a tad too exuberant, but Tony didn't seem to notice, or if he did, he kept it to himself. He waved over a waiter and ordered them two more cocktails. When Anna finished hers in less time than it took him to take more than two sips, he ordered her another, but now his gaze was a bit more assessing.

Anna answered this with more high-spirited jollity and another deep gulp of her Manhattan. "I still remember the first night a boy invited me to the local Palais on a Saturday night. Graham threatened him with violence if he tried anything fresh. When I slunk back home hours past my curfew, he was sitting in the parlor smoking his pipe and doing the crossword. He never raised his voice, merely invited my date out on the stoop to see his old Enfield rifle. The next time I saw that poor boy, I think he tripped over himself fleeing in the opposite direction."

"Nothing like waving a deadly weapon about for keeping the men away."

When had she finished off her drink? Was it her fourth or fifth? Stymied of a liquid distraction, she toyed with her napkin, folding and refolding tiny pleats in the linen. "Prue was usually the one you had to be careful about. She didn't suffer fools gladly and had no problem expressing herself. I thought she would be the one to lose her temper when I told them I'd volunteered with the BRCS, but it was Graham. He'd served in the last war, you see. He knew what I was getting myself into, knew it would be worse than I could imagine. He tried to tell me, but I ignored him. I saw myself as Florence Nightingale with her lamp out to save the world. Then the Germans invaded France and . . . well . . . Graham was right."

Tony laid a hand over hers, putting an end to her manic napkin pleating. "You must miss them very much."

"I . . ." There was that internal stutter-step again, like she'd missed her footing and landed hard, punching the breath from her lungs. She made a small noise somewhere between a hiss and a gasp, barely noticeable above the din of the club, but Tony immediately drew her from her chair. She made no protest as he collected her coat, simply allowed him to ease her through the dancers to the stairs leading back to the crisp wintry street.

Searchlights speared the sky and the glow of fires reflected on the heavy smoke off to the east. Distant antiaircraft fire bounced and echoed like summer thunder. He didn't speak but simply started walking slowly up Coventry Street, clasping her hand in his. Damp snow sifted onto her shoulders, stung her cheeks. In the hours they'd been in the club, it had drifted its way into alleys and under awnings, coating the buildings in dingy frosting. For some reason, she found herself thinking of Nanreath Hall and the way the snow there glowed in the wintry moonlight against the far hills or drifted beneath the bare trees along the path to the village.

"Given any more thought to what I said this afternoon?" Tony asked, breaking into her thoughts.

She rubbed her temples against a headache that threatened to ooze out her ears. "I can't go back. It's too humiliating. My name is Trenowyth, but I don't belong there." She looked around helplessly at the dark street, the city a collage of gray on gray shadows smelling vaguely of soot and mud and death. A scent she knew she would never forget should she live to be a hundred. "I'm not sure where I belong anymore."

"You belong with people who care about you. With Tilly, Sophie." He paused. "With me." She couldn't see his expression in the dark but she felt the intensity behind his words like a slap to the face.

"Oh" was all Anna managed to say until she swallowed the lump in her throat. She pulled her hand from his. Stood hugging herself against the cold. The moment stretched thin and brittle. No words spoken. Only the soft puffs of their mingled breaths in the air between them.

Tony leaned in for a kiss, but instinct had her turning away before she did something she'd regret.

He gave a small self-deprecating sort of laugh. "I didn't expect you to swoon at my feet, but well . . . I guess my bloated ego expected a bit more of a reaction."

"I'm sorry, Tony. I'm honored . . . truly . . . but . . . you see . . . I . . . I can't even think like that . . . of that . . . it's impossible . . ." Her evening's diet of Manhattans swirled uneasily in the pit of her stomach.

The top half of his face was lost in darkness but for the refracted gleam of the sweeping searchlights in his eyes.

"Please don't be angry. Tonight's been lovely, and I don't think I could bear you to be upset with me for ruining your leave."

She'd come to rely on Tony's friendship and trust in his common sense. She didn't know how much so until there was a risk of it being withdrawn. She felt her breath catch in her chest as worry slid cold over her shoulders.

He tipped her chin up and kissed the end of her nose. "Silly thing. I can't say I'm not disappointed." He didn't smile but there was humor in his voice. "But I'm certainly not angry. And I can't think of anyone I'd rather spend my leave with than you, prickles and all. I warn you, though, I don't give up easily. Not once I've set my mind on something—or someone."

An air-raid siren broke the quiet hiss of falling snow, growling louder and louder as the searchlights coalesced to the south where the Thames acted like a great big silver arrow to the armadas of German bombers who followed it on their nightly runs. The dissonant rise and fall broke the spell. She jerked as if she'd been slapped, her skin crawling as every frayed nerve unraveled at the same time. She clamped her teeth and her knees together. She'd already made herself look a complete fool. She wouldn't add to her humiliation by throwing herself to the ground and trying to burrow through the cement.

The streets filled with citizens streaming out of the buildings toward the nearest shelters or underground stations. A man clutching a Bible and an extra pair of shoes; a woman carrying a framed photograph, a teakettle, and a hairbrush; a couple each with a small dog under their arms. Whatever, in their haste, they had decided was worth saving.

"Let's go," Tony said.

Anna forced her legs to move, her feet to follow the others down the street. She balked at the entrance to the station, a hand on the gate. Already the air grew thick with the mingled smells of sweat, onions, and wet wool. It would be worse the deeper they went, as the sensation of being buried alive crawled along her skin and squeezed her lungs.

She looked back over her shoulder to see an ominous red glow riming the clouds. The guns grew louder and closer as the hum of the bombers increased, and the ground shook with the nearing explosions.

"Anna?" Tony took her hand and offered her a reassuring squeeze. "I won't let you go."

She inhaled as if she were going under for the last time and followed him down.

Anna arrived for her appointment with the JWO early the next morning and was promptly shown to a tidy office. The middle-aged Red Cross administrator regarded Anna across a scrupulously organized desk, official-looking forms of every description stacked in tidy piles alongside trays of correspondence, color-coded files, and a bookended row of ledgers. Only a single framed picture of a uniformed young man standing in front of a Hurricane offered any hint this no-nonsense woman had a life beyond this dreary building.

"Your file makes for an interesting read, Miss Trenowyth." Every

tap of her pencil smashed against Anna's skull as if she were shooting off rounds above her head, but at least the throbbing headache
distracted her from the queasy pitch and roll of her stomach. She'd
never be able to smell sweet vermouth again without a nauseated
shudder.

The administrator paused in her tapping to turn a page, her gaze
flicking to scan the fine print of the report. "Three months nurses
training at St. Barts here in London before you left to join the Red
Cross. Anxious to do your part?"

"I was afraid the war would be over before I got my SRN li-
cense."

"Fat chance of that."

The clock on the wall ticked over to 9:00 A.M. Back at Nanreath,
she would have been on duty over an hour and a half already. Probably cleaning up from breakfast or working with one of the sisters
on morning rounds. There had been an increase of pneumonia and
other respiratory infection admittances, which kept everyone hop-
ping round the clock.

The officer continued scanning the pages. "Posted to France
with the BEF in January of last year. Served until the evacuation
of forces in June where you suffered an injury to your"—another
pencil tap, another flick of her pale eyes—"right shoulder when your
ship was hit."

"Actually it was my collarbone, upper right arm, and two ribs.
We probably would have survived the strafing. It was the mine that
did us in."

"Three nurses died."

It wasn't a question. Anna threaded her hands in her lap. Cold
sweat trickled down her spine. "Along with twenty-eight stretcher
cases and six of the ship's crew . . . ma'am."

Her fingers tightened. She felt her eyes wandering back to the clock. Tilly was probably up to her armpits in dirty laundry, and the boiler was tricky if you didn't set it just so. It had taken Anna two months to learn the knack.

"It also says you didn't speak for three weeks following your arrival in hospital for your injuries. And that there were episodes of troubling emotional behavior determined to be a direct result of your . . . unfortunate experience."

"Yes, ma'am."

*Unfortunate* was puncturing a bicycle tire and being late for 10:00 P.M. roll call or being set to polishing keyholes and bed hooks by Sister Murphy. Not wading through roads scattered with the pulverized body parts of refugees fleeing the German advance or unceasing days hunkered on the beach deafened by the constant noise of exploding mines, screaming dive bombers, and artillery shelling, unable to sleep or eat or scrub the sand, grease, and blood from your skin.

The administrator set the file down, eyeing Anna with a schoolmarmish grimness. "I assume this was why your original request for an overseas posting was denied."

"They thought I needed more time to heal. They sent me to Cornwall to work at the convalescent hospital at Nanreath, instead."

Nanreath, where the wind always tasted faintly of salt and the ocean's constant purr lulled her to sleep when sleep seemed impossible.

"Which brings us to the present." The woman placed her pencil in a perfect right angle to the folder and leaned back in her chair. Her row of World War I medals gleamed. "I've been informed that short of my finding evidence of out-and-out lunacy or some other diagnosis that would assume you unfit for duty, I'm to offer you a transfer wherever you wish." Her eyes dropped to the pencil, as if she were dying to edge it to the left a half inch. "You have a friend in high places, Miss Trenowyth, to take such care over one lowly VAD."

"I don't know if *friend* would be the most appropriate term."

"No, I wondered about that, as well. As I said, your report makes for interesting reading." She rose to pace the small office, her eyes flicking ever so faintly to the portrait of the young man. A brother? A son? Alive? Dead? "Is it your wish to leave the hospital at Nanreath?"

"I've spent these past months working hard to prove I'm fit for an overseas post."

"That wasn't exactly an answer, was it?" She smiled, giving her stern face an unexpected warmth. "Or perhaps it was." She sat back down and lifted her pen, dipped it in a great glass inkwell, hand poised atop the forms. "You will be billeted in London until your reassignment. See my secretary for details and additional paperwork."

Anna's stomach rolled. Her head threatened to split down the middle. Her heart dropped into her toes. As the pen touched the page, Anna lurched to grab it away from her, the ink dribbling out to stain the pristine paper. "Wait."

The woman merely glanced up, as if VADs losing their minds in her office were par for the course. "Yes, Miss Trenowyth?"

"I appreciate your help, really I do. And . . . well . . . I thought I wanted to leave. I thought it right up to the moment I saw you lift that pen."

"And now?"

"I want to stay at Nanreath Hall. Not because I'm scared. Or unfit for duty. But I don't like being pushed around. If I get an overseas posting, I want it to be on my own merit, not because you've been ordered to do it."

"You realize you've wasted more than an hour of my time, Miss

Trenowyth, as well as valuable resources as we shift manpower around in order to place you in your requested post."

"Yes, ma'am. I'm very sorry."

The officer ripped up the forms. "Be on the next train west and see that I don't have cause to hear from your friend again."

"Lady Boxley isn't my friend, ma'am. She's my aunt."

The officer leaned back in her chair with a pinch of her brows. "All smells a bit odd if you ask me."

Anna ventured a grim smile. "Take my word, ma'am, you wouldn't believe the half of it."

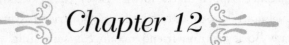

# Chapter 12

*June 1914*

Summer sunlight woke me from a dark dream where no matter how I swam, the sea dragged me from shore, the lights of Nanreath Hall dimming until they winked out and I was left all alone. I started awake, out of breath and heart thudding in my chest, to stare at the familiar and comforting crack in the ceiling above the bed. A dream, nothing more.

"Good morning, beautiful." Simon stood in the doorway already wearing his hat and coat. "Sleep well?"

"Like a baby," I lied.

He dropped a chaste kiss on my forehead, though his gaze burned with desire. "Break a leg today."

"That's what you say to actors."

"What's good luck for artists, then?" he murmured.

"Break a paintbrush?"

He chuckled, and this time when he kissed me, it was a hungry, demanding kiss that had me twining my arms behind his head as I sought to pull him back into bed with me.

"Tempting, love, but I have a train to catch."

"I wish I could come with you this time."

"I wish it, too, but my parents are as stodgy and old-fashioned as yours. They don't understand, and there's no use trying to make them. It's just easier if I go alone."

"Perhaps if we took rooms in separate hotels or—"

He glanced at his watch. "I have to run, love. I'll be home the day after tomorrow. We'll talk then." He broke away with a sigh, and a few moments later I heard the door to the flat close.

I banished my momentary disappointment as I smiled and rolled over, drowsy and satisfied and content with my life in a way I'd never been before. Somehow, becoming a fallen woman was much less tiresome than worrying about how to avoid becoming one.

Still basking in the afterglow, I rose, throwing a wrapper over my shoulders as I made my way into the tiny kitchen to fix myself an egg and boil a pot of tea. I was due to meet Jane in an hour, and the two of us would head to Miss Ferndale-Branch's studio together. My employer had arranged for us to sit for an artist friend of hers. He would pay four shillings each for a day's work.

Jane might have been an old pro at posing in front of strangers, but it was the first time I'd been asked to sit for money, and I was slightly nervous, though keen to try. The wages I received as Miss Ferndale-Branch's assistant were meager at best and while they were enhanced by the classes I was able to take at the Byam, I couldn't eat lessons on composition nor feed the gas meter on what I learned about human musculature. Simon never reproached me, but I felt my dependence keenly. It was one thing to be a fallen woman, but I despised the idea of being a kept one.

After breakfast I dressed in my smartest plaid walking dress and a Dolly Varden hat trimmed with burgundy ribbon, said a frosty good-morning to the old disapproving German couple who ran the bakery next door, and turned my steps to the tram stop on the corner. Halfway down the street, a newsboy shoved a paper in my face.

MURDER OF AUSTRIAN HEIR AND HIS WIFE.

I paid my halfpenny and shoved the paper in my handbag to read later.

The tram took me as far as Victoria, where I met a very flustered Jane. "There you are. I've been waiting forever. It's no use trying to get a bus. A coal wagon's overturned and traffic is snarled in every direction. We'll have to walk."

"If we cut through St. James's Park, we should arrive in plenty of time."

We made our way north, hurrying as best we could through the growing morning crowds. "By the way, I bumped into Doris last week," she dropped casually into our conversation as we passed Wellington Barracks.

"Did you?" Our estrangement remained a sore point.

Jane threw me an encouraging look. "She'll come around sooner or later, Kitty. Just give her time to stew a bit."

I smiled brightly and let the conversation drop, refusing to have my break with Doris mar what was otherwise a perfectly glorious June day of warm sun, soft breezes, and the anticipation of four bob in my purse by evening.

"Has Simon gone to see his family?" Jane asked.

"Yes, he says as long as he continues to draw an allowance, he has to check in at least once every three months just so they know he's still alive. I was hoping to go with him, but I couldn't take the time from work, and they're a bit . . ."

"Disapproving?"

"They wanted him to follow in the family profession, marry the right girl, have fat, dimpled babies, and be a proper Lincolnshire gentleman."

"You'd think catching an earl's daughter counted for something in their eyes."

"Perhaps if we were married."

"So why don't you?"

A question I'd asked myself more than once, but whenever I broached the subject with Simon he refused to talk about it or turned it into a lecture on outdated societal customs. "He has his work, I have my schooling. We will someday, but right now it's enough that we're together."

"You're a brave woman, Kitty. It's not many who'd throw convention to the wind and hold their head high while they're doing it."

As long as Simon held firm, there wasn't anything else I *could* do, but Jane didn't have to know that.

She checked the watch pinned to her lapel and our steps increased apace. If we were to make our appointment, we needed to hurry. We followed the gravel paths through the well-tended park, over the footbridge, and on toward Charing Cross. Here Simon and I had paused to throw bread to the ducks, there we'd sat on the grass and read each other passages from Dickens and Trollope. One fine afternoon we'd even explored the aviary on Duck Island and admired the pelicans there. Small, mundane moments, but they made up a new life; one I could never have imagined even a few short months ago. I felt a different person; alive and energized. I told myself that marriage and children would come in time. Right now I would revel in the freedom to be and do exactly what I wanted.

Since coming back to London, I studied my surroundings with a new eye, observant to every detail, keen to note every subtle nuance, more aware than ever of the emotions hidden behind a bland expression. It had been an advantage in the studio—and the bedroom.

Everywhere there were stories to tell if one looked hard enough: the tired lines biting deep into the face of the man trimming the shrubbery along the path where I walked; the jaunty whistle of the chap in the boater just ahead of me, face lifted to the sun, hands shoved into his pockets; the young couple standing under the trees up ahead. He wore a uniform. She, a dress of pale yellow to set off her ash-blond hair. There was no doubting their affection for each other or the pain of their imminent separation; the way they stood close but not touching, as if to do so might cause physical pain, the haunting sorrow in the woman's eyes while the man murmured softly and reassuringly into her ear.

I came closer, and my heart and feet stumbled at the same horrible moment. I pulled myself together, slowing to stare stupidly as if I were hallucinating. Caught back in my nightmare of last night, the storm dragging me from shore, the lights of Nanreath Hall fading behind a veil of rain.

The woman who wore her grief like a mantle was Cynthia, but that was not William wiping her tears nor kissing her cheek. I had never seen this gentleman in my life, though it was clear he and Cynthia were on intimate terms.

I prayed Cynthia didn't look over, prayed our months apart had altered my appearance enough to create doubt in her mind. I dropped my head, as if searching through my bag for some misplaced item. And then . . .

"Oh no, Kitty," Jane shouted. "Your paper . . . it's getting away."

Jane chased the lost pages across the grass as both Cynthia and her officer looked over. Chuckling, he bent to speak to her, his golden-blond hair gleaming in the morning sun. But Cynthia's face was drained of color. Her lips a flat, disbelieving line, her eyes two burning coals focused on me as I stood flustered and apologetic as Jane handed me back my crumpled paper.

"Now we really will be late for our sitting. Come on, Kitty," she said, sounding a bit too much like my old nursemaid for comfort. "There's a bus stop at the edge of the park. I think I've enough fare for both of us if we sit on top."

So much for reading the news. Clutching the wreckage of my paper, I raced to keep up, still feeling the scalding heat of Cynthia's unblinking stare between my shoulder blades, my morning's confidence shattered.

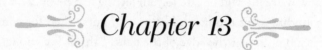

# Chapter 13

*January 1941*

Anna returned to Nanreath Hall amid a rush of new patients. Ambulances lined the gravel sweep, and stretchers lay in untidy rows outside the house's main doors. The sisters moved briskly among the patients, their scarlet-edged capes thrown back as they checked identity disks against the stacks of forms they carried. Tilly knelt beside a stretcher, holding a cup of water for a young man with his arm in a sling. Two more VADs were directing the stretcher bearers as they continued to unload while Sister Murphy was haranguing an ambulance driver who'd had the misfortune to wedge himself into one of the many bottomless potholes dotting the sweep.

Matron stood at the top of the steps. "Get these men inside as soon as possible. It's too bloody cold out here. We don't want them catching pneumonia on top of everything else."

Tilly and an orderly took hold of each end of the first litter and clumsily carried it up the steps and inside. But even with all the or-

derlies, bearers, and VAD working together, it would take hours to
shift them all. Anna abandoned her luggage to join those hastening
to move the patients out of the damp cold and the icy rain that was
beginning to fall.

"Hiya, nurse. You're a blessed sight."

"I reckon I've died and gone to heaven. Nothing but old dragons
at that last hospital."

"An angel, you are, love. An angel from above."

Each soldier offered a grin or a wink, their tired gray faces lifting
in apologetic gratitude.

"Hate you to go to so much trouble."

"Wish I could get out and walk, Nurse. Save you the bother."

"You shouldn't be trundling an old porker like me about, miss."

Anna joked and smiled in return as trip after trip was made
until her arms and legs ached from hefting the unwieldy stretchers and her right shoulder burned and tingled under the unceasing
strain.

Inside, Matron worked the receiving end of the operation, directing the stream of traffic to the correct ward where Captain Matthews moved one by one down the beds assisted by Sister Murphy,
who by now had managed to bring the earlier ambulance driver,
two stretcher bearers, and another VAD to tears.

As Anna settled a gunner from Perthshire with a bad case of
mumps into bed, the sister caught sight of her. By now Anna's overcoat and three-button tunic had been shed, her blouse sleeves rolled
back, and her storm cap sadly askew.

"Trenowyth!" Sister Murphy barked. "Quit flirting with that
boy."

Since the boy in question looked to be at least forty with a face
as lumpy as risen bread dough, Anna ignored the order though she
did give him a sly wink as she tucked him in.

"Don't stand there mooning, Your Highness." Sister Murphy checked a thermometer, wrote the results on her clipboard, moved to the next victim ... er ... patient. "If you're to be of use to anybody, get yourself into proper ward attire and meet me back here in ten minutes. We'll need all hands on deck if we're to get through this bunch before midnight."

As if Sister Murphy's barked command were the signal, the hospital staff's eyes seemed to swivel on stalks until it felt as if every person in the place was staring at her. Most offered a businesslike nod of greeting or a hasty smile. Captain Matthews glanced her way with an oh-so-nonchalant straightening of his uniform that had Tilly, who'd staggered in with yet another case of mumps (must be an epidemic), clamping her lips over a giggle before mouthing "Welcome back" from across the room.

Anna smiled her thanks as she rushed from the ward. The sweep was now empty, the patients having all been moved into the main hall, but even here the initial chaos seemed to have slowed to a manageable crush. She picked her way between stretchers on her way to the main staircase, dispensing words of encouragement and smiles as she passed.

"Nurse Trenowyth." A voice called to her just as she'd reached the landing. She turned to find Matron staring up at her, a hand on the baluster. Despite the effort of the past hours, she remained crisply put together and her voice maintained the same strict edge. Her nod was as sharp as her creases, but the expression in her face warmed Anna as if she'd been wrapped in a hug. "Glad to see you back."

"It's good to be back," Anna replied and realized she meant it.

"We need you on the wards, but if you take an extra five minutes to change, I'll be sure to smooth it with Sister Murphy." She gave her a significant yet unreadable look.

"Uh, thank you, Matron."

"Go on, then. Get yourself settled then come find me. I'll need someone experienced in stores or we'll be in a sad muddle by tonight."

Slightly confused but grateful nonetheless, Anna raced to the top of the landing and down the passage. Gray light filtered from a few office windows into the corridor, shadows speckled with falling snow. She passed the staff dining room and rounded the corner at a dead run right into the arms of Hugh.

"Bloody hell." He staggered, his hands gripping her elbows, his leg nearly buckling. "Anna?"

She wrenched away from him, losing her cap and half a dozen more hairpins in the process. "Can't talk."

He grabbed her arm before she could escape. "Wait. I thought you were gone." He frowned. "You *were* gone. I distinctly remember that bit. The rest is a tad fuzzy. Actually, there's about a week I can't seem to recall, but . . . your departure is quite clear."

"I left. I came back. I'm in a titch of a hurry so if you'll let me pass, please."

He dropped her arm immediately, though he didn't step aside. He looked as though he'd dressed blindfolded in a closet, a moth-eaten wool cardigan that might once have been blue and a pair of khaki trousers smeared with liberal amounts of motor oil—at least she hoped those ominous dark stains were oil. If Anna looked hard, she could just make out the faintest of bruising around one bloodshot eye. All in all, he looked dismal. Served him right.

"Mother was wrong to lose her temper with you," he said. "I told her so as soon as I sobered up. Unfortunately by that time, you'd left for London."

"I thought I would do better somewhere else. That my coming here was a mistake."

His gaze softened, and a dimple winked at the side of his mouth. "I'm glad you changed your mind."

"I had some help changing it, but I think it will be all right now." She tossed her head, dislodging her storm cap completely. "And it'll take more than a few nasty words and a glare to chase me off."

He bent awkwardly and retrieved the cap, handing it back with a dry laugh. "You're a Trenowyth, all right. Hardheaded to the core and too stubborn to notice—or care."

"Bloody right." Anna tossed off a careless, fleeting smile and a "must dash" before ducking round him on her way to the crooked narrow staircase that would take her to the VADs' attic quarters, but her earlier stomach-rolling tension expanded like a warm bubble until her whole body seemed to fizz. "I *am* a Trenowyth," she pronounced to the attic passage's stretch of whitewashed plaster. "And there's not a bloody thing anyone can do about it."

By the time she reached the door to her old room, her careless smile had grown to a bright grin of pure pleasure, and she flung herself inside in a frenzy. In that split second as she simultaneously unbuttoned her blouse, untucked it from her travel-rumpled skirt, and chucked the cap onto the nearest bed, she noticed someone had very considerately brought her trunk up.

She also noticed what looked like a flea-bitten bear in a fetal curl on the bunk opposite.

"Sophie?" Anna asked, one arm still trapped in her blouse, her skirt hanging about her knees.

Her friend might have slept within the old coat's furry folds but for the queerish manner of the stillness, almost as if sheer willpower was the only thing keeping her from flying into a million jagged pieces. Her cap of dark curls was a tangled mess, the fur collar hiding her face.

"Sophie?" Anna repeated, the hairs on the back of her neck lifting, the bubble of joy growing lead-like in the pit of her stomach.

That was when she spotted the edge of the telegram. It lay where it had fallen, half under the bed. Anna pulled it out and read it.

*. . . received the news this morning . . . Lady S. wanted you to know as soon as possible . . . Charles loved you very much. . .*

Five extra minutes, Matron had said.

Anna took ten.

As January turned to February and then March, air attacks picked up. At least two or three nights a week, Anna donned her tin hat, piled mattresses in front of the windows, and assisted her patients under their beds or down into the cellar shelters to wait for the all clear. Newquay was bombed again. Truro. The airfields at St. Eval and Exeter. London continued to be targeted. Despite its reputation as the safest restaurant in town, two bombs struck the Café de Paris, killing scores of dancers and diners and beheading its graceful, sinewy bandleader.

The newspapers and wireless were filled with reports on the campaign in North Africa and the mounting North Atlantic shipping losses. Civilian casualties clogged the hospitals on top of the steady stream of returning wounded soldiers, sailors, and airmen, and the atmosphere was one of grim determination in the face of ongoing bad news.

Anna had been working three weeks of nights, and this morning her head had barely touched the pillow when an orderly knocked on the door with a summons from Matron. "Be dressed and out front as soon as possible. A car will be waiting."

Rubbing the grit from her eyes, she rose and dressed, being sure her ward uniform was in perfect order, her veil straight and crisp, her face smoothed of any nervous uncertainty. By the time she arrived on the front steps of the house, Matron was waiting in company with Captain Matthews.

"Is there a problem, ma'am?" Anna asked, trying not to reveal the quiver in her question. Lady Boxley had made no more attempts to have her transferred, but she'd be a fool to think the woman didn't resent her continued presence and would leap at any opportunity to have her sent away.

"There's been a road accident. The car carrying the blood transfusion service's medical staff has gone into a ditch. The medical officer and two of the nurses accompanying him have been injured. Not seriously, but they've been admitted to hospital for observation. That leaves them shorthanded for today's scheduled visit. I'm sending them Captain Matthews and yourself to assist."

"Yes, ma'am."

The MO smiled, though she was quick to note it was not in the least flirtatious or wolfish. More the encouraging look of someone's kindly indulgent father. A look Graham might have given her. She smiled back and allowed him to hold the door as she slid into the front seat of the Buick. He joined her at the wheel, and the two pulled out of the sweep and onto the long, tree-lined avenue toward the main gates.

"We won't be on our own if you're worried," he said, glancing over with a smile.

For one horrible moment, Anna thought he was flirting with her. "No?"

"We'll still have two of the VADs, a medical orderly, and both FANY drivers to assist. That's the usual crew on these outings," he said as they bowled down the drive and onto the road into the village. "It's a well-oiled machine compared to the last war."

She let out a shaky breath and laughed at her irrationality. "You fought, sir?"

"No, but I cleaned up after those who did, and a bloody great mess it was, too."

She clamped one hand on her veil and another on the door handle as they took the turn at the station road and down the steep hill over the creek. A rumble as they crossed over the bridge, followed by the roar of the engine as the captain gunned the accelerator, and up the hill they sped.

"The fighting in this war is still a bloody great mess, but at least we've come a long way in the patching-them-up-afterward department," he added.

The village hall had become a mini hospital ward with beds separated by screens and a row of folding chairs set by the door for those waiting their turn. A young woman wearing a white coat sat at a table taking donors' information as they arrived while a VAD ushered each one back in turn. Anna and the MO were met with a row of filled beds and a second frazzled VAD who was sporting a bruised cheek and a bandage on her arm.

"Just in the nick of time," she said. "They're already stacking up in the street waiting. They've been checked for blood type and had their particulars taken. It's just a matter of drawing the pint, letting them rest a bit after with a nice cup of tea, and sending them on their way."

"Never fear, Nurse. We'll have them in and out in double time." Captain Matthews immediately took charge as if he'd done this sort of work for years rather than being routed from his rounds by a frantic phone call just this morning. "Let's get cracking, Trenowyth."

As Anna and the other nurses moved from bed to bed, swabbing arms, administering anesthetic, and hooking up the receiving bottles to each donor, the captain supervised their work and kept up a steady stream of one-sided conversation, as if he were delivering a lecture to a hall full of medical students. "Amazing how far we've come since 1917. Conditions in the forward hospitals and clearing stations were crude at best. Always crowded and the stench . . . but we saved lives, we did. Took blood from those less injured and gave it to those with no other chance of survival. Type O usually. Less chance of a cock-up that way."

Normally, Anna would have gritted her teeth as she tried to tune him out, but after a full night on the wards, she struggled to stay awake and only the need for responding at the proper intervals kept her from dozing off on top of some unsuspecting patient. She could have kissed the girl who brought her hot tea and a bun about lunchtime.

"Have a sit-down and let the others have a go," she said. "You look ready to drop."

"Only got off duty at seven this morning," Anna replied, scalding her mouth on a restorative gulp of tea. "Had an hour of kip before we got the call you needed help."

"A damned herd of sheep is what done it. A whole mob of 'em crossing the road. Vera swerved, but it was too late. Into the ditch we went. Never saw such a kerfuffle."

By two in the afternoon, the line of donors had dwindled, but Anna kept busy with paperwork while the two VADs and the remaining driver worked on preparing the bottles for shipment in the refrigerated lorry parked outside.

"Two more for you, Nurse. Then we're just about finished." Anna looked up to find the driver working the table out front flanked by Hugh—and Lady Boxley.

She hastened to plaster a stiff smile of welcome on her face as she rose to greet them.

"You running the war single-handed these days?" Hugh joked. Lines bit deep into his face, but his eyes gleamed mischievously.

"Bang-up on the road this morning. We're filling in," she answered.

"I'm sure we are all happy to see Miss Trenowyth so ably managing, but I have a meeting of the Women's Vestry Society and would appreciate prompt attention," Lady Boxley said imperiously.

Hugh made a face over his mother's shoulder, which Anna sought to ignore as she led them back and settled them each onto a bed before pulling the screens around. She leafed through her clipboard, made a note of Hugh's Type A and Lady Boxley's Type O for the attending nurse. "Nurse Ayers will be with you in a moment."

"Aren't you doing it?" Hugh asked.

"Sorry. I'm up to my ears in forms this afternoon, but you'll be fine."

"It's not me I'm worried about," he warned.

Just then a shout went up from the bed next door, followed by a soothing murmur and then a crash. "Need some help here!"

Anna abandoned Hugh to find Nurse Ayers struggling with Lady Boxley, who must have gone down like a ton of bricks, taking the screen and a metal folding chair with her. "Didn't even get as far as the needle. Swabbed her arm with alcohol, and she passed clean out."

The two of them helped Her Ladyship onto the cot before Ayers raced off for a cup of tea to offer upon revival.

"Is it over?" came a weak, groggy voice.

Anna turned to find Lady Boxley woozy but conscious. Her face was gray as the silk suit she wore. "No, ma'am. You fainted."

"Did I? It must have been the heat in here. It's quite warm and I was kept waiting outside for almost a half hour."

"Has this happened before?"

"Perhaps once or twice." The color deepened. Was Her Ladyship embarrassed because she fainted or because Anna had been the one to witness her momentary lapse of aristocratic control?

Here was the perfect opportunity to offer Lady Boxley the same dismissive contempt she'd meted out. Anna opened her mouth to offer her a dose of her own medicine, took a breath, and smiled reassuringly. "Let me get Captain Matthews. He can have a look at you just in case."

"I don't need a physician."

"But . . ."

"Stop fussing and get on with it, Miss Trenowyth."

"Of course." Ayers returned with the tea. "Here's something to perk you up. Nurse has just made a fresh pot, so it should be good and warm."

"I'm not an invalid so you can stop your fussing."

"No, ma'am. Of course not. We'll be very quick, and it won't hurt a bit. Nurse Ayers has done this millions of times."

Nurse Ayers took this as her cue and quickly completed her preparations and left with a promise to return shortly to check all was well. Anna started to follow.

"Miss Trenowyth, if you'd be so kind to attend me."

Anna couldn't help the surprise on her face, but she took the chair beside Lady Boxley's cot. "Is there something you need?"

"I'm concerned for my son. He's not strong, and I worry he's jeopardizing his health by giving blood. I've told him, but he refuses to listen."

"The nurses with the service as well as our MO will make sure he's well taken care of. You've nothing to fear."

"Don't I? You've obviously never had a child, Miss Trenowyth. Motherhood is a lifetime sentence of worry and fear from the time they take their first breath until the day they lay you in the ground . . . or God forbid . . . you lay them."

"He's out of the fighting, ma'am. You've no more need to fear for his safety."

"That's what they told me when my husband was wounded. He lingered for a bit, but the war killed him as sure as if he'd died on the battlefield instead of his own bed."

"I'm sorry. That must have been terrible."

"I'll not let Hugh end the same way. I've given up too much for him to see his life wasted."

Nurse Ayers's return prompted an end to this odd tête-à-tête. But not before Lady Boxley grabbed Anna's hand, pulling her close. "The past is dead and buried, Miss Trenowyth. If you care for my son as I think you do, you'll leave it that way."

"The only past I'm interested in is my own, Lady Boxley."

She seemed to be warring with herself. Her eyes speared Anna with a look of decision. "Come see me tomorrow afternoon, Miss Trenowyth. We should speak."

Dark walls. Dark furniture. Lady Boxley wearing a black dress barely brightened with a double strand of pearls. And a temperature hovering somewhere between uncomfortably warm and jungle steamy. Any fantasies Anna might have had of a tearful family reunion withered on the vine.

Dressed in her best pencil skirt and pinched waist jacket, legs decorously crossed at the ankle and hands resting in her lap, she felt a growing sense of claustrophobia as she faced Hugh's mother across a rather sparse and dreary tea tray. To combat the urge to leap from her chair and throw open the windows to let in a breeze, or indeed even a sad little breath of air, Anna fiddled with her locket.

"Will Hugh be joining us?" she asked, hopefully.

"He's been delayed. A pressing matter to do with a leaky roof, I'm told." Lady Boxley's petulant tone reminded Anna of a tired child denied a prize. Her face, despite its stately beauty, possessed a nitpicky, unhappy expression. "Knowing my son's constitution, he'll overexert himself and be laid up for weeks, but who am I? Just his mother. What do I know?"

The silence that followed grew thick. Anna shifted upon her lumpy chair and choked down what passed for a scone in these rationed times. It tasted like wood shavings.

"I was surprised to hear you'd returned to Nanreath." If the woman had a lorgnette, she'd be lifting it to her eye to study Anna as if she were a strange form of insect. Her expression was cool and unwelcoming. "I'd assumed my personal assistance would be enough to send you wherever you wanted to go."

Anna had a feeling she knew exactly where Lady Boxley wanted her to go. "You were very helpful, my lady. But my parents always taught me running away never solved anything."

"Parents?" Her Ladyship uttered the word as if someone had laid a dead mouse among her scones and jam. "I was under the impression you had no living family."

Anna clenched her jaw, refusing to display even a hint of weakness in front of this woman. "After my mother's death, I was fortunate to be taken in by the Handleys, who raised me as their own daughter."

"They gave you their home, but not their name. Curious." Lady Boxley took a bite of her gingerbread, her little white teeth reminding Anna of a neighbor's terrier who'd once nipped her for coming too close.

"I had a perfectly good name already."

Another snap. Another condescending look that spoke volumes.

Anna's temper began to fray. She'd given up her precious half day for this inquisition? Even Sister Murphy's sour personality would have been preferable to this. "I know you're unhappy I'm here, ma'am, though why, I can't imagine. It all happened so long ago. Surely it's water under the bridge."

"Is it?"

"I don't want to stir up trouble. I just want to learn what I can about my mother."

"You know nothing of the scandal that drove her from Nanreath Hall? Or the reason for her estrangement from the family? Or . . . anything?"

"There was a man."

Seeming to relax, Lady Boxley gave a soft, unhappy laugh. "There always is. It's a regrettable but oft-repeated story."

"Did you know Lady Katherine, ma'am?"

"Of course I knew her. Katherine was barely eighteen when I married her brother, and already overly indulged and headstrong. I could see which way the wind was blowing as soon as that young man walked in the door, but no one heeded me. Heads in the sand, the lot of them. It was the summer before the war. Our world was perfect and we thought nothing could change. We were wrong." Lady Boxley poured herself a cup of tea. Her hands shook very slightly, sloshing it onto the silver tray. It spread slowly across the tarnished surface.

"Here. Let me do that." Anna took the pot from Her Ladyship and proceeded to fill her own cup. "Milk and sugar?"

"Milk only." She watched while Anna prepared her tea and handed it to her. Accepting it with a curt nod. "We live in graceless times, Miss Trenowyth. I used to have a maid to serve. Now I must do it myself. The ungrateful girl up and left. Chose a dirty, noisy factory over working in service to the family."

Anna sat back with her own steaming cup. "Perhaps she felt the need to do her best for the war effort."

"Girls did their best in the last war, too." Lady Boxley plucked another gingerbread from the plate and nibbled daintily. "Here you are to show for it."

Manners aside, enough was very much enough. Anna set her teacup down with a decided clatter, her blood pushing hard and fast until she flung herself out of her chair with reckless abandon. "Look here. I may not be your idea of what a proper young woman should be or even what you would wish for a relation. But if you think I'll sit here and allow you to insult me, you're much mistaken." And because she'd been taught to respect her elders, she added a grudging, "Good day, ma'am."

She started for the door, already angry with herself for losing her temper but refusing to be made a fool of for another minute.

"You've the look of your mother, you know," Her Ladyship said with an almost wistful note in her otherwise imperious voice.

Anna paused at the door, a hand upon the knob, a breath held against the knot in her chest. "So I've been told."

Lady Boxley continued worrying at her pearls, rings flashing in the velvet-shrouded gloom of her sitting room. "It's that hair of yours, the very same shade of red as Katherine's. I always envied her that luxurious mane. She would brush it out and it would reach almost to her waist, so thick and curly. Mine always took ages to crimp."

Anna knew she was being toyed with. Knew it as soon as Lady Boxley tossed her that scrap of information, like a bone to a mongrel dog. But she couldn't help the lift in her throat and the thrill at even this tiny reminiscence. She turned from the door, though her hand remained on the knob.

"Are you waiting for an apology?" Lady Boxley pouted. "Fine. I'm sorry. Now, come sit down. There's a draft in the corridor and I wish you to slice the sponge cake."

Anna pushed the door closed and crossed back to her chair, unable to walk away, yet not willing to accede complete surrender. "I'll stay for now, but don't think I shan't walk out if you continue as you've started."

"Impudent young woman, aren't you?"

"Not normally, but these are unusual circumstances."

Lady Boxley's lips twitched in what might, for someone more congenial, pass for amusement. "To put it mildly." She accepted a slice of cake, though it remained untouched as she stared sightlessly into the distance. "Who would have thought we'd be fighting the Hun again? I lost two brothers, a dozen cousins, and I can't count how many friends to the Germans last time around. My husband was injured at Bazentin. Hugh was barely three when it happened. He was four when William finally died, his lungs shredded by gas."

"He told me."

Her Ladyship refocused on Anna, leaning slightly forward in her chair, brows lifted. "Did he? What else did my son tell you? I must say, it's disconcerting thinking an absolute stranger knows your family's secrets."

"That's just it. I don't know anything at all. My mother never spoke of her life before I was born. It was like this place and her family never existed."

Now she was sure that Lady Boxley relaxed, her tension sliding from her squared shoulders, her face losing its closed harshness. "I see. Well, that does change things, doesn't it?"

For the first time Anna sensed Lady Boxley's internal battle between distaste at being faced with an old family scandal and curiosity at what that scandal had wrought. Perhaps Anna's efforts at reconciliation weren't doomed to complete failure. "It's rumored the Trenowyths are cursed."

"Is that so?" Lady Boxley sniffed and sat back, the mask of frozen civility slipping to expose a more unguarded vulnerability. "I suppose we've had our share of misfortunes, though we weathered them all." The uncertain light tossed shadows across her features, highlighting the sag along formerly sharp cheekbones, the droop of a once firm jaw, the faded gold of her hair. "Until now. Look at us, Miss Trenowyth—intruders in our own home. Shoved aside as if we don't matter while this uncouth rabble runs rampant."

"I thought you donated Nanreath Hall to the government." Anna felt herself worrying at her locket in an instinctive gesture of nervousness.

"That was my son's doing, not mine." Gone was the milder expression of fragility. Perhaps it had only been a trick of the dim light or Anna's own wishful thinking. She clamped her hand around the locket, the edges digging into her skin. Just when she thought perhaps . . . just perhaps . . .

"Really, Miss Trenowyth, must you fiddle about? It's most disconcerting. What have you got there that has you so itchy and unpleasant?"

"Nothing."

"It's obviously *not* nothing. Let me see."

"It's my locket."

Lady Boxley leaned closer. "An ugly little cheap thing, isn't it? Like something won at a fair."

"It was my mother's."

"Was it? Let me see it more closely." When Anna hesitated, Lady Boxley glared at her. "I'll not steal it, Miss Trenowyth."

Reluctantly, Anna drew the chain over her head and handed it to her.

Her Ladyship pulled a pair of glasses from a case on the table beside her and settled them on her nose. "'Forgive my love'? What is that supposed to mean?"

"I thought you might know."

Lady Boxley unsnapped the locket. Her brows nearly disappeared into her hairline. "Who on earth did her hair? And that dress. Kitty never did have proper fashion sense. Always tossing on whatever suited her with no idea of personal style. But him . . ." She sniffed again, her expression grim. "Even in a uniform, he looks exactly the same."

"You recognize him, don't you?"

She looked up from her study of the photographs. "Of course. I'd not forget that slippery customer. All shallow flash and pleasing smiles—just what a sheltered young woman would fall for. Didn't I tell you I was on to him as soon as he stepped foot in Nanreath's drawing room?"

Anna licked her lips, trying to draw moisture into a mouth gone suddenly dry. She swallowed. Her heart fluttered. Her stomach tightened with nerves. "Who is he?" she asked, though she thought she knew the answer already.

Lady Boxley removed her glasses to look into Anna's face. While the rest of her had faded into middle age, her blue eyes pierced with a tensile inner strength. "You mean to tell me you've gone through life not only without a father, but without even knowing who the man was?"

"My mother never spoke of him to anyone."

"Not surprising. He was hardly a catch for an earl's daughter, was he? A would-be artist without tuppence to rub together. And Kitty throwing herself at him like a wanton. Enough to make one ill to see them carrying on. 'Forgive my love,' indeed! He ruined her life."

"Who is he, Lady Boxley?" Anna heard the quiver in her voice and didn't care. So long she had stared at the photo of the dark-eyed soldier, imagining his laugh, the way he smiled, his strong shoulders carrying her as a baby. She thought she knew, but she needed the confirmation of her growing suspicions before she'd truly believe it. "Tell me, please."

"His name was Simon Halliday."

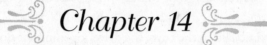

# Chapter 14

*August 1914*

Just past seven in the evening, I stepped out onto Campden Street in time to admire the end of another perfect August day of breezy blue skies and picnic temperatures. A brief shower had passed, leaving puddles on the pavement, and the air smelled fresh with just the hint of an overnight chill to come. I scanned the street, shading my eyes against the lowering sun, feeling the pinch of taut shoulders and a decided crick in my lower back.

The rest of the female students at the Byam had ended their classes at four, but I had stayed behind, hoping to add to the household accounts with a modeling job. For the last three hours, I'd been dressed in a scant drapery of raw linen with a crown that weighed at least a stone crammed onto my head while a gentleman painted me down to the dimples in my elbows and the curve of my white thigh where it emerged tantalizingly from the sheer fabric.

Arms outstretched, my right hand gripping an enormous spear, my hair streaming behind in a red tangled wave, I portrayed the battle queen Boudicca riding forth to meet her enemies. The final product—after horses, chariot, and suitable background carnage were painted in—would be used as an enlistment poster. The Red-Haired Wanton was going to war—or at least urging others to fight for king and country. Mother would be apoplectic.

A taxicab slid to the curb, the driver opening the door for a tall, elegant infantry officer who emerged with a brush of his hair from his brow before he resettled his cap. "Hallo, Kitty old girl," he said, as if we'd only parted that morning rather than nearly a year ago. "Care for a lift?"

"William!" I leaped at him, staggering him off balance and knocking his cap askew before he recovered and returned my embrace. He wore his usual sandalwood cologne, but beyond that, he smelled of starch and soap, and perhaps even a hint of lilacs, Mother's perennial scent. "It's been ages, not even a letter to let me know how you were getting on," I said as he detached himself limb by limb until he stood before me unfettered. "What are you doing here?"

"Hoping to take you to dinner." He cleared his throat, suddenly looking horribly young and uncertain. "I was in town for a few days, but I'm due to report back to my regiment tonight. I wanted to see you before I left."

"I didn't even know you'd enlisted." I tried to keep the hurt from my voice.

He gave a careless dip of his shoulder. "Bit of a hectic spring, really. No time for chatty letters."

"Of course. I understand." I blinked away the mist forming at the edges of my vision and stepped back, taking him in head to toe. "Good heavens, you look quite dapper in uniform. The women will be throwing themselves at you."

Delight glittered for a moment in his eyes. "I took the plunge when word first came that things might heat up. Father was livid and Mother wept buckets, but it seemed like the right thing to do; really the only thing to do." His eyes dimmed briefly before brightening once more. "It's been mostly camping out and marching with a smattering of rifle practice tossed in. Like a boy's summer camp more than the buildup to battle." He jangled the change in his pocket. "So, are you on for dinner? I thought Maxim's in Piccadilly Circus."

My shoulders tensed. Unlike the elegant Les Lauriers or the respectable Queen's Hotel, Maxim's had a reputation as a discreet rendezvous for a less than spotless clientele. Was this my brother's way of protecting me from the hostile, condemning stares of society—or himself? "I don't know, William. I'm hardly dressed for an evening out."

"Won't matter. They're not nearly so stodgy as the usual places. It's what made me think of it."

The growl of my stomach overcame the uncomfortable feeling squirreling my shoulder blades, and I shook off my misgivings. I'd missed William too much to pass a chance to spend even a few hours in his company. Besides, Simon was away on his quarterly visit to his family in Lincoln and not due back until tomorrow. "I'd love to."

The taxi ride around Hyde Park and up Piccadilly to Wardour Street took barely enough time to get us through the stilted commonplaces such as weather—lovely; London—crowded; and the spreading war in Europe—unavoidable, before we were stepping out onto the street in front of the restaurant's white facade with its funny domed turret.

I couldn't help the shiver of pride as my handsome brother escorted me into the crowded brass and palm interior. Red-shaded lamps lit each table and the deep carpet was a matching rose color.

A band played on an upper balcony. Slick military officers of every stripe packed the place, most escorted by fashionably attired women wearing an air of recklessness along with their lavish perfumes and gaudy jewelry. I smoothed my hands down my simple dark blue skirt before resting them in my lap, unsure of where to place them, unsure of where I belonged.

Our orders were taken, and we were left alone, silent and suddenly uncomfortable with each other in a way we had never been.

"Are you . . ."

"Are they . . ."

We spoke over each other in our haste to fill the deafening void.

Tiny smile lines crinkled the corners of William's eyes. "I hope Mr. Halliday won't be alarmed when you . . . I mean you are still . . ."

"Living with him?" I straightened my spine, refusing to be ashamed. "You can say it, William. Lightning won't strike you down."

"No . . . no. I expect it won't."

"We have a small flat above a shop in Ralston Street. Simon hopes to take over the downstairs lease in the New Year and convert it to a studio and gallery. I'm studying at the Byam and working. It's been amazing, William. I'm in control of my life for the first time ever. I'm not merely a puppet or a piece on a board to be pushed about by others."

"Jolly good." William twirled the stem of his wineglass, unable to meet my eyes. Our dinners were placed in front of us. Roast lamb and mint sauce for William and capon for me with a lovely side of crisp potatoes and green peas. I tried not to gobble my food, but I hadn't eaten since breakfast, and the aroma of duck fat and rosemary was nearly overpowering. Afterward, dessert was ordered and another bottle of wine. William sat back, eyeing me cautiously.

Small lines tightened his mouth, and he fidgeted nervously with his napkin.

"I'm glad you've found happiness, Kitty, really I am, but frankly, things just aren't the same without you around."

"I'm sure Mama and Papa are quite happy to pretend I never existed."

"Not true. In fact, though she'd never admit it, I think Mother misses you. Cynthia's ensconced herself in Cornwall with a nonstop string of friends to keep her company. She rarely even comes up to London anymore except to shop. Father's been practically living at the Foreign Office, and Amelia's staying with a friend in Lucerne all summer. I wonder if she'll ever come back after leading such a glamorous life abroad."

"And you've been playing soldier."

His eyes flashed to meet mine. "It seemed the right thing to do. Cynthia says I'll more than likely put a bullet through my foot or catch my death sleeping in a drafty tent and where will that leave her and the baby? I tried reassuring her, but well . . . it's just easier to let her have her head than argue."

Here was my chance to bring up Cynthia and the man I'd seen her with in St. James's Park. I waited for our server to leave our pudding and depart before I summoned the nerve to speak. "Perhaps she's just lonely. You've been gone so much, William. It can't be good for a couple to live such separate lives."

"I don't know. Plenty of marriages thrive on less, and it seems to suit us both."

"But what about Hugh? He probably doesn't even recognize you."

"He's a baby, Kitty."

"He won't be one forever. He needs his father. You should go

home to Nanreath, William. Enjoy this time with Cynthia and the
baby before—"

"Enough, Kitty." He smacked his hand on the table, making the
glassware jump. I felt as if the whole restaurant was staring at us.
"Do you really think a woman living in sin with a man should be the
one doling out marriage advice? Leave it alone."

I'd never been spoken to like that; not by William. I focused on
my pudding, flushed and hurt. "You're right, of course," I mumbled.

Contrition flooded his face. "Damn it, I'm sorry. Let's not spend
what time we have together arguing. Who knows when I'll see you
again?"

I pushed my melting Glace Chantilly around my bowl. "Do you
really think the war, if it comes, will last more than a few months?"

He sighed, seemingly as relieved to change the subject as I was.
"It's not if it comes, but when. The British have given Germany an
ultimatum. If they don't comply with our demands, we'll be standing with France and the rest of them against the Kaiser and his
allies."

"You sound as if you want to go."

"I don't want to fight . . . I certainly don't want to die, but I have
to do what's right. After the initial row, Father agreed, though he
may just be seeing the political advantage to having an heir in uniform. Mother keeps going on about the tailoring and loading me
up with supplies for the front, as if I'll ever use a fur waistcoat or a
sleeping helmet. I think she's under the impression we'll be doing
our fighting in a Paris ballroom."

"Sounds perfectly mother-like. But ballroom or battlefield,
you'll be brilliant wherever you are."

"I hope so."

We finished our meal in pleasant if self-conscious accord. William laughed and joked and chatted about his time abroad and his

new life in the army. I offered him amusing anecdotes about my fellow art students and Miss Ferndale-Branch's eccentricities as an employer. He didn't speak about Cynthia. I avoided talk of Simon. It wasn't until we were standing on the pavement outside that the wall between us crumbled for a brief moment. "Are you all right, Kitty? Truly?"

"Of course. Why do you ask?"

"I care about you. I don't want to see you hurt or . . . unhappy."

"But that's just it. I'm not unhappy. In fact, I've never been more gloriously content in my life. I'm sorry for the way things turned out, but not sorry I left. Simon loves me."

William's face was grave, his voice quiet but questing. "If he loves you, why hasn't he married you?"

A familiar pang twisted my innards, but I'd not burden William with my growing unease. He had enough to worry over without adding me to his list. "I wouldn't say you're exactly a poster for matrimonial bliss, brother dear."

He responded with a snort that told me I'd cut close to the truth. "Perhaps given time, things will change between the two of you, especially now that you have Hugh."

"Right. Hugh. He does change things, doesn't he?" William said with a puzzling ambiguity, then he took my hand in his own. "I only want your happiness, Kitty."

I stood on my toes and brushed a sisterly kiss on his cheek. "I'll be fine. Promise. You concentrate on staying safe and coming home."

It ended the conversation as I hoped it would, and no more was said about Simon or my unorthodox lifestyle. Still, long after William dropped me at my flat, his question haunted me. I had always allowed Simon his avoidance. It was easier than arguing. Besides, I was too taken up with my work, my art, and my new freedom to want to change anything at all about our relationship, or so I told myself. But growing doubts crept into the empty side of my bed where Simon normally slept, and by the time I rose bleary-eyed the next morning, I had convinced myself to hash things out with him once and for all—no excuses.

I didn't have long to wait. I heard Simon's footsteps on the stairs as I spooned sugar into my morning tea and nibbled a piece of buttered toast. My stomach clenched, and I closed my hand to keep it from trembling. I hadn't been this nervous since confronting my mother in the park that long-ago autumn, a comparison I found disconcerting.

He burst into the room, bringing with him the pungent smells of train soot and bus exhaust, burnt coffee and damp socks. His face shone with excitement, his black eyes snapping, and I had a moment's shame for thinking ill of him as I awaited his marriage proposal. "Have you heard the news, Kitty love? It's official. We're at war."

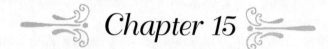

# Chapter 15

*May 1941*

Despite the black news of the war, spring still came to the English countryside. Fields and high moorland meadows became a sea of wildflowers, and the trees burst into an artist's palette of pinks, yellows, and whites. The icy coastal gales softened to soggy gray drenches that left the landscape veiled behind a slanted misty curtain or trapped in a blanketing fog.

Anna was both amazed and relieved when a letter arrived from Mrs. Willits, recounting the bombing that had left her homeless—again. Seeing it as an omen, she'd promptly returned to London, and only now been settled enough to send word. Anna wrote back immediately, barely able to contain her joy at this unexpected resurrection. It gave her hope there might be similar news from Sophie's Lieutenant Douglas, whose whereabouts continued to be unknown.

Sophie continued to do her work, but there was a new vacancy to her gaze and a bleakness to her smile. She rarely joined Tilly and Anna for evenings of sherry and gossip anymore. Her thoughts of an overseas posting were abandoned. The beautiful red dress remained packed away at the bottom of her trunk.

"I'm worried about her, Anna. She's barely eating enough to keep a bird alive and I know she's not sleeping. It's been months since Charles—"

"Don't say it, Tilly. He's not dead. He's missing. And until we hear otherwise, that's all it is. He'll turn up. We have to believe it so Sophie will believe it."

Now that winter's rush of measles, scarlet fever, and influenza patients had been discharged, there was time for a walk into the village of an evening. Tilly and Anna sat at a smoky corner table in the pub, pints of bitter between them. Sophie had declined their invitation, as she declined all their attempts at breaking through the bleak resignation in which she'd wrapped herself.

"Sophie's not a fool," Tilly argued, lighting a cigarette with Marlene Dietrich sophistication. The tweedy farmer sitting at the bar nearly swallowed his tongue. "Even if he's alive, he's most likely in some German prisoner of war camp."

"But alive and well and with the hope of return." Anna scowled. "Say it."

Tilly sighed, her gaze floating past Anna's shoulder to the pair of airmen just now coming through the door. "Alive and well and with the hope of return."

"Not exactly with conviction, but it'll have to do."

Tilly straightened, a smile curving her red lips as she flashed Anna a sidelong look. "Look who just wandered in. Tony dreamboat Lambert and some chaps from the airfield."

Anna's head snapped around to spy his familiar broad shoulders and sun-bronzed face as he pushed his way through toward their table. Her stomach did that little flip-flop it always did when she saw him, and her heart sped up.

"May I join you?" he asked.

"Please do." Tilly eyed him up and down as if he were a three-course meal. "I was beginning to think we'd wasted our evening. Nothing but boys and old men here tonight."

"And every single one of them would crawl over themselves to buy you a drink," Anna teased.

Tilly smirked. "There is that. Perhaps I'll test your theory out on that cute mechanic over by the dart board. Ta, ducks." She rose with a feline grace that quieted conversation as all eyes watched her saunter her way across the room.

"She's incorrigible," Tony commented, watching Tilly in action. "That poor chap doesn't stand a chance."

"She's honest and uncomplicated. I wish I had half her courage."

"You have a different sort of bravery, I think." He sipped at his beer.

The evening crowd thickened as airmen from St. Eval mixed with the local population. Across the room, Hugh ducked beneath the lintel, his golden head like a beacon in the dim, smoky interior. He came alone, though that didn't last as a small group coalesced around him, the women flirting, the men laughing at his ribald jokes.

"Lord Melcombe—the life of every party," Tony said, placing the glass in front of her. "I just hope I don't have to carry him home tonight. I'm growing weary of babysitting, and Lady Boxley's gotten wise to me. The last time I brought him home, I had to hide in the shrubbery for ten minutes. Now I know how a fox must feel as the hounds bear down."

"He looks like he's found a new minder."

Tilly had abandoned her mechanic, and now she and Hugh sat at the bar, laughing over drinks. Anna watched as Hugh's arm came round Tilly's shoulder. She smiled up at him, her eyes sparkling.

"You needn't worry, you know," Tony commented. "Hugh's a charmer, but he's not a rake. He'll not let things get out of hand."

"Won't he?" She sipped at her beer. "You think Tilly will stop him? She's half in love with the sod."

"I think Tilly's smarter than you give her credit for. She knows Hugh's game and plays it twice as well."

"Maybe you're right."

"I know I'm right. You worry too much. If it's not Sophie, it's Tilly or Hugh. If I weren't such a cocky bastard, I'd be jealous."

"You needn't be," she said softly.

He covered her hand with his own. She let it rest there for a moment before sliding free. Her throat went dry, her nerves jumping. He released her without comment, but his second pint went down much faster. "Now that you're back, have you managed to pry loose any of Nanreath's secrets?"

"Oh, just a little something . . . like . . . maybe . . . the name of my father." She eyed him with a proud smile.

His stare focused with a new intensity. "Did you?"

"His name was Simon Halliday. I had my suspicions, but Lady Boxley confirmed it."

"You finally spoke to her."

"It was more like a royal audience, but yes."

"What else did she tell you?"

"He and my mother met when he came here one summer to assist with portraits of the last earl's daughters and Her Ladyship. According to her, he was brash, arrogant, and without scruples."

"You don't sound as if you believe her."

"I should, I suppose, but I can't. Something makes me believe there was more to it than that. He might have been all those things Lady Boxley claims, but I truly believe in his own way he must have loved my mother." She pulled the rolled catalog from her bag and handed it to Tony with the page marked.

"Bloody marvelous," he said on a small, impressed gasp.

"My father painted it."

"She's . . . very beautiful." He cocked her a shy smile. "Though she can't hold a candle to her daughter." He handed her back the catalog. "So why didn't they marry and live happily-ever-after?"

She picked at the table where the wood splintered under decades of wet glasses and dirty plates. "Sometimes love isn't enough. Life gets in the way."

*Forgive my love.*

Anna focused on her drink, the bar, the door—anywhere but at Tony. Tilly and Hugh had disappeared, their stools empty. A raucous game of darts in the corner drowned out conversation. Cigarette and pipe smoke burned her eyes, and she felt dizzy after so many beers on an empty stomach.

"Want to get out of here?"

She nodded.

Outside, she inhaled the fresh, salty air. Clouds obscured the moon, and the street was barely a paler shadow among the thick, cloying dark. They passed a warden making his rounds and a doctor headed on a house call as they meandered down toward the sea, where the shingle crunched under their feet and the water slapped at the fishing boats moored at the harbor's wall. "Why do you suppose she did it, Tony? What would make her pose in such a way for him?"

"You said it yourself. She loved him."

"Fat lot of good that did her. Do you think she ever regretted her choice? Do you think she ever regretted . . . me?"

He didn't answer at once. But after a suitable weighty silence, he cleared his throat. "There were plenty of options for women who regretted their choices, Anna, but she did the best she could by you." He ground out his cigarette under his heel. "I don't think you can ever doubt she loved you very much."

They sat on the harbor wall, legs dangling above the water. Tony leaned back on his elbows to stare up at the sky. Anna enjoyed the comfort of his quiet presence. She'd come to rely on his friendship despite her intention to keep him at arm's length.

"I can't get used to how dark it is out here," she said. "I mean, London's dark since the blackout, but it's still different. Here, the sky seems so close and the stars . . . I've never seen so many."

"Do you know your constellations?"

"Only the Big and Little Dippers, and Orion. His belt is an easy one."

She felt rather than saw Tony smile. "They're up there." He pointed above the horizon and off to their right. "Those two stars there are Castor and Pollux. They make up part of Gemini that sinks below the ocean there. And off to the left and above is Leo. See, you can just make out his head and follow it around. There's the star Regulus and his body goes back from there."

Anna tried to follow his hand as it painted its way across the sky. The beers at the pub left her warm and relaxed as she listened to him explaining the stars and their positions. His voice held a deep, resonating certainty as he spoke. "My dad had a telescope when I was a kid. He was always dragging it out to show us lads what was what up there. Who knew it would come in so handy?"

"Do you miss your family?"

"It's just my dad at home and old Mrs. Sinclair, our housekeeper, who keeps him in proper nabob style. One brother's in the navy, the other working in RAF ops outside of London. My sister's married

and living in Edinburgh." A shadow lay across his face like a crescent, his cheekbone honed to a knife edge. "I miss them, of course.
But we'll be together at some point, then I'll wonder what I ever saw
in the pesky lot of them."

Anna gave a soft laugh. "It must be wonderful to have such a
big family. It was always just the three of us in Aldersgate. Now,
well . . ." She tipped her palm up in a gesture of futility.

"Now you have Hugh and Lady Boxley and mysterious Aunt
Amelia and that wild daughter of hers. A whole different family."

Anna stared up into the sky and kept silent.

Tony seemed to sense the wild sawing of her thoughts. He
pulled a pack of cigarettes from his pocket. Lit one behind a cupped
hand, the tip glowing against the dark. "The Lamberts are a noisy,
uncivilized bunch. Dad's the first generation who didn't have to
scrabble to make ends meet, and it shows. You should have seen the
horrified faces when he'd turn up at my school's prize day, speaking
like a collier's boolie. He did it on purpose, you know? He thought
it was hilarious to shock a reaction from all the old money who
looked down on him despite the fact he could buy them ten times
over." He chuckled under his breath. "My family argues and they're
messy and uncouth at times, but they're a good lot. Solid, you know
what I mean?"

Anna lay back beside him, her hands behind her head, and
smiled up at the milky trail of starlight. "I know exactly what you
mean."

It was May, and Anna took advantage of the lovely warm spring
afternoon to take a blanket, book, and flask of lemonade out onto
the lawn. She settled beneath a greening elm tree, her back resting
against the trunk, knees drawn up. Clouds pulled thin as candy

floss spread across a milky blue sky. On days such as this, it was hard to believe men were fighting and dying and the world bucked and growled as it sought to tear itself apart.

A nurse and soldier strolled arm in arm along the path leading toward the cliffs. She wore the same uniform as every other VAD, but the gleaming blond chignon and movie-star figure gave Tilly away. Anna was pleased to see her back to normal. She'd returned from a week's leave far too quiet—at least for Tilly, and twice she'd turned down an evening at the pub. Anna hoped it didn't have anything to do with Hugh, who'd been visiting London around the same time. Tony tried reassuring her, but she couldn't help fearing that Tilly would be the one to suffer for Hugh's increasing restlessness.

A group of recovering patients played a game of cutthroat cro- quet on the lawn by the back terrace, the mingled, laughing voices of Lancashire and Perthshire, Isle of Dogs Cockney and flat Cana- dian drawl. Hardly more than boys, and when left to themselves reverting to young boys' games and young boys' vocabulary. If she were back home, she'd have been shocked by such crude vulgarities spoken within her hearing. Here and now, it was part of life, and the real vulgarity was playing out in the skies above her and on the far-off battlefields of North Africa.

"Enjoying this fine afternoon, Nurse Trenowyth?"

Anna looked up to find Captain Matthews at her elbow. "Sorry, sir. A million miles away."

"So it would seem," he said with a genial smile. "I didn't mean to intrude. A nurse's half day off is too precious to use in chatter- ing away with an old doctor." He cleared his throat and ran a finger along his thin, pale mustache. "Matron says you have a real aptitude for nursing. That's quite a compliment coming from her."

"I hope to continue my nurse's training after the war, sir."

"A worthwhile goal. If you ever have need of my assistance in pursuing the field, let me know. I have contacts at St. Thomas's in London that would be happy to put you in the way of a suitable posting."

"Thank you, Captain."

He shifted from foot to foot, swiped a hand through his thinning brown hair, and looked as if he wished to share her blanket but was unsure of his reception.

"What ho, Captain. Nurse Trenowyth." Anna looked over her shoulder to see Hugh approaching across the grass. His gait remained awkward and crab-like as he traversed the uneven ground.

Matthews stiffened, as if to attention. "Good afternoon, my lord."

"At ease, sir." Hugh laughed good-naturedly. "Last I checked, you still outranked me."

"On the battlefield, perhaps." Matthews smiled like an indulgent parent. "Actually, I'm glad to run into you. I want to thank you for coming to dinner with the men last night. And for taking the time to stop in this afternoon, though I'm not sure if your offer of brandies all around went over well with Matron."

"Had to give them something to cheer after all the bad news recently, sir. Greece gone, Hungary, Yugoslavia. I'm only sorry I couldn't offer them enough to drown their sorrows into oblivion. The Nanreath wine cellar houses more mice than bottles these days."

"It feels odd inviting the owner to his own house, but ignore Matron and come anytime, sir. The wards can always stand a bit of a shake-up."

"Thank you, Captain. I think I shall. Now if you don't mind, I was hoping to steal Miss Trenowyth away."

"Of course." Hands clasped behind his back, the MO strolled

away, leaving her alone with Hugh, who eyed her as if enjoying an enormous joke.

"I'd heard the two of you were an item."

"You've been speaking with Tilly."

"Among other things." He shot her a wicked grin that would have set any woman in the place to swooning. It only irritated her, especially considering Tilly's growing moodiness. If Hugh had hurt her in any way . . .

"What do you want, Hugh? I'm busy."

"Really? You look positively slothful." He leaned against the tree, arms folded, a smile continuing to hover. But she knew it was all show. He couldn't sit beside her on the blanket without revealing his handicap, and the tree offered him support without being obvious. That moment of naked despair she'd glimpsed New Year's Eve had been buried deep. He'd not let her that close again—not without being blind drunk. "I've a surprise for you, but if you're too busy you can forget all about it."

"Oh? Another lovely tea with your mother? A sack of poisonous snakes would be preferable."

"She can be a bit of a handful, but you seem to have come to an understanding. I don't hear her crying for your head on a plate anymore."

She slumped back against the tree. "No, though I still think she's watching me to see I don't make mischief for the family. What is she so scared of, Hugh? Lady Katherine ran off over twenty years ago. What can it possibly matter to anyone now?"

"It matters to you," he answered quietly.

"It shouldn't." She shoved her book in her bag. "Lady Katherine gave me life, but the Handleys raised me. That counts for more."

"It does, but we all like to know where we come from. Where we fit." He held out a hand. "Do you want my surprise or not? I swear it has nothing to do with my mother. She doesn't even know what it is I've found."

"All right." Anna stood with a smoothing of her skirt. Shaking out her blanket, she folded it and added it to her bag. "But this better be good."

"That's a girl," he said, leading her toward the house.

They passed through the croquet game that was fast becoming a rugby match and entered through the terrace doors into the salon. A few men looked up from their papers or the wireless, but most ignored them. The main hall was busy. Sister Murphy glanced up from her files and scowled. Sophie pushed a trolley of medicines to Ward A, grief turning her bright, rosy looks to ash. The telephone rang. An orderly rushed to answer it. A young man sat in a wheelchair in a patch of sun by the front doors, a blanket across his knees, his eyes trained on the sky, face gaunt and grim.

"To set the record straight, I have no interest in Captain Matthews," she said, apropos of nothing, but wanting to be absolutely clear.

Hugh took her hand as they climbed the stairs, though she couldn't be sure whether his act was born of spontaneous familial bond or his lack of balance. "You're right. He's far too upright and forthright. Hmm . . . who can we pair you with?"

She thought of Tony Lambert, and warmth burned her cheeks. She focused on the scratched paint of the wainscoting, the creak of the stair treads, the faint squares of light spilling across the corridor. "Maybe I'm not looking to be paired with anyone."

"No? I thought you girls were constantly sizing up men for our matrimonial potential."

She tried to remain stern, proof against his potent charm. "Not all of us pine for a wedding ring."

"The woman who says that is the woman I fear the most."

Together they continued through empty rooms and up stairs, which he took slowly and painfully until they reached the top floor in a wing of the house she'd never been. A bare bulb hung from the low ceiling, and mildew snaked along the peeling paint of once cream-colored walls. Hugh fit a key into a lock and pushed wide a creaking iron-hinged door. Snapping on his torch, he swept its light back and forth. The room was enormous, open beams crisscrossing a sloped, cobwebbed ceiling. The air was stale and sour. Boxes and crates were piled high amid a layer of thick dust.

"Where are we?"

"Nanreath's attics."

She followed him into the long, windowless chamber under the eaves, trying not to stumble over either the clutter of past genera-tions or Hugh, who paused before a battered rolltop desk to shine his light upon a dusty leather portfolio case. "Welcome home, cousin."

She rubbed a hand over the dusty cracked leather, revealing a brass name plate, scratched and tarnished with age. "This belonged to my mother."

"I came across it when I was repairing the leak in the roof. Yes, I was telling the truth, thank you very much. This house would crumble around our ears if I let it. Anyway, the portfolio must have been up here for ages."

Anna stared at the loopy script upon the plate, her mind spin-ning until she sank onto a rickety stool to catch her breath. Her hands tightened on the case as she fought to control their trem-bling.

"I didn't look inside," he said. "Figured you might like first crack at it."

"Yes, uh, thank you." She snapped open the latches, drawing it wide. Froze at the deep growl of airplane engines. Her brain went blank. Her heart skipped at the unmistakable whistle of falling bombs.

"Anna, get down!"

Hugh threw himself over her, knocking her to her knees as the first explosion rocked the house, showering them with dust and chunks of plaster. More explosions sounded, shattering windows, spraying glass and splinters of wood. The sound pushed the air from her lungs.

"They must be after the airfield, and bloody smashing everything within twenty miles," Hugh said, levering himself onto one elbow.

"Tony," she whimpered.

"Will be quite safe, I'm sure. It's us I'm worried about."

An airplane engine sputtered in and out before ominously rising in pitch. The whine vibrated painfully along her bones, setting even her teeth on edge.

"It's going down!" Hugh shouted.

The sound intensified, the growl coming closer, louder. The pressure along her skin lifted the hairs along her arms and the back of her neck. The noise deafened her.

" . . . not going to make it to the water." Hugh grabbed a nearby tarpaulin, dragging it over them both as a bone-rattling boom brought down a heavy beam along with a section of ceiling. Plaster, lathing, bricks, and tiles rained down. With a curse and a grunt of pain, Hugh pressed her into the floor. She couldn't breathe beneath the heavy canvas. She gulped like a dying fish, flailing to free herself from the confining weight. Just when she thought she'd go mad, Hugh shoved the canvas aside, letting in a rush of smoky air. Heavy splintered wood lay in jagged pieces on the floor. A ragged hole above them opened to a blue sky smeared with black smoke. She could hear the crackle and spit of flames above the pounding of her heart.

"You're bleeding."

She touched her scalp, her fingers coming away red. Drops speckled a torn page from her mother's portfolio.

"So are you."

A cut slashed Hugh's cheek and there was a spreading red stain on his shoulder. He held his left arm close to his body. "We need to head downstairs before the whole bloody roof caves in."

Blood dripped onto Anna's hand. Warm and sticky and bright red. Smoke spread thick and black. She choked on a sob, shuddering against the panic overwhelming her. This was not France . . . this was England . . . and yet . . .

Harriet's blood spattered Anna's face, its scalding heat seeped through her fingers and drenched her uniform. Someone gripped her under the arms to pull her clear of the twisted steel wreckage as men screamed. She passed out, coming to in the cold, salty plunge of seawater. She gasped and sank and surfaced again, her body gnawed by an unspeakable pain. Screams and shouts accompanied by the groan and scrape of a dying ship and the incessant whip of bullets across the greasy water. She struck out for the shore, sank once more and this time, let herself submerge, too exhausted to continue.

"Damn it, move or you'll get us both killed." She was jerked to her feet, a voice shouting over the noise. "Downstairs now!"

"But Harriet . . . I can't leave her! I can't . . ." She lashed out, but a hand gripped her by the arm and forced her to focus.

"It's me, Anna. It's Hugh. You're safe. But you have to move. Can you do that?"

She nodded, turning her back on her friend—again.

Downstairs, shattered glass from blown-out windows sparkled like diamonds across the lino amid splintered wood and toppled furniture. Cracks spread dark, spidery lines across the plastered walls, and the front doors hung crooked off their hinges, beyond which burned two cars and an ambulance that had been parked in the sweep. Smoke billowed above the distant tree line.

Nurses and orderlies rushed to move patients out of the damaged wards under Matron's sharp eyes and quick commands as Captain Matthews and Sister Murphy worked triage. Those injured by flying debris sat against the wall or leaned upon their friends as surgeon and nurse moved calmly and efficiently assessing need and dispensing reassurance.

A soldier tore through the door. "The plane went down just outside the village! Took the whole church out, and three streets round about."

"Dear God," Hugh gasped. "My mother was attending a Women's Institute meeting. Anna, I have to go." He was covered with dirt, dust, and blood. He gentled his left arm close to his body, a tear in the sleeve revealing an ugly laceration. His face was streaked with ash, a wild look ringing his eyes.

"Your arm."

He waved off her words. "I'll have it bound up, but you . . . will you be all right if I leave you?"

She nodded then wished she hadn't. Her skull felt scrambled as an egg. "I can manage."

He threw her one last uncertain look before fleeing.

Anna hurried to assist a young man leaning drunkenly against a doorway, his wheelchair and blanket gone, his eyes looking everywhere at once as the chaos of sounds bombarded him from every direction.

"Are you hurt?" she asked.

"A Dornier. Engine on fire. Tail shot away. Must have jettisoned its bombs hoping to ditch in the sea." He continued staring out at the greasy black smoke as it rolled upward and was seized by the winds to smear itself across the spring sky.

"Let's find you a place out of the way to sit down."

He seemed to return to himself. He stared at her, his pale eyes fringed by long, dark lashes, his lip fuzzed with the beginnings of a mustache. So impossibly young and yet bearing an old man's burdens. "Don't be scared, Nurse," he said in a firm voice. "I'll see you come through all right."

She started to lead him toward an alcove in the shadow of the stairs where the hospital's main telephone sat. It was out of the way and somewhat sheltered should any more of the ceiling decide to fall. But with each wobbly-kneed step she took, the floor heaved and dipped under her feet, and strange dancing spots flickered at the edges of her vision. She stumbled over a fallen chair, banged her hip against a table. She drew a deep breath, hoping to stave off her dizziness, but her ribs ached and she gasped against a shooting pain down her side.

"Nurse?" the young man said, his brows low. "What's wrong?"

"I think . . . I think I need to sit down." She sank onto the bench and leaned back, letting the roll of voices wash over her. She closed her eyes against the smoke and to ease the throbbing pain at her temples. "I'll be all right. Just need a moment." She couldn't lie about here—just five minutes and then she'd get up, find Sister Murphy or one of the VADs and help where she could . . . just five minutes . . .

"Nurse?" The airman's voice seemed to call from a long tunnel. "Nurse Trenowyth, listen to me. Anna . . ."

She wished he'd stop shouting. She tried to tell him but gave it up as too much work.

"Anna? Anna, can you hear me?"

She swam up toward consciousness like a deep-sea diver emerging from the ocean floor. For a moment she was unaware of either where she was or how she had arrived. Weight pressed uncomfortably upon her, the air hung thick with old smoke and dirt, and she had a moment's panic of being trapped once again amid the burning sinking ship.

She opened her eyes, squinting against a blinding glare. She licked her lips, her mouth dry, her tongue fuzzy. The pain in her side dulled to a bearable, yet uncomfortable ache.

"Welcome back, sleepyhead." The silhouette burning its way into her retinas slowly focused itself into the familiar form of Tilly. Anna was in her bedroom, tucked up under a pile of blankets. Late-afternoon sun streamed in through the window.

"Oh, thank heavens," Anna said, suddenly remembering the soldier and Tilly walking out toward the cliffs just before the bombing. "You're all right."

"I'm fine, but how do you feel? You've been out for hours."

"Horrid." Anna tried to sit up and winced. "Ugh, my aching head." She shifted and decided she shouldn't have. "Ugh, my aching body."

"No wonder. You've got a goose egg the size of a cricket ball and you're sporting a beauty of a bruise from your hip to your shoulder. Your orders are to stay in bed for a few days in case of concussion or cracked ribs."

"I can't possibly. There's far too much to do. The hospital must be a mess and the patients—where's that nice soldier who helped me?"

"Trooper Young is fine, though you gave him a fright." Tilly poured her a glass of water. "Drink this. It will help."

The water slid chill down Anna's parched throat. "Tell me,

please . . . is Tony . . ." Her hands trembled, and she felt a wild, anxious fluttering in her chest. Pushing her panic down where it couldn't touch her, she began again, forcing her words out slowly and clearly, both frightened and relieved at how easily she was able to banish her emotions to a place where they couldn't touch her. "Was anyone hurt?"

Tilly's expression tightened, her normally cheerful face taking on a rather gray and worried look. "One of the bombs hit the old stables where the firefighting crew is billeted, and an orderly died when a wall came down in an office on the second floor."

"What of Hugh? And Lady Boxley?" Would she lose this new family as she'd lost her old one? Just when she'd found them?

"They're both fine, though the village is a bit the worse for wear. They've been bringing the wounded to us all day. We're not equipped for surgery, but the MO has done what he can." She tucked Anna beneath her blankets. "Speaking of Hugh, he stopped by to see how you were doing." Tilly's voice seemed almost shrill, as if fighting off her own black thoughts. "He brought you this."

The leather portfolio from the attic.

Tilly set it on the bed beside her. A long, deep scratch defaced one side, and the clasp was torn away. "As for gifts, I've one of my own. It's much better than a battered old case, but if you're caught, I don't know anything and I had nothing to do with it."

"You haven't been dealing with the black market, have you?"

Tilly merely offered a mysterious smile as she rose to open the door. "You'll see. Now, close your eyes."

"But . . ."

"Go on. Don't be a wet blanket." She flicked her hands in an impatient gesture.

Anna closed her eyes and folded her hands upon the coverlet in patient resignation. Footsteps sounded and the turn of the doorknob followed by a stir of cool air from the corridor. She heard Tilly whisper, and even with her eyes closed, Anna felt a change in the atmosphere. A quivering expectation, as if someone stood watching her, breath held.

"Can I open my eyes?"

"Go ahead," replied a familiar deep voice.

Her eyes flew open to find Tony Lambert standing sheepishly in the doorway. "Surprise."

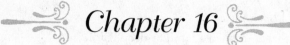

## Chapter 16

October 1914

I adjusted the sumptuous drape of the doll's velvet gown before setting it back amid the rest of Mr. Byam Shaw's collection that he housed in a spacious upstairs studio cupboard at the school in Campden Street. I'd been using it this afternoon as part of my still-life class; I was instructed to create a composition that required me to exactly duplicate the rich nap and bold color of the fabric as well as the way each shadow fell within each soft crease as the skirt brushed the floor. I enjoyed these classes but found them difficult to master. I much preferred Saturday's exercises, when I was able to submit an unsigned work for evaluation. This might be a quick pencil sketch of the newsboy on our corner or a pen and ink of our windowsill where the landlady's tabby lay sunning amid pots of scraggly herbs. This was where my gifts lay, in distilling a scene down to its essential properties. Not cluttering a scene with a cast of thousands each in period-perfect costume and props.

Today my mind lacked the concentration needed to master the

delicate layering of dark and light that would turn a flat canvas into a three-dimensional white velvet gown. Cramps pinched my stomach and my lower back ached. All I wanted was my bed and a soothing hot water bottle. These symptoms, along with the inconvenience of dealing with belts and menstrual pads, should have had me grumbling and unhappy. Instead, I was relieved at my regular monthlies, which only served to irritate me further. A child was a complication I didn't need, but as the war's casualty lists grew, so did my unreasonable wish for a part of Simon I could call completely my own.

Just as I finally settled into work, the creak of a floorboard and a draft from an open door alerted me to an intrusion into my self-pitying disgruntlement. I wanted to hurl my brush across the room in frustration before I realized it was Simon, dashing in gray flannels and a jaunty panama hat.

"They told me you were down here. It's a lovely day outside. I thought we'd take the bus to Richmond and go to the Hippodrome. Afterward, we can take a punt out on the river while the weather is nice."

For some reason, his pleasant invitation grated my already strained nerves. "I can't. I'm trying and failing to wrestle this ridiculous painting into some semblance of art."

He eyed my half-finished wedding scene of bride and attendants standing upon the porch steps awaiting the first strains of Mendelssohn. "Maybe it's the subject matter that has you stumped."

His gaze held a teasing gleam, but I was not in the mood for jokes. My face grew tight and hot, and my tongue ached from biting back so many words for so long. "I wonder whose fault that is?"

He had the grace to blush, the skin around his eyes tensing in dismay. "Here we go again. How many times do we have to discuss this before you realize you're being ridiculous?"

"Once would be nice, but every time the subject comes up, you dodge it."

He took my hand, his gaze both cajoling and rueful. "Come on, love. Leave your painting for now. The day is perfect, and if you're nice to me, I'll take you to the Fountain Tea Room for luncheon and an ice cream. You'll come back with fresh eyes and a full stomach, and we can talk all about it tonight."

"See? You're doing it again." My voice shook, and I knew even as I picked this fight that it was pointless. "Is the idea of marriage so terrifying that you won't even consider it?"

He dropped my hand and stepped back, his face grim. "Of course not, but now is hardly the best time, is it?"

"When is the best time, Simon?"

He sighed, as if I were a recalcitrant child and he the long-suffering adult. "How about when you've completed your studies? Or when I've established the gallery and can afford to keep you in the style an earl's daughter expects? It hasn't been easy since the war began, you know. Commissions have been thin on the ground, and my parents aren't doling out the blunt the way they used to."

"Is that what this is about? Do you really think I care about how much money you have?"

"I care." He pressed his lips together, as if he was trying to control his temper. "We both have dreams we're chasing, Kitty. Do you really want to throw everything we've worked for aside just so you can have a day of orange blossom and white tulle? Frankly, I'm surprised you're so determined. You're always so contemptuous of your sister and her obsession with marriage."

"Amelia is obsessed with weddings, not marriage. She likes the idea of a big party where she gets to be the center of attention. I'm talking about building a life together."

"I thought that was what we were doing."

It was my turn to inhale a deep, calming breath before my head exploded. "You once asked me if I thought you weren't good enough. Well, I would ask you the same question—am I not good enough for you? Don't"—my voice wavered and broke—"don't you love me enough to marry me?"

He seemed to sway, as if I'd physically struck him. His face was white and pinched, the muscle in his jaw clenched tight. "How can you even ask that?" Desperation filled his gaze. "I love you more than I can possibly say. It was as if every choice I'd ever made led me to that first moment when I saw you on the stairs at Nanreath Hall. I was struck by lightning. There was no going back. No denying it. I love you, Kitty Trenowyth. And you love me. Why do we need a priest to murmur some words over us to make what we have real?"

*Because I'm afraid of losing you. Afraid of waking up and finding this has all been a beautiful dream.* That was what I wanted to say. Simon watched me closely, and I could feel his tension in our clasped hands, see it in the lightning-shot depths of his green eyes. If winning this fight meant losing him, was it really a victory?

He must have sensed my weakness. He pulled me against him, his body hard, his muscles taut as wires. If possible, his kiss spoke more eloquently than his words, drowning out my last sputtering argument. Scalding liquid heat slid along my limbs, his devouring passion teasing me into velvety surrender. I closed my eyes. "Richmond sounds lovely."

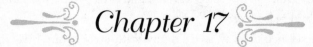

# Chapter 17

*May 1941*

T ony, what a nice . . . uh . . . surprise." Even as her heart thrilled to see him alive and safe, Anna darted swift glances around the room as if Matron or, heaven help her, Sister Murphy, would leap from behind the wardrobe like a diabolical jack-in-the-box.

"Your words say nice yet your face says horrible."

"You can't be here. This is very, very against regulations. If we're caught, I'll be in heaps of trouble. And you . . . oh dear." She threw herself from the bed, ignoring her state of undress and her sudden wash of dizziness to shove him back out the door into the corridor. "You have to leave. Now. Immediately. Sooner than immediately. Oh dear," she repeated weakly as her legs turned to jelly.

Tony caught her before she fell flat on her face, amusement clearly written in the lift of his brows and the twitch of his lips. "Are you supposed to be out of bed?"

She ignored his question as well as the shivery tingle firing every nerve ending and dragged him toward the door. "Quick before anyone sees."

Voices echoed hollowly from the far end by the stairwell.

"Wait, someone's coming. You can't leave." Anna pulled him back inside, shutting the door with a soft click, before leaning an ear against the panels. Her heart banged against her sore ribs and the room continued to swim in and out of focus as she sought to calm her breathing, which came in hoarse gasps.

Tony was clearly enjoying her consternation. The smile in his eyes drifted to his mouth.

"Shhh!" she scolded as she listened. The voices passed by and faded. She let out a sigh all the way to her toes. "That was close."

"I feel like I'm trapped behind enemy lines." His voice was a low, accented purr at her ear.

She squeaked and whirled around, once more struck with a world-tilting dizzy spell that had her groping for something solid to grab. Unfortunately, the something solid was Tony Lambert, who'd crept up behind her and now stood at her shoulder. They collided chest to chest, his arms coming round her waist as she leaned woozy against him. She could swear she heard his heart pounding through the layers of uniform, or maybe that was hers.

"Careful now," he said. "You're a bit unsteady on your feet." His brown eyes seemed to darken, his expression no longer amused, but something more somber that clenched her innards and doubled the spinning of her head.

"Oh God, Tony. When they said it was the airfield . . ." She tightened her arms around his waist.

"I'm fine, but it's nice to know you worried over me."

"Despite my best intentions, I'm afraid."

"I think that's a compliment, but dashed if I'd lay odds on it."

She stepped free of his encircling arms, unexpectedly disappointed when he let her go without protest. She snatched her dressing gown from its peg and hastened into it, yanking the sash closed before collapsing on the edge of the bed, dropping her head into her hands. "You must think I'm completely mad."

"Yes." She glanced up through her lashes to see him leaning against the door, arms folded across his chest, looking incredibly handsome. Her wobbly stomach did another flip. "But in a good way."

She rubbed her face, trying to look less like a case for asylum and more like a capable and confident nurse. Once more, she sought to lock away her feelings, but this time she found them slippery and uncontrollable. Excitement buzzed in her chest and a smile fought its way through her stiff upper lip. "You have a very bad habit of turning up unannounced and in the oddest places. First London. Now my bedroom. I fear where I'll find you next."

"I was at a meeting with the brass hats when I heard about the bombing. I stopped here on my way back to the airfield to see for myself that everyone was all right."

"You weren't even there."

"No, but I'm still gratified to know you worried I'd been blown to smithereens along with two latrines and a supply shed. I'd just about given up hope I'd ever win you over."

The conversation was veering in a dangerous direction. Anna scrambled to pull herself free before her better judgment was overcome by wide shoulders and a pair of devilish brown eyes. There was no place in her life for romance; especially not with someone she could grow to love. "Hugh found my mother's portfolio in the attics."

"Did he? Just when you think the chap's a lost cause, he does something gallant and you have to like him all over again. Well, now that I'm assured you've not dented your skull and you see I haven't been disintegrated by a stray bomb, I'll make my escape while the coast is clear and leave you to it." His hand moved slowly round the rim of his cap before he put it on. "Good-bye, Anna."

She reached out a hand, as if she might hold him back. "Don't go."

He paused with a slight lift of his brows. "I promise to steer clear of the sisters. None will ever know I was up here. I promise."

This was foolish, so bloody foolish. She chalked it up to her head wound. "It's not that, but since we're already breaking about ten different regulations, you may as well stay a little longer. I'm not as brave as I make out, and this feels as fragile as an unexploded grenade." She ran a hand over the soft leather.

"Let's hope less deadly." He returned to sit beside her.

She continued to caress the case, as if she might read the contents through her fingertips, then with a resolution born half of fear, she snapped open the latches, drawing it wide.

The pages were loose, yellowed or spotted with age. Some quick sketches done in pencil had faded almost to oblivion, while others remained crisp and vibrant as if Lady Katherine had only now laid them aside. There were countless watercolors. Some of places Anna recognized; the stained-glass window in Ward B, the carved stonework above the house's main door, the stone bridge over the creek. Others were unknown; a meadow purple with heather, a cottage garden set for tea amid a backdrop of summer flowers, the chimney stack of an old tin mine.

"They're quite good, aren't they?" Beside her, Tony leafed through those works she'd already laid aside, pausing now and then with a grunt of approval or a cock of his head, brows scrunched in thought. "Who's this, do you suppose? It's not Hugh's father. I've seen snaps of him. He was wiry as a whippet with a square face straight off a

Roman coin. I always joke that Hugh must have inherited his good looks from the milkman."

He held out a picture of a man in profile leaning against a crumbling archway, staring heavy-lidded out at a gray, choppy ocean, the horizon nearly lost between sea and sky. A cigarette rested in one long-fingered hand, the other was shoved in the pocket of his jacket. "It's Simon Halliday," she said softly. "My father."

Tony eyed the sketch more closely. "Has Lady Boxley told you any more about him? Or about the circumstances surrounding your mother's elopement with him?"

"I'm afraid not. We may have called a truce, but she still eyes me like a plague."

"What about the village? I'll wager you'd find any number of people who'd be happy to gossip about the scandalous earl's daughter who ran away from home. What else do they have to do around here but talk about their neighbors?"

Anna perked up. "Of course—Minnie Smith. I nearly forgot about her invitation to tea. You're brilliant, Tony."

"Happy to help, Nurse Trenowyth." His eyes grew dark and intense again as he brushed the hair back from her forehead. She felt her lungs constrict as his face filled her vision, his expression both amused and something else, something that sent a shivery aftershock through her. Her bones seemed to melt, and she felt herself falling, her stomach floating into her chest as if she were on a downward lift. He leaned in for a kiss, and this time Anna surrendered to her desire. She lifted her face to his, her lashes fluttering closed.

"Anna." A scratch at the door threw them apart. "It's Tilly. Hate to break up the party but Sister Murphy's on her way upstairs."

Tony rose and grabbed up his cap, raking a hand through his hair before settling it on his head. He seemed to fill the room, his smell, his heat, his calloused hand on her cheek. "You realize now that I know how you really feel, it's going to be very hard to shake me."

"Don't get cocky, Flight Lieutenant."

He quirked her a last smile. "Good luck, Sherlock," before sliding out through the door.

Foolish, she repeated to herself, hugging her arms to her body against a sudden chill. Bloody foolish.

But at that moment she didn't care.

In fact, it took Anna more than two weeks before she had a spare afternoon to walk into the village. In the aftermath of the army's chaotic evacuation from Greece, activity on the wards increased as the main hospital at Southampton sent their spillover to Nanreath. Anna's days were spent at a constant run to keep up with the stream of demands. No sooner had one patient recovered than another would arrive to take his place. Names and faces made no difference to her tired mind as she moved in a fog of rote procedure, pausing rarely for a quick bite to eat or a few hours of sleep between shifts.

Tony's whirlwind visit faded into her tired memory, only occasionally surfacing to pinch at her with worry and fear. He would be all right. He had to be. Someone so vital and alive couldn't simply cease to exist in a split second's violence. Still, there was plenty of evidence that it could and did happen. More telegrams arrived announcing the deaths of brothers, fathers, husbands, sweethearts. As she'd done after France and in the aftermath of Graham's and Prue's deaths, Anna locked the horrors away. It was the only way she could cope without crumbling.

The crush of new patients was only complicated by the ongoing repairs to Nanreath Hall. Hammers echoed the bone-deep hacking coughs, and saws resembled the raspy breathing of men suffering from asthma and bronchitis. No matter where her duties took her, she found herself stumbling over workmen, their loud adolescent innuendo following her from the basement storage rooms as she folded mountains of laundry or scrubbed and boiled equipment for the next day's use to the second floor's offices as she filed medical forms and dusted and cleaned the staff dining room. Anna half expected them to pop out at her in the shower huts or when she opened the lid to her locker.

Hugh surprised everyone by taking charge of the project. He had a knack for channeling the workmen's reckless enthusiasm. She never heard him barking orders or even raising his voice, but what he asked, they did. Anna hoped this was a hint of things to come.

By the middle of June, the flood of patients slowed to a manageable trickle, and Anna was released by Matron for an afternoon to do what she wished.

Like a prisoner emerging after years of captivity, she stepped out onto the gravel sweep, blinking against the glare. Rain puddles sucked at her boots and created rivers of mud from the narrow tracks and lanes, but she ignored the discomfort as she stretched legs cramped from weeks of running in circles and gazed on the wide mackerel skies where summer's larks and thrushes had replaced winter's Blenheim bombers from Chivenor and the slowgoing Henleys flying in and out of Cleave.

"Anna. Wait a moment." Hugh strode around the corner of the house. His bruises had faded to a dull green, but his arm remained bound in a sling. "I was hoping I'd find a chance to catch you alone. May I walk with you?"

"I'm headed to the village."

"Perfect. So am I." He fell into step beside her. Once the house was lost from view, he pulled the sling off over his head and tossed it behind a bush. "I'll pick it up on my way home. Mother's been badgering me to rest my arm one more week, but what she doesn't know won't hurt her."

"Seems as if you conduct most of your affairs that way."

"What's that supposed to mean?"

She shrugged. "Just an observation."

They followed the avenue across the park to meet the lane headed south and west. A few military trucks passed by and an ancient Wolseley coupe, but beyond that, they had the road to themselves. The narrow byway followed the turn and curve of the rocky creek until it met and crossed the stone bridge.

"Anna, I wondered . . . I mean after the bombing . . ." She eyed Hugh curiously, dreading his next words but unable to stop him. "Who is Harriet?"

Sophie and Tilly had asked her the same question. She kept her gaze on the path, the trees, the line of silver ribbon as it made its way toward the sea. Tried not to let her mind's eye turn back, but it was difficult and she was tired after so many weeks of frantic work. The memories crept insidious as a storm tide. She couldn't hold them back. "She was a nurse in France."

"She died."

It wasn't a question. The silence filled with ghosts until Anna felt them pressing on her from all sides. The present faded like mist, drawing her back to that long-ago June sunrise.

"Yes."

"And you were wounded in the same attack."

The tickle of a thought pierced her confusion. "I survived. Unlike too many of my friends."

Her pace increased, her spine brittle, her ribs aching as if she'd been punched. Her throat hurt and her temples throbbed, the memories battering themselves against the inside of her skull.

"Anna—wait." He labored to keep up.

She spun on her heel. "Why bother asking all this, Hugh? You know what happened already. You checked up on me, didn't you?"

His eyes gave him away. "Not me. Mother."

"Bugger all, Hugh! Did she think I was an imposter out to swindle the estate of its teeming millions?"

"Of course not. She can see the likeness between you and Lady Katherine as well as anyone. Look, if you must know, Mother's not been well for months, and then you turned up out of the blue. It's rattled her. She wanted to know with whom she was dealing. When she learned your war record, she couldn't help but be impressed. We both were."

"So glad I passed inspection, but have either of you ever considered I might be just as rattled coming back to a family that doesn't want anything to do with me? I spent my entire life as 'that girl.' Not quite acceptable or decent. The one mothers didn't want their daughters hanging about with in case my bastardy rubbed off. Every other child had parents with the same last name. Every other child had aunts and uncles and cousins, a family history that didn't start when they were six. My parents were nothing but two faded pictures in a cheap locket."

He took her arm, and they hugged the verge to let a removal van pass. It rumbled into a lower gear as it slowed on its way down the hill into the village. "Anna, I know you don't think it, but I'm on your side. I know what it's like to look at a faded photograph and dream about what might have been."

"At least you had your mother's memories of him."

"And if her memories were truth, they'd have canonized him by now. No, it was everyone else I spoke with who painted the picture I have in my head. Their opinion might be more cynical, but it definitely made my father more likeable."

"That's exactly what I'm doing. Your mother has done her best to persuade me Lady Katherine was either shameless or gullible. Now I'm on my way to see Minnie Smith in the village. Perhaps she can offer me a new picture."

"Old Silas Smith's daughter? What would she know of Lady Katherine? I can't imagine they would have ever found themselves in company."

"I'll let you know after tea."

He paused, and she realized with a start they'd arrived in front of the pub. A pair of gaffers sat smoking and chatting on a bench beneath the pub's creaking sign. One tipped his hat to Hugh. The other nodded. Both studied her with a knowing eye and a wink.

"My stop," he said. "An appointment with a builder. Supplies are scarce. And while the government will pay for some of it, there are parts of Nanreath that need more than Churchill is prepared to offer. Mother doesn't like to dicker with tradesmen, she says it's beneath her, so it's up to me to grease the wheels."

"And your throat at the same time?"

He grinned and dipped his head in a self-conscious gesture.

She rolled her eyes and started to walk away.

"Anna?" He remained in the doorway, leaning a shoulder against the weathered wood of the jamb, his hands in his pockets, eyes pale against his pale skin and the afternoon sun gleaming strands of his golden hair. "Be careful."

"I'm sure Miss Smith is perfectly harmless."

"Not her. I'm talking about this search for answers about your mother. Take my word, truth can be a double-edged sword." He paused, his gaze lifting to the sky. "Be very sure you want to hear the answer before you ask the question. Sometimes it's better not to know."

L eaving Hugh to his appointment at the pub, Anna continued
on to Minnie Smith's cottage. While repairs at Nanreath proceeded quickly, the village remained scarred and blackened. The
vestry hall was a roofless burnt shell, the church windows boarded
over and the bell tower leaning dangerously. The narrow, hilly
streets leading to the harbor possessed a dingy grayness, and the air
hung heavy with rot and mold and smoke. Rope cordoned off a side
lane where the occasional timber stuck black and spear-like into the
sky amid a jumble of brick, stone, and tumbled ruined furniture.

Anna turned down the lane running parallel to the narrow strip
of pebbled beach and the long low harbor wall and followed along
until she came to the last stone fisherman's cottage in the row. A
beautiful fairy garden had been tenderly cultivated from the rocky
patch of ground out front, and the door was painted a lively peacock-
blue. She rapped sharply and waited.

The door cracked the width of a chain and an eye peered out.
"Who's there?" a man's thin raspy voice squeaked.

"I'm Miss Trenowyth. I've come from the hospital at Nanreath."

"None's sick here. Go 'way."

A murmured conversation between people Anna couldn't see
ensued, then the eye withdrew to be replaced by Minnie's faded
countenance, peering out at her through the crack. "Don't mind my
da. He doesn't like strangers." The chain was removed and the door
opened. Miss Smith wore an enormous white apron over a spiffing
dress. She grabbed Anna by the arm and dragged her inside. "Come
in, Miss Trenowyth. Thought you forgot about me, I did, but then
I told myself to be patient. You'd come if you had the time. It's just
Da and I don't get many guests. It's hard to wait when it's only his
grumpy face I've got to see every day."

"Thank you for inviting me to tea, Miss Smith."

"It's Minnie, Miss Trenowyth. Told you all my friends call me Minnie."

Removing her apron and smoothing her hair, she led the way into a tiny front room where Anna stopped dead in her tracks. Four ladies with cups of tea and sandwiches were already seated on the lumpy, doily-covered furniture.

"You remember Mrs. Crewe." Minnie nodded toward the plump, middle-aged woman with a Marcel wave and a friendly smile. "That's Mrs. Polley and Mrs. Thompkins in the corner there." Two graying ladies looked up from their half-completed scarves, which trailed from their needles, over the chair arms, and across the floor. "And of course, you remember Miss Dawlish." The steel-eyed woman looked no happier to see Anna now than she had at the New Year's social.

"Very nice to see you all again. I'm afraid you've caught me a bit off guard. I didn't expect a crowd."

"You never invited her without telling her we'd be here, too," Emmaline Crewe complained. "That was poorly done."

Mrs. Polley tsked her distress. "Ambushed right and proper."

"Thought this was a rum do."

"Minnie Smith, you're as daft as a day-old fawn. Not a straight thought in that head of yours."

"Oh, it's fine. Really," Anna said, hoping to ease the dagger looks being shot in Minnie's direction. "I'm just happy to see you all came through unscathed."

"Unscathed? If that's what you call it," Miss Dawlish complained. "I'm staying with my niece and her five children. I'm ready to stick my head in the oven."

"It's just for a bit, Louise," Mrs. Crewe soothed her with another biscuit. "Just until the authorities tell you it's safe to go back."

"And when is that supposed to be? I've been waiting two weeks and not a soul's even come round to inspect the damage."

Minnie offered Anna an apologetic look over the heads of her chattering guests. "As soon as I told them you were coming, they fell over themselves to be here."

"I had no idea I was such a celebrity."

"Aye, not much doings in the village since . . . well . . . since your mother." She giggled. "I'd have had a houseful if I wanted, but Da don't like company, so I kept it to these four. They all knew your mother real well. Mrs. Crewe and Mrs. Polley were in service for the old earl as maids, Mrs. Thompkin's family farms a tenant holding. I worked as maid to Mrs. Vinter, who owned a house at the bottom of Cliff Lane. Doesn't sound like much, but Lady Katherine spent more time there than she did at her own home, so I couldn't help but know what was what."

"And you, Miss Dawlish?" Anna asked.

The tall, thin woman looked up from her cup of tea. "My father was a chemist here in the village. Lady Katherine and I shared a mathematics tutor one summer. I was intended for university."

"And Lady Katherine?"

"For marriage, I assume, though she bollixed that up pretty thoroughly." She added a grudging, "Good at figures, though . . . for someone of her ilk."

"What did you study at university?"

"I didn't go. The war came and I enlisted in the FANY. Drove ambulances. By the time hostilities were over, university seemed the height of self-indulgence. I just wanted to be left alone."

Mrs. Crewe and Mrs. Thompkins moved aside for Anna, who settled between them with tea and a plate heaped with sandwiches.

Minnie hovered like a giddy mother hen. "The bread's not much and it's only margarine, but the strawberry jam's from a batch I put up last summer, and there's real egg in the egg and cress."

"What have you brought in that case?" Mrs. Crewe asked between clicking needles and finger sandwiches.

"Lady Katherine's portfolio. I've heard she was an aspiring artist."

"Aye, she was," Mrs. Polley confirmed. "Always carrying that dingy old bag about with her or squirreled away in a little attic room she took as her studio. Paint under her fingernails and smelling of linseed oil and varnish no matter how many baths she took."

"Remember the time her mother found her behind the dairy sketching that old tinker from up Boscawen way?"

"Lordy, the ruckus. You'd have thought the old badger was going to kidnap her for the white slave trade, the to-do that went on."

"And what about the time she went off the morning before the village fete and never come home. Beaters out looking for her with lamps after dark."

"And there she was at the Cheswick farm having supper just like she'd not been given up for dead."

As Mrs. Crewe and Mrs. Polley reminisced, Anna opened the case, laying out some of the pictures on a table. All the women craned their necks to see.

"Why, that's the old mine near Witch's Edge."

"There's Pete Kelly's boat. See here with the blue trim and always him going out with his old dog."

"Heard he liked that dog better than his wife."

"She was a Wesley, wasn't she? All those Wesleys are mean as badgers."

"Careful, Miriam. Dom Wesley's a cousin of mine on my mother's side."

"My point exactly."

Minnie gasped, her weathered face breaking into a grin. "Why, there's me. Ha, don't I look smart . . . and ever so young." She pulled a loose page from under another. Her hand paused above the sketch, a slight wrinkle between her brows. "Look at this, girls. Should have known there'd be a drawing of the ruins."

"The ruins? Are they nearby?" Anna asked.

"A few miles up the cliff, north of the village," Mrs. Crewe replied. "It's a lonely spot, but very romantic."

"If you like old, mossy stones and sloppy kisses," Miss Dawlish commented.

Minnie pointedly ignored the comment. "All the young 'uns do their sparking there." Her tongue flicked to the corner of her mouth, a troubled expression shadowing her features. She dropped the sketch back to the table, as if wanting to rid herself of it. "Lady Katherine had a real gift, didn't she? Mrs. Vinter always said that she did."

"Do you know why she didn't pursue it professionally?" Anna asked.

"Mrs. V wanted her to, but girls like Lady Katherine didn't work at dabbing at pictures, did they? They married a swell and had lots of rich babies. If they doodled a bit, it weren't to be paid for it."

"But Lady Katherine didn't marry her swell." Anna laid the picture of Simon Halliday on the table.

Mrs. Polley sighed. "He was a handsome bloke, wasn't he? No wonder she fell in love with him."

"You know who this is?"

"'Course I do. That's the chap that ran off with your mother. Only saw him when he was here that summer before the war, but he was a hard one to forget. All the maids were half in love with him."

Minnie giggled. "I can still see Mrs. V facing down the old earl when he come barreling down to her house by the sea, threatening all and a hatchet for her part in corrupting his daughter. She never even blinked. Tough as nails, she was. Not an ounce of give in her."

Anna leaned forward. "Why would the earl have come to Mrs. Vinter?"

"Why, it was her that set the girl to pining for art school when the old earl and his wife forbid it. That's what started the whole mess, if you ask me." Minnie seemed surprised Anna didn't know this already.

"Nah, it was that painting that did it. Flaunting herself with no clothes on was just asking for trouble," Mrs. Crewe declared.

"You mean *The Red-Haired Wanton?*" Anna asked. "The painting Simon Halliday did of her?"

"Don't know the name, but remember the stink," she said. "I traveled to London that fall with the family. The hullabaloo when they found out, dearie me. The rows and carryings-on, weeping and slamming of doors. Lady Katherine marched out and never a backward glance."

"And then later, she run off with him. Could have knocked me down with a feather when I heard. Never thought she'd bolt the traces. Always such a good girl, if a bit scattered."

"A shame it didn't last."

"'Course it didn't. What girl would stay, knowing the man she left her whole family for had a string of mistresses."

*Forgive my love.* Anna's hand closed around her locket.

"Well, I saw Lady Katherine with my own eyes when she come back to Nanreath carrying Miss Anna here," Minnie said with authority. "She was a woman who'd lost her greatest love."

"Sentimental hogwash," Miss Dawlish piped up.

"Are you saying I'm making things up?"

"I'm saying she should have known better than to take up with a shiftless nobody. What did it bring her in the end? Scandal, ruin, exile, and a pointless death without anyone from her family by her bedside."

"You're just sour, Louise, and have been for over twenty years. It wouldn't be the first time a girl's fallen in love with a man what's not good for her," Minnie said angrily. She took up the picture of Simon Halliday once more. "He sure was fine-looking and so young. They were all young, though, weren't they, Miss Trenowyth? Your da . . . the old lord's son . . . so many who died in that war."

"I thought Lord Melcombe's father was invalided out," Anna said.

"Aye, gas tore up his lungs. That's why your mum came back. She wanted to see her brother before he died." She stared blindly into her teacup. "But they sent her away." She looked up, memory sheening her eyes with tears. "It wasn't right not letting her in to see the young lord. Not when they were so close."

"The old earl was always a hard, unforgiving man," Mrs. Polley said.

"And a coward. Didn't even do his own dirty work," Minnie added. "Sent Lady Boxley in his stead."

"She's as cunning and hard as the old earl. Looks soft, but she's sharp as an adder. Always was," Miss Dawlish intoned down her narrow hook nose.

"At least the young Lord Melcombe takes after his father," Mrs. Crewe said.

Minnie sipped at her tea, her fingers tight on the cup, her eyes focused on the sketch of the ruins. "So Her Ladyship's always said."

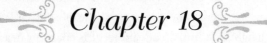

# Chapter 18

*May 1915*

Waterloo Station was crowded with soldiers. The platform rolled and swirled like the sea with a crush of hats and coats, bobbing umbrellas slick with spring rain, and here and there the slender white flash of a waving hand as each loaded train moved out with a mournful hoot of its whistle. Even the moaning rise and fall of voices as loved ones were parted with a final glimpse through a grimy window reminded me of a mournful ocean gale.

I pushed my way through the sobbing wives and lovers wiping red eyes on white handkerchiefs, the swish of their long black skirts, as if they already counted their men dead and gone, the stoic fathers with white bristling mustaches guiding stooped and faded mothers by the arm, their eyes still glassy with shock.

I paused, scanning the lower platform where William's train waited, hoping to spy him through the mob. He'd been evacuated home to recover from a bullet wound to his upper arm, barely a trifle amid such appalling losses, but for a month I breathed easier, knowing he was safe in South Audley Street. I might be forbidden from seeing him, but I could lay aside the tiring weight of my fear for a short time.

Now I stood on tiptoe, withstanding the buffeting currents as people came and went. There . . . just to the left of that last column. William's height lent him an advantage, his chestnut head standing like a flame among the sea of brown and gray surrounding him.

Even from here I could see he wasn't the polished barracks officer of last fall. His face bore a thin, haunted look; his mouth was a twisted line. His shoulders were stooped, as if he were in pain or braced for the blow poised to fall. Looking around, it was easy to pick out the veterans from the raw recruits. A year in the trenches had swept away the crisp pleats and shining brass, the swagger and the arrogant sense of superiority. What remained was a gritty, cynical, dead-eyed cadre of survivors, leading ranks of starry-eyed boys who dreamed of honor and glory as they marched off to avenge the dead of the *Lusitania*, the passenger liner sunk by the Germans three weeks previously off the Irish coast.

William spotted me, and I waved before plunging back into the descending current. The stairs were slick, and I nearly fell, only the press of people to all sides holding me upright as they carried me along with them. I broke free with a well-placed elbow and a poke of my umbrella, finding myself alone at the far edge of the platform.

William smiled then his gaze passed beyond me, the pleasure fading from his face. I turned in time to see my parents descending the stairs behind me, their expressions strained, their posture rigid and unapproachable as ever. Before they spotted me, I stepped back into the shadow of the column, letting them pass, unaware their wayward daughter was only feet away. I smelled Mama's perfume, Papa's cigars. It might have been my imagination but I could have sworn I caught a whiff of lemon oil and beeswax, and even the briny tang of Nanreath's sea air caught in the folds of her coat and his fur collar.

I ached for my home as I had not done since I'd walked away from my aunt's house in Simon's company.

William greeted them stiffly and the three stood in quiet conversation. I looked around, expecting Cynthia to appear just behind, perhaps with Hugh in tow. My brother, too, seemed to gaze up the stairs as if expecting his wife to wish him good-bye, but a small shake of Mama's head seemed to answer the unspoken question. He shrugged and glanced my way, his voice low, his words unmistakable.

Mama spun, her hands curling into her chest, as if protecting herself while Papa's icy stare nearly froze me breathless. Then William's eyes met mine, clear and insistent, and I wasn't afraid or ashamed.

I stepped free of the column. "Hello, Mama . . . Papa. I hope you're well."

I had seen those twin looks of disgust and disapproval many times, usually when we'd had to mingle uncomfortably with the unwashed masses; though never had they been aimed at me. I felt my insides curling, my confidence failing beneath the sneering, hardeyed condescension.

Papa turned his back. It felt like a knife to the chest, and I think I gasped out loud. A flash of pain crossed Mama's face and she reached a hand for me, so quickly that I wasn't sure I saw it, but at a clearing of Papa's throat, she firmed her narrow chin, dropped her arm back to her side, and followed Papa's lead.

"What are you doing?" William growled.

"We no longer know this young woman. Nor should you if you care for your reputation. Her indecency and lack of morals are all too clear just by looking at her."

I admit I wasn't dressed in the first stare of fashion. My skirt was heavily mended, my blouse washed so frequently that the fabric was worn nearly translucent and my coat had come secondhand from a market stall. But my hat was new, the violets in the band perfectly complimenting the blue of my scarf and the blue of my eyes.

"My reputation?" William's bark of laughter was ugly to hear. "There is a far more disgusting indecency going on across the Channel. Would you really shun Kitty for following her heart?"

"One's heart doesn't enter into it. Sentimental youth sees love in every charming smile and nervous flutter. Those smart enough to understand this realize there are greater considerations to take into account. Your sister was a fool and she will end as all fools do, lamenting her folly."

As always, my mouth ran away with me, my anger outstripping my tact. "Is this how you convinced William to marry Cynthia? By pointing out those greater considerations of duty, honor, and the family reputation?"

"Kitty . . ." William warned.

Papa brushed off my accusations with a gruff snort, but at least he was acknowledging I existed. "William knew his worth to the family and to himself and behaved accordingly. You behaved cheaply and thus were bought for a tinker's price."

I swallowed back the tears. I refused to let this man see me cry, but his words hurt like a physical pain. I wanted only to hurt as he hurt me. To cause pain equal to that inflicted, but as anyone knows who lashes out blindly in fury, it's not only the intended target that gets hurt.

"So where is Cynthia now? Shouldn't the perfect daughter-in-law be here to see her husband off to war? After all, it wouldn't be the first time she kissed a lover good-bye before battle—maybe not the last, either."

"Kitty, stop," William said quietly, but I was too far gone to halt the stream of anger.

"Perhaps she's not as dear a prize as you thought, Papa. Perhaps her affections can be bought for far less than you believed. Why don't you ask her when you see her next? Ask her who the lucky man is."

"Kitty, enough."

It was not my parents' sputtered fury but William's cold, clear, knifing voice that dragged me back to my senses. He stood vibrating like a coiled spring, white ringing his mouth, his eyes painfully bright. Hands clenched.

I wiped my face, drew a breath. "I'm . . . William, I'm so sorry. I have to go. I shouldn't have come. Take . . ." I met his gaze for one long, painful moment. "Take care of yourself."

I turned and ran, never getting to hug him good-bye or offer one last kiss. But I watched from the farthest corner of the upper platform as his train pulled out. The young soldiers who hadn't yet experienced the horrors of the front sang songs. As my nose ran and tears burned my eyes, I hummed along as they raised their voices in "The Homes They Leave Behind."

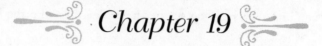# Chapter 19

*June 1941*

The ward scullery, an old anteroom converted and improved with a sink and a small burner ring when the house changed hands, still bore the orange and gold damask wallpaper of its heyday and a chandelier, which sparkled down on a metal table, two chairs, and an enormous ugly army-issue cabinet. The room was noisy, too close to Sister Murphy's gimlet eye for comfort, and the upper doors of the cabinet had a disconcerting habit of swinging open at odd times and catching one in the face. But the biscuit tin was always full, the kettle always at the boil, and the talk always juicy.

Coming off duty, Anna retired to fix a restorative cup of tea before climbing the stairs to her room and falling into bed, hopefully for six hours of dreamless sleep.

"Thought I'd find you here." Hugh dropped into a chair beside her. "I'd kill for a whiskey."

Anna poured him a cup of tea instead and set it at his elbow. "Has Lieutenant Forbes's wife arrived yet?"

"No. That's three times she's canceled." He stared into the mug, hands plowed to either side of his head. "Bloody bitch."

"It's hard to see someone you love suffering."

"You mean it's hard seeing them with half a face and no hands. Forbes shouldn't even be here, Anna. Why hasn't he been sent on to Basingstoke or the Queen Victoria?"

"He's due to be transferred any day. He's only here now because Southampton ran out of beds."

"Bloody fucking war." Hugh pulled a flask from his pocket, pouring a generous amount of whiskey into his tea. Swirled it around. So much for sobriety.

"Surely it will make a difference, now the Russians are on our side," Anna remarked, nibbling a shortbread biscuit.

"I'd like to say Hitler's bitten off more than he could chew, but who would have thought he'd manage as much as he has in such a short time? The damned little corporal in Berlin may look a clown, but he's no bloody fool. He'd not attack Stalin if he didn't think he'd beat him."

"It must do us *some* good. We're not alone in this fight anymore. That has to count for something."

"Meanwhile, the Lieutenant Forbeses of this war languish while the people who profess to love them shy away out of revulsion and fear." A hand fell to his thigh, kneading what was left of his leg. "We're damaged goods set out for the refuse heap."

"Stop it," Anna snapped. "Stop behaving as if your life is over because you've lost a damned leg. Look at Forbes. Is he complaining? You're perfectly capable of doing anything you put your mind to if you took two seconds to be grateful for what you have rather than always moaning about what you've lost."

He offered her a wry if somewhat apologetic smile. "You know, I wonder sometimes if the advantages of gaining a new cousin are worth the grief. Nobody else scolds me like you do. Well . . . no one but Mother, though her reprimands are far less vocal. She can make me feel guilty with no more than a lift of one perfectly plucked eyebrow and a sorrowful half smile."

A voice barked, "In there."

Speak of the devil. Anna looked up in time to catch Sister Murphy jabbing a finger in her direction and Lady Boxley offering a curt empress-like nod of gratitude.

She wore a pale green dress with a fashionable close-fitting hat to match. Her hair and makeup were impeccable, and she moved in that brisk yet patronizing way of all upper-class women, as if she had just swept out of her chauffeur-driven Bentley after a day of shopping at Harrods and taking tea at Brown's Hotel.

Hugh stood as his mother entered the room. Anna noted the way his hand clutched the table and the sudden leaping pulse in his jaw. No doubt, Her Ladyship expected Anna to hop to attention like a doorman or a housemaid with a submissive curtsy, but she was too tired and her feet hurt. She stayed where she was and spooned honey into her cup.

"Set an army of her ilk on the Germans, they wouldn't stand a chance," Lady Boxley grumbled after Sister Murphy departed.

Anna caught her gaze, and for a moment they shared a feeling of mutual accord. Then Her Ladyship ruined it with a cool, dismissive look down her regal nose as she addressed Hugh. "I'm glad to see you safe and sound, Hugh dear. I thought something must have happened when you didn't turn up at the station with the car."

"Blast! I'm sorry, Mother. It completely slipped my mind. I was working with Anna all morning and lost track of time."

"That's all right, my darling. I'm sure your business here was more important." She made a sweeping study of the cluttered scullery and the table set with tea and biscuits. "Overseeing repairs?"

"Helping on the wards, actually."

"Were you? What an odd thing to do." She offered him a thin smile and patted his cheek as if he were ten. "It's all right. Mr. Gough was at the station with the estate wagon. I was able to ride along with him . . . plus four cans of paint, a case of tools, five bags of wheat seed, and a small motor. A diverting if somewhat grubby journey." She sighed. "I'm sure after a hot bath and my medicine drops, I'll be right as rain again. Don't give it another thought."

"Truly, Mother. I am sorry. How was London?"

"Horrid. Traveling is always a travail, more so now when one can't count on any sort of timetable, and proper decorum seems to be a thing of the past. We were delayed over an hour, then our driver turned out to be some young snippet of a girl, and Claridge's is not up to its prewar standards. Everything is make-do and catch as catch can. I don't know why I continue to make the journey."

"Because you can't invite your friends down here any longer now the hospital's been taken over."

"Would you have me entertain them in my boudoir? Or the housekeeper's room, perhaps? We could huddle round a camp table and play at being on a picnic."

"It won't be forever."

"Won't it? By the time this war is over, will there be anything of the Nanreath Hall I remember worth returning to?" Lady Boxley's face narrowed, and she glanced round the scullery, no doubt sizing up the wreck the military had made of her home. Anna couldn't help but feel a pang of sympathy.

"Cheer up." Hugh gestured toward an empty stool. "Join us for a mug and you can tell us all the juicy gossip from the big bad metropolis."

Lady Boxley wrinkled her nose. "Not now, dear. I'm all done in, but perhaps you can help me upstairs."

"I can't just now, Mother. I've promised one of the lads to help him write a letter to his mum. He wants to assure her he's quite all right and comfortable here in hospital, and she needn't worry."

"And Nurse Trenowyth can't accomplish this complicated feat of secretarial work?"

Hugh's face bore a hard, mulish look. "It's more than that. You see, he's . . ."

"Trooper Murphy is dying, ma'am," Anna said, stepping in. "His mother works in an aircraft plant and can't make the trip to see him."

Her Ladyship seemed at a loss, her eyes still crackling, but an obvious shifting of gears going on behind the scenes. She relaxed into a gracious yet somehow condescending smile. "I know you're trying to help, Hugh my love, but isn't that why we've invited these lovely young women into our home? They're far more adept at handling these unfortunate situations than you could possibly be."

"Hugh's been invaluable, actually," Anna replied.

"Thank you, Miss Trenowyth, but I think I know what's best for my son. I won't have him overtaxing himself with unsavory hospital work. He's suffered enough death and sorrow to last a lifetime."

"But that's what makes him so wonderful. The men look up to him. They see how he's managed to move past his injuries and they take heart from that."

"Has he, though?" Lady Boxley argued. "Is that what you call nights spent carousing at the pub until he can barely see straight?"

"That's enough, Mother," Hugh muttered.

"Nightmares from which he wakes screaming and drenched in sweat?"

"Please."

"Constant pain and open sores as he adjusts to that ugly contraption he wears in place of a leg?"

"Mother! I said enough." Hugh was almost shouting. He swallowed back his anger, jaw jumping.

Lady Boxley pressed her lips together, her eyes hot and anguished. "Hugh needs to forget this war. Not have it relived every time he walks onto those wards." She drew herself up. "Hugh, please escort me upstairs. Now, if you will."

He offered Anna an agonized look as he pushed away from the table. "Of course. Tell Trooper Murphy I'm sorry, Anna."

She shouldn't. She really shouldn't, but Hugh's defeated, resentful attitude goaded her into action. "No. You tell him yourself."

"What?"

"You lost a leg, Hugh. You didn't lose your brain or your heart. You've got plenty left to contribute if only you'd see that instead of acting as if you're already dead and buried."

"How dare you talk to him that way?" Lady Boxley growled.

"I dare because no one else will, and if he continues to listen to you, he'll be no good to anyone—least of all himself."

Lady Boxley's face went the color of porridge, which only seemed to accentuate the blue tinge to her otherwise scarlet lips. Her body grew rigid with fury. "You rude girl. Not that I expect anything more from someone of your . . . repute."

"A bastard, you mean?"

"For God's sake, why can't you leave well enough alone?" Her Ladyship flattened a palm against her chest, as if she was having an attack of some sort, and her voice was harsh and wheezy. "Why can't you leave *us* alone?"

Her porridge look gave way to an even worse shade of gray-green like an old bruise, her eyes rolled up into her head, and she sagged like a deflated balloon to the floor.

Hugh caught her just before she hit the edge of the metal counter, but for a split second, he and Anna shared a look. And she truly thought he might let her fall.

The shingles case in Ward B says you punched Her Ladyship," Tilly exclaimed with fiendish delight. She sat on her bed reading her latest *Vogue* while Sophie worked on her mending. "Serves her right, the nasty cow."

Sophie wet her thread before spearing it through a needle. "I heard Lady Boxley suffered a stroke. I wouldn't be surprised. She's not been looking well for ages."

"Do you think you killed her, Anna?"

"No." Anna stood up. "But I *am* going to find out what's going on."

"How?"

"I'm going to see the MO. He'll know."

Anna ignored the look that passed between Tilly and Sophie, and departed her billet in search of Captain Matthews. She found him in his office.

"But no one's allowed in," his clerk informed her. "He's got Matron and Lord Melcombe in there with him."

"Perfect," Anna said, clasping her hands together as she pushed her way past and through the door to the strains of the poor harried clerk's protests.

She arrived in the midst of a heated conversation between the MO and Matron while Hugh perched on the arm of a chair looking unusually stern-faced and grim. Her heart sank into her shoes.

" . . . firmly advise against it," Captain Matthews said rather sharply. "She shouldn't be moved until we can be certain she's stabilized."

"But we're nearly at capacity. We've not the staff to accommodate Lady Boxley, and should the expected patients arrive, we'll be in a right muddle." Matron was on obvious edge. Her normally calm demeanor seemed strained under the potential addition of an aristocratic and demanding patient under her care.

"Anna?" Hugh said, catching sight of her. "What on earth are you doing here?"

She glanced uncomfortably at the circle of somber faces before gathering herself for the attack. "I've heard Lady Boxley's been taken ill. I want to do what I can to help." She wrung her hands before dropping them at her sides and meeting the incredulous gazes head-on. "It's my fault. I'd make it right if I could."

"Rubbish," Hugh shot back. "It's not your fault. Mother's had a bad ticker for ages. Her doctor's told her to take it easy, but she refuses to listen to him."

"Nevertheless . . ."

Captain Matthews folded his arms along his desk as he regarded her. "If you *are* the reason Her Ladyship collapsed, perhaps your presence might not be the most beneficial medicine."

"That may be, but she's"—Anna cast a helpless glance at Hugh— "she's my aunt. Family should be able to count on one another, shouldn't they?"

"Are you sure, Anna?" Hugh didn't look convinced. "She's not exactly an easy person to deal with at the best of times. She'll be grumpy as a poked badger."

"I'm sure." To Matron, she said, "Is it all right with you, ma'am? My half day is tomorrow anyway, and if I'm needed longer I'd make it up. Perhaps double shifts if things get busy."

"It does solve our problem perfectly." Captain Matthews leaned back in his chair, polishing his spectacles. "Lady Boxley can remain under her own roof, where she'll be most comfortable. Trenowyth here isn't on duty anyway, so she won't complicate the rota unnecessarily. And we keep it in the family. A winning situation all the way around?"

"I don't know . . ." Matron hedged. "What if Her Ladyship doesn't want her there? She might be family, but she's not exactly welcome, is she? Naught but the cold shoulder since she arrived."

"You let me worry about my mother," Hugh said. "She'll welcome Anna with open arms—or else."

"All right." Matron offered a grudging nod of approval. "But I hope you know what you're getting into, Trenowyth."

"Yes, ma'am. I hope so, too."

That afternoon, over Tilly's and Sophie's strident objections— "Are you certain you're not still suffering from that bump on the head?"—Anna reported for duty.

Passing through the gallery, she couldn't help but glance toward the painting of Lady Katherine with a feeling of growing comradeship, but it was the larger more prominent painting of Hugh's father, the late Lord Boxley, where she paused. He stood at awkward attention in the ceremonial uniform of the Royal Artillery, his auburn hair, a few shades darker than her own, slicked back from a slight widow's peak, his piercing blue eyes seeming to regard her with insolence, though a curve to his lips bore less the smirk of entitlement and more the good humor of a born prankster.

As Anna regarded him in the gray light of evening, something niggled at the back of her brain, a sense of not-quite-rightness. She tried to place her finger on what about the painting worried at her like a loose tooth, but the idea slipped and slid away from her each time she reached for it.

"Are you dawdling on purpose?" Hugh joined her in front of the painting. "I've told Mother you're coming and made her promise to keep her claws sheathed if she knows what's good for her."

"Your father was very handsome, wasn't he?"

"Every man looks handsome in a uniform. Apparently, dressing in ill-fitting khaki works as an aphrodisiac on any female between the ages of fourteen and ninety."

"Or RAF blue?" Anna slid him a sidelong look.

"My days of flashing a pair of wings and a devil-may-care attitude in order to lure the women are long over," Hugh said, seeming only half in jest. "Not that my ancient title and teetering fortunes have them lining up, either."

"That's a load of rubbish." Anna looked from the painting to Hugh and back again. That same odd dissonance struck at her like a note out of tune.

"Captain Matthews is finishing up," he said, and the sensation faded and was lost. "Mother will be waiting for you."

"With pistols loaded?"

"I've warned her to be on her best behavior." They walked together toward Lady Boxley's apartments. "You're right, you know. You *are* family. Mother needs to realize that."

"The same way she's realized you need to stop hiding from what happened to you in Norway and live again? Why don't you stand up to her, Hugh?"

"Fine words coming from you, cousin. Maybe I'll stop hiding from my past when you stop hiding from yours."

She had no time to frame a suitable response before they reached the door to his mother's rooms, bringing their conversation to an abrupt end.

Lady Boxley was in bed, propped against a banquette of pillows, her normally strong features uncharacteristically haggard, her fading blond hair hanging loose about her shoulders.

The MO snapped a black bag shut. "She's been dosed for the evening and shouldn't require more than peace and quiet. I'll be back in the morning." To Lady Boxley, he said, "Get some rest, my lady. I leave you in capable hands."

"Against my will." She speared Hugh with a hard stare.

He stiffened, but his smile remained fixed. "Easy, Mother. You'll work yourself into a froth and be no good for weeks."

"As if you cared a whit. I'm only the woman who gave you life, but does that matter a jot? Not at all. If you were trying to hasten my descent into the grave, you couldn't have picked a better way to do it."

He planted a quick kiss on her forehead. "I'm going out for the evening, but I'll check in on you tomorrow. Pistols and kippers at dawn?"

"I don't like you going out." Her lip jutted in an almost girlish pout. "It's not safe."

"The Germans have already blown us up once. What are the odds they target us again?"

"I'm not speaking of the Germans."

He laughed as if she'd made a joke, but Anna knew she was dead serious. As he left the room in a cloud of good humor, Lady Boxley's eyes met Anna's and once more they seemed to share a moment of understanding. She smoothed her hands down her apron as a way to calm her nerves before plowing into the situation. "Is there anything I can do for you, my lady?"

"I'd say you've done more than enough already." She worried at her bedspread. "And now Hugh's off gallivanting again. He's not well. He hasn't been since that horrid business in Norway."

"He drinks to forget, ma'am."

"And yet you want to force him to relive everything over and over with those men downstairs." She fluttered a hand to her heart, her face paling as she gasped and lay back. "Family, you call yourself.

The only family I have left is Hugh. All I've ever done has been for his sake. I won't let you hurt him."

"I'm sorry. I never meant for any of this to happen."

"No," Lady Boxley replied faintly through shallow breaths, "but your coming here started it all, didn't it?"

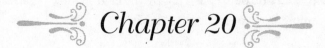

# Chapter 20

*August 1915*

It was hard to fathom a year had passed since the start of the war. We celebrated the anniversary with none of the patriotic fervor that marked the past twelve months. Instead, a small party gathered at Miss Ferndale-Branch's flat for a comfortable dinner followed by a string of dramatic readings, and now we lounged about her front room, drinking and chatting while someone banged away on a piano in the corner. Talk ranged from admiration for Rupert Brooke's collection of posthumously published poems to the new ballet being staged at Covent Garden and round to the horrors in Armenia. Those we'd lost seemed to hover close like fluttering moths, invisible and silent but never far from our thoughts, and despite the jollity of the evening, we were unable to overcome the growing sense our world was sliding toward some great abyss.

I sipped at my wine and tried not to worry over William, away at the front. His last letter spoke of his imminent return to the line. Written four days ago, the news within it was already old. He would be in the trenches by now. He could already be dead and I'd have no way of knowing. Papa would never write to tell me nor would he allow anyone in the household to communicate. He had cut me from the family like a cancer.

As if sensing the dark turn of my thoughts, Simon looked at me from across the room and we shared a secret smile. He stood in conversation with a young man in uniform. The two had been in deep discussion since dinner to the exclusion of almost everyone else, but now as if concluding a business transaction, he shook the man's hand and excused himself.

I thought he would join me in my corner. Instead he stepped into the middle of the room with a raise of his hand. "Quiet, everyone. Quiet. I have an announcement to make."

The conversation dulled to a murmur of curiosity as we looked to one another for answers before focusing on Simon. He held a drink in one hand, which he tossed back as if hoping for strength. Once more he caught and held my gaze, his dark eyes crackling. My stomach leaped and dove and I found myself clutching the arm of the chair, an icy cold splashing across my shoulders.

"I know you've all been wondering what took me so long to take the plunge, and frankly, I haven't a good answer. I suppose I just never thought it would last." He spoke to the room, but his eyes held mine. Attention shifted in my direction, and my cheeks warmed under the scrutiny. "But, well . . . I'm convinced we're in this for the long haul." He drew a breath, his smile widening to a grin. "So, you're looking at the newest officer in the Fourth Suffolk regiment. I report for training next week."

My smile froze in place. My nails dug into the chair. I nearly humiliated myself by throwing up all over Miss F-B's Turkey carpet as a crowd formed around him. The men shook his hand and offered encouragement and advice. The women kissed his cheek or enveloped him in weepy, perfumed hugs.

I tossed back the rest of my wine then went in search of whiskey to thaw the frozen ache blossoming beneath my breastbone. I said nothing of my blind, unthinking terror. I bit my tongue and smiled and laughed, though the knot in my stomach rose into my throat, cutting off my breath.

If Simon suspected my true feelings, he kept it to himself, though whenever the night drew us close, he squeezed my hand, touched my arm, caressed my hip, or kissed my cheek, as if to mollify me or as if he wished to claim me as his own for those weeks and months we would be apart.

That night we lay in bed listening to the rain, the darkness complete but for the red tip of his cigarette as he rested with an arm behind his head. I still felt the memory of his touch upon my sensitive skin, and tiny aftershocks of ecstasy pulsed outward from my center. I rolled over and up on one elbow, trailing my other hand over his chest and down over the rippled muscles of his abdomen. He hissed in response, his body reawakening. He chuckled, stabbing out his cigarette before rolling me over onto my back, settling himself between my legs. "You're shameless, my beautiful wanton."

I relished the weight of him, the press of his erection. It meant he was here. He was mine. He was safe. If this was all I would have of him, it would have to be enough. I cupped his cheeks between my fingers, feeling the stubble against my palms. "No. Merely frightened."

I sensed his frown in the shift of his body, as if he braced himself for an argument. "I know I should have told you first, but I was afraid you'd try to talk me out of it. Or worse, that you'd actually succeed."

"But why do you need to go?"

"Since Mr. Balázs was interned with the rest of the Boche in the spring, things here aren't going as I'd planned. I haven't had a commission in over a month, and well . . . this is an opportunity unlike any other. A chance to experience and record the fighting man's daily existence in a meaningful way. I've spoken to Mr. Weiss and he's interested in commissioning a series of war sketches. This could be the spark I need."

I couldn't argue with his reasoning. I'd seen him stooped over the household accounts late into the night, trying to make income and expense add up as he eked out our diminishing funds. I'd watched his dream of a studio fade as fewer jobs came his way. The space below our flat had been let for a millinery shop, the chatter of shopgirls and clacking sewing machines starting before dawn each day. In desperation, he'd even begun advertising as an art teacher, which I knew he hated and brought him splitting headaches along with a string of pimply, sighing schoolgirls looking to better themselves with watercolor lessons.

He paused as if gauging his words. "I need to let my parents know. I'll travel north tomorrow. Best do it in person rather than a letter."

It was as if someone doused me in cold water, my slick, heated desire congealed to a hard lump in the center of my chest. This time I was the one who chose my words carefully. "Let me come with you, Simon."

I felt rather than heard him sigh. "You know I can't."

I looked away toward the window and the summer storm. A rumble of thunder echoed off the buildings like the sea below Nanreath, like the cannons along the Somme.

"Look at me, Kitty."

I rolled over. He caught my arms, his body hard along the length of me. I felt the tension in his muscles, the thrum of it vibrating between us. His eyes blazed, the ferocity of his words as heated as my blood. "Whatever happens, Kitty Trenowyth, know that I love you more than life itself. You . . . and none other. No matter what happens, you must believe that. Tell me you believe me."

"I believe you." Tears pricked my eyes as his mouth found mine. I lifted my hips, sheathing him inside me. Our joining sweeter and more urgent for the shadows growing ever nearer.

I woke early the next morning after a restless sleep of dark dreams, still feeling uneasy and slightly restless. As usual, Simon was up first. I lay in bed and listened as he fixed a pot of tea and boiled eggs for our breakfast in the tiny kitchen. He whistled the refrain of "Send Me Away with a Smile," a cheerful tune, as if now that he'd made his decision to become a soldier, he felt no fear, only excitement at doing his bit.

He poked his head round the door. "Get a move on, sleepyhead, or we'll be late."

I rolled up and stuffed my feet into my slippers. "You've changed your mind about Lincoln? I can go with you?"

His face fell. "You know I can't do that, Kitty." Then a corner of his mouth curved up in a coaxing smile. "But if you hurry, I have a surprise for you, and believe me, a much better one than lukewarm tea and dry cake in the edifying presence of my parents."

Rather than eliminating my sense of ill-usage, my annoyance grew as I dressed and ate. I knew I shouldn't pout, but as he chatted about his new regiment and the list of supplies he would need to lay in, and the worry over what his family would say, I felt as if he'd already moved on to a new adventure where I could not follow, even with all my newfound independence.

I gave no sign of my continued distress, but I'm sure he sensed it. We were too close not to feel each other's moods, and there was a strain to his gaiety and a force to his smile. He tried to talk to me during the cab ride—a rare treat after an unprofitable year—but I turned away and did not answer, and he soon gave up and left me alone.

We were let out in front of a photographer's studio in Grosvenor Road. From an open door emanated the sour chemical smells of citric acid and ammonium. The window held a melancholy collection of photographs; mostly men in uniform, but there were matrons in wide hats decorated with scarves or ornamental flowers, and children holding bunches of violets or posed with puppies in a basket.

We passed inside where the odors were almost overpowering, and a pudgy man in shirtsleeves and vest stood behind a long, wooden counter. He smelled of spirits and his appreciative gaze wandered over me a bit too freely as he oozed salesmanship.

"I want a portrait, Kitty," Simon explained softly. "I want a picture of you to take with me."

He touched my face, and this time I let him kiss me. My hand touched his chest above his heart. I was sure I could feel it beating beneath my open palm.

"When the battle is at its worst, I need something to prove to me you're real, that this precious life we've built together still remains." Once again his voice held an almost piteous note and his smile was wistful, as if he'd already begun cutting the threads that wove our lives together.

When Simon departed for his regiment, he took with him a small silver locket bearing a picture of me, stiff with nerves and unhappiness, tucked inside.

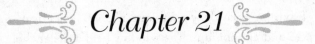

# Chapter 21

*June 1941*

Lady Boxley's lunch consisted of a fillet of sole, new potatoes, and whipped carrots. Anna eyed it longingly as it grew cold on its tray. It certainly beat the tinned ham smeared between two slices of National Loaf she'd eaten two hours ago with her milkless tea.

Her Ladyship had been resting since just after breakfast, and Anna, albeit somewhat selfishly, had chosen to let sleeping ladies lie. She'd expected Hugh to stop in, but the morning and then the afternoon had passed with no sign of him.

While Anna preferred the quiet over the constant carping and demands of her patient, it made it hard to stay awake after only a few hours of stolen sleep on a beautiful if uncomfortable satin divan in the dressing room. In desperation, she'd taken to leafing through the magazines and books on the nightstand when she came across a large leather-bound photograph album lying open at the bottom of the pile. A small shock of excitement curled through her seeing

Nanreath's past—her family's past—encapsulated in pages and pages of sepia-toned moments.

Each photograph had been lovingly placed and captioned, though the glue at each edge was loosening. Holidays, weddings, christenings, and family get-togethers; Anna's gaze traveled over the faces of these affluent, fashionably dressed people she'd never known, unable to stop imagining herself growing up among them.

Hugh from chubby, towheaded infancy to dashing adulthood. Stiff studio portraits of the late Lord Boxley, though only two of husband and wife together: a wedding shot as the two of them left the church and a painfully awkward-looking picture of the new young family shortly after Hugh's birth.

Lady Katherine appeared in more than a few of the photographs. Taller than most of the women, she seemed to stoop to compensate for her height while her round almost childish face was strengthened by a firm chin, a straight, thin nose, and a pair of flashing eyes that stared down the camera like a challenge. Laughing, carefree. No sign of the shadows soon to overtake her and her family. Then she simply disappeared. No more pictures. No more references to her in the penciled captions. From the fall of 1913 onward, Lady Katherine ceased to exist.

Her absence seemed barely to be marked. Instead, the pages were taken up with images of a young and pretty Lady Boxley, always one amid a group in various poses in front of various landscapes from Italian villas to Paris cafés to the familiar Nanreath gardens. Every photo carefully captioned.

Then, on a separate page, Anna came across two or three smaller photos of Lady Boxley and a gentleman standing at the same rocky cliff ruins she'd seen in her mother's sketches. A line of sea lay behind them. His blond hair was tousled by the wind as he smiled for the camera. She looked up at him, her gaze touchingly vulnerable and unsure. But unlike all the others, these pictures weren't captioned. She cast a swift glance toward Lady Boxley before picking the glue from the edge and pulling it away from the page. There on the back in faint pencil—*Eddie and me at the cliff ruins.* And more interesting, another photo lay hidden behind it.

"What have you got there?"

The sharp, barking question startled Anna into releasing the album. It slid onto the floor, the dried crumbling glue giving way to scatter pictures across the carpet.

Lady Boxley uttered a small shriek. "Clumsy girl. What are you doing?"

Anna dropped to her knees, raking almost everything back into the album. "I thought you were asleep."

"Waiting for the perfect time to poke through my personal belongings?"

"The album was open on the table, my lady. I hardly had to snoop to find it."

"So because I didn't have it locked away, it gives you the right to pry where you don't belong?"

Dipping her hand in and out of her apron pocket, Anna resumed her seat, replacing the album on the table. "Why are you so determined to push me away, my lady?"

Her Ladyship scooted herself up against the bolster. Small and frail within the starched white expanse of her bed, she was far less intimidating, but while she might have been physically weak, her manner maintained its razor edge. "Why are you so determined to shove your way in where you're not wanted?"

"Is it wrong for me to want to learn more about my mother and her family?"

"Of course not, but you'll not learn anything of value from

Minnie Smith. She's soft in the head, has been for years. Her drunken sot of a father is even worse." Her breathing grew rough and Anna poured a glass of water from the pitcher on the lunch tray, which she helped her sip. Lady Boxley lay back against the pillows, her face drawn and hollow with exhaustion.

"How did you know I'd gone to see Miss Smith?" Anna asked.

"Not much happens around here that I don't learn sooner or later, and Kitty's natural daughter taking tea with the village biddies makes for scintillating talk." Lady Boxley ran a hand over her bedspread, her rings large on her thin, bony fingers. "Silas Smith was a gardener here on the estate when I first arrived as William's bride. A nice enough chap, whiz with flowers, but that changed after his sons were killed in action. Four within the same year. Shattered the man. His daughter, too. Neither of them recovered."

"That's horrible."

"But all too common when brothers joined the same regiment. William's father offered them a lifetime gift of the house at the harbor when work grew too much for him. An excessive sentimental bequest, he could ill afford it as it turned out. I suppose he did it out of sympathy. William had only just been invalided out and sent home to us."

"That was the summer of 1916."

"Yes, August. A horrible hot month. No respite to be found. Not even here at Nanreath."

"Minnie told me Lady Katherine traveled down here from London when she had word your husband was ill, but they wouldn't let her see him."

Lady Boxley's face stiffened. "None were allowed to see him."

"Is that what you told her when you met her at Mrs. Vinter's?"

She barely blinked at the accusation before recovering her usual aplomb. "If you must know, I told her she was a fool to run off with

Halliday and a fool to think she'd be welcomed home again once he was gone."

*Forgive my love.* "Do you know what happened, Lady Boxley? Why my father left her when he knew she was pregnant?"

"Left her? No, my dear. You have it all wrong. Simon Halliday didn't leave her. She left him."

The MO interrupted their conversation to listen to Lady Boxley's heart, and their moment's intimacy ended in whining complaints and peevish scolding, which lasted the rest of the day. The following morning Anna rose kink-necked and sore from her makeshift bed but twice as determined to question her further. Her chance came over Lady Boxley's breakfast of unsweetened porridge, a piece of plain toast, and prune juice.

"This mockery of a meal is that horrid excuse of a doctor's fault, isn't it? If he had his way, I'd be living on boiled parsnips the rest of my life."

"Boiled parsnips aren't so bad. Have you tried the kitchen's carrot and pigeon surprise?"

"Death would be preferable."

Anna fixed a fresh pot of tea on the spirit burner in Lady Boxley's sitting room and brought her a fresh cup along with a plate of Cadbury's milk chocolate biscuits. "Don't tell Captain Matthews, but this should make you feel a little better. Compliments of Mrs. Willits. She sent them to me in my last care package."

"A friend of yours?"

"A neighbor in London. I believe she traded an onion she'd won in a raffle for two packages of chocolate and sent one on to me."

Lady Boxley eyed them askance before shoving her breakfast tray aside in favor of tea and sweets. "Thank you."

Anna drew up a chair. "When we talked yesterday, you mentioned that Lady Katherine left Simon Halliday."

"Ah, so that's your ploy, is it? Chocolate for information."

Anna offered her the plate. "Is it working?"

Lady Boxley glowered over the proffered biscuits before taking two and settling back with a prim smile of triumph. "You're an impudent little baggage, aren't you?"

"Just determined, ma'am."

"There's little enough to say. Kitty kicked him to the curbstone—as she should have done from the first. Said it hadn't worked out. I could have told her it wouldn't. He smiled too much. A sure sign of an unstable temperament."

"She didn't say why she left him?"

"Why, you ask?" Lady Boxley fiddled with the buttons on her bed jacket. "Not that I recall, but I didn't much care. We hadn't seen each other in more than three years and we'd never been close. It was all over and done with, the damage complete." She eyed Anna up and down. "Kitty was round as a Christmas ham. There, now you have the whole sorry tale. Satisfied?"

Not even close, but what could she do? It was obvious Lady Boxley couldn't tell her anything more.

"Bring me a mirror," she demanded, growing weary and waspish. "I'm sure I look a fright."

Anna retrieved a silver-backed hand mirror from the dressing table.

"Dear God, it's worse than I thought." She turned her face side to side, slid a hand up her sagging cheekbones. Regarded her gray roots with a frown before tossing the mirror aside, lying back with a dramatic sigh. "I look like a haggard crone with both feet dangling over the grave."

"You've been ill."

"That's no excuse for lack of grooming. If only Mademoiselle Rousseau were here to color my hair. Or that lovely girl at the Max Factor counter at Harrods. No wonder Hugh won't come near me. It's like being in the presence of a corpse."

"I can't do anything about the color, ma'am, but I can arrange your hair and do your makeup if you like."

Lady Boxley's expression remained frosty, but Anna noted the gleam in her eyes. "Let's start with a bath. That should make you feel human again." Without waiting for approval, she passed into the adjoining bath. Despite its size and outdated grandeur, the room was chilly, the paint faded, and the tiles chipped along the base of the enormous claw-foot tub. But the hot water was ample, and there were jars of bath salts in a cupboard. Soon steam rose from jasmine-scented water.

"Come along. A good scrub will make everything better," Anna said as she helped Lady Boxley out of her dressing gown and hunted out towels, thin with use and rough as sandpaper, which she placed alongside the tub.

"I'm perfectly capable, Miss Trenowyth."

"Of course you are. So I'll see to my mending while you soak. When you're finished, give a shout. We can get you settled in a fresh nightgown, and then I'll see to your hair and face."

For the next half hour, Anna knitted and listened through the old cathedral radio's static to Tommy Handley bumble his way around the Ministry of Aggravation and Mysteries accompanied by Mrs. Tickle and Funf.

"What's that horrid noise?" Lady Boxley appeared from the bath pink, damp, and jasmine scented.

"*ITMA*, ma'am," Anna said, snapping off the radio. "Thought we could use a chuckle." She gathered up what she needed from the dressing table and set it all out on a tray beside the bed. "This might hurt. You've more than a few tangles back here."

"I have a scalp like iron."

Anna used slow, easy strokes, only tugging when she had to in order to free a rat's nest or two. Lady Boxley held her head still, her shoulders slowly relaxing, her body going pliant. "Did Hugh happen to stop by while I was bathing?"

Anna could sense the effort it took for Lady Boxley to unbend enough to ask this. She almost felt sorry for her—almost. "No, ma'am. I haven't seen him since the day before yesterday."

Lady Boxley sniffed. "He claimed he had a meeting in Newquay. Does he think I'm stupid? Meeting, my foot. I know where he goes. One of these days not even that old swaybacked nag of his will save him from breaking his neck."

Hair dried and brushed out, Anna worked a row of pins across the back. "He needs something besides alcohol to take his mind off the fact that his mates are all away fighting while he's trapped at home."

"You mean safe at home."

First, Anna rolled one side up and over the pins, securing it in place. Then the other. "I don't think he sees it that way, ma'am. Prue used to say, 'Idle hands are the devil's workshop.'" Then taking a section at a time, she rolled the back up and over the pins and sprayed the whole with lacquer. "There. How's that?"

Lady Boxley checked the arrangement in the mirror. "Adequate for the boudoir, though you'd not catch me in public looking this way."

"Now your face?"

Lady Boxley nodded, quite happy now to let Anna set up the tray of cosmetics beside her and begin applying foundation and powder. She seemed to relax under the quiet hypnosis of the hairdresser's

confessional, her eyes drooping, her face losing its taut almost squir-
relish nervousness. "It took every ounce of determination I had to
keep this place going after my husband's death, Miss Trenowyth.
The last earl was no help. He was a wreck after William died. He
let his business managers and lawyers nearly run things into the
ground. Lady Melcombe couldn't rein him in. She was just as bad.
Spent as if there was no end to the wealth."

Scandal, debt, death; that was what Sophie had said. Despite
their callousness, Anna couldn't help but feel sympathy for her
mother's parents. They must have felt as if their world were crumbling from under their feet, the privilege and power they had always
thought was theirs by divine right stripped away within a few tumultuous years.

"It was left to me to keep things from coming apart," Lady
Boxley continued almost peevishly. "No one believed a woman had
any chance of managing the reins, much less recovering from such
staggering losses, but I did it—for Hugh. All for Hugh. He won't
be handed an empty title with nothing to show for it but debt. Not
if I can help it."

"If it's for Hugh, perhaps now is a good time to hand it off to
him. He could use an occupation of some kind to keep him busy,
and you would gain some much-needed rest," Anna offered in a
casual, offhand way.

"My heart's strong as ever despite what that detestable doctor
says. If Hugh wants an occupation, he should try marriage and fa-
therhood. Both would give him plenty to fill his time."

"Is that his only choice?"

"Hugh's the last in a line of belted earls stretching back to the
time of Queen Anne, not some collier's brat with dirt under his
nails and a puffed-up sense of himself." She paused, as if awaiting

Anna's response. Disappointed when she didn't rise to the bait. "The world's run mad."

Anna positioned Lady Boxley's head while she carefully applied eyebrow pencil and shadow.

"It was the same way last time around, you know. The war changed everything. It turned our lives upside-down until no one knew their proper place, and proprieties flew out the window. Life seemed so fleeting, one felt every moment needed to be seized in both hands."

Dry rouge, powder again, then mascara. Anna worked quickly and deftly, choosing a lipstick in a lovely shade of cochinelle.

"You young people think the world will change to suit you." Once more Lady Boxley regarded herself in the mirror, tilting her head to all angles, pursing and smiling at her reflection. Gone was the washed-out sickbed pallor and the gray hollows of cheek and eyes. Replaced by the Max Factor glow of false health that accented the sleek bones and aristocratic planes of her face. "It won't, though. It will grind you up and spit you out." She set the mirror aside, clearing her throat as her expression faded to its usual stark reserve. "I'm tired now and would prefer to rest. Please leave. I'll be perfectly fine without you hovering."

"I'm supposed to stay in case you need anything."

"Then stay somewhere else."

"Yes, ma'am." Anna drew the curtains closed against the late-afternoon glare and switched off the light. "I'll be in the sitting room if you need me."

"I can assure you that you won't be needed." As Anna began to close the door, Lady Boxley cleared her throat. "But you may leave the door ajar . . . if you like."

Anna smiled.

A week later Captain Matthews proclaimed Lady Boxley well enough to leave her rooms.

"As long as you stay away from rich foods, tobacco, alcohol, and caffeine, take your medications, and refrain from undue stresses and activity, there's no reason you shouldn't outlive us all."

"Living like that, I'd rather be dead." She regarded Anna with the lift of one carefully plucked eyebrow. "I suppose you'll abandon me now happily enough."

"My duty lies with the men downstairs, my lady. I did this as a favor."

"For Hugh?"

"No, ma'am. For you."

Lady Boxley looked away for a moment, her hands running along the seam of her coverlet. "And what am I supposed to do, starving, drugged, and bored? Who's going to help me with the crossword or sort my correspondence and reply to all those dull charity ladies' requests for assistance or fix my tea the way I like it?"

"I'm leaving this wing of the house not the whole country. I can stop in from time to time."

"See that you do," Lady Boxley ordered, already dismissing her from her thoughts as she began reading the newspaper.

Anna departed Lady Boxley's room for the clockwork chaos of the hospital where she would find the comforting routine of bedpans, daily rounds, and endless scrubbing a relief after the minefield of the last week.

She passed through the gallery, the transition from the family's opulent wing to her plain attic billet like stepping through a door into another world. The elegant, beeswax-scented sanctuary of heavy polished furniture and fresh-cut flowers fading into scratched and dented walls covered in ugly institutional green, the incessant noise from the wards, and the constant odor of carbolic and rubbing alcohol.

"There you are. Sophie said I might find you up here." Tony climbed the stairs toward her.

"Don't tell me you're depositing Hugh. Even he can't be soused this early in the day."

"Actually, I had a free afternoon and thought I'd ride over. Wasn't sure when I'd get another chance."

"I don't know. I really should report to Matron."

"It can't wait for a few hours? She'll never know you're missing. If anyone wonders, they'll think you're still encamped with Lady Boxley." He gave her a wounded look. "You don't want to turn down a chap on what might be his last free afternoon for ages."

She relented with a laugh. "All right. I'll get my sweater and meet you out front." She paused. "No, wait. I'll meet you at the side door by the stairs to the kitchens. Less conspicuous."

"A devious mind and a pretty face. A potent combination."

Outside, a swirling salty breeze kept the afternoon sun from being too warm, and the lawn stretched green away to a line of trees. "I have wheels . . . of a kind," Tony said. "I borrowed a friend's motorbike. Care to ride pillory? We could drive to Newquay for tea."

She eyed the battered motorbike with trepidation. "I have a better idea. I've always wanted to see the cliff ruins. Now would be the perfect time."

He cocked her a curious look. "What do you know about the ruins?"

"Nothing yet." She took his arm.

"It's a rough hike. Sure you're up for it?"

She turned to look back at the house, the tall windows gleaming

in the sun. She almost felt as if the eyes of Lady Boxley were upon
her as she set out across the grass. "Definitely."

At the edge of the lawn, they turned onto a narrow rutted
footpath leading away through a thick wood. As they neared the
cliffs, the path grew rockier, the trees giving way to wide, sweeping
moorland punctuated by enormous wooden poles sticking up into
the air and crisscrossed with deep roughly dug trenches to keep
enemy aircraft from landing. The sea shone like silver off to a cloud-
hung horizon. Seabirds floated on the breeze, lifting up above the
cliffs before diving like Stukas to the sea and the swirling tide pools
below.

Anna had never walked this way in her hikes. The village lay to
the south, where the roads were paved and the way easy; this constant clamber over rocks as the wind shoved with invisible hands
and tore one's breath away was a battle for every step. Still, she
didn't tire as she might have just six months ago. The endless hours
of hard physical labor and the miles of passages and stairs she'd
walked since coming to Nanreath Hall had toughened injured
muscles and restored her strength. They crossed a deep gully lined
with broken shale that slid under her feet, turning her ankles. As
she hitched herself up out of a ditch, she froze, her heart lifting into
her throat with delight.

"Voilà." He presented the cliff ruins with a sweep of his arm.

"They're amazing." She hurried toward the ancient stone and
earthworks hanging precariously out over the edge of the cliff face.
Steps cut from the ground led down and then back up where a circle
of mossy blocks rose into the air in a crumbling tower. Beyond it,
more steps, these carved smooth by the wind and slick with spray,
climbed even higher toward an empty window arch and a second
stone floor. "It's just like my mother's drawings."

After the initial awe of discovery wore off, she saw the more recent evidence of habitation. Stones sprinkled with graffiti, an empty wine bottle tossed in the high grass, cigarette butts, even a few bits of charred wood from some long-ago prewar bonfire. "Rumor has it that all the young couples in the neighborhood come here when they want some privacy," she commented.

A corner of Tony's mouth broke upward, his brows lifted in cocky amusement. "Is that why you brought me? I'm flattered."

Anna flushed. "Forget I mentioned it."

"I don't know. That's a pretty hard thing for a chap to forget." His smile curved mischievously. "It's not every day I'm pursued by a beautiful woman."

"That's not what I hear."

The mischief in his gaze deepened. "Then you're listening to the wrong people, my dear."

He stepped toward her, his intention to kiss her obvious. She wavered, trapped between wanting to meet his advance and give herself up to his affection and run as far and as fast as she could back the way she'd come. Taking the coward's way out, she flung herself away with a hard swallow and made for the ruins, nearly running the last few feet. Tony called out, but she ignored his cautions as she slipped and slithered down the earthen steps and back up again into the outer circle of stones.

"Anna, wait!"

Unheeding, she climbed the worn stone stairs toward the archway, the wind tearing at the pins in her hair, snapping at her skirt.

"Careful," he called out. "It's unsteady the higher you go. Bits are always falling off."

"I want to see the view," she shouted back.

He didn't chase after her but stood at the wall's base, shielding his eyes with his hands as he watched her climb. "It's water. Same as down here."

"Coming up?" By now she was about twenty feet above him, the stair twisting back upon itself as it rose within the toppled tower with naught but sky overhead.

"I think I like my head attached to my neck, thank you very much."

She stepped onto the upper floor and right up to the open edge where the wind curled around the crumbling tower wall to snatch her breath away. A flight of Beaufort bombers roared overhead and out to sea where a plume of ominous smoke rose from the horizon. She watched them grow smaller and smaller until they were naught but dots, no bigger than the birds. She lifted her face to the sun, dizzy as the sky wheeled above her, her stomach rising like a balloon into her chest.

"Anna!" Tony shouted.

She stumbled, curling her fingers into the chinks of the balustrade as the wind slammed her back against the archway. She froze as a piece of the floor tipped upward sending a scattering of broken rocks shearing from the tower to drop with a smash of pebbles down the cliffs.

"Sit down very slowly," Tony said in a calming voice. "And don't move—don't even breathe—until I get there."

Anna backed from the edge in small, shuffling steps until she came up against the far wall of the tower then inched her bottom down, reclining against the base, her knees drawn up, heart thrashing. A moment later Tony was kneeling beside her. Sweat beaded his forehead. He wiped it with his sleeve. "Are you mad? I just lost five years off my life watching those rocks give way with you standing there."

"My life just flashed before my eyes. Sad to say, it wasn't very interesting."

Tony's shoulder pressed along her arm, his hip neighboring hers.

This time when he sought her hand, she took it. "Let's just rest for a minute before we descend, okay?" he said, still trying to catch his breath.

She risked a sheepish smile. "I'm sorry, Tony."

Would he recognize her apology for what it was? Their eyes met. She noted the amber flecks surrounding his irises, the thickness of his lashes. She felt the tension stringing his muscles everywhere their bodies touched. Anticipation mixed with confusion.

Then he put his arm around her with a smile and the moment dissolved. "You *should* be sorry. If I died of a heart attack, it would have been your fault. I'd like to have seen you try to explain that to my commander."

She leaned her head on his shoulder. "A brave pilot like you scared of heights? I don't believe it."

"Not for myself, mind you, but when I see someone I care about tipping precariously toward a gruesome death, I get a bit squeamish. Now, had you been surrounded by spiders, I might have left you to your fate."

"Spiders?"

He shrugged. "Blame my sister for that personal phobia. What about you?"

"Hmm . . . it would have to be Kewpie dolls. Something about those sweet little faces and those dewy eyes." She shuddered.

He laughed. "I'll bear it in mind if I ever take you to a fair."

"Funny. All this death and destruction around us, and it's spiders and dolls that give us the collywobbles."

"Maybe it's better that way. One can't be frightened all the time." He leaned his head back against the stones, lifting his eyes to the wind-riven clouds. His arm felt nice draped around her shoulder. The breeze was chilly despite the sun and her light jumper wasn't enough to keep her warm. His heat was welcome, his strength reas-

suring. Then she remembered the flight of Beauforts and the smear
of black on the horizon. Personal strength counted for nothing.
Stronger, more skilled men died every day in this war. One could
only take each day as it was offered and reach no further. Planning
for the future only invited heartbreak. And loving someone was out
of the question. She'd suffered enough pain for a hundred lifetimes.

She followed his gaze, wondering what he saw in the ragged
contrails. "Are you ever frightened? I mean when you're up there."

He took a moment to answer, and when he spoke it was barely
audible. "All the time."

There was another long pause. His breathing seemed to shallow
and the hand gripping his cap tightened. "I think I'd be more worried if I wasn't frightened because it would mean I'd stopped feeling
anything. And that would be a far greater tragedy."

The sound of explosions traveled over the sea, echoing against
the cliffs like thunder. The smear of darkness at the horizon thickened and boiled, flames licking red and curling as serpent's tongues.
Like the rocks under her feet crumbling and falling away, Anna
felt cracks fissuring the hard shell surrounding her heart. The pain
made her gasp. She began to shake. Memories flashed like lightning
or the red-hot burst of an explosion across her mind.

"Anna? Are you all right?"

She nodded, drawn back by the sound of his voice, the strength
of his clasp, the warmth of his body beside hers. She scrubbed her
face until her cheeks tingled before curling her knees to her chest,
arms wrapped round them. Stared dead-eyed out to sea.

"Do you want to tell me?" Tony asked.

"Not really."

He gave a half smile and a sheepish shrug. "Numbing yourself
to life isn't the answer, Anna. And it may be self-serving, but I want
you feeling everything to its fullest."

"Oh?"

He leaned closer and before she knew it, he kissed her forehead. Then his mouth moved from her hair to her cheek to her lips. Gentle, almost shy at first, until she responded, then the heat between them increased until she felt it down her spine, between her breasts, along her inner thighs.

"Oh," she repeated breathlessly.

Anna ached to touch him and be touched. To find solace in his hand on her waist, her rib cage, the line of her back. She laid a hand on his chest, which rose and fell with quick, shallow breaths. He murmured into her hair. She knew this was wrong, but for so long she'd felt nothing, that even guilt was a welcome emotion. Emotion and sensation merged into a maelstrom of experience from the tingling gooseflesh lifting the hairs on her arms to the damp ache between her legs to the slam of her heart against her rib cage. He was the cause. She couldn't let him go. She wouldn't make him stop.

He came to his senses when she could not. "Not that I wouldn't happily finish what I've started, but this is neither the time nor the place." His eyes burned dark, lips swollen from her kisses, shirttails hanging loose, and his dark hair adorably stuck up like a rooster's comb.

She dropped her eyes, all too conscious now of what she'd almost done. How far she might have traveled down that path if he hadn't stopped them. Like mother, like daughter? And look how that had turned out.

As if reading her thoughts, Tony caressed her cheek before tipping her chin to meet his gaze. "You're not Lady Katherine. I'm not Simon Halliday. And we're not doomed to repeat their mistakes, Anna."

She nodded, escaping the intensity of his stare by following the track of a lone seabird rising and falling on the warm sea drafts.

He seemed to accept her silence. He lit a cigarette, drawing a soothing pull into his lungs. "I wish . . ." She closed her eyes, her voice trailing off in a sigh, unable to put her dreams into words.

"What do you wish?"

She inhaled the crisp air and let it out on a breath, sidling away as if that might protect her from this new and almost painful awareness of him. "It doesn't matter. Wishes are for birthdays and evening stars." She shivered in the lengthening shadows. The day's magic faded with the sun. "I have to get back." She rose on shaky legs to begin the slow, careful climb down from their perch. She had only made it a few steps before ducking back behind the arch.

"What's wrong?" Tony asked.

"It's Tilly and Hugh," she whispered. "And she's crying."

# Chapter 22

*January 1916*

The New Year dawned with no end to the war in sight. Every day brought new stories of tragedy until we became numb to the pain. Life went on, but it had lost its optimistic exuberance. We endured because we must, but no one was immune from the shroud of sorrow hanging over the world. Of those I was closest to, Miss Ferndale-Branch lost a brother to chlorine gas, Jane's merchant seaman went down with his ship in the Med, and Agnes's new husband—she gave up her dreams of a duke to settle for a corporal in the Royal Irish fusiliers—succumbed to trench fever. Our tragedies did not set us apart in any way. Color seemed to seep from the world, leaving only dreary shades of widow's weed black.

William had been posted to the French frontier near Lille while Simon continued in training at Grimsby with the Fourth Suffolk, though he anticipated a transfer to the front by spring. It got so I dreaded the step of the postman on the stair and shrank from telegram boys as if they carried plague.

Money grew tight. I survived on beans and toast, tinned beef, and gallons of Horlicks. Simon sent what he could, and once a letter from William contained a five-pound note. I hated to accept his charity, but the landlord was blustering and I decided a roof over my head meant more to me than my tattered pride.

Then Miss F-B decided to join up as a Red Cross nurse. I pondered whether to accompany her into the service, or perhaps take a job in a munitions factory, as so many women my age were doing, but in the end my health was too fragile. Twice, I had been brought low with a recurrence of scarlet fever, which the chilly damp only seemed to exacerbate. I would be little use to either endeavor, saddled as I was with weak lungs and a fluttering heart.

I laid aside my studies at the Byam in my determination to find a new position. I could not crawl home a second time. That part of my life was a closed door.

A man on the corner bought women's hair for wigs. His sign said eight shillings a head. One evening after my bath, I stared hard at myself in the mirror, my red-gold curls tumbling glossy almost to my waist. Could I go through with such a desecration? What would Simon say when he saw me?

As winter closed in and the days grew darker, shorter, and colder, my desperation increased. I slowed each afternoon before that sign, my pockets all but empty. Before I had to make a decision, Jane offered to introduce me to her employer. Madame Duchamp owned a fashionable dress shop in Soho and was on the prowl for new girls to act as mannequins. While I didn't relish the idea of parading about in front of strangers, my continuing work as an artist's model gave me some experience of being on display. Besides, my options were shrinking to nothing.

The morning of my interview dawned wet and cold with a spitting sleet that iced the pavement and made walking perilous, but

I couldn't waste precious coins on the bus. Thus, by the time I arrived, my dress was drenched and muddy from being splashed by a passing tram, and the wind and rain had frizzed my already wildly curly hair.

"I'm surprised you came. I wagered Agnes a half crown you'd shy off." Jane eyed me doubtfully from beneath a drippy umbrella. I couldn't blame her. I was hardly the stuff of fashionable elegance.

I tried straightening my wilted hat. A trickle of cold water slithered under my collar and down my back. "I can't afford to be timid. If I don't find something soon, I'll be out on the street and out of ideas."

Jane led me, not toward the main entrance, but through an alley to a set of stone steps leading down to a wooden door and then into a narrow passageway. "Be sure to talk to her in that posh way of yours. She'll hire you on the spot. She's always looking for girls with a bit of polish."

"I hope you're right." I followed Jane and the clamor of voices through an archway into an enormous set of dressing rooms.

After a quick neatening of my hair and a rather ineffective brush at my muddy skirts, I followed Jane through to a spacious office papered in cream and green with thick Turkey carpets on the floor and heavy damask draperies at the window. A desk took up one wall. A large worktable took up the other. Bolts of colorful fabrics leaned in corners or were spread out on a wide chintz-covered couch as if recently used. A comfortable set of chairs flanked a cheerful pink marble fireplace.

"Good luck," Jane whispered as she closed the door behind her.

I threw a strained smile over my shoulder as I smoothed my hands down my skirts and tucked a stray curl behind my ear. Elegance may have been beyond me at this point, but I could at least strive for presentable.

I had not noticed the small side door papered to blend into the surrounding wall until it swung open and Madame Duchamp entered as if making her entrance upon the stage. She wore a stylish outfit of brown and gold and her blond hair was perfectly waved and dressed. A pair of wire spectacles hung on a chain around her neck. She waved me to a chair.

I ignored my squirming stomach and faced her boldly, trying to meet her austere elegance with a measure of calm. She was my last hope, though I'd not give her the satisfaction of knowing it. "I was told you were looking for young women to work in your showroom."

After a long silence that had me mentally squirming in my seat, she finally spoke. "I must say when I agreed to this interview you were the last person I expected." She made a great show of lighting a cigarette, closing her eyes on a sigh as she blew a stream of smoke before leaning back in her chair. "The infamous Red-Haired Wanton working as one of my mannequins? The idea is delightfully intriguing."

I sat up. "You know who I am?"

"Everyone who's anyone knows, my dear. You're quite notorious." She continued to eye me from behind a veil of blue smoke. My cheeks burned, but I refused to cower or squirm.

"Who would have thought the daughter of such a well-respected member of Parliament as Lord Melcombe would end up on display half-naked and obviously more than"—she smiled—"fulfilled."

I bit back on the words rising to my lips, and instead, offered her a practiced smile. "A good businesswoman might use that notoriety to their advantage."

"I like your thinking, Lady Katherine, but alas our partnership is not to be. You see, I need a girl who can display herself and her wardrobe to perfection, without upstaging the outfit she wears." Her smile was cool as she tapped the ash from her cigarette into a cut-crystal ashtray. "When the girl overshadows my clothing, she is no longer effective and thus no longer of use to me."

I clenched my empty handbag and tried not to glance toward the crowded tray of food. I hadn't eaten since last night.

"Someone like yourself . . . well . . . there would be talk, but it would not be about the cut of my gown or the drape of a sleeve. Surely you can see how that would serve neither my needs nor yours."

"Of course." I tried to keep the disappointment from my voice as I rose to take my leave. "Thank you for your time."

She gave a small moue of sympathy. "A piece of advice, if I may? It can be a slippery slope for a girl in your situation. But there are always ways to claw your way back to the top if you're willing to do what it takes." She handed me a small white calling card. "I know people. With your reputation, you could make a tidy sum."

I laid the card back on her desk. "Thank you, but I have to decline the offer."

Her gaze narrowed, her manner chill. "Please yourself, but don't say you weren't given a chance."

That evening, I passed the smashed and shuttered German bakery on the corner, the disapproving baker and his wife long since sent away, and paused in front of the wig maker's sign. I closed my eyes, said a prayer, and entered the shop.

A half hour later when I stepped back out onto the pavement, the wind froze the back of my exposed neck, but I was eight whole shillings wealthier.

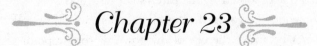

# Chapter 23

*September 1941*

Listen to this, Anna. *'The details are secret, but I can say that in general terms it means that by using a great number of small radio sets of modern design, technicians posted at ground points all over the British Isles will be able to detect enemy airplanes in the air and direct antiaircraft fire with deadly precision.'* What do you think of that? I reckon that'll stick a fork in old Hitler's eye, eh?"

Anna was scrubbing out the sink in the ward scullery. Tilly was supposed to be piling a trolley with dishes to transfer down to the main kitchens but had lapsed into reading an abandoned newspaper.

Both had been on duty since seven thirty that morning and had another four hours to go before the night staff relieved them. But at least the day had been quiet.

"I say it's a tiny bright spot within a dismal summer, but at this point, I'm happy to cheer about anything."

September seemed to cap off a season of mounting losses by

their so-called allies as the Jerries rolled through Lithuania, Latvia, Ukraine, and Belarus on their way toward Moscow. Every time Anna turned on the news another city had fallen, more troops had surrendered. At this rate, the Germans would reach the Pacific by Christmas.

"Speaking of the Air Ministry, did you ever hear back from that friend of yours?"

Tilly's head snapped up. "What friend?"

"The one you were writing to last week. You said she worked at the Air Ministry."

"Oh, right . . . her. No, she hasn't written. I suppose she's too busy. We weren't that close anyway. A bit of a slag, if you ask me." She buried herself back in her newspaper.

Strange, but then Tilly had been acting strange for the last few weeks; almost secretive. Letters she didn't want Anna to see, frequent trips alone into the village. And more recently, Anna had woken to soft weeping into a pillow.

"Tilly, is anything wrong?"

"Why do you ask?"

"I don't know. You seem . . . preoccupied. Unhappy."

"It's nothing," she replied before relaxing into a reassuring smile. "Just run off my bloody feet. What I wouldn't give for a nice long holiday by the seashore with oodles of good-looking men fawning over me."

Anna knew she was being put off. "If you're certain . . ."

"Jones," Sister Murphy snapped, standing hands on ample hips in the doorway, veil twitching. "When you're finished daydreaming, that trolley should have been down to the kitchens ages ago. Then get back here double-quick. If you're so interested in rooms full of men, I've an entire ward of them who need their bedpans emptied."

"Every girl's fantasy." Tilly leaped off the counter. "TTFN,

Anna dear." She hustled out of the scullery, pushing the squeaky trolley ahead of her.

"Don't think you're getting off scot-free, Trenowyth," Sister Murphy growled. "I need you to change the dressing on Greenwood in Ward B."

"Greenwood, Sister?"

"Are you deaf or just lazy? I've got a list of duties long as your arm, and not near enough staff to see to it all. You have more experience than any of the other girls. So get cracking, or do I need to bring you up on a charge of disobedience, Your Highness?"

"No, ma'am." Moments like these made her almost miss waiting on Lady Boxley.

She stopped at the dispensary to gather her supplies, trying not to recall Greenwood's last dressing change. The VAD who'd attempted it had ended with three stitches in her head.

The young airman had been admitted to Nanreath Hall, allegedly to recover from an emergency appendectomy, though most of the staff agreed his wounds ran much deeper than the incision in his abdomen. Unlike most of the boys, who were cheerful and cooperative, if a bit cheeky, Greenwood was stony and disobliging. He never smiled. Never spoke. And spent his days staring blindly out the long windows toward the northern wood. But that was better than those unpredictable moments when he snapped into a blind rage and it took orderlies and an occasional guard to subdue him.

Ah, well. She couldn't get out of it, and as Prue always said, "soonest begun, soonest done."

Most of the up-patients in Ward B were in the salon or taking tea across the main hall, so the room was almost empty. Greenwood's bed was at the far end of the room. His dour attitude normally kept his corner unoccupied; even the other soldiers steered clear of him. So Anna was surprised to see Hugh sitting beside his bed, the two engaged in conversation. Greenwood was even smiling. She didn't know the man had teeth.

"...got sick in his oxygen mask," Greenwood recounted. "Froze straightaway, of course, and he nearly passed out before they got him free of it, idiot bugger."

"I can top that," Hugh replied. "My first solo flight, I pissed myself at twenty-five thousand feet. Was nearly castrated peeling off my trousers."

Greenwood laughed, losing at least twenty years in the process. He was actually a nice-looking boy when he wasn't threatening to rip one's head off. Come to think of it, Hugh seemed more relaxed, as well. His usual waxen pallor from too many hours spent hunched over a whiskey at the village pub had brightened to an almost healthy pinkish glow. Both chatted and laughed as they traded stories with a soldier's grim gallows humor.

"The run to Haamstede was the worst," Greenwood said. "Lost four planes from my squadron the first time. Seven the second. Could have walked on all the ack-ack the Jerries put up."

"Wish I could say I had been there. Had a smashup during the Norway campaign last spring and lost the blasted leg."

"Do you miss it, sir?"

"The flying or the leg?"

Greenwood cracked a smile. "Either, I suppose."

Anna hated to intrude. She hovered just beyond the edge of their conversation until Hugh glanced up and spied her. "If it isn't the lovely and talented Nurse Trenowyth."

"It's time for a dressing change. Sister's orders." She held up her tray to prove her innocent intent.

As if someone flipped a switch, Greenwood's face shut down, his body stiffened, and he turned away to stare once more out the window.

"The MO says you're doing splendidly," she said, striving for professional yet friendly and nonthreatening. "A few more days and you'll be released back to your unit. I'm sure you'll be glad to see your mates."

Greenwood didn't answer.

"I'll toddle off now," Hugh said, standing up, "but let me know when you're leaving, Sergeant. We'll toast the skies before you go."

"Wait." Anna and Greenwood spoke nearly in unison.

Greenwood's face was nearly the color of pea soup, his eyes wide and hard. He licked his dry lips. "Please, sir. I mean . . . I don't mind if you stay. I . . . was enjoying . . . I mean you understand what it's like, sir. You . . ." His gaze dropped to Hugh's leg. "You survived, didn't you?"

"Most of me anyway," Hugh answered grimly.

Anna offered Hugh a look of near entreaty. "This won't take long. If Sergeant Greenwood wants you here, I don't see why you can't stay."

"Right." He smiled and gave a quick bite of laughter. "I'll stay, but you'll be sorry, old chap. You might have had Nurse all to yourself. Now you've got me to contend with, and I've had a soft spot for this one since she arrived. I'm not sure but I think I'm wearing her down."

"I suppose she's pretty," Greenwood reluctantly offered, though he remained pinch-lipped and scowling. "A bit old for me, though."

"Why, thank you, Sergeant—I think." She smiled, drawing up a stool and laying out her supplies beside her. "Let's have a look, shall we?"

She unbuttoned his pajama shirt and carefully peeled back the old dressing on Greenwood's abdomen. As the cool air hit his stitches, he twitched, his chest heaving as he sucked in a breath. Out of the corner of her eye, Anna saw his hands close to fists. He was a tall boy, not bulky but definitely strong enough to snap her like a pencil should the desire arise. Hopefully Hugh's presence would suppress his more violent tendencies.

"Where are you from, Sergeant?" Hugh asked.

Silence met his opening gambit.

"How about you, Nurse Trenowyth?" Hugh continued smoothly.

"London," Anna replied automatically, working as quickly as she could. "Aldersgate."

Tension threaded Greenwood's body. Sweat glistened in the hollow of his throat and dripped from his temples. She felt every jump of his muscles and every hitch in his breathing. As quickly as she could, she bathed the area with warm water, noting the fluid seeping from the wound as she examined it for signs of infection. Nothing out of the ordinary. She began the process of packing the incision with gauze.

"I flew with a lad from Brixton. His name was . . . Jim . . . Jim . . ." Hugh rubbed a hand over his chin. "Damn if I can remember his last name, but I can see his face clear as day." He glanced at Greenwood, whose lips were pulled back from teeth clenched tight enough to crack. "I was in London this past summer. The Jerries certainly have made a mess of things. Guess they figure to pound us into surrender. Bloody Krauts don't realize the more bombs they drop, the more determined we are to keep fighting. Only wish I could still land a few blows of my own. Damned satisfying feeling to know you're making the bastards duck and run."

His steady stream of babble steadied her nerves. Anna hoped it did the same for her patient.

As she inched the gauze carefully into the incision, Greenwood's back arched off the bed. Faster than Anna could react, he had her by the hair. His left arm came around her neck to choke off her breath.

His face was close to hers, his breath hot on her cheek, hoarse and frightened.

Her lungs burned, but she didn't flail or fight back. That would only make him worse. She forced her body to go limp and sought to gain Hugh's attention with a weak, keep-him-talking gesture.

Hugh gave an almost imperceptible nod as he struggled for words. "So . . . uh . . . Nurse is from Aldersgate, you're remaining coy and keeping your hometown to yourself. Me . . . I'm from here . . . a jolly place to be from, I always say. Of course, everyone thinks owning a great heap like this place means I'm rolling in the blunt, but have you ever tried buying coal enough to heat sixty-five rooms?"

Greenwood's hold wasn't easing, but it wasn't tightening, either. Anna could just manage a thin stream of air if she held her chin just so and to the left. At least she wasn't in danger of strangulation. On the other hand, a broken neck might still be a possibility.

By now she noticed through the spots dancing at the edges of her vision that Tilly and Sister Murphy had come at the first notice of trouble. A few patients milled uncertainly nearby. And was that really Lady Boxley just beneath the archway, hands clasped under her breasts, eyes wide in a frozen expression of worry? Couldn't be. She hated the wards.

Anna blinked, trying to force more oxygen to her brain to keep the hallucinations at bay. No. Still there.

Over the roaring in her ears, she heard Hugh, still in that even, calm voice. "Let Nurse go, and you and I can continue our chat. Let me tell you about the attack on the airfield at Stavanger."

Greenwood's grip loosened slightly.

"That's right. Nurse Trenowyth's a good egg." Hugh eased his way closer. "She'll have you fixed right as rain. Just settle down. We're all friends here. No one wants to hurt you."

She felt the tension slowly ebbing from Greenwood's body, though he remained jittery. "I'm from . . . from . . . Manchester," he muttered. "My mum still . . . lives there with my younger sister. Ain't got a dad."

"Me, neither," Hugh chirped, his manner overly hearty. "I've heard they're extremely overrated." He placed a hand on Greenwood's shoulder and shot Anna a look. "What's your sister's name?"

Anna gasped as she slid free of Greenwood's grip. She didn't care if it was against the rules, she slumped down on the next bed in the row. Her knees shook. Her hands trembled, and she had a horrible urge to either burst into tears or laugh hysterically. Instead, after a few calming minutes, she resumed her stool and her work.

"Gladys." Greenwood sagged back against the pillows, sobs shaking his body. "Her name's Gladys."

Hugh never missed a beat, continuing his steady patter as Anna inspected the wound in case the sergeant had dislodged something in his struggle, her movements slow but her hands steady as she concentrated on covering all with the new bandage and securing it. When she finished and had buttoned him back into his pajama shirt and drawn the sheet back over him, she rose as calmly as if this were just another task.

"There now," Anna said. "I'll have one of the orderlies bring you a nice cup of tea and I believe we even have some Brown Betty left over from dinner last night. After that, I want you to have a nap. Be right as rain afterward."

Greenwood didn't answer. He had a hand over his face. His white-blond hair was dark where sweat plastered it to his scalp.

She stood to leave, ignoring a few concerned and muttering patients and Sister Murphy, who continued to glare but remained blessedly silent.

"Are you all right?" Tilly asked. "He could have broken your neck like a toothpick."

Anna gave a weak nod.

"I need a drink, and so do you," Hugh said, catching Anna under her arm just before her wobbly knees gave way. He hustled her out of the ward before she could resist. "That was amazing, you know."

"You were pretty amazing yourself." Adrenaline continued firing, so every breath felt as if her heart might leap from her chest. She slumped on a chair in the scullery, suddenly too tired to even fill the kettle.

Hugh moved deftly to fill the kettle and set it to boil. "I don't want to think about what Mother's going to say when she hears."

"I think it's too late for that."

When the kettle whistled, he fixed her a cup and pushed it toward her. "Why do you say that?"

"She was there. I'm sure of it. Just at the doorway."

"I didn't see her."

"You were otherwise occupied." Steam rose enticingly from the surface and she took a sip. It burned a path all the way to her toes.

"Perfect," Hugh huffed. "She barely survived the last shock to her heart. I'd better go find her and make sure she's all right."

"Hugh?" Anna called after him. "I couldn't help but overhear you and Sergeant Greenwood talking. He asked you a question . . ."

An odd look of almost pain crossed his face, his bright eyes vacant, as if lost in thought. Then he offered her a melancholy smile. "I miss the flying more."

Anna didn't see Hugh on the wards for the next few days, though she hadn't heard any rumors of Lady Boxley succumbing to another attack of angina. Hopefully, he was merely busy with estate work and hadn't succumbed to his mother's strong-arm tactics in keeping him away. She tried to convince herself it wasn't her problem—Hugh was a grown man, for heaven's sake. But she couldn't quite forget his self-pitying desolation the night of the New Year's social or the excited spark in his eyes she'd seen recently.

Not that she dwelt on it. Her schedule didn't allow for too much dwelling on anything—a gift disguised as exhaustion. This morning, for example. Her alarm didn't go off, the nurses' showers were broken, and her hair refused every attempt she made to pin it neatly beneath her veil. She'd just enough time to snatch a quick glance at her fading Technicolor bruises in the mirror before she needed to be on the ward in—she checked her watch—three minutes.

She raced from her room, tearing down the steps toward the first-floor landing, her shoes scuffing the carpeted treads.

"... should have known it would turn out this way. I'm fine for a few laughs, but not the right sort to bring home to meet Lady High and Mighty."

Anna sucked in a breath as she dragged to a halt at the bottom step, thankful the carpets silenced her footsteps.

"That's not true. You wait, it'll come out all right. Give it a few more days."

Tilly and Hugh in hushed conversation. Anna held still, ashamed at her eavesdropping ... but not too ashamed.

"A few more days? It's been three weeks, Hugh. When do I officially stop playing the fool? She doesn't approve of our relationship. I'm not the right sort for her precious boy." Tilly was clearly angry, her voice staccato sharp, biting her words through clenched teeth. Hugh soothing as he offered excuses. "I know I'm not like Sophie. I can't trace my family tree back to William the Bloody Conqueror, but, sod all, I'm not some gold-digging slag."

"She's not as bad as all that. Just . . . hold tight. She'll come around and everything will be tickety-boo. I promise."

"I'm holding you personally responsible if it's not." There was a pause and what sounded like a kiss. "Come on," Tilly said, obviously mollified. "You can escort me back to the wards before Sister Murphy catches me sneaking off again. She'll not kick up too much of a fuss with you there."

Anna hugged the staircase as the couple headed down the remaining steps and through the baize door to the back passage. She let out the breath she was holding, but the questions lingered as she trailed her way into the main hall. Hugh and Tilly in love? They'd grown close over the last months, but Anna never once suspected things had escalated so far. Why would Tilly keep such a secret?

"Trenowyth!" Sister Murphy's bellow rattled the chandeliers, jolting Anna from her growing anger. "You're late. We've got a dozen beds that need to be stripped and remade by this afternoon. If you manage to get that accomplished without a problem, the ward scullery, duty room, and dispensary need to be scrubbed top to bottom, and the ward floor waxed. I want to be able to eat from the lino . . . or else."

"Yes, ma'am," Anna replied, shelving her annoyance to meet the buzz of activity as she jumped into the fast-flowing currents accompanying morning rounds.

An orderly nearly knocked Anna over as he pushed a trolley loaded with bedding, and VADs scurried up and down the stairs with buckets and pails. The sisters moved efficiently from bed to bed, checking medical charts as breakfast trays were removed. Anna found Sophie on Ward B in the midst of fighting with a mattress. If Sophie's breathless cursing and disheveled appearance were any indication, the mattress was clearly winning.

Since the bombing, the ward's beautiful tunnel of stained-glass windows had been re-glazed in cheap plain glass or in some instances boarded over completely. The walls bore the carved or penned inscriptions of hundreds of patients, and the hastily erected flimsy plank partition shielding a row of metal sinks wobbled with every swipe of the orderly's enormous bumper as he polished the floor.

Sophie straightened from tucking in the last crisp hospital corner, grimacing as she arched her back and wiped her face. "I feel like a pretzel."

"How long have you been on duty?"

Sophie looked at the clock. "Since five this morning. I couldn't sleep. I spent a few hours in stores and then I came here." She bent to begin the next bed in the row.

"Have you had breakfast this morning?"

"I'm not hungry."

"You're never hungry."

Sophie shrugged and turned back to her work as an orderly entered, pushing another trolley of bedding. By the time they broke for a cup of tea, the beds were done, anything that could be polished had been polished, and no speck of dust lingered in even the darkest corners.

Aprons limp and gray with dirt, veils askew on hair hanging loose and draggled from their pins, they stood outside the scullery door in the fresh air of the courtyard, sipping from steaming mugs. Anna tried not to look surprised when Sophie lit a cigarette. "When did you start smoking?"

"Does it matter?" Sophie answered dully, sucking in a lungful of smoke.

Anna sipped at her tea. "Has Tilly spoken to you at all about Hugh?"

"What about him?"

"Nothing, really. It's just they seem very close these days."

"Do they? I haven't really noticed, but you know how Tilly is. She doesn't mean anything by it. And Hugh flirts with anything in a skirt. I wouldn't worry."

Just then, Tilly rounded the corner of the house, no trace of this morning's encounter with Hugh on her face. "Post's arrived, girls. Thought you might not want to wait until tonight. There's a package for Sophie at the duty nurse's desk from Fortnum and Mason. Mater's been shopping again."

"Anything for you?" Sophie asked.

"Nothing today. I expect I'll see a bunch come all at once tomorrow. You know how the mail is." Tilly shrugged, but it was clear she was disappointed.

Anna sifted through her letters. "Two from Mrs. Willits." She hadn't heard from her in a few weeks and she'd begun to worry. The German bombers seemed to have turned their attention to other cities, but London still bore the brunt of near nightly air raids. She scanned the first of the two letters. "She thinks her daughter Ginny might be able to help me look up Simon Halliday's records at the War Office."

"Golly. That would be fabulous, Anna," Tilly said. "A trip to London *and* news about your dad. What do you think, Sophie? Should we go along to keep her out of trouble? I've heard the dance halls are a gas, full of soldiers and sailors from all over. Beats the lot at the pub, I'd wager."

Sophie didn't answer. She stood frozen, one hand to her mouth, the other clutching a single thin page of pink stationery. Tears ran down her cheeks.

"Crikey! What's wrong, Sophie?" Tilly grabbed her by the shoulders. "Say something. Say anything."

"Is it bad news?" Anna asked quietly.

Sophie handed Anna the letter. "I've known it for months. I

always felt like I could sense Charles out there somewhere . . . and then one day a few weeks ago, I woke up, and there was nothing. Just a horrible blankness where he'd been."

"Bloody hell." Tilly peered over Anna's shoulder, both of them reading the confirmation of Lieutenant Charles Douglas's death as a prisoner of war at an Italian transit camp.

Sir Giles and Lady Douglas's boy? A sad shame, but at least they have two others and he wasn't the eldest. We should be grateful for small mercies." Lady Boxley eyed her physician-approved dinner of boiled potatoes with distaste.

Anna clenched her fork to prevent her from jamming it into her hostess and ending this farce of family harmony once and for all. How in the hell had Hugh managed to convince her to join them for dinner?

"I'm sure Sophie doesn't see it that way," Hugh admonished as he sipped at his wine. He had a bit of a hostile gleam in his eye, as well. Perhaps he was having the same violent thoughts.

"Would she have preferred to have him back horribly burned or disfigured?" Immune to the dagger glances being shot her way, Lady Boxley continued as she started. "Better a clean death than to linger on crippled and unable to function. What would Miss Kinsale have done had she been tied to such a man for life?"

Hugh placed his wineglass carefully on the table, his knuckles white, his face horrifyingly blank of expression. "I'd hope she would love him for the man he was—and is, even scarred or crippled." A gleam lit his eyes. "As you did when my father came home from the last war maimed and sick."

Anna felt like a spectator at a tennis match.

"That was different. I was already married to your father when he was wounded. What else could I have done but care for him?"

"Would it have been different had you not been married? Had you not loved him?"

Lady Boxley stiffened, her shoulders squaring before she dropped her gaze to her plate, suddenly very interested in her potatoes. There was a drawn-out silence as if the room held its breath.

"Miss Trenowyth. I hear you're heading to London," she said, smoothly turning aside the question.

"I have a friend who works in the War Office. She's going to help me sort through the old military records."

"To what purpose?"

"I'm hoping I might be able to learn more about Simon Halliday."

"Are you so dissatisfied with your mother's side of the family, you must hunt for relatives on the other side of the tree? It's obvious they wanted nothing to do with you, otherwise they'd have stepped in when your mother died."

"Neither side stepped in, though, did they?"

Lady Boxley pushed her boiled spuds around her plate and ignored the question. "I don't like it. London's not safe. Bombings nearly every night. People living in their cellars. Hugh, tell her she shouldn't go. She won't listen to me."

Hugh shrugged but tactfully remained silent on the matter.

"What about that boy of yours—Lambert?" Her Ladyship persisted. "What does he have to say about you leaving to pursue a pipe dream? Or how about that military idea of a physician? He can't want a dearth of nurses at such a busy time."

Her spine straightened. She hadn't told Tony. For some reason, confiding her plan meant she'd be admitting to herself that she cared for him. Denial meant she could continue pretending he was just another bloke and nothing special. "It's none of Tony Lambert's business what I do."

She must have sounded sharper than she intended. Hugh shot her a curious look across the table. She met it with a smile and continued. "And the MO and Matron have both signed my travel warrant, so I'm all set. I promise to be careful if it makes you feel better, ma'am."

"It doesn't. Not at all. Just when things are settled, I'm to be turned all inside out again. It's always thus. My feelings are never taken into consideration. I'm the last to be advised and never heeded."

"London's my home, ma'am. I won't abandon her now that she's lost her luster any more than Sophie would have turned her back on Charles if he'd come home injured."

Lady Boxley threw up her hands. "So I'm to have that thrown back at me, am I? I should have known I'd be outnumbered. Forgive me for seeing the practical within the tragedy. Life goes on and must be lived whether it suits us or not. The girl has suffered a grave loss, and I'm sorry for it. But she can't simply surrender to her grief." She pushed her plate away, her ringed hands barely trembling. "I lost your father, Hugh. But I didn't wallow and fade away to nothing. I had you and your future to think of. It kept me going and made me look beyond my own loss to something bigger. Perhaps Miss Kinsale can find the strength to do the same."

Hugh ran a tired hand over his face, shoulders slumped. "Perhaps she can, Mother, but give the poor thing time to grieve before you shove her back into the fight. It's only been a few weeks since she received word."

"Oh no, Hugh. I made that mistake once." She looked at him steadily, her hand barely trembling. "Now I begin to see what damage unchecked time and grief can do."

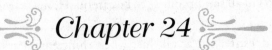

# Chapter 24

*June 1916*

One night was all we had. Simon had been given a week's leave but spent most of it in Lincolnshire with his parents, only returning to London the last evening before his ship was due to depart. I didn't even try to argue with him this time. I knew by now it was a hopeless cause.

I heard Simon's pocket watch chime midnight as I slid from under his arm and left our bed to pad across the bare floor. Light shone ghostly silver from a full moon that scraped the sky and gilded a few ragged scraps of cloud. It poured through the grubby window to fall on Simon's face like a spotlight as he slept.

Curling in a chair by the window, my journal open on my knees, I sketched the dagger-sharp line of his jaw, the sloping cheekbones, the arched brows beneath the muss of his dark hair. He was no longer the affable idealist I had fallen in love with. War had changed him. Boiled him down to a concentrated nihilism that seemed always at the edge of fury . . . or passion. Even if he survived, I wondered if he would ever completely recover his zest for life. He had seen too much death. Experienced too much horror. Ghosts crowded his once bright gaze.

The light dimmed, casting a veil across Simon's face. Outside, the rooftops were edged in long shadow, though no windows glowed with life. As I watched, a long dark shape blotted the moon like an insidious eclipse. There was no sound as it passed high above the city, at least none reached my ears, but that only made its approach more terrifying.

"Simon," I whispered, as if speaking aloud would draw its attention. "Simon, come and see."

"What is it?" he said, instantly awake, his body vibrating like a plucked note.

"A zeppelin." I found myself reaching for my journal, my heart thundering, my skin prickling with excitement and fear.

He joined me at the window as searchlights suddenly speared the sky like swords. The behemoth seemed to turn, and as my hand raced across the page, explosions rocked the ground and the thin silver clouds were met by plumes of red-laced black smoke.

"A mere taste of the horrors our soldiers gorge upon daily." Anguish burned in Simon's voice.

The zeppelin disappeared as quickly as it arrived, floating gracefully east and north. We were too far away to hear the sirens or see the destruction, but now lamps shone from every window and voices could be heard in the once quiet street.

From behind, Simon put his arms around me so that I stood cradled in the circle of his embrace. I felt his tremors quick and sharp, his breathing labored and rasping hot against my shoulder. Panicked like a wild thing caught and frozen by the hunter's lamp.

I turned so that I faced him, pressed skin on skin, chest to hip. He shivered as if he were cold or aroused. Or both. I felt his racing heart beneath my palm, laid a kiss to the hollow at the base of his collarbone as he plowed both hands into my wild crop of hair so that I must lift my face to his.

"Come, darling." I led him back to bed, knowing only one way to combat death in the dark hours of the night.

Afterward, he lay on top of me, his head upon my breasts as he traced the line of my ribs with one finger. "'Doubt thou the stars are fire, Doubt that the sun doth move, Doubt truth to be a liar, But never doubt I love,'" he quoted softly.

I answered with a kiss. "Shakespeare."

He laughed but it was without humor, only a dull resignation. "He's not the world's greatest poet for nothing. I was dead before I met you, Kitty. I existed, but I didn't live. You changed that. You changed everything."

"'For where thou art, there is the world itself . . . And where thou art not, desolation.'" I brushed the hair back off Simon's forehead. "The man had a way with words."

"You don't understand." He rolled up so that I was pinned between his arms, his gaze hot as a brand on my bare flesh. "This isn't the war talking. Or rather the war has only made me realize how stupid and selfish I've been. It's too late to go back and make things right, but I want you to know . . . I need you to know . . . I love you, Kitty." His coiled intensity pulsed the air until I felt myself stirred to take him between my legs once more. "I've spent so long chasing an elusive dream when all along it was right in front of me. You were right in front of me, and I was too foolish to realize it. You are my dream." He looked away, but not before I caught the almost desolate ferocity in his gaze. He hung by a single unraveling thread. "Can you ever forgive me?"

"There is nothing to forgive," I soothed. "Whatever happens, these few years have been the most wonderful gift you could have given me. I wouldn't change one second of them."

That seemed to comfort him. He relaxed, his face losing some of its wild desperation. "I'd be lost without you," he said quietly.

I smiled through my own tears. "Then it's a good thing I'm not going anywhere."

By dawn, the bed was empty, and last night might have been a dream but for the drawing in my journal and the eight people killed in the bombing of a tram.

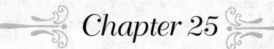

# Chapter 25

*September 1941*

"A re you certain you're all right? I can phone Mrs. Willits and let her know I'll be delayed," Anna suggested.

She stood with Tilly in the main hall awaiting Mr. Gough. He'd agreed to give Anna and Sophie a lift to the train station when he went to pick up supplies from the depot.

"Are you mad? I'll have the room to myself for four whole days. The thought of so much privacy makes me positively giddy. Besides, someone needs to see to Sophie on the trip to London. The way she's been sleepwalking, she's liable to get on the wrong train or ride past her station to the end of the line."

"Right, but if you wanted to talk, if you were upset about anything at all, you know I'd be there for you, don't you?"

Confusion colored Tilly's expression. "Uh . . . of course. But I'm *not* upset, and if we don't stop talking, you're going to miss your train." She chivied Anna toward the door. "Go before Matron changes her mind and decides to keep you here."

"Right. Well, then I suppose I'll see you in a few days. Enjoy the room."

She hoisted her bag onto her shoulder and headed for the door.

"Anna?"

She turned back.

Tilly gave her a wistful smile. "Thank you. You're a good friend."

Outside, Sophie stood on the sweep, bag in hand. She had traded her VAD uniform for a simple frock, making her seem fragile and childlike while her dark hair accentuated the tragic pallor of her face and heightened the emptiness of her large blue eyes.

Anna smiled brightly. "Ready to push off then? Mr. Gough's probably waiting for us."

Sophie nodded and followed Anna around the side of the house to a row of Nissen huts set up as supply sheds where Hugh leaned against a cherry-red sports car parked between two Bedford cargo lorries and an old Ford motorcar. "Let's get a move on, ladies. I've traded in my trusty steed for this beauty."

"I thought Mr. Gough was driving us to the station."

"You're not taking the train. I've decided to drive you to London myself. I've been hoarding petrol coupons like gold. I've enough to get us there and back with a gallon or two to spare."

"That's awfully nice of you, Hugh, but if you're doing this on my account, it's not necessary," Sophie said, though the slight breathy tremor in her voice belied her brave words. "I won't shatter from a little rough usage."

"Rubbish. I'm acting out of pure self-interest. The car's been under a canvas in our stables for months. Thought she needed an outing, and London seemed the perfect destination."

"What about Tilly?" Anna asked.

"What *about* Tilly?" Hugh replied. "If she's hoping to cadge a ride as well, she's out of luck. It'll be a squeeze already with the three of us plus luggage."

"I just thought you might want to hang about here in case she needs you."

He gave Anna an odd look of confusion. "I'm probably the last person Tilly needs—or wants, for that matter. Stop stalling, Trenowyth. I won't run you into a ditch if that's what you're worried about." He helped them stow their luggage. "Come on. Pile in. We need to get on the road if we're to make London by tomorrow morning."

"What happens tomorrow morning?"

He smiled mysteriously and held the door as they smashed themselves into the passenger seat.

"Wait! Don't go!" Lady Boxley appeared at the top of the steps beneath the portico, waving a handkerchief.

Hugh muttered under his breath, but it was Anna she approached, handing her a picnic hamper. "It's a bottle of good claret, a sturdy wool blanket, and the last of the biscuits made with our butter and sugar ration. Should you be forced to take refuge in one of those hellish shelters, you'll at least be comfortable." Surprised, Anna accepted the bag from Lady Boxley. "I don't like you going off to who knows where in search of answers. Seems to me as if you've learned more than you need to know about that horrid man and his wicked ways."

"He was my father."

"A father is the man who makes you the person you are, not the man who simply makes you. Remember that, Miss Trenowyth."

Should she? Dare she? Anna pressed a swift kiss to Lady Boxley's cheek. "I'll be careful."

Lady Boxley didn't smile exactly, but her permanent scowl lines definitely softened. Then she turned to Hugh. "Take care and drive with some sense, Hugh. Nothing's lost by going at a sedate and measured pace."

Sliding behind the wheel, he started the car with a sputter, a cough, and a roar. Lady Boxley retreated to the portico to wave them off. "If Mother had her way, we'd be making the royal progress at a sedate ten miles per hour, time enough for the common folk to tug their forelocks," he muttered.

He put her into gear and they were spitting stones in the gravel sweep before roaring down the avenue, wind slapping their faces and stealing any ability for conversation.

The drive to London took two days with an overnight stop outside Newbury. Sophie and Anna shared a tiny hotel room while Hugh bunked in his car, afraid someone might siphon off his precious petrol. Dinner was fish and chips from one of the ubiquitous British restaurants washed down with hot strong cups of tea to warm the chill from their fingers and loosen their wind-stiffened faces. Breakfast was more tea and buttered toast eaten on the fly before they bundled back into the car for the remainder of the trip.

Sophie's presence made questioning Hugh about Tilly impossible, and Hugh's presence made discussion with Sophie out of the question, though it was doubtful she'd have been much help. She barely spoke, her face set, her eyes distant. She bore all the personality and warmth of a marble statue. Anna hoped Sophie's parents would be able to break the frozen look of bewildered shock from her face. All her attempts had failed utterly.

By the time they entered London, Anna was ready to forgo the splash and glamour of Hugh's sports car for the relative comfort and warmth of the bus. They dropped Sophie first. Birds fluttered in the trees along the wide terraced Kensington street, and an almost prewar serenity pervaded. Nurses pushed prams, a spit and polished bobby walked his beat, and women in heels and hats emerged from taxis with shopping bags in hand.

Sophie's parents met them at the door, both wearing worn and anxious faces. They murmured pleasantries, and Sir Edmund shook Hugh's hand. "Damn ugly business this. But I want to thank you for getting her safely home to us, Melcombe. Had she been here in the first place rather than gallivanting about in Cornwall, we could have helped her from the start rather than hearing everything secondhand."

"Has she said anything?" Lady Kinsale asked. She was a nervous, harried-looking woman, though it was obvious where Sophie got her pretty, dark looks.

"Not much," Anna answered.

"We'll take it from here," Sir Edmund broke in. "A good long rest is what she needs. She's done her bit. None can say different, but it's time she was home where proper young ladies should be." It might have been Anna's imagination, but she felt certain Sir Edmund cocked her a disapproving glance as he said this.

"Really, Pater," Sophie argued. "It's not the Dark Ages. And I'm an adult. Not some little girl who needs a nanny to take care of her."

"I don't care how old you are, you're my daughter."

"A change of scene perhaps," Lady Kinsale broke in, as if used to smoothing over arguments between her husband and her daughter. "A nice trip to the country for some fresh air. My sister lives in Hastings by the sea."

"I don't want a change of scene or country air," Sophie argued. "I need to be busy. I want to find work here in the city, something useful."

"You don't know what you want, my dear. You're all done in over this business with Charles. A few weeks of rest at your aunt's will do you a world of good. You'll see. Your cousins will be happy to have the company."

"Mater, please." Sophie looked on the point of collapse.

"We'll discuss it over dinner." Sir Edmund's tone brooked no argument.

Hugh and Anna each offered Sophie one last hug before they left the quiet, elegant house. "And I thought my mother was bad. No wonder Sophie joined the VAD."

Anna tried to smile, but her last sight of Sophie nearly prostrate in her chair, pale as a snowdrop, her eyes wide and lost, haunted her.

"She'll be all right now, won't she?" she asked as Hugh shoveled the traveling rug across Anna's knees. It was September but every inch of her ached with the cold of the road.

"I hope so." Hugh shook his head. "Charlie Douglas was a damn good chap. A bloody waste, if you ask me."

He peeled away from the curb, and for the next half hour Anna held on for dear life as he wove with a race driver's reckless disregard for human life and property through the increasingly crowded streets. As they headed east, the city was a maze of roped-off areas that even Hugh had to respect. Their pace slowed, the snazzy roadster turning heads and eliciting whistles and shouts from passing pedestrians now that it was less than a cherry-red blur leaving catastrophe in its wake. Anna noticed Hugh's smile grow wider with each complimentary yell and every little boy who chased after them screaming for a ride. They'd gained a tail of them by the time they arrived at the narrow three-story brick house in South Hornchurch where Mrs. Willits lived with her youngest daughter, Ginny, in a third-floor flat.

Anna spotted her standing in a queue of women awaiting their turn at a mobile laundry truck run by the Women's Voluntary Service, a floury apron tied over a frock in a dismal shade of brown. But she was plump and laughing and looked completely at ease among the chattering women with their sacks of clothes.

"Anna, my pet!" Mrs. Willits enveloped her in an enormous hug. "I was worried sick for you on the road. You never know when Jerry's going to take it in his head to strike a highway." She spotted Hugh, her face creasing into a wide, approving smile. "And this must be your fella."

Anna blushed but Hugh laughed and accepted her hug with his usual easy charm. "Actually, I'm her cousin. Her fella's much better-looking."

Mrs. Willits's painted eyebrows disappeared beneath her kerchief as she stepped back, smoothing her apron and tucking her hair, primping as she blushed a schoolgirl shade of pink. Anna could tell she had half a mind to curtsy. "Your lordship, sir. It's an honor to meet you."

"The honor is mine, Mrs. Willits."

"Imagine me hugging on an earl. The girls at Woolworths won't believe it."

"I can't stay," Hugh said, handing over Anna's luggage. "I've a meeting this afternoon and errands to run for my mother all day tomorrow, but I'd love to take you all to dinner tomorrow evening. What do you say? The Ritz?"

"We'd love to, your lordship," Mrs. Willits jumped in before Anna could answer.

"I'll give you a ring."

"Hornchurch two-oh-five-three. There's only the one phone in the house, but Mrs. Grayson the landlady's good at taking messages."

Hugh offered one last tip of his hat as he leaped into the car, roared it into life to the delight of the swarm of schoolboys, and sped off.

"Imagine going to dinner at the Ritz with a real earl." Mrs. Willits traded her ticket for her sack of cleaned laundry from the uniformed WVS woman on duty, and together she and Anna walked the half block to the flat. "Guess that family of yours surprised you after all, eh, ducks?"

Anna hooked Lady Boxley's satchel higher on her shoulder, smiled, and looped her arm in Mrs. Willits's. "I guess they did at that."

The next morning at eight, Anna followed Ginny Willits in her smart WAAF uniform through the doors of a tall, official-looking building and down the lift to an enormous room stocked with rows and rows of shelves, each shelf containing rows and rows of boxes. Overhead bulbs shone on a set of metal tables with another three desks by the lift.

"Welcome to hell," said a smart young woman in khaki, an open box in front of her, stacks of pages to either side.

"That's Lizzie. Ignore her. She's all giggles and butterflies."

"My eyes are shot, my backside is spreading from all this sitting, and I'm seeing veteran pensions in my sleep."

Anna glanced at Ginny for an explanation.

"Last fall, the War Office's repository was bombed. Over two million service records from the last war were destroyed. It's up to us along with the Ministry of Pensions to piece it all back together as best we can."

"That could take decades," Anna said.

"Centuries, but who's bloody counting," Lizzie chimed in. "Meantime, we're trapped in this hole without even a proper look at the sun. We emerge like moles at night and stumble home for a few hours' kip then back we come. They should have hired miners to do this work, not us."

"Quit your whinging," replied Ginny. "It's not so bad. You could be on the top floor dodging bombs."

"At least I'd see the sky once in a while. Down here, what do I see but you ruddy lot."

"Who is he, then?" Ginny asked. "I'll see if he's among the boxes we've sorted."

"If he's not?"

Lizzie blew a curl off her forehead and rolled her eyes. "Come back in 2041 and maybe some poor blind, pale mole girl from the future will have found him by then."

Anna ignored Lizzie and directed her answer to Ginny. "His name was Simon Halliday. I don't know his regiment or rank or anything really. I do know he died during the Battle of the Somme in September 1916."

"Right. That might narrow it down a bit."

Ginny left Anna at the table where she sat at a desk and watched Lizzie and the others quietly working through the piles of crumbling, discolored pages. The only sounds seemed to be the scratch of pens, the shuffling of paper, and the steady mind-numbing tick of the wall clock. At ten thirty the clank of the lift signaled the arrival of a tea cart, which the girls descended upon with speed and excitement.

Ginny arrived back amid the clamor as cups were drunk and biscuits devoured while the young lad who'd brought them grinned his delight over being the center of so much female attention.

"Nothing yet, but I've oodles of files to sort through. What say, you go on. If I find anything out, I'll jot it down and bring it home tonight. Mum will want to be in on any grand secrets anyway."

"Sounds perfect."

"Leaving us so soon?" Lizzie commented as Anna shrugged on her coat. "What's your hurry? Uncomfortable accommodations, bad lighting, catty girls, and enough paper to giftwrap the earth. You'd be daft to give up such an opportunity."

"Very nice meeting you," Anna said.

"Say hello to the war for me," Lizzie grumbled, turning over a new set of folders.

Ginny left Anna at the lift. "Don't mind her. She wanted to serve on a naval base or an airfield. Somewhere romantic and full of action. She's gone a bit sour being stuck down here with us lot."

"What about you?"

"Me? I'm glad enough. I like being in London and I like the job for the most part. It's almost like being a detective, isn't it? Piecing a bit from here and a bit from there and seeing the whole picture."

Something nudged at Anna's consciousness. "Yes, it is, isn't it?" She couldn't put her exact finger on what she was missing, but she sensed the answer lay close at hand. "Can I ask one more huge favor, Ginny? I mean, if it's not too much bother."

"Ask away."

"Would you be able to find me another military record?"

"How many fathers are you looking for?"

"No, it's nothing like that. It would be my uncle, Lady Katherine's brother. His full name was William Algernon George Burnside Trenowyth. His title would have been Viscount Boxley. He served as a captain in the Royal Artillery."

"Died in battle?"

"No. Wounded and gassed at Bazentin Ridge. He was invalided out and died in 1917."

"Oh, that should be easier. Soldiers discharged due to injury weren't among the files burned. I can ask around and see what I find. Anything I should be looking for in particular?"

"Would it be trite to say I'll know it when I see it?"

Ginny grinned. "The game's afoot."

Hugh was as good as his word. To the delight of Mrs. Willits, he arrived in a taxi that evening to sweep them off to dinner at the Ritz. Introduced to the other occupants of the house as His Lordship and a particular friend, Hugh made sure to bow over each lady's hand, his noblesse oblige on full display, his immaculate evening wear and blond cinema-star looks melting hearts up and down Cherry Tree Lane.

Mrs. Willits settled herself in the back of the taxi, wrapping a rather forlorn stole about her shoulders as the feathers in her enormous hat tickled the roof. "Ginny's running late. She said she'll meet us there if it's all the same to you, my lord."

"We'll keep her cocktail warm, madam."

She tittered like a schoolgirl as Hugh and Anna exchanged a smile.

The lobby of the hotel was packed, but Hugh moved them through with an ease born of innate superiority. Arrangements were made, doors were opened, and staff acquiesced to every request with surprising speed. Hugh never batted an eye, just behaved as if this was par for the course, which Anna expected it was. An advantage of wealth and rank that inferior folk could only look on with envy.

"If only Tilly were with us," Anna said oh-so-casually.

Hugh chuckled. "I can picture her now slinking her way through here like Rita Hayworth. The hens would be cackling for certain."

"Would that bother you?"

"Have you ever known me to be bothered by cackling hens? I go out of my way to toss petrol on a fire."

"True. You do have a love for causing a spectacle." Which made his furtive relationship with Tilly so odd. Hugh would be more likely to flaunt her in his mother's face, just for spite.

Even with the dust and debris clogging the nearby streets, the

Ritz remained relatively unscathed and the famous Palm Court as glamorous and opulent as Anna had always imagined. She tried to match Hugh's nonchalance but felt herself straining to catch every glittering sight, and she knew her eyes must have been bulging. Mrs. Willits, on the other hand, had gathered herself together in the taxi and now moved with the same careless disinterest as the most jaded of society matrons.

Over the rare treat of oysters, roast lamb, and fresh garden vegetables rather than the soggy tinned substitutes relied upon by the hospital, Hugh nudged Mrs. Willits to recount story after story of Anna's misspent youth on Queen's Crescent. "Oh, the times we had. Mr. and Mrs. Handley were good respectable folk. Never a bad word to say about anyone and always there to help when you needed it. Do you remember when . . ."

A lump formed in Anna's throat even as she laughed over events and people she'd nearly forgotten.

" . . . a real close street, you know, my lord? Everyone knew everyone. Of course, it's not the same now, is it? People uprooted, families split up. I expect things won't ever be the same again."

Not even close. Anna swallowed her food with difficulty, her stomach knotting.

Ginny arrived, still in her WAAF uniform and carrying a sheaf of papers as they nibbled on cake and sipped tiny cups of strong espresso. Anna had refused dessert and sat fingering her locket, aching for one of Graham's warm, pipe-smelling hugs or a cup of Prue's honey and ginger tea with scones straight from the oven.

"Sorry I'm late. It's a mess out there. Took me hours to get a bus," Ginny said as she slid into the chair Hugh held for her. "Golly, is that chocolate?"

"We think so, though heaven only knows where they got it," Hugh replied. "We've decided not to ask just in case we hear it's ground pencil shavings or some other putrid concoction meant to trick us."

"I often wonder if Lord Woolton eats some of the meals he dreams up for the rest of us. Mock fried egg, pilchard pancakes, carrots à la king." Mrs. Willits wrinkled her nose and forked in another spoonful of cake. "Who on earth comes up with these recipes?"

Hugh waved to a passing waiter, and immediately plates of food appeared in front of Ginny.

"Blimey," she murmured as she looked on dazedly at the bounty before her. Between bites, she recounted her day in spectacular fashion while Anna sat on her hands and tried not to reach across the table and throttle her impatiently.

Mrs. Willits leaned back in her chair. "Yes, dear, I'm sure we're all sympathetic to your trials with the section's temperamental mimeograph and laddering your last pair of good stockings was horribly careless of you, but poor Anna is all aquiver. Did you or did you not find reference to Simon Halliday?"

Ginny carefully examined each pea before she scooped it into her mouth. "Oh, well . . . you see . . . about that . . ."

Mrs. Willits rapped the table with her knuckles. "Virginia Willits, stop that infernal mumbling and answer the question."

"Sorry, Mum. I don't mean to mumble. But you see . . ." She threw her mother an agonized look.

Out of patience, Mrs. Willits snatched the file. "Here now, Anna. Open it up and let's have it once and for all. No sense wondering and worrying. Lady Katherine was a sweet thing, and if she loved that man enough to have a child with him, then he couldn't have been all bad."

"No, but Mum . . . it's complicated . . ." Ginny stammered.

Anna was torn between Ginny's reluctance and Mrs. Willits's determination. She glanced at Hugh, whose face bore a grim expectancy, hand resting against his bad leg, fingers curled to reveal white knuckles. "Remember what I told you. Be very sure you want an answer before you ask the question."

"I have to know, Hugh."

"Right." He gave a faint smile as Anna flipped the folder open. Seven pages clipped inside; an entire life neatly summed up in a few columns of type and handwritten scrawls. "Simon Edward Halliday. Born on December twelfth, 1887, in Wragby, Lincolnshire," Anna read aloud. "Occupation: artist. Enlisted August 1915. Lieutenant Fourth Suffolk. Died September sixteenth, 1916, at Flers-Courcelette."

Anna's eyes followed the page down and stopped—dead. The names blurred. Her eyes burned.

*Forgive my love.*

Don't ask the question if you don't want to hear the answer.

It all made sense now. Awful, perfect sense.

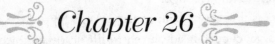

# Chapter 26

*August 1916*

A ll right, you two. Take five minutes to stretch."
Agnes put down the Chinese fan she'd been holding while
I grabbed a heavy dressing gown to throw over my naked body. For
the last two hours, we'd been arranged like dolls in a series of come-
hither poses while a photographer snapped countless pictures to be
turned into lurid penny postcards.

Desperation had finally led me to accept Mrs. Duchamp's suggestion for alternate employment, which was how I found myself
in this nondescript house off Brixton Road where tenants came
and went and no one noticed anything for the right price. It was
a job, I told myself. And if I had to remove my clothes in order to
be paid, I could at least take comfort in knowing that was as far
as it went.

"Have you heard anything from Simon?" Agnes asked as she
sipped a cup of tea in barely more than a pair of lacy garters and
stockings.

I shook my head as I nibbled a cracker, my stomach quivering with the nausea that had plagued me for the last month.

"Well, take heart. No news is good news as they say. He'll write when he can."

I drank my tea and tried not to envision Simon as one of the hideously scarred faces or limbless shambling men who now populated the city's streets. It was hard. Since one short letter in June, informing me he was headed a few miles behind the lines for forty-eight hours of leave, I'd heard nothing. That was six weeks ago.

"Does he know about the baby?" Her gaze flicked to my stomach. I had yet to start showing, but I felt as if the whole world could tell I was carrying my lover's child.

I clenched my dressing gown tighter. The coarse fabric itched my swollen, tender breasts. "I don't know. That's the worst part. I don't know if he received my letter. I don't know anything." I swallowed to keep the quaver from my voice.

"Perhaps his parents have heard something. Have you written them to ask?"

"I don't expect they'd answer a letter from me. They've never approved of Simon's profession or his life in London. It would be ten times worse if they knew I was working here."

"If you ask me, you need to go visit these Puritans and let them know you're going to have their grandchild."

"What if they don't care?" I'd yet to tell anyone besides Agnes and Jane that I was increasing. I hadn't even written to William with the news. I didn't want to give him more to worry over.

"If something's happened to Simon, surely they'd want to know some part of him carries on, even if the child's . . . you know . . ."

"A bastard?" The weight of that horrible word seemed to press on my shoulders, and my hands unconsciously cradled my growing stomach. I hated the thought of bringing an innocent into this world saddled with the guilt of its parents' sins, a shameful burden through no fault of its own.

"Didn't you say his family owned some big machine works in Lincolnshire? They should be willing to lay out a few quid to the woman carrying their son's baby. And if not, maybe they'd be interested in paying a few quid to keep your mouth shut. Either way, you win."

"Agnes!"

"Don't Agnes me." She tossed her head, gray eyes flashing. No hint of embarrassment or shame in her bold gaze. "You can't be squeamish, Kitty. You have to look out for you and the mite. No one and nothing else matters."

"You sound well versed on the subject."

"My mother was in service down south when she found she was pregnant. Did she turn up her toes? Not a bit of it. Came to London and did whatever she had to in order to scrape the pennies together. It wasn't always pretty and it wasn't always decent, but it fed me and clothed me and in time she found a boatman living in Limehouse who married her and made her a respectable woman. I knew how hard she had it, and I never looked down on her. Not once. Yours won't neither. I guarantee it."

"Ladies!" The photographer returned, grinding out his cigarette as he prepared to resume his work.

Removing my dressing gown, I lay back down on the bed amid the silken sheets and tasseled pillows, staring straight ahead as indifferent, tobacco-stained hands arranged my naked body. My nipples puckered despite the stifling heat of the studio, but I never flinched or blushed. I became the bold wanton of Simon's painting, who offered no apology and met every challenge.

I carried that confidence through the week, and thus it was that I found myself following Agnes's advice and traveling north to Lin-

coln. I shared a hard wooden bench in a third-class carriage with
an old woman loaded down with baskets and bags, a sleeping boy,
and a young woman trying to soothe her squalling baby. Soldiers
crowded the rest of the remaining dirty cramped space, sharing
cigarettes and the occasional flask, their laughter harsh, bitter, and
overloud. To take my mind from the coming confrontation, I spent
the time sketching my traveling companions with a scrap of pencil I
found at the bottom of my handbag.

When I finally emerged in Lincoln, I was tired and grubby. Por-
ters who would have fallen over themselves to carry Lady Katherine Trenowyth's luggage ignored Miss Kitty Trenowyth with her
one shabby bag, though they did—reluctantly—offer me assistance
when I asked directions and pointed me toward the tram that
would take me to the uphill neighborhood north of the river where
the Hallidays owned a fine big house on a fine big street.

I had not long to wait. I gathered myself together and pressed
into the tram along with a number of fellow travelers and soon
found myself dispensed on a corner by a church. A wide, leafy
avenue stretched north and the air smelled more of new-cut grass
and summer gardens than it did of river mud or diesel fumes.

Set off the road and approached by a wide gravel drive flanked
by a pair of brick pillars, stood a large house of golden stone. A
fountain murmured, and in the shrubs by the front doors, a gardener worked on his knees, pulling weeds. He spied my approach
and sat back on his haunches, a spear of grass tight between his
lips.

"Servants' entrance is around back," he said.

"Is it?" I said coolly as I climbed the steps to pull the bell.

He moved his grass from one side of his mouth to the other but
didn't go back to his work. Instead he hung about, all too interested
to see what happened next.

I clenched my handbag tighter in front of me and waited for someone to answer my ring.

"May I assist you, miss?" The Halliday butler was twice as toplofty as comfortable Burton, the man's livery immaculate, his manner chilling.

"I was hoping to speak with Mr. and Mrs. Halliday."

Apparently, the oddity of my shabby appearance placed against my obvious aristocratic bearing confused him. He seemed uncertain whether to shut the door in my face or invite me inside. I used that moment to my advantage and slid past his guard into the hall.

I couldn't help staring around me at the garish opulence wrought from the cogs and wheels of farm machinery and now military hardware. Nanreath's stark dignity seemed positively shabby in comparison.

"I'm sorry, miss. The Hallidays are not at home."

"I'm happy to wait."

When he realized I was not going to be gotten rid of so easily, he bowed stiffly. "I shall see if they are accepting visitors."

"Snaffle? Who was at the door?" A voice called down from the upper stairs. A head poked over the bannister, a woman perhaps a little older than myself; thin-faced with arrow-straight hair pinned up ruthlessly against her head. She wore an elaborate afternoon gown riddled with bows and beads, and diamonds sparkled in her ears. "Oh, hello. Are you here about the job? I believe Mrs. Nuttle is interviewing the girls in her office."

"I'm here to see Mr. and Mrs. Halliday. It's about their son, Simon."

Her wan complexion blanched to bone, though in no other way did her expression change. She hurried down the stairs, her hand tight on the baluster. "Have you heard something? We've been worried sick, and my father-in-law hasn't been able to get any news out of the War Office no matter how many strings he pulls."

"I should wait to speak to his parents."

"You can tell me. I'm his wife."

She continued to speak, her hand plucking at my coat like the twitting of a bird. I heard nothing beyond that one heart-stopping declaration as the truth clicked one into another like artillery shells shattering my world, one crumbling piece at a time. My stomach turned, and I thought I would be sick right on this woman's expensive pumps. I don't remember what I said to escape that house and that woman, but when I came to my senses I was back on the tram, heading to the railway station, the shredded pieces of Simon's last letter flittering the air as I released it out the window to catch the wind.

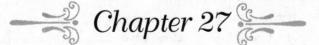

# Chapter 27

*September 1941*

The debris had been cleared, the empty lots swept clean but for a few pieces of broken tile and smashed glass. A set of worn marble steps rose from the pavement to nowhere. The pale slash of searchlights bounced off the underside of a barrage balloon tied six or seven streets over; a new addition to the neighborhood. But low clouds and a misting drizzle kept German bombers grounded, and no growl of airplane engines broke the normal sounds of a city bedding down. London was quiet—for now.

Anna stood across the street, unable to tear her eyes from the hole where her life had once been, unable to tear her thoughts from Graham's scratchy wool cardigans and gentle laugh and Prue's wire spectacles and inevitable wise sayings. These should have been enough for her, but beyond these memories lay dim, half-formed impressions conjured from her own imagination. Lady Katherine's paint-stained fingers and devilish grin, Simon Halliday's rugged good looks and bohemian temperament. Never in her wildest fantasies had she ever imagined—his wife.

Last October she had lost the two people she loved most—her family. Tonight, she lost the two people she held against her heart like a talisman—the dream of a real family.

She had nothing and no one left.

She yanked the chain from her neck and cocked her arm back.

"Don't do it." Hugh approached from the corner where a taxi waited with shuttered headlights. A gleam of light silvered his blond hair and picked out the white of his shirtfront. His false leg scraped against the pavement with each step.

"Why not? Everything they meant to each other was built on a lie."

He caught her wrist, gentling it down to her side and taking the locket from her. "You don't know that."

"I know all I need to know. He was married, Hugh. He ruined my mother, got her pregnant, never with any intention of making it right. Your mother had him pegged. He was a bounder and a rake."

"Does that matter?"

"Of course it does. I spent my entire life dreaming up bedtime stories about the great and beautiful lady and her handsome prince. But *The Red-Haired Wanton* was just that; the portrait of a woman who threw herself away for lust and lost everything. Nothing more." She rested against the cold brick of the building, her chest aching as she fought to breathe. "No wonder Graham and Prue asked me to come home before I was posted. They must have wanted to warn me what I'd find if I asked too many questions about my parents."

"But they weren't your parents. Not really," he said softly.

Anna's body braced, as if expecting another blow.

"I listened to Mrs. Willits tonight, did you?" he continued. "She spoke of two people who loved you as their own. Who never once thought of you as anyone but their daughter, no matter that you didn't share a drop of blood." He paused, as if gathering himself. Eyes distant. Expression stern. She was vaguely aware he spoke to her in the same gentling tone of voice he'd used on Sergeant Greenwood. "Lady Katherine and Simon Halliday are a pretty child's story or a tragic romance, whatever you decide, Anna. But it doesn't take away from who you are or where you come from—or the people who love you."

Piano lessons . . . evenings waiting up . . . stray kittens . . . broken arms . . . Sunday school picnics . . . hugs . . . kisses . . . advice, support, encouragement, and love.

Anger and resentment and horror seeped out of her as Hugh's words and her own memories filled her with warmth and a new calm.

"You were upset and where did you go, Anna? Home." He gave a soft, dry chuckle. "It doesn't matter if you live at Nanreath Hall among Trenowyths for the rest of your life—though for sanity's sake, I don't recommend it—your heart will always remain here in Queen's Crescent with Graham and Prudence Handley."

She threw her arms around him. He staggered and recovered, his own arms enfolding her more slowly. He smelled of aftershave and soap and the wine from dinner. But if she closed her eyes she could smell salty wind, wild gorse and garden roses, beeswax polish and musty wood.

It was the first time she thought of Hugh as the Earl of Melcombe, inexplicably twined with Nanreath Hall and that unbroken line of ancestors stretching forever backward in time and on into a dim future that seemed so uncertain right now.

"Thank you," she whispered.

He dropped the locket into her cupped palm. She closed her hand around it, and together, they headed for the waiting taxi.

The first time Anna arrived at Nanreath Hall it was as a reluctant stranger.

The second time she arrived at Nanreath Hall it was as a determined nurse.

The third time she arrived at Nanreath Hall, she was coming home.

It would never take the place of Graham and Prue's little house in Aldersgate, but there were people here she cared about who cared for her in return. That was as good a place to start as any.

Hugh tore up the avenue, the lime trees flashing past in a blur of green and gray, the snap of a sea wind pulling her hair from her scarf. The hill steepened and the car seemed to lift as it sprang over the rocky drive and there was the house, standing like a sentinel above the parkland with the line of the cliffs behind it and the blue sea beyond. The noise and the wind made talking impossible, but Hugh grinned at her and Anna smiled back.

They had departed from London before dawn that morning, spending the day on the road with only a stop to picnic from the brown shopping bag packed for them by Mrs. Willits. Beetroot sandwiches and sausage rolls washed down with bottles of beer upon an old blanket at the side of the road. Nothing more was said of their midnight conversation, but Anna felt the bonds between them coiling firm and fast.

By the time they reached the gravel sweep in front of the house, the illusion of Nanreath's prewar elegance revealed itself as the workaday convalescent hospital it had become. A queue of ambulances waited by the supply sheds, a mechanic in military khaki serviced a refrigerated delivery van with its bonnet up, and a group of up-patients in regulation pajamas accompanied by two sharp-dressed VADs and a scarlet-trimmed sister relaxed on the lawn. Still, the house, for all its battered neglect and dingy grandeur, retained a quiet dignity, as if the passing calamities of men could never touch it.

"We're home," Hugh announced as he pulled into the old buttery now serving as his garage and parked the car.

Anna gave a decisive nod. "I like the sound of that."

As if she'd been watching for their arrival, Lady Boxley met them at the door. Whether it was a result of Anna's new perspective or Lady Boxley's recent illness, she seemed far more approachable than ever before. She wore a peach floral frock that warmed her pale, blue-veined skin, and her hair had been carefully waved to soften her long, narrow face. Even the set of golden topaz at her throat seemed gentler than her usual set of harsh, cold sapphires.

"Hallo, Mother." Hugh brushed a brisk kiss upon her cheek. "You can relax now. We're back safe and sound."

"You're a filthy mess, Hugh. No doubt you ran yourself ragged without a care for your health. I'll fix you a drink before dinner and you can tell me all about your meeting with Samuels at Whitehall."

"I would, Mother, but I didn't meet with Samuels. Didn't go to Whitehall at all, actually."

"Hugh! Why not? I set up that appointment specifically. It was difficult to persuade him to meet with you in the first place and now this . . . what am I going to tell him?"

"Tell him I lost my leg and couldn't hobble there on my stump, tell him I was in bed making mad passionate love to a woman I met in a shelter, I don't care. I got as far as the lobby and then . . . couldn't go through with it. Ended in a pub near Cheyne Walk."

"I should have known. I thought you wanted a purpose. Something to keep you busy."

"I do. Just not that purpose."

She sighed and pinched her forehead, as if a headache were coming on.

"Anyway, love to chat but I can't. I'm meeting someone. I just have time to drop my bags and scrub the dust off."

Her sculpted brows arched, her eyes hardening. "Not five minutes home and you're off again. Some floozy, no doubt. I've seen those land girls working the farm over at Whitecross Halt. A lot of cheeky good-for-nothings with their minds in the gutter."

Anna stiffened, her eyes flashing to Hugh. But he gave no outward sign of being upset by his mother's accusations. Instead he laughed and tweaked her chin. "A gentleman never kisses and tells, Mother dear."

She turned to Anna, her nose almost twitching with suppressed anger. "And you, Miss Trenowyth? I hope your journey to London was more successful than my son's."

"In a manner of speaking."

"What's that supposed to mean?"

She smiled politely. "Excuse me, ma'am. Matron will expect me on the ward within the hour."

As she climbed the front steps, she heard Hugh and his mother in their usual barbed exchange. She should have known Her Ladyship's illness wouldn't change her personality *that* much. " . . . as headstrong as her mother" followed her inside.

Upstairs, Anna began unpacking. Clothes folded and put away, cosmetics bag back on her dressing table. She was hanging up her best dress when Tilly came in, fresh off duty.

"Welcome home. Did you have a nice trip?"

"I did. Hugh even treated us to the Ritz one evening for dinner."

"Sounds posh. Anyone there worth seeing?"

"No one I recognized, but in uniform they all look the same, don't they?"

"I don't know. Some fill out their uniforms better than others."

Tilly flashed her usual cheeky grin before sobering. "How did Sophie seem when you dropped her off?"

"As if a cold wind would blow her away. Sir Edmund only mentioned her unfortunate nursing business twice within my hearing."

"Damnable war. I hate it." Tilly's eyes shone with anger. "Just when you're happiest, it all comes caving in."

Anna was reminded of Tony. She'd tried so hard to keep him at arm's length, and still he'd finagled his way into her heart. He'd become someone she could count on . . . and that was dangerous. She'd already lost Graham and Prue and witnessed Sophie's devastation at the death of Lieutenant Douglas. She couldn't bear to grieve again.

"Is anything wrong, Tilly?" Anna asked, selfishly hoping someone else's worries would ease her own.

"Of course not," she replied sharply, unpinning her veil and tossing it away. "A drink and a dance, and I'll be right as rain." Pulling off her apron, she presented her back to Anna, who helped her unbutton her dress.

"With Hugh?"

Tilly craned her head round. "I don't know. Is he headed into Newquay?"

"He rushed off as soon as we arrived back. Said he was meeting someone."

"Probably one of those land girls from Whitecross Halt. He better watch out, or he'll find himself in the suds."

"Are you still arguing?"

"I'm not arguing with Hugh. What gave you that idea?"

"It doesn't surprise me if you are, but if he's hurt you in any way, I . . ." Her words faded along with her nerve, especially considering Tilly stared at her like a Billingsgate cod.

"You think Hugh and me are an item? Oh dear, Anna. I can't

decide whether that's the most amusing thing I've ever heard or the most offensive." Tilly shook off her momentary stupefaction and was now moving about the room, grabbing up a blouse and skirt from one chair, a pair of pumps from under her bed, a scarf from the hook beside the mirror, though she did it all while avoiding Anna's gaze.

"But you're always flirting with him and then there was the conversation in the stairwell and I saw you walking with him on the cliffs and you were crying."

"Oh, so that's what this is about." Comprehension lit Tilly's eyes as she brushed and repinned her hair. She smiled into the mirror at Anna's reflection. "I'm not in love with Hugh if that's what you're worried about."

"But you're in love with someone. You said so. Someone whose family doesn't approve."

"I said I didn't want to talk about it." She applied her lipstick, pursing and primping, wiping the edge of her mouth, blotting it on a handkerchief.

"You talked to Hugh about it."

"That was different."

"Why?"

"Fine." Tilly swung around from her place at the mirror, hurt and anger in her face. "You want to know what happened? I'll tell you what happened. I met a chap. He told me he loved me. I believed him. Then he scampered, and I feel the biggest clot in Christendom. End of story."

"Why didn't you say anything?"

"I . . ." Tilly sank onto a chair, Tangee lipstick rolling between her thumb and finger. "Oh, I don't know. I wanted to. I was so close to spilling everything to you and Sophie, but Jamie wanted us to keep it quiet. That should have been the knock in the head I needed to see it was all a hum, but he made it seem so logical. He wanted to tell his grandmother before she heard it from anyone else."

"Wait. Start at the beginning. Who is Jamie?"

"Pilot Officer James Meadows. He and Hugh were mates in Norway. Now he's flying Blenheims out of Chivenor. We started walking out together. It was going swimmingly. He told me he loved me, even asked me to marry him—"

"Tilly! You didn't."

"No, but I would have. I also knew if I told you or Sophie, you'd talk me out of it. You both always thought I was too frivolous and silly for my own good. Anyway, he left to speak to his grandmother about it months ago. She raised him after his parents died, and he feels an obligation. Then . . . nothing. He didn't write or call. I tried phoning him at his base and they acted as if I were a Jerry spy. Wouldn't tell me anything."

"You think his grandmother told him he couldn't see you anymore?"

She blinked away tears. "I know he was awfully worried about telling her. She's quite old and very particular. Hugh knew about Jamie and me. He'd caught us at the ruins one night, but he kept his mouth shut—for once in his life. Anyway, he asked around for me, but he ran into the same stone wall." She dabbed at her eyes. "You can call me a twit to fall for that old flyboy's line, it wouldn't be any worse than what I've called myself. But he really was a peach, Anna. So old-fashioned and proper—a real gentleman, not like these swaggering half-pint heroes with their wide smiles and their quick lines. I couldn't help myself. I fell—hard."

"It happens to all of us."

"Not to you. You're much more sensible. You've both feet too firmly on the ground to ever let anyone sweep them out from under you like that."

It was Anna's turn to look uncomfortable.

"I'm so glad I told you. It was killing me to hold it in, but I just wanted to forget about it. Jamie Meadows could arrive on his hands and knees and I'd not give him the time of day." She rose from her chair, her earlier distress buried under a layer of powder and paint. "Got to run. Me and some of the other girls are hitching a ride with one of the MTC to Newquay. There's a new band playing at the Blue Lagoon. I hear the singer looks exactly like Sinatra. Ta."

And just like that she was gone in a cloud of Shalimar and hair lacquer.

Anna continued unpacking, using the chore to make sense of Tilly's confession and her own misunderstanding, but she couldn't help but return to Tilly's offhand assertion. Was it really practicality that kept her from giving herself up to love or something else?

At the bottom of the valise lay the file Ginny had brought to the restaurant. Anna sat on the bed, opening Simon Halliday's folder to reread notations she'd long since memorized. Simon Halliday married to Edith in June 1911. No children.

Her mother—and now Tilly—had both given themselves up to love and had their hearts crushed. Was it so wrong to want to prevent the same thing from happening to her? To want to hold a part of herself back from the chance of more and possibly greater loss? It was just good common sense, that was all.

Turning over the page, she discovered a second set of reports clipped underneath—William Algernon George Burnside Trenowyth.

She'd completely forgotten about her request for Hugh's father's file. She started reading entries on service medals, regimental details, medical reports. She read through the facts of his shrapnel wound in July 1916 exacerbated by the lung-shredding effects of the chlorine gas. Evacuated to a battalion hospital, where he was given a transfusion of Type O blood.

Anna paused before reexamining the report from the doctor in charge. William Trenowyth possessed Type O blood. According to the questionnaire filled out at the blood drive in the spring, Lady Boxley also possessed Type O.

So why did Hugh have Type A?

Anna went to her locker and pulled out the purloined photograph of the blond man kneeling in the grass beside the tumbled remains of the old cliff ruins. Standing with him, chubby with baby fat, his wispy blond hair peeking from beneath a cap, was a very young Hugh. A picture hidden away for years. A scandal that could turn a family inside out.

Same narrow face. Same smirk to the full mouth.

Eddie at the ruins.

Was this her answer?

Two days later Anna cornered Captain Matthews in his office after her last shift—or perhaps interrupted might be the better word. The QA sister collecting files from the MO looked positively flustered, her eyes bright as her cheeks. "I look forward to seeing you at the concert tomorrow night, Captain," she cooed on her way past.

The MO had the grace to look chagrined, but it didn't keep the pleasure from his own earnest gaze. "It will be my honor to escort you, Sister Evangeline."

Anna watched the exchange with relief. Surely this would end the persistent rumors linking her and the captain once and for all. And if she were to select the perfect woman for him, she couldn't have done better than Sister Evangeline. Unpretentious, level-headed, and endlessly patient, she would make a textbook doctor's wife.

He closed the door with a tug of his shirt collar, a blush creeping up his neck. "Sister Evangeline and I were just archiving old case files. She's very good at organizing, so I thought I'd set her loose on me . . . that is . . . my office."

"I'm sure she'll do a wonderful job, sir." In either case, she thought, though she didn't say it out loud.

"Yes, well." He cleared his throat as he gestured for her to take a seat. "I hope you had a good time in London. When did you get back?"

"Day before yesterday. I had a lovely time."

"Good. Ready to jump back in? I have a feeling we're going to be busy. Things are heating up and not in a good way for us. Between the Japanese stirring things up in the east and the Russian collapse at the Dnieper, it's looking bleak."

"We've managed this far, sir. I suppose we can keep muddling on."

"Mm," he grunted. "But for how long, is the question." He rubbed his forehead, as if it ached, before reaching for his pipe. "I don't suppose you sought me out in my office to talk about the war. What can I do for you, Trenowyth? Though if it's about Sister Murphy, my hands are tied. I've suggested she be parachuted into Berlin on a one-woman crusade to take out the top brass. If anyone can do it, she can."

"No, sir. It's not Sister Murphy. I wondered if you might explain blood typing to me. I mean, I have a general idea of how it works, but I want to be certain."

Obviously relieved to be back on a professional footing, he lit his pipe and sat back in his chair, once more in firm control. "Of course. Always happy to educate. What do you need to know?"

"The genetics of it. It's like hair and eyes, isn't it? I mean, certain traits get passed down through the parents."

"That's right in a nutshell. There are four main types; A, B, AB, and O. Two As have an A child, Two Bs have a B child, Two Os have an O child."

What if one parent has one type and one has another?"

"Well, in the case of an A and a B, the child will have AB type blood."

"And in the case of O and another type?"

"The O is a recessive trait so the child would end being A or B." He eyed her curiously. "Why all the questions? Still thinking about my offer to set you up with a recommendation to St. Thomas's? They're in need of qualified nurses, and with your wartime experience, you'd do well."

"No, sir. I was just curious." He continued to regard her oddly, making her scramble to come up with a convincing explanation. "You see, while I was in London, I was telling the story about my afternoon filling in with the blood transfusion service, and it got me wondering about the science of it. That's all."

He smiled. "Well, not to sound selfish, but I'm glad you're not planning on leaving us just yet. Now that Kinsale is gone, we've few staff with extensive experience."

"There's always Sister Murphy, sir." Anna rose to leave.

He shuddered. "By the way, did you and Lady Boxley ever come to a détente?"

"I think so, sir. For now."

"I'm happy for you. She's a hard woman, but in times like these, we must cling to family with both hands. You never know, do you?"

But Anna knew. She knew everything. Now she just had to decide what to do with the information.

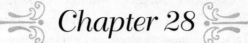

# Chapter 28

*November 1916*

"Kitty?"

I didn't answer. Instead, I continued to paint, throwing color on the canvas, shade after shade, layer after layer, until the canvas dripped with thickly spattered gobs of cadmium red and crimson, vermilion, carmine and rose adder. My smock was covered, my face and hair speckled while my hands were sodden up to my wrists.

"Kitty? Please come away. It'll be all right. You'll see."

I knew Jane and Agnes stood in the doorway. I could feel their concern, could picture them sharing worried glances as they pleaded with me. I slapped a gob of earthy brown sienna that cut across the brighter shades like a bayonet slash, an open wound.

Was this what it felt like to go mad with grief? I'd heard the phrase before; who hadn't in these last few years of annihilation, but I'd always assumed the women who tore their hair and slashed their wrists in their agony were a weak, overly dramatic bunch given to hysteria simply to gain attention for themselves. Now I began to understand the truth. This had nothing to do with anyone else. This was a storm within that could not be contained no matter the humiliation. One had to simply give in to this howling, wild, insatiable fury. It could not be stopped, merely aimed.

My only release came with sleep, and so I spent hours in my bed, curled beneath the blankets with my face buried in one of Simon's old shirts. I tried to forget for those long hours, tried to pretend all was as it had been before the war, before I knew the truth.

But solace was not so easy to find, even in oblivion. In my dreams, we lay entwined, his lean strength cushioned between my legs. He would laugh away my sorrows and explain his betrayal. Their marriage had been a loveless contract wrought from duty and convenience, which neither had been sorry to set aside in order to pursue independent lives. He anticipated a life dedicated to his art in London. She happily pursued her charitable works in Lincoln. All was easy until we met and fell in love, then he'd been forced to make a choice: tell the truth or live a lie.

My dream always ended with his tears scalding my breasts as he asked what choice I would have made had the decision been mine. I would wake before I could answer him, cold and cramped and nauseated as our growing child spun within my belly, but with the question ringing in my ears as if he had only just now whispered it.

I grabbed up a handful of bright canary yellow, smearing it in long, thin, snaking streaks like tears. I looked at my paint-covered hands, fisting them so the paint oozed out the sides to fall to the floor in large, ugly, wet plops.

"Kitty! Stop it now!"

The voice froze me in place, still feeling the cold, glutinous colors slick between my fingers. I turned to see Doris, her familiar features haggard now and pale with losses of her own. She took off her hat and coat, as if coming into my flat was a daily occurrence, though we'd not seen each other in years. "Agnes, fix a pot of tea. Jane, run down to the grocers and purchase bread, cheese, and a good thick slice of ham if they have one."

The two jumped to her bidding as Doris eyed me as a mother might a child she despaired of. "Look at you. You're an absolute mess. Let's get you cleaned up."

She guided me to the lavatory at the end of the landing. Plunged my hands under the faucet. The water was icy cold. My fingers ached. The bowl of the sink turned red and pink as Doris scrubbed me clean, the paint swirling toward the drain. I closed my eyes, sickened at the bloody, frothy mess. "I was sorry to hear about your husband."

She had married a rabble-rousing socialist, a writer for a trade-unionist paper. The marriage had lasted barely six months before he'd been killed; one among thousands pounded into dust along the Somme in July. She waved off my sympathy. "I'm sorry, too, but it won't bring him back or keep bread on my table, will it?"

She guided me back into the tiny cramped rooms I'd taken in Fitzrovia when I could no longer pay the rent on the more spacious flat in Ralston Street. Pushing aside the pile of letters strewn across my wobbly dining table, she sat me down with a cup of tea and began to rummage efficiently through cupboards for the makings of breakfast.

Soon enough, I was eating a soft-boiled egg with toast and a bowl of porridge. I found myself surprisingly ravenous and ate every morsel, sopping up the last of the yolk with my bread in a manner that would have horrified my mother's idea of good manners.

"When was the last time you had a proper meal? Or a proper rest?"

"I don't know," I answered honestly. When I dreamt it was of

Simon. And food had lost its flavor, my stomach constantly uneasy so that anything that went in soon came up again.

Her gaze fell on the letters, the handwriting growing increasingly messy and hard to decipher, as if the writer was losing patience with each unanswered missive.

. . . never know how sorry I am . . .

. . . loved you beyond measure . . .

. . . for God's sake, please write and say you forgive me . . .

"It's been three months since you found out about his wife. From the look of this mess, he must have written you every day. Did you ever answer him?"

"What was there to say? Nothing would have changed." I picked at the edge of the table where the veneer pulled away. Paint remained under my nails and in the creases of each knuckle.

"Yet you kept them, Kitty," she said quietly, forcing me to meet her gaze. "All of them."

"I won't receive any more." I went to the desk scattered with unpaid bills and returned with a single bloodstained envelope, which I handed to Doris. "This came two days ago."

She pulled free the nearly ruined pages, bringing with them a thin gold chain and locket that fell onto the tabletop.

"One of Simon's friends found the letter among his things after he . . . he died in hospital," I explained, my eyes unable to pull free of the dull glint of cheap metal worn smooth by the dirt and sweat from his chest where it had lain against his heart. "He sent it on to me with a note enclosed. It was a belly wound. It took Simon two days to die. At least he wasn't alone. It's little enough comfort, but it's all I have."

Doris read the pages slowly before laying them aside. "He loved you very much."

I couldn't help but recall our last night together and his almost tearful declarations, the ferocity in which he sought to convince me of his undying passion. Had that been as false as all the rest, or was that the truth amid all the other lies? Was love enough to justify deception?

"I don't want to talk about it anymore, Doris. I just want to put it—and him—out of my mind."

"You can't just push the last years aside like they didn't happen."

"I have to try or I'll go mad. Simon wasn't ever mine, not really. No matter how many letters he wrote to me. He belonged to her."

"Will you give up the baby?"

My hands caressed my stomach where the flutterings of tiny limbs rippled like waves. "No," I answered, almost daring Doris to argue. "Whatever happens, this baby belongs to me."

"Right, easy enough to manage with so many widows these days. None will ever question it."

My head came up sharply. "I won't lie."

"Simon's gone, Kitty. You have to think of yourself . . . and the baby that's coming. Do you want the neighbors to whisper? It's not hurting anyone. Who's to know?"

"I'll know." I pushed my tea away. "Lies started this. I won't . . . I can't . . . keep pretending."

"It'll be harder."

I took up the locket, unclasping it to reveal the photos. On the left was the stiff, sour-faced picture of myself taken over a year ago. But on the right had been added a grainy shot of Simon in his uniform. He looked tired but stoic. His hair was shorter and his face thinner, but I smiled through my watering eyes at the familiar slash of dark brows and the long, knifing cheekbones beneath a shadow of beard.

"Perhaps, but not nearly as hard as this."

I snapped the locket closed, running my thumb over the inscription he'd added before he placed it in the envelope to be sent home to me: *Forgive my love.*

There was nothing to forgive. And, God help me, but despite it all, I loved him still.

# Chapter 29

*October 1941*

A few days later Tony and Anna sat side by side on the grass in the shadow of the ruins. It was almost nine at night, but double summertime meant light still lingered in the west, throwing a satin sheen across the sea.

"Now that you know the truth, will you seek out your father's family?"

"Even if they had any idea I existed, do you think his wife would care to make the acquaintance of her husband's bastard child?"

"What of his parents? He might have brothers and sisters. You could have a whole basket of relations you never knew."

She plucked a stem of heather, twirling it between her fingers before crushing the small purple petals to release the woodsy aroma. "I don't know. I've spent my whole life never even knowing his name. He was always just a shadowy idea, never real. Not in the sense of family and houses and a place you can go on a train to visit. And now that I know what he did, the hurt he caused"—Anna tossed away the broken stem—"I just don't know."

Wind moved over the grass, and she pulled her cardigan onto her shoulders. The temperature had dropped with the setting of the sun, the night growing cool with the changing of the season.

Tony sipped from the beer they shared between them. "Hard to believe it was Hugh that kept you from tossing away the locket."

"Don't sound so surprised. He hides more behind that devil-may-care smile than you'd think."

"I've known that for years. Smartest chap in school without cracking a book. We'd have hated him if he wasn't so damnably pleasant. I just didn't know he'd finally decided to stop playing the jester. It's past time."

"Perhaps events have forced him to sober up."

"What sort of events?"

Anna shrugged, her gaze drawn to the first glimmer of stars showing through a haze of clouds.

"You've been awfully quiet," Tony commented. "Penny for your thoughts?"

She let out a breath as she made her decision. "Right. I didn't know whether to show you, but I need to speak to someone. Maybe you can help me decide what to do." She pulled the photos from her pocket and handed them to Tony. "I found these in Lady Boxley's room."

"This was taken here." Tony studied the first photo in the fading light. "Who is he? He looks familiar."

"His name is Eddie. I don't know his last name."

"So Lady Boxley holds a tendre for a long-lost love, so what?" He handed Anna back the photos, casting her a doubtful look. "I thought you were here to find out about your past, not Hugh's."

"I am, but the longer I'm here, the more things don't make sense."

Anna sat up, tucking her legs beneath her. For some reason, the space between them seemed to yawn wider than the inches would indicate. "Why was Lady Boxley so afraid of me coming here in the first place? She practically warned me away from Nanreath Hall and Hugh in particular. And then there's the portrait in the gallery of Lord Boxley."

"What of it?"

"It doesn't look a bit like Hugh. He's auburn-haired, Hugh's blond."

"Lady Boxley is blond."

"So is the mysterious Eddie. And maybe he looks familiar because he looks like Hugh. Then there's this." She handed him the folder.

"What am I looking at?" Tony asked.

"It's Lord Boxley's wartime medical report. I had Ginny Willits retrieve it at the same time she searched for my father's."

"So you already had your suspicions."

"But this proves them."

"Does it?"

She felt his sharp response like a slap to the cheek. Not that she hadn't expected him to play devil's advocate, but his forcefulness caught her off guard.

"Look," she hammered, pointing out the bits she'd underlined in black pen. "Lord Boxley was wounded at Neuve Chappelle. He was treated at a battalion aid station and returned to his unit, but while he was there his blood was tested for possible transfusion use. He was Type O."

"So?"

"Lady Boxley is Type O, as well. But Hugh is Type A. That can't happen—unless Lord Boxley is *not* Hugh's father."

"I suppose you think this chap Eddie is?"

For some reason, his defense of Hugh felt like an attack on her. She carried on, but her earlier enjoyment of the evening had evaporated, the atmosphere between them now as chill as the weather.

"It all makes sense. Lady Boxley has a fling and finds herself pregnant. Easy enough to pass off the child as her husband's. Then he's gassed in the war and dies soon after. She's a widow with no ties to Nanreath Hall or the title but for Hugh, the supposed heir. It fits. You have to see that." Her voice rose. She took a breath and tried to relax.

Tony looked out on the ocean for a moment, as if pulling his thoughts together before speaking. He made a small dismissive gesture with his shoulders before turning back to her. "All right, say this is all true and Hugh's illegitimate. There's nothing anyone can do about it now. Hugh's been Lord Melcombe since he was thirteen. No going back even if he wanted to hand the whole thing over and become a hermit in Tahiti. He's stuck with the whole bally lot."

"That's just the point. Hugh's trapped. Trapped by this house, by his mother's expectations, by history and family. If I tell him . . ."

"If you tell him? You mean you want to show him this? And then what? Have you even thought that far ahead?"

"I'm sorry I asked your advice."

"You didn't ask my advice. You sought my approval."

Stung, Anna got to her feet. The shadow of the ruined tower stairs cut across the grass, and wind purred through the crumbled mortar. She had allowed Tony to bring her to the cliff ruins, but it wasn't the same. She wasn't the same. With Russia's slow capitulation, the war drew dangerously close again. How long before Tony's luck ran out? Perhaps their quarrel was a sign that she needed to end it before she fell too hard and lost too much.

"I don't understand what you're trying to accomplish, Anna," Tony said quietly. "I wonder if you do."

"You can't possibly understand. You have a big family, women hanging after you, wealth and position." Questions ate away at her composure. She could feel her voice rising with her temper. "You've never felt trapped or alone or wondered where you fit. You've never had a care in the world."

"Is that what you think?" He rose and dusted himself off, his own voice growing tight. "That I'm just some ruddy playboy looking for the next notch in my belt?"

Anna couldn't face the hurt in his eyes. She turned away. "That's what happens, isn't it? War changes everything. It makes us behave as if there's no repercussions, no tomorrows. We never stop to think how our careless flings will impact those who follow after us."

"I thought we were talking about Hugh."

"We are."

"I don't think so. I think this all comes back to you and your fear of reliving Lady Katherine's mistakes."

"That's unfair."

"Your mother followed her heart. So it didn't work out. That doesn't mean it won't for you." He stepped toward her. Paused when she stepped back. He stood, hands in his pockets, the wind teasing his black hair, his face lost in the ruins' shadow. "You can't let fear rule your life, Anna."

She looked up at the stark tumbled stones jutting against the darkening sky. "You don't know what I fear, Tony. No one does."

"I think you've spent the past year afraid of everything." He didn't say it, but the word rose like a specter in the dark—Dunkirk. "I know what you're feeling, Anna. I was there."

Her breath iced in her lungs. She froze, unable to breathe or move. Then ice was replaced by fire, and she felt a rage boiling up from a churning pit in her stomach. Unexpected and uncontrollable. It was no longer about holding Tony at arm's length. It was about making him hurt as she had been hurt. "Were you? Really? Funny, because I never saw you. I never saw any of the RAF flyboys who were supposed to be protecting our retreat. The only planes I saw belonged to the Jerries as they strafed our ambulance convoys, shot up refugees, and dropped bombs on the boats sent to bring us home."

By now the memories strangled her thoughts. Even as some small part of her knew she was being irrational, she hurled her fury at him, enjoying the look of wounded confusion in his eyes. "Damn you all, you left us to die."

She fled the cliffs as she had not been able to flee the disaster at Dunkirk, praying she might leave the horrors behind. She glanced back only once. Tony stood in the graying twilight, a black silhouette against the crumbling tower brooding above him.

He had it all wrong. She didn't fear she would make her mother's mistakes.

She feared she already had.

Captain Matthews was right. The wireless and newspapers were full of the worsening news from the Russian front. Every update seemed to bring new casualty numbers and reports of more ground lost to the panzer divisions racing for Moscow—Odessa, Kharkov, Sevastopol. The hospital was alive with speculation over how soon Stalin would capitulate to Hitler and what that might mean for the beleaguered British.

At least the rumors kept Anna from dwelling on her row with Tony. She shouldn't have spoken to him like that. Harriet's death wasn't his fault. She rang him to apologize, but the clerk who answered the phone was singularly unhelpful and she'd been too ashamed to leave a message. She would find him at the pub one evening or cycle to the airfield at St. Eval on her next afternoon off and grovel in person. Hopefully, it would be enough to make amends. She might not agree with him, but she'd come to rely on his being there when she needed him.

Her shift over at seven, Anna went in search of Hugh. He'd not been on the wards at all today and no one she asked knew where he might be. She climbed the stairs and turned onto the corridor leading to the gallery and the family's private quarters. By now she felt easy strolling the long, pillared room with its walls of Trenowyth ancestors, and no one from the hospital questioned her right to be there.

Rain washed the long windows, blurring the grounds and sending a cold draft over the creaking floorboards. With no lamps lit, the space was dim and she shivered in the cardigan she'd thrown over her uniform. Another long, dreary winter lay on the horizon. Would the New Year show a turn in the tide for the Allies, or would the war drag on endlessly?

She pushed her dismal thoughts aside as unhelpful. Instead, she began comparing faces as she passed beneath the rows of portraits; noses and eyes, the tilt of a head, the strength in a jaw. She touched her own cheek and chin, smoothed a hand over her curling red hair pinned viciously into a neat victory roll beneath her veil.

As always, she paused before the portrait of Lady Katherine, as if seeking a connection between this silent, staring young woman and herself. Was she the only one to notice the way her mother's lips curved in a smile of flirtatious excitement, the sparkle of secrets in her eyes? Or the way her body looked to escape the prison of her frame, as if she couldn't wait to be caught up in her lover's arms?

*Forgive my love.*

Had Lady Katherine forgiven Simon's betrayal?

She had left her home and family for him, though they could not wed. She had borne him a child. She had worn his locket until her death and passed it to her daughter to carry forward.

Was that Anna's answer?

She tucked her locket beneath her blouse and over her heart.

"Back to lurking about the gallery like a skeleton at the feast, Miss Trenowyth? I'd hoped we'd turned you from that habit. It's disconcerting. I feel as if you're sizing us up and finding us lacking."

Lady Boxley stood in the far doorway. In a stylish aubergine suit with a jaunty ribboned hat perched on her blond hair, and handbag clasped in her gloved hands, she appeared to be just arriving home.

"I'm sorry. I know it's against the rules."

Her Ladyship waved off Anna's apology. "You've earned the right to a few concessions on our part. Freedom to wander the gallery is hardly an onerous request."

"Thank you, ma'am. I don't remember much about my mother, but here I feel . . . close to her in a way I never have before."

Lady Boxley's heels tapped across the floorboards as she joined Anna in front of the painting. She gave it a quick, disparaging glance and sniffed. "A nice sentiment, but proximity doesn't always bring happiness." She paused, her gaze uneasy. "You discover things best left buried."

Anna sucked in a quick breath of realization. "You knew all along."

Lady Boxley's face took on a pinched, shuttered expression as she ran an agitated hand up and down her strand of pearls.

"You knew Simon Halliday was married," Anna badgered. "That's why you didn't want me to go to London."

"Of course I knew," Lady Boxley finally snapped. "Simon Halliday was a cad of the first order. Kitty only found out about the wife after it was too late. Then he died, and Kitty was left with you. Life moved on."

"That's when she came back to Nanreath, isn't it? She needed help, and all of you turned her away."

"William was unwell. Frankly, he was dying, though no one would admit it."

Generations of Trenowyths watched from every corner of the gallery in seeming curiosity as Anna left her post beneath Lady Katherine's portrait to pause in front of the nearby painting of the late Lord Boxley. "Was that the reason, or was it because you were afraid my mother knew the truth about Hugh's paternity and would tell your husband?"

For a moment Lady Boxley's face was wiped clean of all expression, the color draining away to leave her ghostly white. She swayed, laying a hand on the back of a chair to steady herself, and her hand touched her chest. But the weakness lasted only moments. As if a metal rod was inserted into her spine, she straightened, her chin lifting in defiance, her eyes crackling with—amusement?

"Is that what you thought?" she asked mildly. "That I drove Kitty off to prevent her from exposing my infidelity?" A dark smile hovered on her lips. "You do have a rather sinister view of me, don't you?"

Anna frowned. This was where Lady Boxley was supposed to explain her actions in a tearful pleading confession. Not take a seat on one of a pair of sofas and beckon Anna to sit opposite her on the other. Not clear her throat with businesslike composure as she folded her hands across her handbag, eyes grave but far from horrified or guilt ridden. Anna felt as if the bombers had struck again and the floors beneath her had shifted under her feet.

"I found the pictures that you tried to hide. And the information in Lord Boxley's military record confirms he's not Hugh's real father."

"I wondered where those pictures had gone. I should have known it was you."

"So you admit it?"

Lady Boxley heaved a tired sigh, her shoulders rounding, as if she bore up against a great weight. "I sent Kitty away when she came home. That much is true. But I sent her away on her father's orders, not my own. The old earl had always been a stickler for society's hidebound proprieties. Kitty's affair with Halliday put all he held dear at risk—his position, his reputation, his connections. When she left, he cut off all communication. It was as if she never existed."

"Yet, her portrait remains."

"I returned it to the gallery after the late Lord and Lady Melcombe died. Despite its unfortunate subject, it's a Balázs. His works carry a hefty price tag. I wasn't going to let a potential source of future revenue molder away in Nanreath's leaky attics." She clasped her hands in her lap, her diamonds winking. "As for William, he guessed long before Hugh was born that he wasn't the father. He chose to overlook it."

"But that doesn't make sense."

"Perhaps it doesn't to you, but times were different. Pride and shame in equal measure kept William silent, and since to divorce me would have been a financial as well as social disaster for the earldom, he did the only thing he could do under the circumstances—he ignored his suspicions. In the end, it turned out for the best."

"But Hugh was the heir. He stood to inherit everything and yet . . ."

"He didn't bear one drop of Trenowyth blood?" Her smile tightened, as if she were in pain. "William was wounded in the war—

I'm sure whatever report you unearthed in London explained just how extensive those wounds were. He would not—could not—sire a child of his own. Hugh was all he had. If it was discovered he was a bastard, the earldom would have passed out of this line of the family to a distant second cousin. So for all those reasons, William ignored what he couldn't change, and Hugh became the earl in due course."

"Does Hugh know?"

Until now, Lady Boxley's manner had been one of almost relief, but at mention of Hugh, her gaze hardened with its old animosity. "Don't be absurd. I only told you to make you understand what's at stake. My son must never find out. You see how he is; he drinks, he smokes, he runs around with a string of cheap women. All to prove he is still the man he was before he lost his leg. Would you add to his despair by telling him that man was a fiction all along? It would destroy him."

"Doesn't he deserve the truth?"

"What good would it do now?" She clutched her bag, and a flash of real sorrow knifed her expression before she was once more a mask of complete self-control. "Eddie is dead, Miss Trenowyth. As is William, Lady Katherine, Simon Halliday. Everyone involved in this story are naught but ghosts. I would leave them where they are; in their graves. I would have you do the same. For your sake. For Hugh's." She stood up, signaling the end of their conversation. "As I said before you went to London, the past is over and done with. We can only move forward as best we can. I tried to do what was best for my son just as Kitty thought she was doing what was best for you when she left you with the Handleys. That is all a mother can do. Muddle through and hope she's not made too big a hash of things. That you turn out well despite our failures."

Anna looked upon Lord Boxley in his frame; stoic and stiff

upper lip as he prepared for war. She glanced at Lady Katherine, forever young and beautiful and poised to make the biggest choice of her life.

"Will you tell him?" She had never heard such vulnerability in Lady Boxley's voice.

Suddenly unable to stomach this house and its generations of Trenowyths all watching her with what seemed malicious curiosity, Anna rose from the sofa. When had life become so complicated? When had the truth become the enemy and the falsehood the friend? When had right and wrong grown so muddled?

"I don't know."

"Anna?" Lady Boxley's use of her Christian name caused her to pause at the door. She turned back to see a fleeting look of entreaty pass over the older woman's face. "I would have thought you of all people would realize that digging up old pains only brings new sorrows. Hugh has grieved enough this past year, don't you think?"

T urn it off, Nurse. I can't take any more bad news."
        "With allies like these, what's the point? These Russian blokes are as worthless as the bleeding French."

"Russian bear? More like a Russian bunny rabbit."

The men's grumbling prompted Anna to snap off the wireless.

"How about a nice game of bridge?" she asked, shuffling a deck of cards.

The men groaned. One stared out at the soggy lawn with longing in his eyes. Another put a record on the gramophone. The first sentimental bars of "London Pride" broke the dismal sound of the wind speckling the windows with rain. It had been pouring for close to a week. Even Anna was beginning to grow bored—and moss. Hugh's decision to visit a friend in Exeter had put any decision to speak with him on hold. Part of her was relieved. Part of her wished for it simply to be over and done with. She changed her mind at least twice every thirty seconds.

"If nothing else, the foul weather's keeping the bombers on the ground. Let's be thankful for small favors," she chirped, hoping to lighten their mood—as well as her own. A Ping-Pong ball crossed her bow. They obviously weren't buying what she was selling.

"Heard Portsmouth got it last week. And Bristol night before last."

"Aye, the ports is getting it the worst. Them and those poor bastards at sea. Blighters running convoy duty are sitting ducks out there."

"What of them boys up St. Eval way? Aren't they supposed to be keeping the Jerries at bay?"

"Ha. I heard they're close to packing it in. Lost near half a flight over the past weeks."

Anna picked up a tray of glasses and set them on a trolley for delivery to the sinks downstairs. Cleared away lunch. Tried to hide her shaking hands as she began her twice daily round of ashtray emptying. Tony would be all right. He had to be all right.

"What ho, chaps! What's the latest from the front?" Hugh leaned against the door frame dressed in official-looking khaki, a white-trimmed cap perched on his head at a rakish angle, his usual cigarette dangling from his mouth.

"Sir!" The men straightened from their various poses of ennui to welcome Hugh. "Where have you been?"

"Thought you'd copped it in that jalopy of yours."

"Or ran off with that blonde you told us about."

Hugh processed down the passage between the beds like a commander inspecting his troops. All eyes followed him like a roomful of lovesick puppies. "Been away, but I'm back now, so you all have to shape up—or else. That means you, Harris." He offered a lighter to a tall, gangly boy with a bad case of stomach ulcers fumbling in the pockets of his robe.

The boy laughed and accepted the light, puffing at his gasper with a sigh of gratitude.

"Where's Rollins?" Hugh asked.

"Sent back to his unit, sir."

"And that chap with the eye . . . what was his name . . ."—he snapped his fingers—"Stewart."

"Him, too."

"Bloody shame. Hell of a good bridge player."

"Garrett's still here."

"Of course he is. Never known a chap to have so many illnesses. What is it this time, Garrett? Bubonic plague with a side helping of foot rot?"

The men laughed, including a blushing Private Garrett.

Anna closed the lid on her box of medicines and set it back on the waiting trolley. "Is that a St. John's Ambulance badge you're wearing?"

Hugh did a model's turn in front of her. "It is. You're looking at the brigade's latest driver. I'm headed for training tomorrow."

"When on earth did this happen?"

"Remember that meeting in London I scuppered out on?"

"Your mother was in a fume over it."

"I ended in a pub, nursing a pint when in walks an old friend of mine. Apparently, he was invalided out of the navy with a steel plate in his head—not that you could have told the difference. He was always a bit of a clod. Anyway, we got talking and the next thing I know he's telling me about his work with the ambulance brigade. Got me thinking. I made a few calls and voilà . . ."

"I thought you went to Exeter to visit a friend."

"I did. I just didn't happen to mention he worked as a district first aid superintendent."

Anna grabbed the trolley and headed for the dispensary. "What does your mother say about it?"

He finished one cigarette and immediately lit another. "When she found out what I intended, she tried to persuade me to get posted to a nice cozy billet in East Dull and Boring, pushing files or answering telephones; something suitably dreary and away from any whiff of danger. But the way things are going, nobody's safe and there's nowhere to hide, so I may as well be doing something worthwhile. I've been stationed in Plymouth. The city needs drivers. I need to be busy."

"I think it's perfect. You'll do splendidly."

The back corridor where the dispensary was situated was dark; two bulbs had burned out and never been replaced. The air smelled of carbolic and sweat. A sister and an orderly passed them on her way to the wards. A VAD waxed the floor. "Can we find someplace private?" Anna asked.

"Of course." Hugh led her to a side door. "What's going on?"

The terrace was chilly in the gray of a rainy afternoon. Or was that Anna's own nervousness lifting the hairs on her arms and at the back of her neck? The boom of the ocean mingled with the deeper distant sound of explosions. Another convoy. Another ship lost to the U-boats prowling the seas off the coast. No matter how many coastal patrols were sent out from St. Eval, it was never enough to keep everyone safe.

Now that she was faced with it, she felt clumsy and indecisive. Should she speak? Banish the ghosts that plagued Nanreath Hall like a fog or hold her tongue for the sake of Hugh and let the dead keep their secrets?

"What's the problem, Anna? Not to rush you, but I have to pack my kit. I leave in a few hours." Hugh was already checking his watch, anxious to be away.

Inside, a phone rang. Footsteps sounded as someone hurried to answer it.

"It's about your father, you see," she began.

The terrace doors opened behind her. A veiled head poked out. "Trenowyth? It's a chap by the name of Johnson on the line. Says there's been an incident at the airfield. They want you there right away. Flight Lieutenant Lambert's been injured."

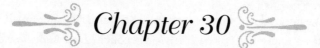

# Chapter 30

*December 1916*

"Lady Katherine, I would say this is a surprise, but I woke this morning with the most delicious premonition that you were coming to see me today."

It had been so long since I had been called by this name that it took a few moments before I acknowledged her greeting. But her patchouli-scented hug was exactly as I remembered it, as were her clacking beads, her expressive hands, and her shrewd knowing gaze, which summed me up from the top of my felt cloche to the tips of my scuffed half boots, pausing only briefly at the rounded swell of my stomach.

"Minnie! Come greet Lady Katherine after all these long years away."

Like Mrs. Vinter, her maid of all work Minnie looked exactly the same, though there was a grayness to her tired complexion I instantly recognized. "I'm sorry for your loss, miss. He seemed like a nice man."

Her awkward compassion touched me, and I blinked tears from my eyes as I hugged her tight, feeling the give of her ribs and the narrowness of her shoulders. "Thank you, Minnie. He was nice— very nice."

We entered the small sunroom where amaryllis bloomed in the windows and a cat curled lazily on a couch. *Don Giovanni* played on the gramophone. I half expected my portfolio to sit open on the table, pages of drawings scattered for Mrs. Vinter's critique, just as if the past three and a half years had never happened.

"Minnie, bring those scones, and we've last summer's preserves, and tea of course," she said, her pleasure infectious. "You'll need it after traveling all day and in this nasty weather. It's been a terrible wet autumn. The cold goes right to my bones. Not as spry as I once was."

"I know I shouldn't have come, but I had no one else I could turn to. I was desperate and well . . . I was afraid if I wrote, you'd refuse me. I thought it better just to sort of . . . turn up."

"I'm offended. Of course you come to me. I'm not one to sit in judgment on someone else's actions. Too many of my own skeletons."

"It's about William, you see," I said as I took a welcome seat in an enormous armchair floating in throw pillows. "I saw the notice in the paper, but that was all. No one would tell me anything."

"Poor Lord Boxley," Minnie piped up. "They say he's lost an arm and the rest of him battered till his own mother wouldn't recognize him, and now they've shut him away where none can see him. I'll wager his wife is relieved or she'd have explaining to do, wouldn't she?"

"Thank you, Minnie," Mrs. Vinter admonished. "I hear the kettle whistling."

She scurried from the room under her employer's gimlet eye.

"You mustn't mind her. She talks a lot of rubbish, especially these days. I've had the doctor round to see her, but he says it's nothing time won't mend." She heaved a great tired sigh, as if the world had grown too much for even her adventurous spirit. "It will take more years than I can count to mend the world after this mess, I think." She turned her shrewd gaze on me. "Though some things are for the good. Women working as ambulance drivers, nurses, running canteens for the boys, factory work; why, I even saw a lady tram driver when I was in London last fall. Imagine that. Things are changing, Kitty. The world is a different place now."

"It still feels like the same old tired world to me." I accepted a cup of tea and a sandwich from Minnie, who returned bearing a tray loaded with more food than I could eat in a week.

"I've been worried about you since I heard about Mr. Halliday and your rather complicated situation." She said this without the usual nervous sideways glance I had grown familiar with since I started showing.

"I'm fine." I hastened to add, "Or rather as fine as I can be under the circumstances. Can I ask you a question, Mrs. Vinter?"

"Of course. Anything."

"Can you love someone and hate them at the same time? I feel like my heart's been torn in two. I despise the lies Simon told me, but I can't despise him. I'm not half certain that I wouldn't have done just the same even if I had known the truth. He was everything to me."

"You can't turn love on and off like a cold water tap, Kitty. 'The heart wants what it wants or else it does not care.' Emily Dickinson wrote that. For an old spinster, she summed it up perfectly."

"That's it exactly. I suppose I should be hiding away from the world, ashamed of the child I carry, but I can't. Is that wrong of me?"

"To face up to your choices and make good on a promise, even if

it's just a promise to yourself? That's never a reason to be ashamed."
She patted my ringless hand. "Now you say you're here to see your
brother. I wish I could offer you more, but it's as Minnie says. None
have seen him since he arrived home. Only the doctor and the vicar,
and both tight-lipped about him, as if guarding state secrets. Makes
the village uneasy, not knowing what's what. You should hear the
old biddies at the village shop. A coopful of pullets couldn't cluck as
much as them."

"He's alive, though. That has to count for something."

"He is, though he may not be the same man who went away
to war."

"None of them are. But we're not the same, either, are we? There's
no going back."

"No, we can't go back. We can only hope we never repeat it."

As we finished off the last scone and emptied the pot of its last
drop of tea, Mrs. Vinter asked, "Are you still painting, my dear?"

I gripped my hands, my knuckles white. "No, I haven't been able
to since Simon died. My mind just refuses to . . . see things as I used
to, and my hands fumble and tremble. I finally stopped trying."

For the first time that afternoon, Mrs. Vinter's lined face sagged
in something that looked like defeat. "Ahh, that's a shame. You were
good, Kitty. You were damn good." I hated the sense of disappointment I saw in her dulled eyes.

Minnie scurried into the room, wiping her hands on a dish
towel. "It's Lady Boxley, mum," she hissed. "She's asking to speak to
Lady Katherine—alone. I've put her in the parlor to wait."

We all exchanged wary glances, but of course I followed Minnie
out into the hall where I stopped her with a hand on her arm.
"Minnie, what did you mean when you mentioned that Lady Boxley
would have some explaining to do?"

"Did I say that, milady? I didn't mean nothing. Mrs. V is always scolding me for prattling on when I should be quiet and know my place."

"But in this case, I want you to speak. Have you seen her with someone? Is that it?"

She eyed the floor with grim determination, mouth pursed tight.

"Please, Minnie. I'll not tell anyone you told me. You're perfectly safe."

She grudgingly nodded, her eyes still on the floor. "Aye, miss. Up at the old ruins. Thought it was His Lordship."

"Did they see you?"

"No, miss. My father would have killed me if I was caught up there with a boy. We slunk off quick and quiet."

I tried not to remember my last sight of Cynthia in the arms of the blond officer in St. James's Park or the tears she shed as she released him with a kiss. Or William's avoidance of Nanreath Hall in the years since Hugh's birth. I tried to comfort myself with innocent scenarios and reasonable explanations, but the conclusions I continued to return to were anything but comforting. Still, whatever suspicions I harbored, I couldn't let Minnie's doubts continue.

"Perhaps it was one of Lady Boxley's brothers come for a visit. She has four of them."

She gave a quick sharp jerk of her head. "Does she? I had four brothers, miss. None left but me now to take care of my da."

"I'm so sorry."

She shrugged off my pity. "Maybe it's as you say, miss. Maybe it was her brother up there in the ruins with her." She opened the door to let me pass into the parlor, her final words spoken under her breath. "But I'd not wager on it."

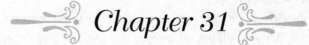

# Chapter 31

October 1941

This wasn't Tony. That was Anna's first thought upon seeing the man lying bandaged and unconscious in the infirmary bed. The same build perhaps, the same thick, dark hair and squared-off chin, but this man lacked the strong angles and handsome lines, the sleek energy pulsing beneath the sun-bronzed skin. This man was merely flesh and blood, a wrapper of skin round a pasty, angular frame too long for his bed, hands large and blunt-fingered across his hollowed chest that rattled as he breathed.

"I expect our boys to be injured or killed by the damned enemy, but when it's one of your own pulling the trigger . . . that's dirty pool." A young man with thinning brown hair and a bristly mustache stood at the end of the bed. He wore the bars and nervous temperament of a flight commander.

"What happened?" Hugh asked. Immediately upon receiving the news, he'd driven Anna over to St. Eval, deeming rightly that she'd never make it on her own. She clasped his hand, using his strength to maintain a semblance of calm.

"Airman Jensen," the flight commander answered. "He simply snapped. I don't know how else to put it. Took a rifle to the top of the old church tower and started shooting at anyone who came too close. Said he'd die rather than go up one more time. After he winged two mechanics and a radioman, Flight Lieutenant Lambert decided to play hero. Jensen was one of his crew, you see. He climbed the tower after him. Tried to talk him down."

"It didn't work?"

The man chewed his mustache, ran a hand through his thinning, pomaded hair. "To a point. He stopped shooting at the men on the ground. Started whizzing off bullets at Lambert. Missed him, thank God. At the last one, Lambert lunged. The stair railing gave way and they both fell. Jensen managed to catch himself." He wiped his brow. "Lambert didn't."

Anna let go of Hugh to take a seat beside Tony's bed. She took his pulse. Placed a palm upon his forehead. It was clammy and cool, his heartbeat rapid and shallow. "I'm so sorry, Tony," she whispered. "About everything."

Hugh and the young man continued chatting, but Anna watched Tony for some sign he knew she was there, some glimpse of the bottled lightning that was his personality in the silent figure under the blanket.

"What does the surgeon say?" Hugh asked.

"It's not good. His spine's been damaged, and no way to know how bad it is."

"He can't walk?"

"Can't feel or move anything from the waist down. It could be temporary. A bruise that heals with time. It could be permanent

if he's severed the cord. We're transferring him to Southampton.
They'll know more."

Anna's hand found Tony's.

"There's Lieutenant Brightwell now. He runs our infirmary. I'll
let you speak to him." The men walked away, leaving her alone.

A heavy weight sat on her chest. Her lungs struggled against
the pressure, her throat closing around a painful knot. Her fingers
trembled. Her brain raced. She squeezed her eyes shut, hoping to
stop the dip and swirl of the room. Her ears roared with the sound
of her heart, of airplane engines, of bombs, of shrieking metal and
dying men, of the raging sea, and the spit of bullets. "Anna! Don't
let me go! Anna, please . . ."

She shook her head, as if trying to dislodge the memory, but
Harriet's voice deepened. The hand holding hers belonged to Tony.
"Don't let go, Anna. Please, for God's sake . . ."

She clutched his hand until her knuckles whitened. Her dizziness became nausea. She wanted to be sick. Her brain seemed
ablaze with horror. A sputter of engines nearly had her dropping
to the floor. Tears slid hot down her cheeks. She must hold on. She
mustn't let go. She was the only thing holding Harriet . . . Tony . . .
in this life. She wouldn't fail them. She wouldn't let them die because of her. Anna tried to suck in a breath, but her lungs fluttered
against her ribs. Cold flooded her body.

"I won't lose you. I won't let it happen again."

"Let what happen?" The voice was threaded with pain and soft
as a moth.

"Tony?" Her mind reeled as it fought to return from the teetering edge where all was scorching flame and icy water. "You're alive."

"More or less." He grimaced through the cuts on his face. One
eye was swollen shut. He winced as he sought to shift and failed.
"Can't seem to move my legs."

"You've hurt your spine."

"Have I?" His brow furrowed, as if he were trying to remember. "Someone mentioned that, but everything's rather vague."

"You could have gotten yourself killed. What were you thinking?"

He swallowed. The pulse in his throat skittered and sweat broke out on his skin. "Mainly that I hoped Jensen was as poor a shot with an Enfield rifle as he is with a Browning machine gun. The man couldn't hit the side of a barn with a cannon. A rotted railing never even crossed my mind." His lids grew heavy as he fought to stay awake. " . . . be all right, Anna . . . weeks in hospital, back to flying ops." His words grew thick and slurred. "You'll see."

"Of course you will. Back to playing the hero, too. The women won't be able to keep their hands off you."

"Only one woman for me. Damned nuisance . . . want to wring her neck, but can't get her out of my head." His hand slid from hers as he drifted into unconsciousness.

"Tony?" Her throat closed, choking off her voice. "Tony, please don't leave me."

"It's time to go, Anna." Hugh had returned. He gave her shoulder a reassuring squeeze. "The ambulance is here."

She rose from her chair as a pair of orderlies moved in. She dug her nails into her palms as they shifted Tony's limp weight, legs flopping uselessly, swollen, battered face void of color or expression. She tried to follow, but Hugh held her back. She turned her face to his chest and closed her eyes on a prayer.

"What did the doctor say? Will he be all right? I told him he would. I had to. He was scared, Hugh. He couldn't feel his legs. But what if I was wrong? What if he's not all right?"

"You told him what he needed to hear."

"Even if it turns out I lied?" She looked up to see him give a small shake of his head.

His eyes held both grief and some other more hidden emotion. "Sometimes a lie can be the kindest truth."

A nna sat beside Hugh in his little two-seater as they wound their way back to Nanreath Hall from St. Eval. She gripped the handbag in her lap as he took each hairpin curve as if he were competing in a Monte Carlo road race. Normally his terrifying manner of driving would have had her praying to any god who might be listening as she held on for dear life. This afternoon she stared straight ahead, though she saw nothing of the view beyond the windscreen. She trembled, but she wasn't cold. In fact, heat washed across her shoulders and splashed up the back of her legs, but still her teeth chattered, and every breath she took came wobbly.

Her eyes ached. Her head pounded with unshed tears. She didn't cry. She couldn't. Other than the teeth-chattering chills and a tightness in her chest, she couldn't feel anything—not anything at all. Not fear or rage or grief or pain. It was as if she viewed life from within a bubble where nothing touched her. She was safe within this cocoon where nothing and no one could hurt her.

Safe—and alone.

The car dipped down a hill, slowing as the road narrowed to one lane ahead of the old stone bridge. Her own vision seemed to narrow, as well, black at the edges crowding closer with each shaky indrawn breath. "Stop, Hugh! Stop!" she yelled, throwing a hand to the dashboard as the car swerved and screeched, the walls of the bridge approaching in a rush, before Hugh's skill pulled them out of the skid, the tires biting into the dirt, the car idling, the silence roaring in her ears as the car skidded to a stop.

Anna threw herself out of the car, nearly falling before she righted herself and half ran half scrambled down the bank to the creek to fall to her knees at the water's edge. She splashed her cheeks, hoping to cool them. Dipped her hand in the water to take a drink.

"Anna?" Hugh had followed her. His shadow fell across her shoulder. "Are you all right?"

She sat back on her haunches, feeling the damp seep through her skirt and stockings. Mud squelched and her hair fell loose from her cap, but she didn't move.

"Drink this." He knelt beside her, handing her his flask. "You need it more than me."

She took a sip, letting the whiskey burn its way into her stomach, but still she shook, her mind spinning. "I need to talk to you. I tried earlier, but now I need . . ."

"Of course. Is it about Tony? He'll be—"

"No," she said abruptly, cutting him off. "It's nothing to do with Tony."

"All right," he said hesitantly. "Go on."

"I wanted to tell you before but . . . well . . . I found something out about your father. I didn't know whether I should say anything or not. Tony and your mother think I should keep it to myself. They both feel that this could be the straw that shatters you, but you're tougher than that. You've had to be."

"A year ago, they might have been right to worry."

She met and held his gaze. "But not now."

"No," he said, his face filled with a new pride. "Not now."

"I had a look at Lord Boxley's medical file when I was in London—"

"Wait." This time it was Hugh who cut her off. "You don't have to tell me this, Anna."

She stared into the curling eddies of water as they washed

against the bank. A stick tumbled and spun on its way past, a bright yellow leaf, a fish jumped. The damp in her stockings seeped through to her knees. Her muscles cramped from sitting so long. "The house . . . this family . . . it's riddled with secrets. One lie begets another until we crumble under the weight of them. I can't keep pretending."

"You don't have to. Remember when I said I learned about Lord Boxley from the people who knew him best?"

"Yes, but . . ."

He lifted her chin, his pale gray eyes solemn but always with that hint of sparkle lurking just beyond the surface. "Whatever happened, whatever lies your father or my mother told, it was done to protect us. It was done out of love. I've made my peace with it. In time, perhaps you can do the same—cousin."

She caught back a swift breath.

"Oh yes, whatever you might think you know, you're not shaking me that easily. We're family, old girl. It's too late to disavow us now."

"Thank you." Her voice emerged as barely a whisper.

"No, Anna. Thank *you*." He stood and pulled her to her feet beside him. "Let's go home. I've a bus to catch." Hand in hand, he led her back up the steep rutted bank.

"Hugh?"

He glanced back over his shoulder. His smile lacked its usual quicksilver charm, but it was all the sweeter for it. "I think we're both stronger than we look, don't you?"

The next days and weeks were a blur. Anna's nightmares returned with a vengeance. She sought relief in work, but even the hardest chores and the endless hours weren't enough to keep the ghosts at bay. Water, fire, and burning, bullet-ridden men filled her mind each time she closed her eyes. Harriet's cries for help pulled her awake, sweat-drenched and gasping for air.

"Trenowyth!" It was mid-October, and Sister Murphy cornered Anna as she retrieved her mail. "Where's Jones? She was due on the wards an hour ago."

Anna stuffed the letter from Sophie into the pocket of her apron to read later. "I don't know, Sister."

"Dillydallying with some young man if I know you girls. She better be careful or she'll end up"—she eyed Anna harshly—"in the family way."

Anna forced herself not to punch the QA sister in the nose. "I'm sure she'll be along."

Sister Murphy puffed away, but from then on Anna watched for Tilly. By the end of the shift, she had still not turned up, and Sister Murphy reported her to Matron for delinquency. By ten, Anna put on her pajamas and climbed into bed with Sophie's latest letter.

She was better. That was Anna's impression as she read of her parents' well-meaning attempts to push her back into the social whirlwind and her own decision to volunteer with the Red Cross in London, working nights at a first-aid post. There was still sadness written into every line, but no longer did she seem lost and dazed by calamity.

Finally, at eleven and with no sign of Tilly, Anna snapped off her light and lay in bed envisioning motorcar smashups, stray bombs, white slavers. The clock by her bed ticked with infernal good cheer.

Midnight. One o'clock.

Anna fingered her locket before realizing what she was doing.

Two o'clock.

She unsnapped the clasp and put the necklace in her jewelry case.

Three o'clock. Four.

Where could Tilly be?

Tap. Tap. It came from the window. Tap. Tap. Tap.

Anna rose and peered through the grimy glass, but the darkness was complete.

Tap. Tap.

Someone was tossing pebbles. She pulled up the sash and leaned out.

"Anna. Down here." Tilly stood below her in the shadow of the house. "They've locked the doors and I don't want to ring the bell. Sister Murphy will have my guts for garters."

"Be down in a tick." Anna grabbed her robe and stuffed her feet in her slippers. Taking up a torch, she raced as quietly as she could down the stairs to the scullery entrance. She drew back the great iron latch with a screech to raise the dead and cracked the door. "Psst! Round here. Quick now."

Tilly crunched through the shrubbery and slid through the door, brushing leaves from her skirt. "Ta, ducks. I was afraid I'd have to sleep out there all night and sneak in with the charwomen in the morning."

"Where have you been?" Anna whispered, casting worried glances over her shoulder.

"I'll tell you upstairs," Tilly replied. They crept back to their room, holding their breath at every squeak of the floor. Safe, Tilly sank onto her bed with a sigh.

"Well? You'd better have a good excuse for disappearing all day. Sister Murphy's preparing the thumb screws."

Tilly flashed the ring finger of her left hand. "Does marriage count?" Anna must have been staring because Tilly laughed. "Close your mouth before you swallow a fly, and I'll explain everything."

"I'd say you will."

"Remember when I told you about Jamie?"

"Your flyer chap with the horrid grandmother."

"That's him." Tilly undressed, tossing her clothes on a chair as she scrambled into a pair of worn flannel pajamas. "I'd given up ever hearing from him again. Chalked it up to experience and moved on a sadder but wiser me. Then you'll never guess what happened."

"You heard from him again."

"He turned up here out of the blue this morning. Apparently, he'd been involved in some cloak-and-dagger hush-hush business and wasn't able to communicate with anyone. When he returned to London, he knew I'd be worried so he skipped out on meetings and traveled down here to see me." Cold cream, curlers, hand cream. The nightly routine, all as if this were a typical evening chat before bed.

"He went AWL?"

"Not exactly, just a bit . . . missing. He's being transferred in a week. He can't say where, but he wanted to make sure we were properly wed before he left. We hitched a ride to Launceston and were married in the registry office this afternoon. Unfortunately, we couldn't find a ride back. Barely a car between here and there. Had to hoof it most of the way. We were almost here when Jamie got picked up by the military police. There was a big kerfuffle, which we finally got sorted, then I borrowed a bicycle and rode the rest of the way here."

"What about his grandmother? Did he ever get her blessing?"

"Not even close. They had a huge row over it and Jamie told her he'd never darken her door again until we could darken it together as man and wife."

"Oh dear."

Tilly crawled into bed and settled back against the pillow with a satisfied sigh straight from her toes. "I know. Could anything be more romantic? I mean it's not exactly comfortable knowing his grandmother detests me, and I have a feeling my parents won't be much happier. They had their hearts set on me marrying one of the lads from the steelyard. Good future, you know? But I don't care. Jamie loves me and I love him, and that will have to be enough." She grew fierce. "It will be enough."

"And what happens if . . . you know . . . it doesn't work out?"

"Do you mean we start throwing pots at each other like two old curmudgeons or something more permanent like a downed plane or a bullet to the head?" Tilly rolled over and lit a cigarette, exhaling a thin stream of smoke as she stared at the ceiling. "I suppose there's not much I can do if Jamie and I start throwing punches, but if the worst happens and he's killed—"

"Don't even say it."

"I can't bury my head in the sand, Anna, and I won't wait until the war is over to start my life. I want my happiness now. If Jamie dies then I'll have had a short, glorious marriage and wonderful memories."

"Can it make up for the pain of losing him?"

Tilly smashed out her cigarette. "I don't intend on losing him."

# Chapter 32

*December 1916*

Cynthia departed, but not before making it very clear that I was no longer welcome at Nanreath Hall. Father wished no further taint to fall on his already shaky ministerial aspirations. Though there were moments I'd longed for the support and comfort of my family, I couldn't claim to have missed them overmuch in the time I'd been away. It was really only William's company I desired; his brotherly advice, his unflagging good humor, that sense of connection we had shared since we were children. To be denied a visit with the one person remaining to me that I loved above myself hurt like a knife to the chest. Worse, that it might be my last chance to see his face or touch his hand made it all the worse.

I went so far as to allude to the secrets I harbored that she might not want revealed. She laughed at my crude attempt at blackmail. She knew I'd never hurt William, no matter how much I wished to make her squirm. Still, I could no longer remain in the house. I paced the rooms like a caged tiger until I could take it no more and drew on my coat.

"I think I'll take a walk. The lane north of the old tin mine is quiet."

"Are you sure you should be walking out on your own?" Mrs. Vinter stood at the door, her bright red and blue dress a tropical vision among the cottage's gray winter landscape. "There's no telling what could happen. You're plump as a medicine ball."

"You forget. I grew up out here. I know every inch of ground between here and the north cliffs. I'll be fine. Besides, I need to be alone to think."

I let myself out the gate and set off, not through the village to the hill leading gently toward the lodge and its heavy iron gates, but across the meadows and over the stile by the empty farm cottage that led into Nanreath's park.

The rain showers had passed, leaving a second horizon between the heavy dark clouds and the orange and pink afternoon sky behind it. Away below me, I saw the chuff of the train as it made its way east to meet the main line, and behind me, the soft echo of the church choir could be heard belting out "Eternal Father, Strong to Save" as they rehearsed for Sunday's service.

The way was rough but familiar. I forded a rocky stream slithering between high, muddy banks, surprising otters and sending a great heron winging between the trees. Passed through the leafless belt of ash and sycamore and beech known as Tandy Wood, and finally emerged on the high open promontory, the ruined tower of tumbled stones before me. Gulls hovered above the ruins, and the sea shone like brass in the afternoon sun.

I had expected to be alone for my communion with the ghosts of my childhood. Instead, a man stood facing the sea, a hand upon the line of carven rocks leading toward the ancient stair. My heart leaped and my insides took flight. Then he turned, and I couldn't help the catch of my breath or the slight recoil.

The skin of William's face was hideously stretched and scarred from the left corner of his mouth back toward his ear, one eye hidden behind a patch. The arm I thought tucked against his side was in fact, gone completely. No more than a stump ending above his elbow, the sleeve pinned to his lapel. What injuries lay masked beneath his clothing, I shuddered to imagine.

Just as I thought to step out of the spinney's cover, a child's laugh broke the stillness and a small boy ran on unsteady legs toward William, who knelt as the boy slammed into him with unbridled enthusiasm, wrapping his arms around William's neck, showering his scarred face with kisses.

"You win, monkey," William laughed.

"I hided, Papa. I hided 'n' you couldn't find me."

So this must be Hugh. His wispy blond hair clung sweaty to his head, his face and limbs only now losing their chubby baby fat.

"You must have dug yourself into a hole like a badger. Look at you. You're a mess."

It was true. Hugh's rompers were sadly muddied, a button torn loose and one shoe gone. But his expression held only excitement and triumph. "I a good hider, Papa. Stones." He pointed back toward the ruins.

"You're an expert hider, but Nanny and your mother both are going to have a fit when they see you."

Hugh's face screwed up in a delightful scowl. "Don't care."

"You may not, but I do."

"Papa's brave. Grandfa says so."

William scooped the boy up with his one good arm. Hugh giggled and, placing both small hands softly upon his father's scarred cheeks, he kissed him on the nose. "Brave Papa."

Before I could be caught spying, I stepped out of the spinney's shadow.

William stiffened. His face wiped clean of his earlier happiness.

"Welcome home," I said, uncertain of my reception.

Hugh wriggled to be let down, but he stayed close to his father, glancing up at him now and again for reassurance.

"I suppose I could say the same to you." William's smile was a tortured mockery of his once handsome grin, but the voice remained the same, warm and welcoming.

Despite myself, tears tracked my cheeks. "I wouldn't have come, I know I'm not welcome anymore, but I had to see you. To see for myself that you were all right."

"Papa?" Hugh mumbled around a finger, his other arm hooked round William's leg.

"Is that your son?" I asked.

Barely a pause and then he nodded. "It is. We've both escaped the clutches of our nurses for the afternoon."

"Not for long. If they know you at all, this is the first place they'll look."

"Perhaps." He glanced around the ruins, as if remembering all our childhood adventures.

I cocked my head and smiled at Hugh. "Hello there. I'm your aunt Kitty. Your papa's little sister."

He shook his head as I grappled to see something of William in the boy's white-blond hair or slate-gray eyes.

"Go on, sprite," William cajoled. "Go see your auntie Kitty. Give her a kiss."

Hugh's face grew red, his scowl deepening. "No. No kisses."

I continued to smile in my most friendly fashion while rummaging in my bag for a toffee. "I've a sweet."

That did the trick. His face cleared. He toddled toward me with arms outstretched. I unwrapped the toffee and handed it to him. He immediately stuffed it in his mouth with a cherubic smile before turning tail and racing off toward the ruins as fast as his unsteady legs could take him.

"He's a bright little sprog. Not afraid of anything." William's proud smile faded. "Not even me."

"And why would he be? You're his father."

Our eyes locked. I could see through his pleasure to the shadows that lay just beneath the surface, the demons he wrestled daily in order to remain sane. Did he suspect the child's paternity? Cynthia was right. There was no way I would ever hurt William with such horrible accusations.

"So much for my motherly instinct," I said, laughing past my uncertainty and the awkward moment. "Hugh seems singularly unimpressed with me."

William's gaze slid to my stomach and away again. A common reaction these days. I barely noticed it anymore. "I'm sure you'll do fine when the time comes. It's like riding a bicycle."

"I was never very good at bicycles if you'll recall."

Hugh fell, his cries startling us apart. William hurried to catch him up, but he faltered, staggering with the same drunken steps as his toddler son. He fought to breathe, his coughing harsh. It blanched his face and shook his thin shoulders until he could barely stand. Hugh's cries grew louder until they were almost shrieks of defiance.

William waved me on in desperation. I found Hugh on his backside in a muddy spot, his face smeared, romper torn and ruined with sticky glop. His shyness vanished. He reached for me, his face screwed in anger, snot and tears mingling on his chin. As I bent to pick him up, he stopped crying and even smiled, patting my cheeks with his small, fat hands. I brought him back to William, who sat upon the mossy wall, his face recovering some of its color, his hand shaking.

"Papa!" Hugh nearly threw himself from my arms to reach his father.

"He certainly loves you."

"He's not stupid. He knows which side his bread is buttered on." He joggled Hugh on his lap. I could see the effort it took not to cough. "Strange though, is how much I love him."

The wind moved over the grass and through the stones. I looked to the skies where the clouds thinned and broke above.

"I didn't want to, Kitty," William said quietly, "but he's the only one who sees me as anything but a monster. How can I hate him when he's all I have left to carry on after I'm gone even if he . . . ?" He ruffled Hugh's hair. "All we can hope now is that the future's better for those we leave behind. That we've learned something from this catastrophe. That our children live the lives we dreamed, but couldn't realize."

My stomach fluttered, and I cradled my belly. I thought my love for Simon had been boundless, but it was a mere drop against the all-consuming wave of feeling that washed over me as I felt my unborn child stir and move beneath my heart.

"What was it all for, Kitty? I did what I was supposed to. I sacrificed everything." William gave a dry bark of ugly laughter. "Look what that got me. I'll be dead in a year. They try to tell me different, but it's just words. I know the truth." He rubbed his face, his cheeks lacking any color, his lips nearly blue. This time when his gaze flicked to my stomach, it settled there. He didn't pretend he didn't notice. If anything, he drank the sight of me in, as if memorizing me. "And you . . . you ran off the rails in spectacular fashion. Poor Mother and Father still haven't recovered from one of their

offspring turning on them like a rabid dog, but you risked everything to follow your dreams, Kitty."

"And mucked it up, but good."

He gave a sad shake of his head. "You did what I was too scared
to do. They call me brave, even gave me a medal for it, but I've always
thought you were the bravest of all of us." He smiled. "Guess you'll
have to be doubly so now, won't you?"

He closed his eyes for a moment, as if gathering his strength.
Hugh sat at his feet, his scrapes forgotten as he played with a pile of
pebbles. Stacking them up and knocking them down.

"Were you happy, Kitty? Did he . . . in the end, was it worth the
pain?"

I stared off toward the sea, the tumbled ruins where Simon and
I had sat and sketched and talked about our dreams and the lives
we had hoped to live. He was dead, and all I had to prove he existed was the child growing inside me—our child. I felt a sudden
longing to hold it in my arms, stroke its tiny soft head and see its
scrunched-up face, pink and white and beautiful. Would he be a
handsome charmer like his father? Would she be a scatterbrained
dreamer like her mother? "Yes, William. It was worth every moment's heartache."

"I wish I could help, Kitty. I know you must be in a muddle, and
I'm useless to you in this state. They don't even trust me alone at
night. Have a nurse to sleep in. She watches me like a hawk."

"I didn't come looking for charity, William."

"No, I didn't think so. You're far too proud to beg, but I wish I
could help just the same."

We heard the crack and snap of approaching footsteps and
turned at the same instant to see Cynthia and a tall manly-looking
woman severely dressed in plain frock and white apron step from

the spinney behind us. "There you are. I told Nurse Baynton we'd find you here. Nanny's beside herself and your father is nearly apoplectic with worry."

A shadow of despair passed over William's face. "I think I can manage a walk without calling out the beaters to hunt me down."

Her steps slowed as she spotted me, the question in her eyes quickly masked with a brittle smile. "I should have known you'd not heed my warning, Kitty dear. You'd think by now you'd realize your willfulness is what landed you in this mess."

"Damn it, Cynthia. Leave her alone." William stepped forward, his one good eye blazing in a face drained of color. He made it two paces at most before he began to wheeze and then cough. Hugh stood up from his pebbles, gripping his father's leg, his tears starting again.

The nurse swooped in, pulling a medicine bottle from her apron. William swallowed between spells where every breath was a struggle. Cynthia picked up Hugh, who by now was screaming at the top of his lungs. He locked his arms around his mother's neck, his shrieks dulling to whimpers.

"Baynton and I will take over now, Kitty. It's best if you leave, don't you think?"

With the efficiency of a sheepdog, Cynthia had effectively cut me out of the scene. Still recovering his breath, William and the nurse slowly shuffled back toward the path while Cynthia confiscated Hugh. By the satisfied smile he shot me over his mother's shoulder, he seemed more than happy to be carried. My last sight of father and son, though I didn't realize it at the time.

I remained behind, the ruins throwing long afternoon shadows over the grass. I touched the stones of the stair, the sun's warmth clinging to the weathered rocks, the moss soft under my palm. The sea stretched away to the west like gray satin capped with froth.

How many times had William and I dreamed among these ancient stones, searching the horizon for a glimpse of our futures?

William had chosen family duty, his fear chaining him to an unhappy path not of his making. Would I have done the same if not for Simon?

He had burst into my well-ordered life like a cyclone and shown me what could be mine if only I had the courage to reach for it. I had leaped at the opportunity and reveled in my freedom. I had been the wanton in word and deed.

And yet for all that he'd inspired my own bid for independence, Simon had been unable to take that final irrevocable step. He had spoken of following his dreams, but his family . . . his wife . . . they held a part of him that I could never touch.

A flock of birds rose from the trees behind me, the breeze carrying the late-autumn scents of burning leaves and cooling earth. They turned and wheeled as one, a cloud of black against the sky. One broke from the flock and darted out over the water, its wings churning madly.

I loosed a silent prayer, turned my back, and walked away.

That evening I hugged Minnie and Mrs. Vinter good-bye. She kissed me on the cheek then took my face between her hands. Her smile was as teary as mine. "The trouble with growing wings is the baby bird eventually flies from the nest. I will miss you, my dear."

"Thank you. For everything." I stepped onto the train that would take me back to London. The carriages were crowded, but I managed to find a nearly empty compartment, inhabited only by a chubby woman in glasses with a cheerful face and wispy brown hair flying loose of its pins beneath her wide-brimmed hat. She waved me to a seat. "Come in, dear. Come in. I frowned off a pair of rowdy-looking gentlemen, and a woman with a dog. It's a long trip, and there's nothing more distressing than to be trapped for hours with

someone boorish or irksome, but you look perfectly comfortable."
She smiled, her cheeks dimpled and eyes like stars behind her wire-
rimmed spectacles.

"Thank you." I settled myself shyly on the opposite bench, rummaging in my bag for my ticket.

"You look positively fagged. Cup of tea? I never travel without
an extra mug and a vacuum flask. It's amazing how often one finds
it useful."

"Thank you," I repeated, feeling dumb and now overwhelmed as
my uncertain future raced toward me through a veil of bittersweet
tears.

She tactfully ignored my embarrassing bout of weepiness as she
poured tea from her flask into a mug. "Here you are, dear. Drink up.
It can't be that bad."

I wiped my eyes. "I'm sorry. You're probably regretting your hos-
pitality."

"Not at all. I'm a vicar's daughter from Whitechapel. What I
haven't heard isn't worth hearing." She held out a hand. "Forgive my
shoddy manners. I haven't even introduced myself. I'm Prue Handley. Nice to meet you . . ."

The train pulled out with a jerk, the lights of the station passing into a blur of landscape as I raced toward the future. For the
first time since I'd learned of Simon's death, I found myself reaching
for my journal. Quickly and almost without conscious thought, my
hand moved over the page, trying to catch the joy and the love I'd
seen in Hugh's apple-cheeked face this afternoon. Re-creating William's almost unwilling affection, coupled with a frail vulnerability
that told its own story.

Without lifting my eyes from my work, I smiled with an almost
forgotten joy. "My name is Kitty . . . Kitty Trenowyth."

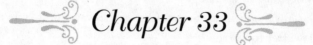

# Chapter 33

*November 1941*

The front desk operator summoned Anna from the ward where she'd been chatting with a young soldier recovering from a bout of malaria. "Telephone call. Long distance."

"Really?" Her stomach didn't fall, but a flutter beneath her breastbone chilled her. Could it be Tony? She'd not seen him in ages and her letters to him were barely more than a cheerful recap of hospital news. Nothing of how she felt or the emotions behind them. Those drafts ended in the fire.

She took the receiver with trepidation. "Trenowyth here."

"About time. I've been feeding pennies into this phone box for ages."

"Hugh?"

"Of course it's Hugh. Did you expect the king of Siam? Listen, I can't chat, so I'll make this short and sweet. I need you to travel up to London. Just for a day or so. Can you do it?"

"I suppose so, but we're awfully busy."

"Think of something. I promise I'll make it worth your while."

"What are you doing in London?"

"It's a long story. I'll tell you when you get here."

"Where are you staying?"

"Garlant's on Suffolk Street. Out of the way, but it suits me. Be here day after tomorrow?"

"I don't know, Hugh . . ."

She heard the pips on the line. "Right. Have to go. See you then."

"I . . ." But he'd already rung off.

Two days later, dressed in her uniform and cap with one small traveling bag, her gas mask slung on her shoulder, she stepped off the train at Paddington into the crush of a morning commute. Businessmen heading in from the suburbs of Ealing and Southall shouldered past white-gloved women in last year's fur collars and smart hats arriving for a day's shopping. Working women bearing a new brisk professionalism as they headed to jobs in offices, factories, shipyards, and ministries paused to buy a cup of coffee or a paper from one of the warring newsboys shouting the latest headlines— the *Times* announcing frozen Germans outside Moscow, the *Daily Mail* crowing over the devastation to Berlin and Cologne by British bombers, the *News of the World* mourning the loss of HMS *Ark Royal* in the Med.

Cabs were impossible to come by. She settled for the 23 bus heading south toward Trafalgar Square then hoofed it the rest of the way. The hotel sat back off the street in a courtyard. Its white painted exterior gone gray and mildewed, the trim a shabby, dingy dust color. One window had been boarded over, and someone had swept up the broken glass into a pile and left it, the broom still standing at attention for their return.

After that less than stellar first impression, the interior surprised with its modest but tidy decor. Comfortable couches and polished tables in the front parlor stacked with newspapers and magazines, bookcases filled with books for those looking for a weightier read than the latest fashions and gossip. The air was redolent of old leather and dusty heat from an old coal furnace, with just a hint of bay rum cologne and pipe tobacco. A gentleman of middle age, red-faced with a cabbage ear and a few greasy strands of combed hair, sorted mail into the cubbies behind the counter.

"Pardon me. Would you ring Lord Melcombe's room and tell him his"—she paused—"tell him his cousin is here to meet him?"

The man eyed her skeptically but did as he was told, making Anna wonder how often Hugh used this place for less savory rendezvous. "Of course, miss."

A few moments later she heard a rush of footsteps on the stairs and Hugh appeared like a blast of fresh air. "Hello, old girl. You made it!"

"I've followed your instructions to the letter and cheesed off Sister Murphy in the process, so what couldn't possibly wait until my next leave?"

"It's a surprise." He grabbed her hand. "Come on. I'll take you there."

Outside, Hugh waved down a cab. "Ashdown Place."

The cab pulled into traffic and Anna sat back, enjoying the luxury of a few moments' rest. Her bag had been getting awfully heavy on her bad shoulder. "What are you doing in London? I thought you were stationed in Plymouth."

"I am. Up here for the past couple weeks on estate business that couldn't wait. I think Mother is finally coming round . . . either that or she's dangling a prize in front of me like a carrot to a mule if only I'll give up this ambulance business. She's turning over some of her trusts to my management. I'm up to my ears in lawyers and business managers, all telling me how best to spend what little we have left."

"Hugh . . . are you certain? I mean Nanreath Hall . . . the earldom . . . you said yourself it's teetering."

"It's not as dire as it might have been. Mother's managed to keep us afloat if not flush. She has me swimming in advice, of course, but there are a few ideas I've been batting around on my own."

"Are you certain this is what you want?"

His expression grew almost mulish. A new harshness to his gaze. "He trusted me to keep it going, Anna. He ignored every impulse to toss me aside or have me sent away. Instead, he gave me his name and more important, his love. I won't let him down."

"I thought you hated the whole ruddy lot."

"No, I hated myself." He cut her a sideways glance. "But things have changed, haven't they?"

The cab crawled along Euston Road behind a convoy of military trucks.

"Have you been to see Tony?" he asked.

Anna dropped her gaze to her hands, tightly threaded together in her lap. "No."

"I hope you're not going to offer me that old chestnut about being unable to see someone you love suffering. That's a coward's excuse."

"It's nothing like that."

"Besides, I hear he's improving. The doctors have real hopes."

Anna continued to fiddle with her gloves, run a finger along her skirt seam.

"Look, I don't know what the two of you argued about, Anna, and I'm not exactly best suited to offering advice, but he's completely batty over you."

"It was nothing, just a silly misunderstanding. Over and done with ages ago."

"Then go see him. He needs you right now . . . and if I'm not mistaken, you need him just as much."

"What's that supposed to mean?"

"It means you can push people away only so long before they take you at your word and leave. Don't wake up and find yourself alone, Anna. Not while there's still a chance for a second chance."

Before she had to respond, the cab drew to the curb. They stepped out into a street that had seen its share of the war. Like so many others, it was gray with dust and ash. A Woolworths sat between a newsagent and a run-down cinema. The most upscale establishment was a Lyons on the corner where a pair of middle-aged housewives chatted over a pot of tea.

"It's just down here." Hugh took her elbow as they threaded their way through a crowd of window-shoppers.

They rounded a corner and continued halfway down until they reached a shop as sad and beat up as all the rest, though the glass in its brightly painted yellow door sparkled with a vinegar and newspaper shine. The shop itself was tiny, barely enough room for Hugh and Anna both to fit, but it was filled floor to ceiling with artwork—sketches in charcoal and pastels, watercolors, oil paintings, even a few choice sculptures in bronze and a few cruder pottery pieces.

An older man, thick-bodied with the weathered features and large square hands of a farmer, emerged from a back room to greet them. "Ah, Lord Melcombe, so nice to see you again. I have everything as you requested. It's in the back now. Would you like to inspect it before I wrap it?" His voice still held heavy traces of his Polish ancestry.

"Thank you, Mr. Burkowski. But first, I wanted to introduce you to Simon Halliday's daughter, Anna Trenowyth."

The man's pale blue eyes lit up as he shook her hand. "Delightful. I've been an admirer of your father's work for years. Ever since I found a sketch of his up for sale at a gallery in Elsham. A shame he was lost so young, his works forgotten. They were truly master-pieces in their touching simplicity."

"Works?"

"Of course. There were a few years when he was quite prolific. Much of this has been lost to us, but every now and then something turns up. I've been collecting what I could." He led Anna to a corner of the gallery where a series of framed charcoal sketches hung. "He did these while he was stationed with the Fourth Suffolk. Sent them back here to his London dealer. They were supposed to have been part of a larger piece, but then he died, and there were other artists with similar ambitions. These quickly faded from public attention, but I find them so moving, don't you? Stark and almost crude in their simplicity, but they convey the real tragedy of that war."

A woman stood in a doorway, her eyes vacant and heavenward as a soldier fumbled beneath her skirt, his head buried in her chest.

Two bandaged and bloodied soldiers shared a smoke in a for-ward aid station over the body of a third, flies gathering in the cor-ners of his mouth and buzzing above his staring eyes.

A boy cried over the carcass of a dead horse lying tangled in its traces, its head nearly blown off.

The wall held at least half a dozen, the paper yellowed, some nearly faded with age and neglect, but all vicious in their honesty. Anna cringed, reminded of her own experiences on the teeming roads of France after the invasion; the fear so rife you could smell it in the air, the numb disbelief as lives were changed in a cataclysmic instant, the almost blessed resignation after one's compassion has been stripped away.

"Hugh, I don't know what to say."

"Don't say anything yet. Follow me." He took her hand and they headed into a workroom. "This was really what I brought you here to see."

On a table ready to be wrapped in butcher paper rested a small oil painting. Despite its dark-hued background and smaller size, the portrait pulsed with life; bold jeweled colors rendering the wild tangle of red-gold hair tumbling loose about a pair of bare white shoulders and lips curved in a teasing smile. More delicate hues wrought in perfect detail the curve of a lifted eyebrow and the playful dimple in an otherwise stern chin. *The Red-Haired Wanton.* The illustration in the catalog hadn't done it justice. This woman glowed from within, an exhilaration captured in the tip of her head and the mischief in her gaze.

"It's an exquisite work of art," Mr. Burkowski stated with all the pride of ownership. "Not as powerful as his war sketches, of course, but still a masterpiece of color and composition. You can feel his emotion in every stroke."

Anna swallowed before turning to Hugh. "But how?"

"Simple, really. When Tony learned about the painting being put up for auction, he tracked down the buyer, Mr. Burkowski here, and made him an offer he couldn't refuse. He would have brought you himself, but well . . . circumstances intervened. I gave him my word I would come in his stead and see to it you and your mother were reunited."

"I don't know what to say."

"Save it for Tony. He deserves the credit. I'm just the errand boy."

"The most wonderful brilliant errand boy ever." She hugged him around the neck, nearly knocking them both over. Kissed him soundly on the cheek.

"Who knew the life of an errand boy could be so gratifying?"

She studied the painting as if she might understand her mother's choices if only she looked long and hard enough. "Funny how much trouble one little painting caused, isn't it?"

"I don't know if *trouble* is the word I'd use." Hugh smiled at her, and she finally felt her doubts melt away. The answers she'd sought when she'd come to Nanreath Hall dwindled to nothing. She had found something greater—a family.

"What do you think, Anna? Let's take Lady Katherine home where she belongs."

May I help you?" Anna clutched her handbag as she faced Seacroft Hospital's very efficient-looking desk nurse. She'd traveled to Leeds on the dawn train after a night of little sleep, wedged between two gentlemen heatedly discussing escalating tensions with Japan, and felt every bit of her grubby dishevelment as she stood before the pristine QA sister in charge. "I'd like to see Flight Lieutenant Lambert."

The sister checked her log. "Is he expecting you?"

"Not exactly."

"Let me call up to the ward." She lifted the receiver and dialed, her stern gaze traveling over Anna's rumpled uniform as she spoke to the person at the other end. After a few curt words, she hung up. "The flight lieutenant isn't taking visitors today."

"Please, if you tell him it's Anna Trenowyth, I know he'll see me."

She didn't look convinced.

"I have to speak to him. It's very important."

She eyed Anna for a long, hard moment before summoning over a pretty young nurse who couldn't have been more than eighteen. "Take Miss Trenowyth to see Lambert. He's just back from therapy. Should be presentable for the public."

The nurse nodded and led Anna up the lift to a long room partitioned by screens. "Third bed down on the right, miss."

Now that she was here, Anna felt uncertain and afraid. Her heart banged against her ribs and she rubbed her damp palms down her skirt. She swallowed her worry as she traveled down the aisle, letting the familiar hospital sounds and smells wash her into a state of calm. The clank of bedpans and trays, squeak of trolleys, the hushed murmur of nurses and the brave conversation of patients, these things she knew. She paused just outside the curtained screen for a final steadying breath.

"Knock knock."

"Anna? What are you doing here?" Tony sat in a wheelchair, a blanket over his legs. He was thinner, his face gaunt, eyes circled by deep hollows, his usually determined expression marked by defeat. "I told them I didn't want to see anyone."

"I know, but I had to come . . . at least once. To say thank you for the painting. I've never received a better or more thoughtful gift. It's absolutely brilliant."

"I'm glad you like it." He stared out the window, though she wondered if he saw any of the view beyond the glass.

"Like it? Tony, you have no idea how . . ." She wiped her eyes with her sleeve. "That's not the only reason I came. I needed to ask your forgiveness. I couldn't do it in a letter, and you weren't taking any phone calls. So I braved Sister Murphy's scoldings, withstood hours of talk about Tojo and oil embargoes and the plight of Hong Kong, and came up to see you in person. Figured you couldn't turn me away if I was standing on your doorstep—so to speak."

"You needn't have gone to so much trouble. You've nothing to apologize for."

"Don't I?" She perched on the bed beside him. "That day at the ruins, Tony. I . . . I was afraid. You were right about that. I was afraid of everything so I simply stopped feeling anything. I thought it would make my life easier, but it's only ruined it. I've ruined it." She felt herself reaching for her locket, forced her hands back into her lap.

"What do you want from me, Anna?"

"I want to tell you what happened."

He didn't answer. Just continued to stare across the lawn toward a low wooden barracks.

So many people had asked her about France; the sailors who'd plucked her from the water, the doctors and nurses in hospital, her friends, her parents. She'd never been able to speak of it without falling into the pit of her nightmares. Denial had been her only recourse against madness. But now, slowly at first, the words halted and painful, she spoke her nightmare out loud.

"We were belowdecks. There was an explosion." She paused and drew a shaky breath, mouth dry, throat sore as she tried to swallow.

Tony remained silent, but at least he was looking at her now, his dark brown eyes locked on her face.

"One of the nurses had been wounded, but I had a hold of her hand. It was dark and hot, and we were all trapped like rats. A fire in the engine room cut us off, the smoke made breathing painful, and I could hear men screaming as they burned alive. We thought we were goners. A wave swamped the ship. It started to roll, and my fingers slipped, and . . ."

She blinked away tears. She'd not cried since that day. It had been as if all her pain had been locked inside with no escape, but now her shoulders shook and her throat ached as she wept. "Harriet was gone . . . just like that. I don't remember much afterward. Somehow, I made it to an upper deck and into the sea. I woke in hospital bandaged and singed, but alive. Others weren't so lucky."

"Her death isn't your fault," Tony said quietly.

Anna's teeth chattered. She rocked back and forth, trying to keep warm. "If that's not my fault, whose is it? Harriet was barely eighteen. She counted on me to see her safe, and I let her down. I let them all down."

"It's war, Anna. It's a bloody awful mess where good people are going to die and bad people are going to live and there's not a damned thing we can do about it. We just have to keep plugging on and hope we don't go mad before it's all over."

"They were my responsibility—my patients, the other nurses. They died, and I lived. I see them every day. I hear them in my head every night. Harriet's parents came to visit me in hospital. They wanted to talk to someone who was with her at the end. They didn't say it, but I could see their loathing and their disappointment that I had survived and their daughter had died."

Tony leaned forward and took her hand. His fingers slid between hers before curling against her palm. She shivered at the intensity in his gaze. "You can't take on their grief and their regret, Anna."

"Why not?"

"Because it will grind you down until you're as broken and self-pitying as Hugh. And frankly, one of you is bad enough."

She sniffled back her tears. "That's a horrid insulting thing to say."

"About you or about Hugh?"

"Both." She wiped her face with her sleeve, a grudging smile tipping her mouth. "Am I too late again, Tony? Or is there still time for me . . . for us?"

"Whether you like it or not, Anna Trenowyth, you won't lose me as you lost Harriet." Tony's legs might be useless, but the power in his grip remained. It was strong and warm and unbreakable. "I won't let go."

Snow dusted the ground and ice glittered along every branch and reflected dark from every frozen puddle. The sea frothed white and choppy, pushed by a wind that bit Anna's cheeks and watered her eyes as she pushed her bicycle up the avenue toward Nanreath Hall.

They'd buried old Mr. Smith today. Anna had attended the funeral and stayed for the tea afterward, so it was nearly dark by the time she parked her bicycle in the shed and headed for the house.

An ambulance stood in the drive, an orderly smoking as he stood waiting while the driver checked the engine. Two VADs stood together on the portico, chatting and stamping their feet against the cold. A sister with an armful of files hurried up the stairs past a group of young men trailing in from the garden at the enticing smells of baking.

A typical winter afternoon, yet an unusual air of excitement pervaded the damp, frosty air. In the main hall, conversation buzzed as knots of patients and staff hovered in expectant groups. One such group hovered around the wireless in the salon.

"...Japs attacked..."

"...Churchill's on the radio now..."

"...place called Pearl Harbor..."

"Trenowyth, did you hear the news?" Sister Murphy fairly beamed, an odd and somewhat worrying expression to those unused to anything but her usual peevishness. "Late to the party, as always, but the Yanks are in it now. Just announced it on the wireless."

"That's wonderful, ma'am."

"Not that there won't be hard times ahead. We've still got work to do." She checked the watch pinned to her apron. "Some sooner than others. You're due on the ward in less than an hour."

Anna started for the stairs.

"Oh, almost forgot," Sister Murphy barked. "A package arrived while you were out. Jones took it up."

"You mean Meadows, ma'am?"

"Jones . . . Meadows . . . call her what you will, I wouldn't give you tuppence for that marriage, and that's the God's honest truth."

Anna left Sister Murphy to her grumbling as she took the stairs two at a time. She recalled how her heart used to lift into her chest with a fool's hope at the arrival of every letter. It had been over a year now. Graham and Prue weren't coming back. And she was all right with that now. She grieved them still—she would grieve them always—but she had found what she'd been looking for when she arrived at Nanreath Hall broken and suffering.

She had found a place to belong.

Upstairs, she snapped on the light, removing her scarf and gloves as she did so. As always, Tilly's side was a clutter of photos and newspaper cutouts of the latest movie stars. A book lay facedown on her bed alongside a half-written letter, a castoff pink frock, and the latest copy of *Tatler*. Only now, pride of place on her nightstand was taken by a wedding snap of Flight Officer James Meadows freckled and beaming with pride beside his beautiful bride in her VAD uniform as she grinned into the camera.

Sophie's cot remained stripped and bare, the locker empty. No silver-framed photograph stood on the rickety dressing table beside the Après L'Ondée perfume bottle or the Fortnum & Mason care package. But her last letter had brought surprising news; Sophie was shipping out for a forward battalion hospital in North Africa within the month. It was too late for Lieutenant Douglas, but there were plenty of men far from home who would benefit from her presence.

On Anna's bed sat a parcel wrapped in brown paper and tied with string. The label had been typed, the return address a solicitor's office in Chancery Lane near Lincoln's Inn. For some reason, a chill swept through her despite her winter coat, and her fingers grew clumsy and numb as they fumbled with the paper.

It was a leather-bound journal. The cover, though ornately tooled, was cracked and blistered, a corner charred black. The fragile pages warped and curled, as if they'd been doused in water.

A page of expensive stationery fell from the book and into her lap dated three days ago. She unfolded it, reading the typed impersonal note accompanying this strange gift.

*Dear Miss Trenowyth,*

*This journal was found among the client files of the late solicitor Mr. Alton Bainbridge of Clements Lane who was killed last November in an air attack. All salvageable material from his office was sent on to his associates at Peckham, Stills and Copper. This journal entrusted to Mr. Bainbridge by the late Lady Katherine Trenowyth was among those items along with instructions for the delivery of said journal to Lady Katherine's surviving daughter at her guardians' discretion. We have ascertained these guardians are no longer living. Thus we are sending this journal directly to you. We regret the delay.*

*Sincerely,*
*Claude Peckham*

Anna sat quietly for a long time unmoving. The ancient radiator clanked and hissed. Frost feathered the cold glass of the window. She rose from her bed to stare down the long, sloping hill toward the sea, the light purpling in the growing dark. To the north, the black fingers of the winter trees marched along the hidden creek bed. Beyond lay the wood and the ancient ruins. On the other side of the closed door sounded the thud of shoes upon the stairs and slamming doors up and down the corridor as shifts changed over. Someone laughed. A chorus of "Yankee Doodle Dandy" broke out.

Despite Lady Boxley's best effort, this was not the Nanreath Hall of corsets and quiet manners, house parties and soft-spoken servants. Lady Katherine wouldn't recognize it now. Yet there was still a dignity about its grand spaces and neglected corners, memories imprinted in its very brick and mortar. Sophie had once said the family was cursed. Anna didn't agree. So many other families had fallen in the years following the last war, their men dead, their wealth scattered. Nanreath Hall had survived. The Trenowyths had survived.

Broken and suffering, they had all come through stronger and more resilient. And God willing, one day perhaps a son of hers and a daughter of Hugh's might play within the ancient remains of the cliff ruins, adding their marks to the marks of those children who'd come and gone.

Smiling, she seated herself back on the bed and opened the journal to the first page. Her hand closed tight around her locket.

And she began to read.

# Acknowledgments

My heartfelt gratitude to my agent, Kevan Lyon, whose enduring faith in my stories has, on occasion, eclipsed even my own. Without her advice, encouragement, guidance, and friendship, I would more than likely still be banging away on manuscripts doomed to eternity in a dusty drawer and an audience of one.

Thanks also to my editor, Tessa Woodward, who took a good story and made it great; her assistant, Elle Keck, for keeping me organized throughout the process (never an easy task); and everyone on my HarperCollins team whose support and enthusiasm made even the most difficult bits easier.

As always, I have to give an enormous shout-out to my critique partners, Maggie Scheck and Do Leonard. You two have been there with me from the very first page of the very first book. You've sympathized with every failure and cheered on every success. You've hacked through the clichés, pointed out the plot holes, and directed me back to the path when I couldn't see the forest for the trees. And you did it all with popcorn and lots of laughs.

Last but never least, my family. I drive them crazy, but they love me anyway.

## About the author

## About the book

Insights,
Interviews
& More...

## Read on

# Meet Alix Rickloff

Creative Focus Portrait Photography

ALIX RICKLOFF is a critically acclaimed author of historical and paranormal romance. Her previous novels include the Bligh Family series, the Heirs of Kilronan trilogy, and, as Alexa Egan, the Imnada Brotherhood series. ❧

# Author Q&A

*What inspired you to write* **Secrets of Nanreath Hall?**

Actually, the earliest seeds were planted
while watching a certain popular BBC show
that shall not be named. My inquisitive
mind passed over the adults' melodramas
to focus on the children. Who were these
three cousins? How would their disparate
upbringings have affected them as they grew
older? And what would have happened to
them during World War II, when they would
have all been young adults? From these
initial questions, I began to weave my own
story, and the book grew from there.

*How did you go about researching the two
time periods in your book?*

I'm a history nerd so I love the research
that goes into a story almost as much as
the actual writing itself. Until now, my
focus has been on Regency England, so
for *Secrets* I had to really utilize every tool
in my thwarted history major's toolbox.
I spent countless hours devouring memoirs
and biographies, film documentaries and
contemporaneous newsreels and newspapers,
and even historically accurate bus and rail
schedules. (Truly, the Internet is an author
and history nerd's best friend.)
   To capture the era surrounding World
War I, I found myself leaning heavily
on Vera Brittain and Lady Cynthia Asquith.
They came from very different backgrounds
and experienced the war in very different
ways, but their collected letters contain
a wealth of historical detail and, more
importantly, the painful emotions of
those living through the war. ▶

I adored Lucilla Andrews's memoir of her time spent as a VAD during World War II. She touchingly captured both the optimistic can-do spirit of that generation as well as the heartbreaking sorrows they endured with typical stiff-upper-lip stoicism.

### *What was the first story you ever wrote?*

I wrote my very first story in Mrs. Larsen's fourth-grade class, probably while I was supposed to be doing something far more important like long division or diagramming sentences. I titled it "The Fuzzy Family" and both wrote and illustrated it. I went on to complete an entire series starring the Fuzzies, which, alas, never made it to a bookstore near you. But I still have the complete set in my attic, so you never know.

### *Who or what inspired your love of books and writing?*

I blame my parents, who are both avid readers and bibliophiles. I grew up in a house overflowing with books on every subject from history and literature to theater, art, and music. The local bookstore was the one place my father kept a charge account that we kids were not only allowed but encouraged to use. I still remember clear as day being about seven years old and curling up with my mother in a rocking chair every evening to read *The Secret Garden*. We still enjoy exchanging and discussing books we've read, and she was the very first person after my editor and critique partners who read *Secrets of Nanreath Hall*. (If you're wondering, she gave it two thumbs up.)

### *This is your first straight historical fiction novel, though you write historical romance under the pseudonym Alexa Egan. How was the transition from one genre to another?*

The one thing the romance novelist in me insisted on was a happy ending, and if a love story turns up unexpectedly, well . . . old habits die very hard. Actually, it turned out that switching genres wasn't as difficult as juggling the dual mother and daughter narratives. There were times when I truly questioned my sanity in thinking this story would ever come together as I first envisioned it. Fortunately, I have a very unsympathetic husband, who knows me better than I know myself. His job over the years has become dismissing my bouts of panicked venting as part of my creative process. After ten novels and three novellas, I am beginning to think he might be right.

*Do you do in-depth plotting for your books or do you fly by the seat of your pants as you sit down each day?*

Authors who create collage boards, color-coded Post-it notes, spreadsheets, and in-depth character studies before they ever type their first word make me green with envy. They just seem so perfectly organized. I tend to start with a character or a vague premise and build from there, though "build" might be a rather misleading term. It sounds far too orderly for the chaos that ensues as my characters run rampant across the page. I've often compared my method to driving through a fog at night in that I can only see a short way ahead before the road is obscured, but as long as I keep driving I'll end up where I need to be.

*You open the book at the end of Lady Katherine's story, which then unfolds as a flashback. Were you concerned about the potential downfalls of this narrative style?*

Not at all. The opening scene with Lady Katherine came to me immediately, and while I tweaked it slightly, there was never a question of not beginning the book at this moment in her story. If I've accomplished what I set out to do, readers will be curious enough to turn the pages to find out what events led her there.

*How do you decide on the overall theme of each book? Is this something you decide before you begin plotting or does it grow organically as you write?*

I never sit down to write a book with a specific theme in mind. But I do seem to unconsciously return again and again to a core story of redemption and the search for one's place in the world. I'm sure an astute psychoanalyst could tell you why. All I know is that it makes for wonderful story fodder.

*What are you working on now?*

I'm working on a follow-up to *Secrets of Nanreath Hall* that tells the story of the third and final Trenowyth cousin, who has departed Singapore for England under a cloud of scandal on the eve of Pearl Harbor. I also hope to soon return to Regency England and my Alexa Egan historical romances. ⌒◡

# Reading Group Discussion Questions

1. The book opens with Kitty looking back on her life and her choices. Did your knowledge of how her story ultimately ends affect how you felt as you read?

2. Anna's story begins in late 1940 when England stood alone against Germany and an attempted invasion seemed inevitable. Despite this threat, citizens never panicked. How would you have felt under a similar situation? Would you have assisted in the defense of your country? In what way?

3. From the VADs to the WVS, the Land Girls to the WAAF, there are references throughout the book to the full-scale mobilization of England's civilian female population. After the war's end, most of these women returned to their homes and families. Do you think it was difficult for them to go back to the way things were after such valuable contributions? Do you think the war was a factor in the rise of feminism that came in later decades?

4. The Hungarian-born artist Balázs was interned during World War I along with thousands of other enemy nationals, including many British citizens of German descent. This same hysteria struck again during World War II when thousands of Italian, German, and, in the United States, Japanese citizens were interned. Do you believe these governments were justified in their actions? Do you see it ever happening again?

5. Lady Boxley tells Anna, "A father is the man who makes you the person you are, not the man who simply makes you" (p. 298). Do you think she was referring to Anna's situation or Hugh's? Or both?

6. Anna thinks she should tell Hugh the truth about his paternity. Tony and Lady Boxley disagree. What would you do if faced with that decision? Why?

7. Secrets are at the heart of both stories, from Anna's white lie when she first meets Hugh to the heartbreaking betrayals that end up tainting the lives of two generations. Have you ever kept a secret? Have you ever had someone keep a secret from you?

8. William followed the rules while Kitty followed her heart. Neither ended with what they wanted. Who made the better choice? Why?

9. Do you feel Simon's deception was justified since he acted out of love for Kitty or do his actions make him a villain?

10. Anna wears a locket with her parents' pictures in it. Do you have a favorite memento you carry all the time? What is it? What does it mean to you?

11. Sister Murphy is rarely seen and speaks only a few times, yet she is one of the most vivid characters in the book. How is her personality conveyed when she is so rarely part of the main action? Would you have liked to have seen more or less of her?

12. Both Anna and Hugh are affected by their wartime battle experiences. How does each of them cope with the trauma? In what ways are their strategies similar? In what ways are they different?

13. Do you know anyone who served during World War II, either in the military or as a civilian volunteer? How did the war affect them?

14. Do you believe the Lady Boxley of Kitty's story acts out of love for Hugh or self-interest? What about the Lady Boxley of Anna's story? What are some examples in both cases that further your argument?

15. Which character did you most identify with? Which time period drew you in more deeply? What will you most remember about this story? ❧

# Alix's Ten Favorite Page-Turners

### *The Finishing Touches* by Hester Browne

This was a book I accidentally happened upon and then couldn't put down. Quirky, fun, and romantic with a little mystery thrown in, it's a book that sparkles with pure enjoyment.

### *The Blue Sword* by Robin McKinley

I've read my dog-eared copy of this book at least a dozen times and will probably read it a dozen more. McKinley's sword-and-sorcery tale of a reluctant heroine and an enigmatic hero is comfortably familiar, but in her capable hands and with her imaginative setting, it becomes something completely unique. I only wish she had written more of her Damar books.

### *The Warrior's Apprentice* by Lois McMaster Bujold

This is the first in Bujold's Vorkosigan sci-fi series to feature the physically impaired but hyperactive genius Miles Vorkosigan. Bujold creates an amazingly realized world of wormholes, space stations, and far-off galaxies that pulls you in, and the character of Miles will make you fall in love if you don't throttle him first.

### *Airs Above the Ground* by Mary Stewart

My mother handed me this book when I was in high school, and I became instantly hooked. The original queen of romantic suspense, Stewart is able to create tension and excitement while painting a vivid description of her setting until it becomes as real an adversary as any of her villains.

### *The Game of Kings* by Dorothy Dunnett

This is the first in Dunnett's Lymond Chronicles. Francis Lymond, a Scottish nobleman of mysterious parentage, is the most captivating and charismatic antihero I have ever read. He's poet, soldier, scientist, fugitive, and lover swashbuckling a path through Renaissance Europe. Dense, lyrical, and with a complex plot so twisted you'll need a compass at times to find your way through, this is not a book for the easily distracted. But if you love sweeping, action-packed historical fiction, stay the course. You will not be disappointed.

### *I Capture the Castle* by Dodie Smith

Another keeper I read first as a child and have since reread as an adult. What's not to like about an eccentric family living in a run-down castle? Smith has written a scrumptious coming-of-age story that's as inviting to dive into at forty-seven as it was at seventeen. And did I mention they live in a castle?

### *The Daughter of Time* by Josephine Tey

While Scotland Yard inspector Alan Grant is laid up, he takes it upon himself to solve the mystery of the little princes in the Tower. Did their murderous uncle Richard III have them killed, as the world has always believed . . . or was it someone else? Tey's historical detective story was completely engrossing and sparked my lifetime sympathy for poor maligned Richard.

### *Winter's Solstice* by Rosamunde Pilcher

When a group of five lonely strangers end up together in an old house in Scotland right before Christmas, magic is bound to happen. Pilcher's novels are the literary equivalent of snuggling up under a blanket with a cup ▶

of tea and a purring cat on a rainy day. Pure bliss.

### *The Martian* by Andy Weir

Who knew NASA science could be so completely compelling? Stranded on Mars alone, astronaut Mark Watney must figure out how to survive while his crew works to bring him home. This one-of-a-kind read combined chemistry, engineering, biology, and physics with edge-of-the-seat suspenseful action that kept me turning pages long past my bedtime.

### *Fiercombe Manor* by Kate Riordan

A haunting, slightly gothic tale of two women separated by time but both drawn to a mysterious old house and the secrets it keeps. Every word seemed to heighten the moody suspense and drew me in until I had to find out the truth at the heart of the dark brooding valley.

Discover great authors, exclusive offers, and more at hc.com.